David Gibbins is the internationally bestselling author of eight novels, which have sold over three million copies worldwide and are published in thirty languages. He has worked in underwater archaeology all his professional life. After taking a PhD from Cambridge University he taught archaeology in Britain and abroad, and is a world authority on ancient shipwrecks and sunken cities. He has led numerous expeditions to investigate underwater sites in the Mediterranean and around the world. He currently divides his time between fieldwork, England and Canada.

DAVID GIBBINS
PYRAMID

headline

First published in Great Britain in 2014
by HEADLINE PUBLISHING GROUP

First published in paperback in 2015 by
HEADLINE PUBLISHING GROUP

1

Cataloguing in Publication Data is available from the British Library

ISBN 978 0 7553 5406 1 (B-format)
ISBN 978 1 4722 2692 1 (A-format)

Typeset in Aldine 401BT by Avon DataSet Ltd,
Bidford-on-Avon, Warwickshire

Printed and bound by CPI Group (UK) Ltd, Croydon, CR0 4YY

Headline's policy is to use papers that are natural, renewable and recyclable
products and made from wood grown in well-managed forests and other
controlled sources. The logging and manufacturing processes are expected
to conform to the environmental regulations of the country of origin.

HEADLINE PUBLISHING GROUP
An Hachette UK Company
338 Euston Road
London NW1 3BH

www.headline.co.uk
www.hachette.co.uk

Acknowledgements

I'm most grateful to my agent, Luigi Bonomi, and to my editors, Marion Donaldson and Sherise Hobbs at Headline in London and Tracy Devine at Bantam Dell in New York; to my previous editors Martin Fletcher and Caitlin Alexander; to Kay Gale for her copy-editing, and to Christina Demosthenous, Beth Eynon, Emma Holtz and Sarah Murphy for their work in getting this book into production; to the rest of the teams at Headline and Bantam Dell, including Jo Liddiard, Jane Morpeth, Tom Noble and Ben Willis, and to the Hachette representatives internationally, including Donna Nopper; to Alison Bonomi, Amanda Preston and Ajda Vucicevic at Luigi Bonomi Associates; to Nicky Kennedy, Sam Edenborough, Mary Esdaile, Julia Mannfolk, Jenny Robson and Katherine West at the Intercontinental Literary Agency, and to Gaia Banks and Virginia Ascione at Sheil Land Associates; and to my many foreign publishers and their translators.

I owe a continuing debt to Ann Verrinder Gibbins for her critical reading of all of my writing, and for her support. The formative period of travel and fieldwork behind this novel was funded by the Winston Churchill Memorial Trust, the British School of Archaeology in Jerusalem, the Palestine Exploration Fund and Corpus Christi College, Cambridge. I'm grateful to the staff of Cambridge University Library for allowing me to examine original documents from the Cairo Geniza when I was a graduate student there, to the Royal Engineers Museum and Library in Chatham for help with research on the officers who appear in this novel and to Peter Nield for introducing me to recent work on the life of the caliph Al-Hakim. Finally, I owe a special thanks to my daughter Molly for organizing a trip to the Black Country Museum in England, where I was able to 'wall-walk' a barge in an underground canal just as I have imagined happening in Egypt more than three thousand years ago.

Pharaoh . . . made ready his chariot, and took his people with him; and he took six hundred chosen chariots, and all the chariots of Egypt, and captains over every one of them. And the Lord hardened the heart of Pharaoh King of Egypt, and he pursued after the children of Israel . . . and overtook them encamping by the sea, beside Pihahirth, before Ball-zephon . . . And Moses stretched out his hand over the sea; and the Lord caused the sea to go back . . . And the children of Israel went into the midst of the sea upon the dry ground: and the waters were a wall unto them on their right hand, and on their left. And the Egyptians pursued, and were in after them to the midst of the sea, even all Pharaoh's horsemen, his chariots and his horsemen . . . and the Lord overthrew the Egyptians in the midst of the sea . . . And the waters returned, and covered the chariots, and the horsemen, and all the host that came into the sea after them; there remained not so much as one of them . . .

Old Testament, Book of Exodus 14: 6-28
(King James Version)

Moses threw down his staff and thereupon it changed to a veritable serpent . . . Pharaoh sent forth heralds to all the cities. 'These,' they said, 'are but a puny band, who have provoked us much. But we are a numerous army, well-prepared.' . . . At sunrise the Egyptians followed them. And when the two multitudes came within sight of each other, Moses' companions said: 'We are surely undone!' 'No', Moses replied, 'my Lord is with me, and He will guide me.' We bade Moses strike the sea with his staff, and the sea was cleft asunder, each part as high as a massive mountain. In between We made the others follow.

We delivered Moses and all who were with him, and drowned the rest . . .

Qur'ān, Al-Shu'Arā' (The Poets), 26: 32-66
(trans. N.J. Dawood)

Omens of fire in the chariots' wind,
Pillars of fire in thunder and storm

Yannai, possibly *c.* 7th century AD
(a Hebrew poem in the Cairo Geniza,
about the Book of Exodus)

Prologue

In the eastern desert of Egypt, in the eighth year of the reign of the pharaoh Akhenaten, in the 18th Dynasty of the New Kingdom, 1343 BC

The chariot swept round in a wide arc in front of the pharaoh, the horses kicking up a cloud of dust and coming to a halt stamping and snorting, their eyes bloodshot and their mouths flecked with foam. The charioteer held the reins while a portly official stepped off the back, and then he flicked his whip and drove off to join the others waiting in the wings on either side of the pharaoh. The official waddled up, his bare belly juddering, trying to fan the beads of sweat that were forming on his shaven head and jowls. He came to a halt, catching his breath, blinking the sweat out of his eyes as he knelt down and prostrated himself.

'Well, vizier, what news from the east?'

'May the light of the Aten shine on you, Neferkheperure-Waenre Akhenaten, King of Upper and Lower Egypt, Lord of the East and the West, Lord of the Worlds, Lord of the Heavens and the Earth and all that lies between them.' The man wheezed, kneeling like a dog in front of the pharaoh, slowly lowering his belly into the dust.

'Yes, yes, you fool, get up. What news, I say?'

The vizier struggled to his feet, his knees and the front of his belly smudged with dust, and then shut his eyes as he declaimed, 'Their kings prostrate themselves and beg for peace. Canaan is devastated, Ashkelon is vanquished, Gezer is taken, Yenoam is annihilated, the land of the Shasu is laid waste, its seed existing no more; Syria is made a widow for Egypt, and all of the lands have been pacified.'

Akhenaten tapped his fingers impatiently. It was the same tired old formula, platitudes he had heard reeled out to his father Amenhotep and his grandfather Thutmose before that. He leaned forward in his palanquin chair, the slaves holding it on either side quickly adjusting their positions to keep it upright. 'Yes, vizier, but what about *Mât Urusalim*, the Land of Jerusalem? That is what I sent you to resolve.'

The man reached into a leather pouch on his belt and pulled out a clay tablet, covered with the punched writing that Akhenaten recognised from the tiresome cascade of tablets he received in his royal capital of Amarna from the sea traders of Canaan, all of them wanting to do trade with him. The vizier gave a little cough and attempted to puff out his chest. 'It is from the King of Jerusalem. It says: "To the pharaoh, my lord. Thus Abdu-Heba, your servant. At the two feet of my lord, the pharaoh, seven times and seven times again I fall. Behold, the pharaoh has set his name in the Land of Jerusalem for ever: so he cannot abandon the lands of Jerusalem! Those who come from Egypt with the golden seal of the pharaoh will be welcome, and may stay.'

Akhenaten sat back under the shade of the parasol, awash with relief. *Everything was as planned*. He waved dismissively, but the vizier remained stock-still, uncertain what to do, expecting further instructions. He waved again and the man suddenly took the cue, awkwardly attempting a bow and then shuffling backwards and scurrying out of sight. The commander of the chariot corps who had been standing next to the chair turned to him. 'With the lands of Canaan vanquished and the King of Jerusalem your vassal, all we have to do now is destroy the renegades in front of us and your conquest of the peoples of the east will be complete. No longer will the kings of Ashkelon or Canaan or Syria side with the Hittites against us. Today the weight of history is in your favour.'

Akhenaten looked towards the red glow of dawn in the east, above the place a mile from them where the level plain of the desert dropped in a cliff to the great gulf of the sea. 'Indeed it is, Mehmnet-Ptah. Are your divisions ready?'

'The divisions of Ra and Seth are formed up, Pharaoh. All we await now is the division of Mina.'

'When the divisions are ready, when the sun glints above the horizon, you will lead the charge in my golden chariot, Mehmnet-Ptah. You will inspire your men, and strike fear into the hearts of the enemy.'

'It should be you who drives the golden chariot, Pharaoh.'

'The Aten has blinded me to everything but his brilliance, Mehmnet-Ptah. I can no longer see to drive an earthly chariot,

3

but the rays of the Aten will reflect from my eyes and light your way. You will charge on my command.'

'It will be so, Pharaoh.' The general strode off, followed by his retinue of staff officers. On either side the chariots of the two divisions stood in long lines as far as the eye could see, the horses drinking from buckets carried up and down the line by slaves, the charioteers and bowmen sitting in the sand behind, resting and checking the torsion of their bows. Their chariots were of a new design, lithe, well sprung, copied from the chariots of the Mitanni that Mehmnet-Ptah had so admired when he had campaigned in the ancient land of the two rivers when he was a youth. It had been Moses the Israelite who had given them the design, who had brought before Mehmnet-Ptah an Assyrian chariot maker from among the slaves willing to trade the secrets for his freedom; Moses who with his people was concealed behind that distant ridge overlooking the sea, waiting for the trumpets to blare and the chariots to come thundering towards them across the desert.

Akhenaten stared again at the horizon, shifting his head slightly from side to side. His eyesight was not as bad as he had made out, but the image of the sun was seared into his eyes from the time he had spent staring up at it in the desert, soaking in the rays of the Aten. He contented himself with imagining the shimmer of the great gulf of the sea beyond, and on the clifftop above it the encampment of the Israelites. He had told Moses to camp there, brazenly so, on the very edge of the cliff, their campfires burning through the night so that when the Egyptian scouts saw them there should be no uncertainty, and the massed army that followed would know where to aim their chariots with the coming of dawn in order to destroy the Israelites once and for ever.

He thought of that word: *Israelite*. It was Akhenaten who had given it to them, plucked from among the multitude of their origins because it was the name of Moses' own tribe, and he who had first written it down for them in a hiero-glyphic cartouche. Yet those few hundred encamped by the sea were of many origins – Syrian, Canaanite, Elamite, Hurrian – from all of the tribes and kingdoms between Egypt and the Hittites and the empire of the Assyrians, prisoners of war and their descendants from the many campaigns waged by Egypt in those lands. To be called Israelite, to accept it, did not give the slaves the illusion of one origin, but the dream of one destiny. It had been the dream of Moses, the one who had been his slave and had become his brother, who had travelled with him to the desert of Nubia and shared the revelation of the Aten, the god whom Moses in his language called *Jehovah*, the one and only god.

After today both men would be able to fulfil the dream they had shared in the desert. Akhenaten would return to his capital stronger than before, a vanquisher of enemies, a warrior-pharaoh like his father and grandfather, unhindered by those of the old religion who would seek to undermine him; Moses and his people could celebrate their miraculous deliverance from the army of the pharaoh and go to the haven that Akhenaten had found for them, far away on the rocky mount of Jerusalem. Together they would build not one City of Light but two, shining beacons of the one god that would unify all of the peoples of the world and make wisdom and knowledge the new religion.

He felt a presence to his right, and turned, seeing past the slaves holding up his chair to a chariot that had drawn up alongside. Through his blurred vision and the dust the chariot seemed monochrome, a coppery red, as if it had somehow driven up from the underworld, and for a second he remembered the cold fear he had felt as a boy when he was still in the grips of the old religion and its superstitions. He then heard the voice of a woman, hoarse and sharp-edged. '*Akhenaten*,' she said contemptuously, looking down from the chariot on him. 'Who is this *Akhenaten*? I know only Amenhotep, the weakling child who always had his head in papyrus scrolls.' She spoke in a language incomprehensible to those around them, the language of their great-great grandmother Ahhotep, first Mistress of the Shores, wife of the pharaoh Ahmose, a language learned in secret by all in the royal line who descended from her.

'A lot has happened since you were last here, Mina,' he replied, speaking in her tongue. 'I am now pharaoh, and you are Mistress of the Shores.'

'Pah.' She spat the words out. '*Mistress of the Shores*. I am more than that. We hold the men of Mycenae in our thrall. They think they control our island that you Egyptians call Hau-nebut, because when they came after the gods inundated our palaces with the great wave we retreated to the mountains and the southern shore. But we seduce their warriors and breed with them and take our female offspring as our own, training them in all the skills that Ahhotep passed down to us. I am no longer merely Mistress of the Shores. Now, I am Mistress of *War*.'

Akhenaten smiled to himself. Minas had come from her island fastness to the north at his beckoning, promised gold but lured more by the prospect of war. Her warriors had sailed across the sea in sleek ships, so unlike anything Egyptian, vessels that Akhenaten would one day use for his own final voyage. Minas had always been one for posturing, but unlike many male warriors who boasted, it was backed up by a bloodcurdling ability on the battlefield, with what she called *kharme*, battle-lust. Mina's female warriors had been the mercenaries of choice for his father and grandfather, preferred over the Nubians who had now become too integrated into Egypt and her intrigues. Minas was perfect for Akhenaten's task. He needed mercenaries who would do exactly as they were bidden, who would leave with their gold and never tell the truth of what had happened on this day.

He looked sideways at the chariot again, suddenly seeing her. She was standing on the platform, one hand on her hip, holding the reins. Her thick black hair was wound around her head and fell in tresses behind her back, hanging over her bow. She wore a skirt and corset, but her ample breasts were exposed, pushed up by her corset. Two big snakes curled over them and around her neck, and with her free hand she slowly caressed them. Behind her Akhenaten could see more chariots drawn up, a division he knew amounted to no more than two hundred warriors but would be easily enough for his purpose.

She gestured towards the cliff edge to the east. 'It will be suicidal for your chariots. Is this your intention?'

He refused to answer directly. 'When I give the signal, you and your warriors will charge ahead of the two Egyptian divisions. They will already be stoked up, and seeing your women take the lead, bravado and lust will drive them further. But only you will know that the Israelite encampment is right on the cliff edge, leaving the Egyptians no room to wheel once they have driven through it. At the last moment before reaching the camp you will wheel to the right and left and leave the two Egyptian divisions to charge straight through.'

'Over the cliff into the sea.'

'Are your chariots up to the task?'

She snorted. 'It is not the chariot that matters, but the charioteer. We all drive the same chariots, your divisions and mine. They all have wheels at the back, six spokes, and the leather harnesses that yoke the horses. They can be driven as fast as the sound of their coming, but drive them that fast and you will never be able to turn them. Your charioteers are inexperienced, and train too little. You have been lazy in war, Akhenaten, unlike your father and grandfather. You have been spending too much time staring at the sun. But today the inexperience of your charioteers will work to your advantage. They think that the ease with which they can gather speed makes them nimble and warlike, when it will just hurtle them to their deaths. My charioteers know how to fly towards an enemy and then wheel at the last minute, to loose their arrows at close range. We will do the same manoeuvre today.'

'Prepare your division.'

She pulled on the reins and turned her chariot back towards the others. Akhenaten remembered the last time she had been in Egypt, when he had called on her to protect the border to the south against nomadic raiding. She had visited him and Nefertiti in Amarna and held their child Tutankh-aten, a sickly boy whom nobody expected to live long enough to be his successor. Minas had suggested that they expose him to the elements, as they did unwanted infants in the mountains of her island; she had said if he did survive he would be too weak to resist a resurgence of the old religion, plunging Egypt back into an obsession with the afterlife and the priests once again in control. Akhenaten had known that she was right, but he could not bring himself to kill his own son. It was then that he knew his legacy would have to be a secret one, not open for all to see as the new Jerusalem would be, but something hidden, secreted away in the most venerated place in Egypt where its presence could be safeguarded for the future by a new priesthood sworn to serve only the Aten.

The line of trumpeters to his left had been gaping at Minas and her bare-breasted warriors, and now looked at him expectantly. To the east the glow of dawn had become stronger, and now a crack of sunlight appeared between land and sky. Akhenaten extended his left hand, and the trumpeters instantly raised their instruments and blew; a ragged noise at first that levelled out and became a deafening blare across the desert. It was the signal to mount up. The men turned from leering at the women and leapt on their chariots, the drivers unleashing the reins and standing with their whips at the ready, the archers pulling arrows out of their quivers and stringing them loosely in their bows. Out of the dust to his right Mehmnet-Ptah appeared in his royal chariot, glinting now in the sunlight, his great curved sword upraised, pulling to a halt just ahead of the start line. Stamped into the gold and electrum shield at the front of the chariot Akhenaten could see the wings of Horus, the falcon-god, and above it the rays of the Aten and the cartouche containing his own name. Behind him Minas drew up with a section of her chariots, and he saw others of her division stream off to the left and right to take up positions on either flank of the Egyptian charioteers, ready to funnel them towards the encampment below the rising sun.

Akhenaten's own chariot drew up alongside. He got up, waved the charioteer aside, and took his place at the reins. He would drive the chariot himself, spurring his army on like the warrior pharaohs of old, but would fall back behind the main body before they converged on the cliff encampment. He stared to the east, narrowing his eyes. The light was stronger now, searing his vision on either side of his blind spot. If he did not give the signal soon the horses might shy away from it and refuse to gallop, but he wanted to wait long enough that it blinded the drivers as they hurtled closer to the cliff edge. The blare of the trumpets had also been the last warning to any of the Israelites who might remain in the camp. Moses should by now have spirited them away along the perilous path just beneath the lip of the cliff, and they should be far away to the north. If all went to plan, after this morning there would no longer be an Egyptian chariot army to pursue the Israelites; they should be able to make their way across the northern isthmus of the gulf beyond the border of Egypt and to safety.

Mehmnet-Ptah looked back to him. Akhenaten raised his arm again, and then dropped it. With a huge battle cry the general whipped his horses forward, his sword flashing. On either side the ground rumbled and, like a great wave breaking on a beach, the line of chariots surged forward in a cacophony of yelling and neighing and screeching of wheels. Then Mina and her chariots followed, hurtling ahead like a spear thrust through the centre of the line. For an instant Akhenaten saw her as he whipped his horses forward, seeing the snakes held high above her head like batons, writhing and turning, her warriors shrieking and ululating as they shot past. Soon they had overtaken Mehmnet-Ptah and disappeared in the cloud of dust that had risen above the plain. Far out on either side he could see the two flanking lines sweeping ahead and closing in to constrict the main force, driving it towards the clifftop encampment. As the dust enveloped the last of the charioteers all he could hear was an extraordinary din, like the sound of a rushing sandstorm heading out from the desert and dropping into the canyon of the sea.

He veered right, reached the cliff edge and turned to look back at the Israelite encampment. The dust cloud had rolled ahead of the chariots and erupted like a huge exhalation from the desert, billowing and swirling out over the sea. An astonishing sight met his eyes, almost impossible to register. In the final seconds as they had realised their mistake in driving too fast at the cliff edge, the first rank of charioteers had tried to rein in their horses, slowing them enough that the following ranks had crashed into them, each successive rank doing the same. The combined momentum of horses and chariots and men had pushed the entire army in one impacted mass over the cliff, the leading edge appearing out of the dust cloud hundreds of feet above the sea. For a moment it seemed suspended in space, like a great frieze of battle carved into the wall of a temple, and then with a cacophony of shrieking and whinnying and bellowing it plummeted to the sea, a thrashing, seething mass of limbs and wheels and spars that fell like some monstrous apparition from the heavens, hitting the water with a mighty crash. Giant waves erupted around the edges, throwing dismembered parts of horses and men far into the air to rain down on either side. Within the tumult it was as if the seas themselves had parted, exposing a sloping sandy seabed littered with chariots that still seemed to be driving forward into the depths, their horses and charioteers gone.

Churning waters enveloped the scene, shattered and burst bodies and slicks of blood lying thick on the surface of the sea. Akhenaten peered along the cliff face to the north, imagining the Israelites who he knew would have been left behind to watch before catching up with the main exodus. He knew that what they had seen today, the destruction of an army, the parting of the seas, would become a legend of their people as they fled along the great canyon of the gulf to the north. It truly had been the work of the Aten, the chariot army having been blinded by the rays of the sun, but only he and Moses would know that it was a deliverance planned not by divine wisdom but by two men intent on saving those whom they had chosen to be the people to carry forth the worship of the one God.

Then on the cliff edge out of the dust on either side he saw a distant line of chariots streaming off to the north and south, looping round to their rendezvous point somewhere behind him; it was Mina's division, their job done. But from the centre of the dust storm there was nothing, no longer any sound, no chariots returning. He had achieved what no enemy of Egypt had achieved in a thousand years, and had driven a pharaoh's army, his own army, to utter destruction, over a cliff into the sea, leaving no survivors and no trace of their passing.

He reined around and turned his back on the scene, looking to the left, then right, and seeing the emptiness where the army had once been, the dust still settling on the scuffed hoof prints and the shallow depressions where the soldiers had been resting mere minutes before. He felt the warmth of the sun on his neck, and looking to the west saw only the burning white disk in his vision that blotted out all but the shimmering sands of the desert. It was with him all the time now, the light of the Aten shining through all of his thoughts and his deeds.

Now was the time for his own destiny.

PART 1

PART I

1

The Gulf of Suez, Egypt, present day

Jack Howard sank slowly into the depths of the Red Sea, injecting a blast of air into his stabiliser jacket and reaching neutral buoyancy only inches above the seabed. Ahead of him the sand shimmered with the sunlight that streamed down from the surface some thirty metres overhead, blocked only by the shadow of the dive boat at the edge of his field of vision. For a few moments he hung there, barely breathing, perfectly at one with the sea. When Jack dived he was always seeking the past, in shipwrecks, in sunken ruins, in humble scraps of evidence or fabulous treasures, some of it dating back to the dawn of recorded history. And yet for him the experience of diving was all about the present, about the heightened awareness and rush of adrenalin that came when every breath was precious and your life depended on it. In more than thirty years of diving he had never lost it, from his first dives as a boy through his academic training as an archaeologist and his time as a navy diver to his years with the International Maritime University, on expeditions that spanned the globe. It was the same allure that had drawn men to the sea for millennia, men whose past receded with the shoreline, their future hemmed in by the vagaries of storm and wreck, whose survival could only be measured as far as they could see ahead. For Jack it was intoxicating, his lifeblood. He knew that even if he found nothing this time, the dive would revitalise him, would push him forward to try again, never to give up as long as the past beckoned him to explore its deepest secrets.

He stared around him. To his left a cliff rose steeply up the western shore of the gulf, the rock furrowed and worn. To his right the seabed dropped off to the abyss at the centre of the gulf, punctuated by the heads of coral that rose out of the sand like giant mushrooms. He strained his eyes, scanning the seabed: still nothing. And yet his gut feeling told him to carry on, an instinct born of more than thirty years of underwater exploration in which he had rarely made a bad call and never given up while the window was still open. For three days now he and Costas had dived repeatedly along this coast, covering more than a kilometre of seabed, and he was determined to use every last second of dive time available to them. The prize that he knew lay somewhere out there was big enough to justify the risk they had taken coming here, and they might never again have a chance like this.

A voice crackled in his ears, its familiar New York tones clear even through the intercom. 'Jack. It's my worst nightmare.'

Jack turned, seeing the sparkling veil of exhaust bubbles at the edge of his visibility some thirty metres upslope, the diver kneeling on the seabed beneath. Costas Kazantzakis had been his constant dive companion for almost twenty years now, ever since they had first met and come up with the idea of an institute for exploration and research. Costas had learned virtually everything he knew about archaeology from Jack, who in turn had come to rely on his friend for engineering expertise and general practical know-how. He remembered the last time he and Costas had dived together in the Red Sea, almost five years before. Then, they had been seeking a fortune in gold lost in a Roman ship trading out to India, following clues in fragments of an ancient merchant's guide found by their colleague Maurice Hiebermeyer in a desert excavation. Now, five years later, they were again following clues in ancient writing, but instead of a newly discovered text it was one of the greatest works of literature ever known, words and verses pored over and memorised by millions. And what was at stake was not just a treasure in artefacts but the truth behind one of the oldest adventure stories ever told, a foundation myth in one of the world's great religious traditions, yet a tradition that may have been torn apart by an event of unimaginable destruction at this very spot over three thousand years ago.

He tapped his intercom. 'What is it?'

'Two sea snakes. Right in front of me, Jack, swaying, working out which bit of my neck to lick. Just like those snake batons from the tomb of Tutankhamun that gave me the jitters in the Cairo Museum. It's the undead, come back to haunt me for violating the temple we found under the Nile.'

'Those weren't snakes, Costas. They were *crocodiles*. A temple to the crocodile god, Sobek.'

'They're all friends, right? Crocodile gods, snake gods. Violate one, you violate all of them. Right now I wish I'd never got involved with archaeologists.'

'Remember our cover, Costas. We're here to photograph the wildlife. Our dive boat captain's probably watching us through his glass-bottomed bucket right now. You need to look the part, but just keep your distance.'

'Don't worry. Every great explorer has their phobia, Jack. Mine's just become sea snakes.'

'Yeah, along with, at the last count, rats, skeletons and anything decayed. Especially mummies.'

'Don't mention mummies, Jack. Just don't go there.'

'That's why I brought you here, remember? To get away from all that. You're always on at me about wanting more down time, and now you've got it. A holiday on the Red Sea, and still you complain.'

'Jack, holiday means sun lounger under a parasol, gin and tonics, the occasional splash in the sea, delightful *female* company. It doesn't mean another Jack and Costas against-the-clock hunt for some lost archaeological treasure. It doesn't mean the entire Egyptian security service on our tails, our lives dependent on some dodgy dive boat captain who probably moonlights as a pirate, and just to cap it all, a major war about to start overhead.'

'You love it, Costas. Admit it.'

'Yeah, right. Like I love being licked by sea snakes.'

'How's your air?'

'A hundred bar and counting. Enough for half an hour at

my depth, twenty minutes where you are.'

'Okay. You see that triple coral head about twenty metres in front of me? At my four o'clock from that, about twenty metres down the slope, there's a cluster of smaller coral heads I want to look at. There's something strange about them. That's as far as we're going to get on this dive.'

'Roger that, Jack. Wait there while I take a picture.'

Jack stared, riveted by the scene. For a long time it had been thought that the Red Sea was fatal for sea snakes, being too saline for them to be able to filter out enough of the salt to make the water drinkable. But reports of sea snakes in the Red Sea had circulated among divers for several months now, and fishermen had brought in several specimens. The captain of the dive boat had spoken of it to Jack the night before, telling him of turbulence he had seen on the surface of the sea at night, patches of disturbed water and phosphorescence that looked like feeding schools of fish but that he thought were writhing schools of snakes. In the Indian Ocean they were known to rise to the surface to drink fresh water after a rainstorm, and he thought that they had reached the northern limit of their tolerance at the entrance to the Gulf of Suez, where the sea becomes even more saline, and were congregating there in a desperate attempt to find drinkable water, drawn in large numbers to a few places where the water was fresher. He had pointed to a desert spring that trickled down the cliff face to the beach at this spot, and had thought there might be other freshwater upwellings below the seabed near the shoreline.

Jack watched Costas reach out and turn the camera on himself and the snakes, and then he pressed his intercom.

'You might not want to alarm them. I'd keep the flash off if I were you.'

'You know what I feel about snakes, Jack. I'm trying not to shake all over. I just need one selfie to show that I've overcome my fear.'

'Did you hear what our captain said about the snakes last night?'

'I heard the word snake, and then I put on my headphones. I didn't want any bad dreams on our final night here.'

'He said the ones he's seen are *Pelamis platurus*, the yellow-bellied sea snake.'

'Got it. Black body, yellow belly. They look kind of Egyptian, the sort of thing you'd see swirling around Tutankhamun in his tomb.'

'Just don't get bitten.'

'Don't say that, Jack. I thought sea snakes were pretty passive.'

'Not when they're thirsty. And these ones might be a little deranged. They shouldn't really be in the Red Sea, and they've swum in the wrong direction if they want to find water that's less saline. The Gulf of Suez would be a death zone for them.'

'Okay, Jack.' Costas slowly withdrew the camera. 'Give me the lowdown. You should have said earlier.'

'I didn't want to break the spell.'

'That's done.'

'Progressive flaccid paralysis, leading to muscle breakdown, renal failure and death. Get bitten out here, and you're a goner.'

'Great.' Costas sounded distant, and had gone still in the water. 'Any suggestions?'

22

'You remember that spring we saw above the cliff face? The outflow should be coming into the sea just opposite. If you slowly ascend and the snakes stay with you, they might sense the fresh water and swim towards it, away from you.'

'Got you.' Costas slowly reached towards the valve that bled air into his buoyancy compensator. One of the snakes slid under the jacket, came out through the neck opening and coiled itself around Costas' hand, hovering over his fingers, its mouth open. Costas had stopped exhaling, and for a moment there was no movement. Jack felt his own breathing lessen, as if he too were worried that the snake might be disrupted by his exhaust bubbles, and he watched, his heart pounding, barely believing what might be about to happen. After all they had been through it seemed absurd that a chance encounter with sea life could put an end to everything, but it was an occupational hazard as dangerous as anything else. He held his own breath, staring. A few seconds later the snake slid over Costas' mask and then uncoiled above him, looking towards the surface, its mouth opening and closing. Costas pressed the valve and slowly began to ascend, his legs motionless, letting the buoyancy do all the work. After about five metres both of the snakes uncoiled and swam up towards the surface, rising on the mass of bubbles from Costas' exhaust. He watched them swim towards shore on the surface, sinuous black shapes silhouetted by the sunlight, and then bled air from his jacket and swam towards Jack.

Jack turned to face ahead, regulating his breathing until he was hanging almost motionless in the water. He thought about what Costas had just said. *A war about to start*. He stared north along the slope to a rocky promontory that marked the limit of their survey area. Earlier that day an Egyptian navy patrol boat had told the dive boat captain in no uncertain terms that he must not stray into the military zone that lay beyond the promontory. Tensions between Egypt and Israel were higher than they had been for decades, with the Middle East closer to meltdown than it had been since the Yom Kippur war of 1973. The extremist hold on Iraq had been tightening again; only Iran remained a beacon of stability, ironically courted by the West after years of standoff. To the north of Israel, the true intentions of the extremists who had flocked into Syria during the civil war had become clear, with their attention turning from fighting the regime to sending rockets and suicide bombers across the Israeli border. To the south, the Israelis had watched the political turmoil in Egypt with dismay, as the newly installed Islamist regime was now itself threatened by extremists, a faction whose sympathies lay more with the jihadists in Syria and Iraq than it did with the interests of the Egyptian people. Most worryingly, it had become clear that the Egyptian army, in the past a force for moderation, had been infiltrated to the highest level by officers in the extremist camp, a process that had been going on in secret for years.

A military coup now would not bring stability as it had done in the past, but would provide clout for an extremist takeover. And everyone knew that if that happened the Israelis would have no choice but to act. A war now would not be a lightning conflict as in 1973, brought to heel by superpower intervention, but a prolonged conflict, escalating into surrounding countries, into Libya, Somalia and Iraq, drawing in Iran and Turkey, with outside powers lacking the strength to mediate a peace, their credibility undermined by the failed interventions in Iraq, Afghanistan and Syria. The war would start on the eastern frontiers of Egypt, in the skies above them now, and could turn into the cataclysm that everyone watching the Middle East had feared since the end of the Cold War: a new kind of world war, one marked not only by a wildfire of conventional conflicts but also by unfettered terrorism, paralysing the world and bringing fear to people in a way that had not been seen since the threat of a nuclear holocaust two generations before.

As if to underline his thoughts, the deep rumble of a low-flying jet coursed through him, one of a succession of warplanes that had been flying towards the Egyptian border over the past few hours. The captain of the dive boat had been jittery enough without the ultimatum from the patrol vessel, and was now standing off from their anchorage point with his engine already fired up. Jack and Costas were here anony-mously, posing as recreational divers, having chartered the boat with the cover of being photographers. The only way now that Jack could extend their time on-site would be for him to blow their cover and tell the authorities that they were on the cusp of a breakthrough discovery, but to do so would be to court disaster. The new Antiquities Director in Cairo was a political stooge and had been shutting down foreign excavations in Egypt on a daily basis. A month ago he had been enraged to discover that Jack and Costas had been exploring beneath the pyramids at Giza, had refused their request to clear the underground passage they had found and had rescinded their permit.

Anything Jack tried now would almost certainly result in the International Maritime University being blacklisted in Egypt, his deportation and the closure of all the remaining IMU projects in the country, as well as threatening Hiebermeyer's Institute of Archaeology in Alexandria, an affiliate of IMU. At this moment Maurice was working desperately to complete his excavation of the mummy necropolis in the Faiyum oasis, the culmination of a lifelong passion for Egyptology that might still produce astonishing finds. For him, every moment now counted just as it did for Jack, but Hiebermeyer's entire soul and career was wrapped up in ancient Egypt and Jack was not willing to risk his friend's chance of bringing his excavation to some kind of completion. There was no leeway: this dive would be their last one on-site, with the chances of them ever returning overshadowed by the cloud that now hung over the entire Middle East, not just Egypt.

Jack closed his eyes for a moment, breathing in slowly and deeply, knowing that each draw on his tank now represented a final countdown to the end of the dive. Over the past few months in Sudan and Egypt he had pushed the envelope further than he ever had done before, and had raised more than a few eyebrows among the IMU Board of Directors. Officially Jack was IMU's archaeological director and Costas its submersibles expert. When Jack had set up IMU fifteen years before he had relinquished control to an independent board because he had seen too many institutes wobble under the control of a founding director who had put too many eggs in one basket. IMU projects were now spread around the globe, encompassing oceanography and geology as well as archaeology, and IMU acted as an umbrella for affiliated institutes, including Hiebermeyer's beside the ancient harbour of Alexandria on the Mediterranean coast of Egypt. One of the board's remits was to rein in any project that had become a political flashpoint, potentially threatening IMU's reputation and wider activities in the region. Through no fault of his own, Jack had endured the Sudanese authorities terminating his diving in the upper Nile and had then experienced the barely contained furore over their pyramid exploration, seeing Jack up against the same extremist element that had infiltrated the regimes in both countries. For some days now Jack had wondered whether it would be the new Egyptian antiquity authorities or the IMU Board of Directors that would cause his final departure from Egypt. Either way, he knew his time was running perilously short.

He glanced at his wrist computer. There were still fifteen minutes of dive time left, precious moments in which he could push aside the modern world and focus all of his being on the diving. For Jack, no amount of equipment preparation, of preparation of body and mind, of bringing a lifetime of experience to bear, could guarantee his ability to see beyond the perimeter of his vision to what might lie ahead. Living for the moment was more than just an intoxication for him but had become a tool of his trade, sharpening his senses and his acuity of observation, clearing his mind and allowing him to see more in a few moments on the seabed than he could do in hours on land. He stared down the slope, and saw the seconds slipping away on his dive computer. He knew that he was going to have to bring all of that acuity to bear if they were to stand any chance of finding what all of his instincts told him lay out there: a revelation that just might shake the foundations of history.

2

Jack stared up at the hull of the dive boat some thirty metres overhead, watching as the captain gunned the engine to keep clear of the shore. Something nudged him. 'Jack.' He heard the suck of another regulator, and turned to see Costas hovering behind him. It was still a double take to see him in rented scuba gear rather than the usual E-suit, an all-environment drysuit with Kevlar exoskeleton and an integrated rebreather that Costas had developed more than ten years before at the International Maritime University engineering lab in Cornwall, constantly refining it since then. Out here anything with an IMU logo was going to attract unwanted attention; even the full-face masks with intercom were a lucky find in the backroom of the dive operator they had decided to hire, and all they had brought of their own was Costas' photo rig and the GoPro camera he had strapped to his forehead. Yet Jack relished going back to basics, to the kind of equipment he had pored over in dive magazines as a boy. Sucking on a battered rental regulator gave him the same thrill he had felt when he did it on his first open water dive all those years ago.

He steadied himself, injecting a small blast of air into his stabiliser jacket. 'What is it?'

'Found something.'

Jack shook his head, staring back down the slope. The coral heads were shimmering with schools of fish, and in the distance he saw the flash of a white-tipped reef shark. 'Not yet. But I want to look at those outcrops down there. It means going a bit deeper, and I know we can't risk extending our no-stop time with the boat having no recompression chamber. But even if we only have five minutes, that might be enough.'

'No. I mean *I* found something.'

Jack turned to him, and caught his breath. Costas was kneeling on the sand holding an object in front of his camera. It was a rusty old rifle, the stock riddled with shipworm and the metal receiver caked with marine growth. Jack lifted it from him, staring at the distinctive magazine and bolt. 'Lee-Enfield Mark III,' he said, turning it over, seeing the magazine cut-off and long-range volley sights. 'First World War issue, early on, before 1916.'

Costas held up a rusted charger clip containing five staggered cartridges with rimmed bases. 'There's more where this comes from, Jack. Strewn down the slope behind me. It looks like the remains of several crates.'

'You sure?'

'All the same. Lee-Enfield rifles and .303 ammunition.'

Jack's heart began to pound. Maurice Hiebermeyer's

Egyptian wife Aysha had been researching old archaeological reports in the Cairo Museum, and had come across a diary written by an archaeologist friend of T.E. Lawrence, Lawrence of Arabia, a man who had served alongside him as an intelligence officer during the First World War and had assisted with the Arab Revolt. She had nearly put the diary aside when her eye had been caught by a remarkable sketch, and she had read the accompanying entry. While loading arms from shore at a clandestine transit point in the Gulf of Suez the dhow carrying the arms had capsized, and in the scrabble to recover what they could the officer had pulled up something else from the shallows, something much older.

Jack had been at the institute in Alexandria when Aysha had shown Hiebermeyer the sketch, and had seen his jaw drop. With its curved shape the object could have been medieval, perhaps Saracen, but there was one particular feature that had convinced Hiebermeyer it was ancient Egyptian, dating no later than the end of the New Kingdom in the late second millennium BC; if so, it was a prestige object owned by someone of wealth and high rank. They had pinpointed the stretch of coast to within a few kilometres and were pondering how such an object could have been lost there, so far from the heartland of Egypt, when Costas had looked up from the submersibles manual he had been studying in a corner of the room and had recited a passage from the Old Testament's Book of Exodus. The atmosphere in the room had suddenly gone electric; for a few moments all of Jack's frustration at their unresolved pyramid quest had gone out the window. Any lingering sense that this new quest was deflecting his attention from the bigger prize, from what lay beneath the pyramid, was overcome as soon as he dropped off the boat for the first dive. For the past three days, after discovering the site where the officer had found the artefact and more evidence of that astonishing biblical event, it had eclipsed all other thoughts.

Jack stared ahead. The words that had been running through his head all through the dive surfaced again, and he spoke them slowly. ' "We bade Moses strike the sea with his staff, and the sea was cleft asunder, each part as high as a massive mountain. In between We made the others follow. We delivered Moses and all who were with him, and drowned the rest." '

Costas swam alongside him. 'Come again, Jack?'

'Do you remember in Alexandria quoting the Book of Exodus, on pharaoh and the Egyptian chariots chasing the Israelites?'

'Advantage of a strict Greek Orthodox upbringing. I know a lot about submersibles, and a lot about the Bible.'

'Well, my quote was from the Qur'an, Al-Shu' Arā', The Poets.'

'Huh,' Costas replied. 'Same prophet, same God.'

'And same pharaoh,' Jack replied. 'That's who "the others" means in the quote. "Lord of the East and West, and all between." I don't know about the parting of the sea, but we're about to find out if the nub of the story is historical reality.'

'You think that pharaoh's our guy? The one we were chasing in the desert? Akhenaten?'

Jack checked his contents gauge. He had only ten minutes of air left. He pointed ahead to the cluster of coral heads. 'There's only one way to find out. Let's move.'

★ ★ ★

Jack powered ahead of Costas, finning hard as he dropped down to thirty-five metres depth, then forty. It was deeper than he had thought it would be, and they were going to have less time. The diffused light at this depth meant that the brilliant colours of the coral heads closer to shore had now been reduced to dark shades of blue, making it more difficult to distinguish any unusual features. With only a few minutes remaining, Jack's thinking automatically switched to free-diving mode, as if he had taken a single breath of air on the surface and had to maximise every moment on the seabed. He reached a central point above the coral heads and sank to the sand. There was no question that the heads were unusual, almost as if they were lined in ranks extending down the slope, more densely concentrated than on the surrounding seabed. He began to look between them, finning quickly over the gaps, scrutinising the sand for artefacts. *Nothing.*

He glanced back at Costas, who was a few metres upslope shining the torch on his strobe array at one of the coral heads, floating slowly around it. 'I've drawn a blank,' Jack said. 'There could be material under the sand, but it could be metres deep. I'm going to ascend slowly just in case a wider view gets anything, and then we've got to go.'

'Wrong, Jack.'

'What do you mean, wrong?'

'I mean, *wrong*. It's not buried. It was *once* buried, but now it's all around us. Get over here.'

Costas began taking photos, the strobes flashing as fast as they could recharge. Jack glanced at the warning light on his dive computer, and then finned over towards him. 'I see coral,' he said. 'An unusual amount at this depth, but that's it.'

Costas switched off the torch on his strobe array, and the brilliant colours that had been lit up in the artificial light were reduced to blue. He pointed to a complex growth of coral at the base of the head. 'Now look.'

Jack stared hard, dropping down in front of a jumble of coral that extended out in front of the head. It reminded him of marine growth on the decayed iron structure of modern wrecks, preserving shapes that would otherwise have disintegrated. He remembered the clandestine First World War shipment at this spot; they might be looking at other material that had fallen off the dhow, encased in coral after a century underwater.

He shifted slightly sideways, and then he saw it. 'A wheel,' he exclaimed. 'I can see the spokes of a wheel, and the curved line of the rim.'

'Not just one wheel, Jack. There's another one on the opposite side. And there's a curved facing in between them, and a shape like a coral-encrusted pole sticking out front.'

Costas dropped behind Jack, taking pictures of him in front of the head. Jack stared in astonishment. 'My God.'

There was no doubt about it. He was looking at the preserved form of a chariot, encased in coral. 'The wheel,' he said hoarsely. 'The spacing of the spokes suggests a six-spoke wheel, typical of the New Kingdom. I think we just hit pay dirt.'

'Bingo,' Costas said. 'Congratulations, Jack.'

'You spotted it.' Jack twisted round, staring. There were dozens of them, hundreds, a cascade of chariots down the slope. He turned back to the one in front of him. The flash of the strobe revealed an unusual colour, a shimmer of pale gold emerging from the sand at the base of the head. 'Good God,' he exclaimed.

'What is it?'

'Get close up and photograph it. There's about a ten-centimetre square section of gold there, maybe electrum.'

'I can see a wing,' Costas muttered, the strobe flashing. 'The end of a wing.'

'It's the falcon-god Horus,' Jack exclaimed. 'Wait till Maurice sees that. The symbol of a pharaoh.'

'It can't get much better than this, Jack.'

Jack pushed off, rising above the head and scanning the others. 'I'm trying to understand how this happened. How these chariots were preserved like this.'

'I've got it. Think bodies at Pompeii, Jack. Bodies preserved as hollow casts in the volcanic ash as it solidified over them. Check out the base of that coral head: you can still see traces of the mud that once encased the chariots, now rock hard. You remember this morning we were scanning the cliff from the dive boat, thinking how unstable it looked? I think those chariots came hurtling over the cliff and caused a massive landslide, enveloping them in earth and debris as they fell to the sea floor. The material in that cliff may contain a volcanic dust like the pozzolana of the Vesuvius area, something that caused the mud to solidify underwater.'

'Got you,' Jack said. 'Like hydraulic concrete.'

'Exactly. The hardened masses were buried in sand but as that shifted with the current over the centuries the masses were exposed, some of them resisting erosion long enough for coral to form and preserve them in the way we see them today. That one with the gold fronting happened to be eroded in such a way that the coral formed over those features just as the mud casing was about to wash away completely, so the features of the wheels and pole are preserved in the shape of the coral. The others masses we can see are probably shapeless lumps now, but raise them to the surface, fill them with plaster, break them open and hey presto, you've got a pharaoh's chariot army reborn.'

Jack remembered the lines of the Book of Exodus that Costas had quoted a few days before:

> *and the Egyptians pursued, and were in after them to the midst of the sea, even all Pharaoh's horsemen, his chariots and his horsemen . . . and the Lord overthrew the Egyptians in the midst of the sea . . . And the waters returned, and covered the chariots, and the horsemen, and all the host that came into the sea after them; there remained not so much as one of them.*

He felt a huge rush of excitement, and punched the water. His dive computer began beeping, indicating that he was now at his no-stop limit. 'Time to go. We've done all we can here. A fantastic result.'

'A few more pictures, Jack. Be with you in a moment.'

Jack glanced at his contents gauge. He was well into the red, with only twenty bar remaining. He knew that if he breathed hard now he would soon feel the resistance of an emptying tank. He needed to relax, to moderate his breathing, but to keep it at a normal rate in order to expel as much nitrogen as possible as he ascended. He finned off the seabed, his hand ready on the vent on his stabiliser jacket in order to expel air as it expanded, keeping his rate of ascent no faster than the speed of his exhaust bubbles. The one thing they could not afford was a decompression incident, with the nearest chamber hours away. He looked up, aiming at the metal bar suspended ten metres below the boat as a decompression safety stop, seeing the two hanging regulators from cylinders of pure oxygen on the boat that would help to flush the nitrogen further. With Costas now having exceeded the no-stop time for his depth, they had all the more need of the oxygen now.

He looked down as he rose, seeing the repeated flash from Costas' strobes as he took as many photographs as he could, finning quickly between the outcrops and dropping deeper to get the best angles. Along with the video from the GoPro camera on his forehead the images should give them all they needed for a press release that would astonish the world. He was already running through the timing; the release could only be after Maurice had wound up his Faiyum excavation, as even with the euphoria of discovery and Egyptian archaeology once again at centre stage, the new Antiquities Director would be bound to pick at the fact that he and Costas appeared to have carried out an archaeological project without his authorisation. The fact that they left the site undisturbed and had been within their legal rights as recreational divers, with the dive boat even under surveillance from the Egyptian navy, would carry little weight; Jack knew that he would have to ensure that all IMU assets were out of Egypt before the storm broke.

By then Hiebermeyer's institute would probably have been forcibly closed anyway and a fresh outburst from the

Antiquities Director would have no effect on the prognosis for future excavation permits, which were already as bleak as they could be. Better by far that Jack give the Board of Directors what they needed to ensure that IMU's departure from Egypt was accompanied by a major archaeological revelation, and not overshadowed by a political firestorm. It would be better still if Maurice were able to add to it with a last-minute discovery of his own from the mummy necropolis, something that Jack now hoped for fervently as he looked ahead to the next hours and days.

Jack's mind returned to the past, to the trail of discovery he had come out here to follow. He thought of the pioneers of archaeology – amateurs, surveyors, soldiers, those who had travelled to the Holy Land in the 19th century seeking what he and Costas had just found, proof beyond reasonable doubt of the reality behind the Bible. Yet he had begun to feel that history had judged those men wrongly, had focused too much on their Christian zeal and their role as imperialists rather than their wider humanity. He thought of the group of officers he had been shadowing as he followed the trail of Akhenaten through the desert of Sudan to the pyramids at Giza, and he remembered what Costas had said: *one prophet, one God*. Perhaps for those men the story of Akhenaten, of his conversion to the worship of the one God, the story of Moses and the Israelites, was about more than just biblical reality. These were men who in the war against the Mahdi in Sudan had come up against the terrifying rise of jihad, and who also knew the extremism that could be preached by followers of their own religion, not least among the zealots and missionaries they had seen in Africa. Perhaps their true zeal had been to reveal the single unifying truth behind both traditions. Perhaps their quest had been fuelled by the burning desire for discovery that drove Jack, but also by an extraordinary idealism. Then, as now, anything that could throw the spotlight on the similarities, on the common tradition, might push the world back to reason, might strengthen the common ground and force the extremists to the margins. Jack stared back down at the receding forms of the chariots on the seabed, and felt another surge of adrenalin. He was back on track again, taking up where those men had left off. Archaeology had more to offer than just the thrill of discovery, far more, and the dark cloud over Egypt and the Middle East made it all the more imperative that he do everything in his power to see this one through. *He would not let it go.*

Costas' voice crackled through the intercom. 'A wing and a prayer, Jack.' He came up alongside, showing where his contents gauge was nearly at the bottom of the red. 'Are we done here now? I mean in Egypt? We can't do better than this.'

Jack said nothing, but seemed to stare through Costas as they came up level, their masks almost touching. 'Uh oh,' Costas said. 'I've seen that look before.'

Jack snapped out of his trance, looked up at the boat and then back at Costas, his eyes burning. 'As soon as we've off-gassed and can fly, I'm going back to the institute in Alexandria.'

Costas peered at him. 'You want to get under the pyramid again, don't you?'

Jack stared at him. 'Damn right I do.'

'What's changed here?'

'It's not because I think what we've found here will give us a glimmer of hope with the Egyptian authorities. If anything, the opposite. That's why we're keeping this discovery to ourselves until the time is right.'

'It's crazy,' Costas said. 'Apart from anything else, the press attention this would get around the world might just remind them of the huge tourist revenue they're in the process of losing by shutting down archaeology in the country.'

'We're talking about a regime whose ideologues might be about to wind the clock back to year zero. I don't think they could care less about tourist dollars.'

'That thug in the Antiquities Department might finally blow a fuse and deport us. It's only the more moderate elements in government that might stop him doing that. Anyway, events could be moving too fast for us. We might be flying back into an extremist coup, in which case we may as well just keep on flying.'

'That's why time is of the essence. If we do still have time in Egypt, it might only be for days or even hours. Are you with me?'

Costas took a final few photos of the scene below, the outcrops now just dark smudges in the shimmer of sand. Jack looked up at the decompression stop, less than ten metres above, seeing the bar vibrate as another fast jet roared overhead. Costas peered again at him. 'I know what's happened. Maurice predicted it. He said that any hope that a discovery out here might allow you to leave Egypt satisfied was misplaced. He said it would just rekindle your desire to get to the bottom of our original quest.'

'Damn right it has,' Jack said.

'And make you take risks. Really big risks that would jeopardise your future and maybe your life.'

'Been there before.'

'Not like this,' Costas replied. 'Maurice's own words. He knows these people. This time we're not just dealing with some maverick warlord. The Antiquities Director may be our bad guy of the moment, but when that coup happens he'll be ousted by someone who'll make the Taliban thought police look tame. Cut off his head, and another one will appear. This time we're up against an ideology, an extremist movement the world has been fighting since the days of the Mahdi in Sudan, and so far it's been a losing battle.'

'All the more reason not to give up. You win the fight against ideology with ideas, not with hardware. That's the lesson of history. If I can find a revelation from the past that adds ammunition to that battle, then it will be worth it.'

'That's a tall order, Jack. This could just be the highest mountain you'll climb.'

'You can walk. I won't hold it against you. I can go it alone.'

'As if.'

'Well?'

'What's in it for me?'

'I've been thinking about that,' Jack said. 'Submersibles. We'll definitely need submersibles.'

'You making that up?'

'How else do we get into passages under pyramids too small to dive through?'

Costas narrowed his eyes. 'Remote operated vehicles, autonomous android excavators?'

'You name it. Any gismo on the books. You just name it.'

'Little Joey Three, my latest submersible micro-robot? I haven't told you about him yet. Lanowski and I were perfecting him in the IMU engineering lab just before I came out here. Amazing bionics.'

'Anything. It's all yours.'

Costas shook his head. 'So much for the beach holiday.'

Jack concentrated on his ascent. Costas had been right: *a wing and a prayer*. They had come here following a report of a find that had suddenly opened up another extraordinary possibility, another part of the trail they had been on for months now, from the ancient crocodile temple they had discovered on the Nile to the pyramids. It was a trail that shadowed one made over a hundred years before in the time of another conflict: the war against the Mahdist uprising in the Sudan, a war that itself foreshadowed what was on the verge of happening in the Middle East today. Yet somehow Jack knew that the story of what had gone on in the 19th century had not yet been fully told, that somewhere in it there was another key to the quest ahead that needed to be found before they could take a new plunge into the unknown.

He looked down and saw a thin black shape had emerged from the encased chariot wheel in the coral head they had examined, wavering like a stalk of seagrass in a current. Others appeared from the surrounding heads, and one detached itself and began to move sinuously towards shore. They were sea snakes, ones that had clearly been dormant within the heads but had been disturbed by their exhaust bubbles and move-ment. Jack remembered the captain's story of a swarm of snakes thrashing on the surface, and be began to see more of them now, rising from the coral heads further down the slope and following the first one towards the place where the other two had earlier sensed the inflow of fresh water from the shore. He felt uneasy, as if by coming to this place they had disturbed something that should have been left alone, a secret that should have died with a pharaoh and his Israelite slave more than three thousand years ago. He saw Costas concentrating on the boat above them as he ascended, and decided not to tell him. There had been enough snakes for one dive, and they needed to look ahead.

Together they reached the metal bar of the decompression stop. Costas turned to him, hanging with one hand on the bar, putting his other hand on Jack's shoulder. 'Before we deactivate the intercom, there's something I want to pass on. Maurice mentioned it to me just before we left but we decided not to tell you straight away, as we thought it would just fuel your frustration about not being able to get back under the pyramid. Apparently, when Aysha was rummaging in the museum she also found a news clipping from before the First World War about some mad old mystic in Cairo who appeared from nowhere, claiming he was a former British soldier who had been sucked from the Nile into an under-world of mummies and the living dead. Something like that, anyway. Maurice thinks it's a typical story made up at the time for credulous tourists, but Aysha thinks it's so far out that there must be something in it. I think it's that husband-wife rivalry thing again, and as you know Aysha usually wins. Anyway, she's following it up. There may be another entrance into our pyramid underworld, that's all.'

Jack stared at him, his eyes gleaming with excitement. He took one of the regulators hanging down from the dive boat, pressed the purge valve to see that the oxygen was on, and then took a final breath from his own regulator, sucking on empty. He pulled off the full-face mask, put the oxygen regulator in his mouth and reached down to the front of his stabiliser jacket for his backup mask, putting it on and clearing it, and then watched Costas do the same. He breathed in deeply, feeling his entire body tingling, relishing the sudden lift that pure oxygen always gave him, as if it were cleansing his soul. He set the timer on his computer, beginning his countdown to surfacing and getting back on the trail they had left off under the pyramid.

He could hardly wait.

3

On the Nile south of Cairo, Egypt, 1893

The man in the dark cape struck a match and raised it to his cigar, cupping his hand to prevent the flame from being seen by anyone who might be passing along the riverbank. Around him the waters of the river were barely discernible, a swirling miasma veiled by a thin mist; the abandoned fort on the embankment was still invisible despite the captain of the boat jabbing his finger into the darkness and assuring them that it was a mere stone's throw away. They had deliberately chosen a moonless night for their venture, and without a navigating lantern their voyage upriver had seemed a blind man's gamble at best. But the captain had raised the huge triangular sail of the felucca and brought them unerringly past the city, using the northerly breeze to sail against the current and bring them to the narrow strip of cultivated floodplain beyond the southern outskirts that fronted the desert. They had left the putrid odour of the Cairo waterfront behind, and now the river smelled musty, like an old camel. The captain had bent the tiller while his boy ran along the spar and furled the sail. For what seemed an age now they had drifted silently, letting eddies push them slowly into the river's shore.

The man strained his eyes into the darkness, still seeing nothing, having no recourse other than to trust the skill and knowledge of the captain. He took a deep draw on his cigar, clenching it in his teeth while he exhaled the sweet smoke into the darkness, trying to calm his excitement. In daylight, if they were in the correct position, he would be able to see the pyramids of Giza just above the horizon to the west, and in front of him the ruined river fort that they had visited on foot the day before. Somewhere below, somewhere under the riverbank, lay the key to the greatest undiscovered prize in Egyptology, greater even than the lost city of Amarna or the tombs of the Valley of the Kings, something that would cap his years of adventure in Africa and allow him to return home in triumph across the Atlantic to the destiny that had seemed marked out for him, the highest offices in the land now surely within his grasp.

Something bumped the boat, knocking him momentarily off balance. He peered over the bows, seeing a small swell on the surface of the river, doubtless marking some fetid unpleasantness beneath. With the annual Nile flood only now abating, they had encountered all manner of flotsam on their trip upstream, from the washed-away wooden structure of riverside *shaduf* irrigation pumps to the bloated carcasses of cows. Most remarkable had been a rotting fishing net tangled up with empty wooden cartridge boxes marked to the Gordon Relief Expedition, the detritus of a botched conflict eight years before that had taken all this time to wash its way down from the former war zone in the Sudan. The boxes had seemed archaeological, artefacts from another era, and yet Egypt, the world even, was still gripped in the aftershock of General Gordon's death at the hands of the Mahdi army in Khartoum, and the ignominious British failure to retain Sudan. In Egypt the British were bent on revenge, and in Sudan the Mahdi army on jihad that threatened to sweep across North Africa and the Middle East as it had done more than a thousand years before, drawing the West into a conflict that would make the wars of the Crusades seem like child's play.

Seeing those cartridge cases had made him ponder his own role in the affair. He had been one of a group of American officers restless after the Civil War who had crossed the Atlantic seeking excitement in Africa, and had been employed by the Khedive of Egypt. From being a captain in the 11th Maryland Regiment of the Union Army, a veteran of Gettysburg and a personal acquaintance of General Grant, now *President* Grant, he had become a lieutenant-colonel in the Khedive's service, and then chief of staff to Gordon after the British general had been appointed governor of equatorial Sudan. With his exotic surname, Chaillé-Long, a legacy of his Huguenot French ancestry, and the manners of a southern gentleman, he had seemed a cut above the other American officers, and had quickly found favour as a kind of honorary European. He had at first struck up a cordial relationship with

Gordon; despite being born on a Maryland plantation he had joined the Union army opposed to slavery, and had been more than willing to assist Gordon in his effort to eradicate the slave trade in the Sudan. Their relations became strained only once Chaillé-Long realised the futility of that enterprise and the impossibility of working under such a man as Gordon. They were broken entirely after the Khedive appointed Chaillé-Long to travel deep into Africa to conduct a treaty with the king of the Ugandans, on the way becoming a celebrated explorer whose name now stood alongside those of Speke and Burton, Livingstone and Stanley.

In 1877 he had returned to America in high esteem, newly decorated by the Khedive with the Order of the Medjidieh, acclaimed as the first American to stand on the shores of Lake Victoria. With Gordon still in charge the Sudan had been closed to him, but he had seen the future in international law and after a degree at Columbia had set up a practice in Alexandria in Egypt. In 1882 he had earned the approbation of the State Department by taking over the US Consulate during the British naval bombardment of the city that preceded their military conquest of Egypt, the circumstance that led to direct British involvement in the Sudan and the debacle of the relief expedition in1885.

After that Egypt too had seemed closed to him. And yet here he was again, drawn back not by the promise of military glory or exploration but by something else, by unfinished business from his time under Gordon in the 1870s. A few of them had become party to an another enterprise, one that had begun with a small circle of British officers around Gordon obsessed with uncovering the truth of the Old Testament, whose quest to find out more had led them on a trail of discovery that had brought him to this place now on the eve of his final planned departure from Egypt. He hoped to show something to the world arising from those years that was not tainted by the guilt and dishonour that pervaded the failure to rescue Gordon.

The boat bumped again, more jarringly this time. There was a commotion from the hold opening in the centre of the deck, and a voice in an English accent cursing. 'God damn you. *God damn your eyes.*' Another man spoke, higher-pitched, in French, remonstrating angrily, followed again by the first voice. 'I didn't mean you, Guerin. I meant the spanner, God damn it. The one I just dropped.'

Chaillé-Long took out his cigar, and peered into the hold. 'Keep your voice down, Jones. We're close enough to shore that we might be overheard.'

Jones' head and shoulders appeared out of the opening, and he spoke in Arabic to the captain. After listening to the reply he turned around, his bearded face scarcely visible in the darkness. 'Don't worry yourself, Colonel. The captain says there's nobody along the shoreline. The fishermen don't bother to come this far along the bank when it's pitch dark, when there's no moon. They're terrified of slipping into the whirlpools that appear during the flood and being sucked down by the monsters they think lie beneath. Nile perch, no doubt, some of them of prodigious size, though who knows what else swims in this river. Even the captain and his boy are afraid. It's only your gold that's brought them here, and you'll probably have to cough up more of it to make them stay. So I can curse and swear as much as I like.'

'In my experience of English soldiery, Corporal Jones,' Chaillé-Long drawled, 'that could keep us occupied to dawn and beyond.'

'The valve of the diving cylinder is jammed.' Jones ducked down again, there was a sound of scrabbling in the bilges, and then he reappeared. 'I've found the spanner, Allah be praised. But I'm going to have to strike the valve to open it, and that sound would wake up all Cairo. I'll need to muffle it.' He paused, looking up. 'Toss me your scarf, would you, old boy?'

Chaillé-Long drew himself up, and snorted. 'I will *not* give you my scarf. It is the purest cashmere, direct from my *fournisseur* in Paris.'

'I don't care if it's rat skin. I never took you for a dandy, Chaillé-Long, but now I'm wondering. How did an American get a name like that anyway?'

'Not all Yankees are Irish, despite the prejudicial views of you English. My great-grandfather was French, from a landed family under the old regime. And before you call me a dandy, I will have you remember that I was a captain in the army of the North at the Battle of Gettysburg, and after that a colonel in the Khedive's Sudanese army, chosen for the task by your revered General Gordon, no less.'

Jones narrowed his eyes, staring at him. 'Well, if you were good enough for old Charlie Gordon, God rest his soul, I suppose you're good enough for me. But I still need your scarf.'

Chaillé-Long snorted again, paused, then unlooped the scarf from his neck and dropped it into the opening. A few moments later there was a sound of dull thumping, of metal against metal, and then a sharp hissing noise that stopped as abruptly as it had started.

'Done,' Jones called up. 'That's the breathing device prepared. As soon as the captain gives the word, Monsieur Guerin will be ready to go. We will help him to kit up.'

Fifteen minutes later Jones lit the small gas lamp inside the hold, turning it down so that the glow would be invisible beyond the boat. He had only known Guerin for a few hours, since the man had joined them from the Cairo dock with his secret crate of equipment, and until now it had been a matter of fumbling around in the dark as he had helped to unbox and assemble the contraption.

Guerin had come straight from the harbour of Alexandria where he had intended to dive on the ruins of the Pharos, the great lighthouse from antiquity, but Chaillé-Long had seen him there and diverted him to their present purpose. Now for the first time with some semblance of light, Jones was able to see it: a bulbous cylinder containing compressed air, above that a complex attachment of pipes and hoses to regulate the supply of air to the diver, and attached to that a face mask with a glass plate and beneath it the mouthpiece. Jones remembered the course in submarine mine-laying and demolition that he had been obliged to take as a recruit at the Royal Engineers depot at Chatham. His greatest fear had been confined spaces, followed closely by being underwater, and he had been petrified that the instructor would select him to demonstrate the bulky hard-hat diving gear in the murky depths of the River Medway. Earlier, in the barracks, the corporal in charge had regaled them with lurid tales of divers being sucked up into their helmets when their tenders on the surface had forgotten to keep the pump going; as it was, the luckless recruit who was selected on the river that day had come up unconscious and blue, temporarily overcome by carbon dioxide.

Jones squatted in the scuppers of the boat, peering more closely. The gear they had used on the Medway had been helmet-diving equipment, in use for more than half a century; Guerin's contraption was very different. He pointed at the regulating valve. 'Does the diver introduce air manually by opening and shutting the valve with each breath, or is it automatic?'

The Frenchman thrust his head through the neck-hole in the suit, and shot him a sharp glance. 'You know something of diving technology, *mon ami*?'

Jones started to speak, and then checked himself. Only Chaillé-Long knew anything of his army background, and it was best it stayed that way. 'From watching salvage divers on the docks at Portsmouth, when I was a boy growing up there,' he replied. That much was true; he had seen divers raising guns from the wreck of the *Mary Rose*, Henry VIII's sunken warship that had been deemed a hazard to the ever-larger naval ships that plied the Solent. 'But of course they were only using Mr Siebe's hard-hat equipment.'

'Then, *mon ami*, you will have seen how *impossible* it is,' Guerin exclaimed, straining as he tried to poke his fingers though the hand-holes, his arms outstretched and his fingers working vigorously against the rubber. Finally his left hand broke through, and he used it quickly to pull through the other hand. '*Premièrement*, it is too heavy for the diver even to stand upright out of the water, firstly because the helmet must be strong enough to withstand the external pressure at depth, and therefore be a great weight of bronze, and secondly because the diver must wear yet more weight underwater to keep the helmet down, because, despite its weight out of the water, it becomes almost buoyant underwater, when filled with air.' His face reddened and his veins bulged where the rubber seal constricted his neck. '*Deuxièment*,' he continued more hoarsely, 'the diver must remain upright on the bottom, to prevent the helmet from flooding and himself from drowning, and thus limiting his usefulness for jobs requiring any, how can I put it, finesse. *Troisièment*, he is tethered to the surface by the air hose, so has even less freedom of movement underwater, and he is entirely dependent for his survival on the man pumping the air down to him.'

'And fourthly,' Jones said, remembering the recruit on the Medway, 'he risks blackout from carbon dioxide poisoning if he fails manually to open the valve and expel the exhaled air from his helmet.'

'Precisely. *Précisément*. You have it.' Guerin got up, climbed out of the hold, lurched and fell backwards, caught just in time by Chaillé-Long who steered him to a plank that served as a bench. The Frenchman thrust his fingers into the neck seal to pull it open, gasping as he relieved the pressure. 'I assure you, *mes amis*,' he said even more hoarsely, his face running with sweat, 'this constriction is relieved under water, but it is necessary to keep the suit watertight.'

'Well, I for one am mighty relieved to hear it,' said Chaillé-Long, looking at the man dubiously and then at the river. 'We shall need to secure that contraption on your back and get you in the water, once our captain has steered this benighted craft to shore.'

Guerin nodded, his face now looking drained. '*Un moment, monsieur*. While I recover my composure.' He gestured at the equipment, and then looked at Jones, suddenly beaming. 'It is, as I believe you have correctly surmised, an automatic valve, the first ever demand valve. When the diver breathes in, the cylinder releases a lungful of air, regulated through the device on the valve.'

'Tried and tested, I presume?' said Chaillé-Long, taking out the butt of his cigar and tossing it into the river.

'Monsieur Denayrouze has been developing a similar device, and Monsieur Rouquayrol has been making cylinders strong enough to hold more air,' he replied, his eyes narrowing. 'But their *régulateur* is inferior to mine, requiring the diver to open the valve manually each time he needs air.'

Chaillé-Long looked at him shrewdly. 'Are you in competition with these other gentlemen?'

'It is why I have had to be so secretive. And there is something else, *mon ami*. This device would revolutionise underwater warfare. Divers could swim freely to attach mines beneath enemy ships' hulls, wreaking havoc. One day wars will be fought underwater, you know. The world's navies would clamour for it.'

'It is a good thing, then, that when I needed a diver for our enterprise, I was not obliged to employ these other gentlemen, and you were to hand.'

'A matter of good fortune that I had travelled to Alexandria intending to test my prototype first in the ancient remains of the harbour and then in Aboukir Bay, on the wreck of the

Oceanus where it blew up in 1798 during the Battle of the Nile. In these days of the British Empire people have forgotten the role of Napoleon in opening up Ancient Egypt to the world, and my discovery of the wreck would have been *pour la France*.'

'You mean it would have brought you the fortune in gold coin that is said to lie in her hold.'

Guerin shrugged theatrically. 'An *inventeur* needs his income, *monsieur*. How else does he buy his *matériel*?'

'So, you do not selflessly give your endeavours to *La France*, then?'

Guerin eyed Chaillé-Long. 'Do you work for the United States of America, *monsieur*, or for yourself?'

The ghost of a smile passed Chaillé-Long's lips. 'It sounds as if you are embarked upon a profitable enterprise.'

'Now you understand how it is that I have not been able to test my equipment like this before. I could not risk prying eyes seeing it.'

Chaillé-Long gave the man a wry look. 'I am grateful to you for answering my question in so *direct* a fashion.' He put his hands on his hips, surveying the shore that was just coming into view, a dark bank several boats' lengths away. 'Now, are we ready?'

Jones eyed Guerin. 'Do you have your lamp?'

'*Mais oui*,' the Frenchman replied exuberantly, lifting an open-fronted metallic box the size of a kerosene lamp but containing an opaque glass ball. 'Another one of my inventions. It contains a battery and an electrical filament. The opaque glass keeps the light from shining too strongly, as the glare off the suspended particles in the water would obscure my view.

I have tested it myself to a depth of ten metres, off the Marseilles docks.'

'You are indeed an entrepreneur,' Chaillé-Long murmured. 'If *liberté, égalité et fraternité* are in truth not your master, then you and I could do business.'

Guerin looked at Jones, his eyes glinting. 'And you, *monsieur*, for your part, you have *les explosifs*?'

Jones carefully lifted up an oiled tarpaulin beside the hatch, revealing a small wooden box attached by a coiled cable to a plunger. 'Borrowed from the Royal Engineers depot in Cairo,' he said. 'Security there is not what it used to be. The box contains eight one-pound sticks of dynamite, packed in petroleum jelly for waterproofing. The cable is two hundred feet long, and the charge should be waterproof down to a depth of thirty feet. If the captain can hold us that distance from the riverbank, the boat should survive the detonation unscathed.'

Guerin stared hesistantly at the box. 'That is, if I find what you are after, and have occasion to lay the charge.'

'I have spent weeks triangulating this exact position from the pyramids, transposing the ancient plan on the most up-to-date topographical maps prepared by the Ordnance Survey.'

The Frenchman tweaked his moustache. 'More *équipement* liberated from the Royal Engineers, I surmise? And you found a theodolite too? You are a man of many skills.'

Jones coughed. 'Let's just say I've had some training.'

Guerin's eyes twinkled. 'Do you mean in the larceny, *mon ami*, or in the military sciences?'

Jones pointed at the riverbank looming out of the darkness, held off by the captain's boy with a pole. A cascade of bricks and mortar lay embedded in the bank, and above it they could make out the ruined walls and gun embrasure of the fort. 'There it is,' he exclaimed, his voice hushed. 'This was the feature that coincided precisely with my measurement, the place I told the captain to find. When I came here in daylight I also measured the movement of water along the shore. It's outside the main river current, but there are strong eddies, enough to keep river silt from accumulating or mud from building up too deeply. Monsieur Guerin, I believe you will be in with a very good chance.' He looked up at Chaillé-Long. 'Are you up to getting your hands wet, Colonel?'

Chaillé-Long bristled. 'I will have you know that I have survived pitiless rain, mud, misery, malaria and the other dread fevers of the jungle, in my years as an explorer of deepest Africa.' He pointed to a faint scar on his cheek. 'This wound, as you will doubtless have wondered, I acquired fighting off the Bunyan warriors of Uganda, alone with my Reilly elephant gun, assisted only by two of my bearers with Snider rifles, together accounting for dozens of 'em.' He took off his silk gloves with a theatrical flourish. 'I do believe, sir, that I am capable of dipping my hand in this river, however fetid and pestilential its waters may be.'

Jones glanced at Chaillé-Long as he squatted down beside him: at the silk top hat, the black cape with its crimson lining, the patent leather shoes. The war in Sudan had attracted all manner of mavericks, some of them genuinely capable, others charlatans, and had refracted their skills in the intensity of the struggle, sometimes brilliantly so; and then it had thrown them out at the other end, propelling some on to greater things and others back to the obscurity from which they had emerged. The American officers hired as mercenaries in the Khedive's service had made the Egyptian army a force to be reckoned with, but had included their share of tale-spinners and egotists. Jones remembered one night by the Nile sitting with his officer Major Mayne and a group of other Royal Engineers officers and listening to them talk about Chaillé-Long and his exploits in equatorial Africa. He had been derided at the Royal Geographical Society for suggesting that Lake Victoria was only twelve miles across, having misidentified some islands as the opposite shore, and for trying to bribe a cartographer to make Lake Kyogo on the Upper Nile appear larger than it was, a blatant act of self-aggrandisement. It was also common knowledge that the wound on his face had not been caused by enemy fire but by his Sudanese cook, who had saved his life by shooting an attacking warrior with a revolver but in the process grazing Chaillé-Long on the face with the bullet.

Yet all the posturing and exaggeration was unnecessary. Chaillé-Long had indisputably gone further south than any other foreigner in the Khedive's service, showing the grit and determination so admired by the British and earning a letter of approbation from Gordon himself, published in the *New York Herald*. And he had no need to embellish his experience of fighting: Jones had respect for anyone who had been through the bloodbath of the American Civil War, and he knew that Chaillé-Long had been in at the sharp end. Beneath the foppery and affectation he had seen the look in his eyes he knew well from men who had faced death on the battlefield, and he had also seen the pearl-handled Colt revolver beneath the cape. Of one thing he was certain: Chaillé-Long was not a man to be trifled with, and Jones knew that having made the decision to approach him in the first place he was now committed to seeing this through with that man in the cape and top hat looming over him, whatever the outcome.

The captain of the boat whistled gently, and pointed to the shore. Chaillé-Long waved back and drew himself up. 'Now, Monsieur Guerin, if you will be so kind as to instruct us, Jones and I will assist you in donning your contraption. We have less than four hours until dawn, when we shall suddenly be conspicuous. We have no time to lose.'

4

Half an hour later Jones and Chaillé-Long watched as Guerin floated on the surface of the Nile, his underwater lamp lighting up a brown smudge of silt in the water around him. With some considerable effort they had heaved him off the side of the boat while the captain and his boy offset the balance on the other side, swinging the boom around and hanging out as far as they could from it without falling in. After they had slid Guerin into the water, trying to keep their splashing to the minimum, Jones had double-checked the regulator valve above the bulbous air tank on his back while Guerin had inspected his face mask for leaks. There were thirty atmospheres in the tank, pumped into it by a steam compressor in some backstreet mechanical shop that Guerin had found in Alexandria, and Jones could only hope that there was more air than fumes in the mix. If all went well, he should have some thirty minutes at the depth that

Jones had estimated for their target, about twenty-five feet below. Guerin had shown him the small safety shut-off he had devised for when the pressure reached ten atmospheres, indicating that it was time to surface but allowing him to open the flow again to breathe the final lungfuls of air from the cylinder before it emptied.

The regulator was hissing now, a froth of bubbles coming out with each exhalation. They watched as he vented the air bladder under his arms that had kept him afloat. As his head began to sink Jones reached out and tapped it. '*Bonne chance*, my friend. Remember to drop your lead weights when you intend to ascend, or else you will never make it back up.' Guerin nodded, raised a hand in farewell and dropped below the surface, the smudge of light quickly disappearing. After a few moments only the bubbles from his exhaust betrayed his presence, along with the detonator cord that Jones fed out as Guerin descended, attached to the dynamite in a box on the front of his suit. 'Damn it to hell,' Jones murmured. 'I forgot to remind him to breathe out as he ascends.'

Chaillé-Long dabbed his wet forearms with his handkerchief and rolled his sleeves back down. 'Breathe out? Why should he need reminding of that, might I enquire?'

'Because the instinct underwater is to hold your breath. We were taught that in diving class at the Royal Engineers School at Chatham. If you hold your breath while ascending, you get something called an embolism.'

Chaillé-Long snapped shut his cufflinks. 'And what might that be?'

'Your lungs rupture like an over-filled balloon.'

'Surely Monsieur Guerin would know of such things.'

'Monsieur Guerin is more an engineer than a diver, more a theoretician than a practitioner.'

'Elegantly put, Jones. You *are* an educated man, I find, more so than I might expect from the ruffians I have seen in the rank and file of your army.'

'Educated, but not a gentleman. A benefactor who visited my orphanage paid for me to go to the Bluecoat School in Bristol. But I was too rebellious and knew I'd never be polished enough to be admitted to the Royal Military Academy, so at sixteen I ran away from the school and joined my father's old regiment, the sappers and miners. They gave me some skills, but the rest is self-taught. I've always enjoyed reading. Done a lot of that over the past eight years, since the war.'

Chaillé-Long tucked his cloak under him and sat down on the bench on the foredeck. He adjusted his top hat, produced two cheroots from his waistcoat pocket, offered one to Jones, who declined it, and then lit the other one with a silver lighter, drawing deeply on it and crossing his legs. 'I've wanted to ask you about that, Jones, now that we have some time on our hands. About the last eight years. About the officer who pointed you in my direction, Major Mayne.'

Jones was looking at Guerin's bubbles, straining to follow them in the darkness as they advanced towards the shoreline and then seemed to veer a dozen or so yards to the north. The bubbles would be pulled further along by the current as they rose, giving a misleading impression of the position of the diver, but even so Guerin would soon be reaching the limit of the detonator cable. He watched anxiously, checking that the plunger box was still secure where he had nailed it to the deck, but then saw with relief that the bubbles were returning along the shore in the direction of the boat, no more than fifty feet away now. He perched on the gunwale, still keeping an eye on them, and glanced at Chaillé-Long.

'Major Mayne. Finest officer I ever knew. Without him, I wouldn't be here. He was the one who mentioned your name as one of Gordon's confidants, and when I came to need a partner for this enterprise you were the only one I could find of those officers still in Egypt. I took a risk in revealing what I did to you, but I knew you had money and without gold to pay for a boat and a diver I was going nowhere.'

'What were you doing with Mayne in the desert?'

Jones paused, looking at him shrewdly. 'He was a reconnaissance officer, and we carried out forays behind enemy lines. I was his servant, his batman.'

'You mean he was an intelligence officer. A spy.'

Jones paused again. 'Not exactly. I cleaned his rifle once. It was a Sharps 1873, 45-70 calibre, with a telescope sight and heavy octagonal barrel. One of your American sharpshooter rifles.'

'Sharps 45-70?' Chaillé-Long exhaled a lungful of smoke. 'Saw a man take out a buffalo with one at a thousand yards.'

'Well, I saw Mayne shoot a dervish across the Nile at over five hundred yards, and that was with a service Martini-Henry rifle,' Jones replied. 'It was the finest shot I've ever seen, so who knows what he was capable of with the Sharps.'

Chaillé-Long knit his brows. 'So, Mayne goes with this rifle on a mission to Khartoum, and a few weeks later Gordon is dead and, apparently, Mayne too, having disappeared and never been seen since?'

'That's what I told you when we first met.'

Chaillé-Long cocked an eye at him. 'All of the most reliable accounts of Gordon's last moments have him on the balcony of the Governor's Palace, surrounded by dervishes, in full view, as it happens, from the other bank of the Nile; let's say five hundred, six hundred yards distant, beyond the dervish encampment and where a sharpshooter might creep up and lie undetected, awaiting the right moment.'

'I know for a fact that Mayne met Gordon in Khartoum, the morning of his death.'

'You know this for a fact? How so?'

Jones checked himself; he had revealed enough. 'I've spent a lot of time amongst Arabs since then, and heard first hand from men who were in Khartoum that day.'

'Was Mayne alone in his enterprise?'

Jones paused. 'I did not see him depart for Khartoum from Wadi Halfa, where he went to be told of his mission by Lord Wolseley. I last saw him the day before on the Nile, where he left me with his belongings. That's when he gave me the inscribed stone that he and his fellow officers had found in the crocodile temple beside the pool, with the radiating sun symbol of the pharaoh Akhenaten that he had recognised as the plan of something underground, with the three temples at Giza clearly shown.'

'The artefact that brought us here,' Chaillé-Long exclaimed, taking another draw. 'The ancient map to something hidden beneath the very feet of all those many who have tramped the plateau of Giza seeking treasures, little knowing what might lie below.'

He clamped his cheroot hard, and then removed it and

picked out a piece of tobacco from between his teeth. He looked to the deck, and then at Jones again. 'Did the thought ever occur to you,' he said quietly, 'that Gordon alive in the hands of the Mahdi would have been a grave embarrassment to the British, a death knell for the Gladstone government, a fatal dent in the prestige of the Empire? Gordon alive, a Christian martyr abandoned to the forces of jihad; or Gordon alive, a willing partner of the Mahdi, a man so disgusted by the failure of his compatriots to rescue the people of the Sudan that he would cast in his lot with the enemy? Would not such a man have been a prime target for assassination?'

Jones kept his eyes glued on the waters below the riverbank. 'Thoughts are for officers, Colonel. I'm just a lowly sapper.'

Chaillé-Long thought for a moment, shook his head, then flicked his butt into the river, leaning back and smiling. 'But not any longer, it seems. You say you've been associating with Arabs. Tell me, Jones, are you a deserter?'

Jones coughed. 'Before Major Mayne left on his mission to Khartoum, he arranged for me to return to the railway construction unit that I'd been working with when I first arrived in Egypt after service in India. He thought railway construction would be safer, and would see me through the campaign. He was probably right, but as far as I could see neither the railway nor the river expedition were ever going to reach General Gordon in time, so I tossed a coin and stayed on the river. Everything was going swimmingly until the Mahdi's boys finally caught up with us at a place called Kirbekan, and there was a terrible twenty-minute battle. One moment I was bayoneting and bludgeoning dervishes, and the next thing I knew I was floating down the river all alone, with only the corpses of my mates for company. I fetched up at the same pool where the major had found the crocodile temple, and the clue in the inscription that he gave me for safekeeping. I stayed there for days, weeks, living off abandoned supplies. I'd been knocked on the head, and was half-crazed. We'd heard rumours of a giant crocodile in the pool, and I became obsessed with the idea of catching it, conceiving all manner of devices to do so. The *Leviathan* we'd called it, after the biblical monster. Then Kitchener and his camel troops arrived, and seeing them put some sense into me. You know Kitchener?'

Chaillé-Long nodded. 'Rising star of the Egyptian army. The man who has sworn to avenge Gordon.'

'I heard him say it. That he'd kill a dervish for every hair on Gordon's head. But I knew that could only be a long time in the future. It was Kitchener himself who told me that Gordon had been killed, and that the British force was retreating back to Egypt and abandoning the Sudan to the Mahdi. It was then that I knew that Major Mayne wouldn't be coming back, that it was a forlorn hope for me to wait for him. Then just before we reached the British camp at Abu Halfa on the Egyptian border I gave Kitchener the slip. I remembered what had happened after the battle of Kirbekan, and how it would look with me having disappeared. An army recovering after defeat is always looking for scapegoats and is never generous to soldiers they think have done a runner. I'd been cashiered before, out in India, even made sergeant once before being reduced. Too cocky for my own good, mostly; too many opinions for certain officers to stomach. But this time it was more serious. I didn't fancy having survived the dervishes at Kirbekan only to face a firing squad of my own mates at Abu Halfa.'

'That was more than eight years ago,' Chaillé-Long said. 'What have you done since then?'

Jones peered at him, and stroked his stubble. 'Master of disguise, I am. That's what Major Mayne used to call me. Within days of our reconnaissance missions behind dervish lines I'd look the part, with a beard and a turban. My mother was Anglo-Indian, the daughter of a British soldier and a Madrassi woman, so I'm naturally dark-skinned. I knew enough Madrassi to pass myself off as an Indian, and enough Arabic from Major Mayne and our time in the desert to get by. I learned to live like an Arab, to blend into the folds of the desert and the crowded souks of Cairo, to live without being noticed.'

'And you read books. You learned about the ancient Egyptians.'

'I joined with the fellahin who are used as labourers on digs and found work at Giza, clearing out the pyramids. I went to Amarna and became foreman of a French excavation there. No questions were ever asked; I looked the part of an Arab and with my engineering skills I could do the job well. I spent days in the Cairo Museum, working from cabinet to cabinet, memorising everything I saw. I learned to read hieroglyphics.' Jones lowered his voice. 'I learned everything I could about *him*.'

'Him?'

Jones leaned forward, almost whispering. 'Long-face. That's what the Canadian Indians called him. We had them with us on the Nile expedition, you know, voyageurs, brought over from Canada by Lord Wolseley to navigate the boats. On the way up they'd stopped at Amarna and seen the crumbled statues of the pharaoh who had built the city, that strange face with the big lips. In the Mohawk language they called him *Menakouhare*, long-face. The name stuck with me.'

'You mean Akhenaten.'

'The Sun Pharaoh,' Jones said, his voice a hoarse whisper. 'Father of Tutankhamun, the boy-Pharaoh. The one who went south to the desert as Amenhotep the fourth, high priest of the old religion, and came back as Akhenaten, *He through whom the Light shone from the Aten, the Sun God*. He went south with his wife Nefertiti and his companion Moses, the former slave who had the same revelation and took away his vision of the one god to his people. They were in the crocodile temple, the one Mayne found beside the pool on the Nile. I saw it myself, steeled myself to go inside in the weeks I spent there alone after the battle, when my mind was unbalanced. I saw the wall carving, with Menakouhare at the head of the procession, the Aten symbol before him. I saw the gap where Mayne had taken the plaque that I showed you. Akhenaten had his vision in the desert, but his City of Light was not to be there: it was to be here, out of sight and hidden in the heartland of ancient Egypt. And we will be the first to see it in three thousand years.'

Chaillé-Long put his hand on his hip, and eyed Jones keenly. 'When we have made our great discovery, you and I will be much in demand. We will be on the front page of the *New York Herald* and the *Illustrated London News*, and around the world. People still reeling from the death of General Gordon, from his *neglect*, will see our triumph as his apotheosis, as proof that he was in Khartoum for a higher purpose, not only to succour the people of Sudan but also to safeguard the clues to a discovery that will be for the enlightenment of mankind. I have little doubt that on my return I will be called to the House of Representatives, even the Senate. You should come with me, Jones. America is a place for a man like you. There are railways to be built, rivers to be dammed. With my connections and good word I can propel you on a path to riches and fame, unfettered by the barriers of class and etiquette of your own country that keep men like you in the gutter.'

Jones turned to watch Guerin's bubbles, the detonator cord still slack in his hands. The lofty intentions, the talk of taking the world by storm, of business collaborations with Guerin, could all be a smokescreen, a play by a man who when the time was right, when the discovery was certain, could as easily sweep them aside and take all the glory for himself. Jones did not know whether the style of the man in front of him was that of a true gentleman, or merely a veneer of decency. He had seen what war did to men, and civil war was the worst, war that pitted brother against brother, men who after that could plumb no greater depths. The America that Chaillé-Long spoke of was a place where ambition might know no bounds, but only in the shattered morality that was the aftershock of the Civil War. He had heard stories of latter-day robber barons carving out fiefdoms for themselves in the west with the Colt and the Winchester. It would be an easy matter on a night like this when the time was right for a man like Chaillé-Long to use that revolver beneath his cloak to dispose of them all: a British army deserter long thought dead, an obscure French inventor who seemed intent on keeping his very existence secret, a Nile river boat captain and his boy, adding a few more to the cargo of unidentifiable corpses swept down annually by the Nile into the swamplands of the delta.

Jones too had been hardened by killing, but not at the expense of his own soldierly brand of morality. As a soldier he had been a maverick, constantly pressing against authority, an enlisted man with the wayward thinking only allowed to officers. Yet not for the first time he found himself missing the army, the moral certainty of those who worked and fought for one another. Out here, in the world beyond the army, he had discovered that the only person you could rely on was yourself, but in so doing all of your flaws and weaknesses became sharply defined, and the personal demons kept at bay in the army rose up to do battle for your soul and mind when there were no others to discipline and protect you.

But he had laid a smokescreen of his own, and had not told Chaillé-Long everything. In the last eight years he had learned to move in the shadowlands, to bend the truth to his purposes. He knew what had happened to Mayne; he had guessed who had ordered it. Chaillé-Long was right; Gordon had become a liability, but so too would be the one ordered to carry out the deed, a deed so shocking to public sentiment that word of it must never be allowed to leak out. And Mayne had not gone to Khartoum alone, but with his friend, his blood brother from their service together years earlier on the Red River expedition in Canada, a voyageur named Charrière. After Jones had left the crocodile pool with Kitchener they had ridden out into the desert to join the route back from

Khartoum to the Egyptian border, and Jones had been astonished one night to see a form he recognised as Charrière slip by, heading north. Jones followed him to Wadi Halfa, where he had seen Charrière go alone into Lord Wolseley's tent. It was then that he knew what Charrière had done. Wolseley had been a patron and benefactor to the Mohawk Indians since he had first employed their services in Canada; Charrière would be beholden to him, and was someone who would disappear back to the forests of Canada as silently as he had crossed the desert from Khartoum, trusted never to tell anyone what he had done.

And there was something else that Jones had not told Chaillé-Long. It was not only the plaque from the crocodile temple that had given him the clue to this place. That night at Wadi Halfa he had risked all and crept into Charrière's tent while he was with Wolseley. In Charrière's bag he had found Gordon's journal of his final days in Khartoum, something that he must have entrusted to Mayne, that Charrière must then have taken from him but clearly decided not to show to Wolseley. In the frantic few seconds in the tent he had seen an incredible drawing inside the back cover, something that had etched itself on his mind. It was another clue to Akhenaten that Gordon himself had uncovered, a more detailed version of the plan on the plaque: it too showed the Aten sun symbol, the lines radiating off from the centre with the cluster of three squares showing the Giza pyramids at one corner. Jones had hastily copied down a series of hieroglyph cartouches that Gordon had inscribed at the bottom of the page, and then packed the diary back in the bag and fled into the night.

It was Gordon's sketch that had been his biggest revelation, and had allowed him to understand the plaque. One day several years later working with the fellahin at Giza he realised that the three small squares exactly mapped the relationship of the pyramids on the plateau; he was then able to use the sketch and the plaque to triangulate their position at the river from the pyramids, following one of the radiating lines from the sun symbol that he believed represented underground passageways. Finding what lay beneath became an obsession for him, not because he was drawn by a promise of ancient riches but because it was about discovering a truth that seemed to give a nobility of purpose to their enterprise in the desert, something that could exonerate Mayne, even Gordon, that would stand in stark contrast to the grim reality of failure and dishonour in their avowed reason for being there. In his fevered imagination, gripped once again by the same mania that had enveloped him at the crocodile pool, he had even felt himself on the same elevated mission as Gordon in Khartoum, as someone who had thrown away all of the shackles to the outside world and his past life in order to devote himself to a higher purpose.

He was barely out of this state, in the grips of the deep melancholia that followed, when he had been begging near Shepheard's Hotel in Cairo and had overheard guests mentioning Chaillé-Long and his law practice in Alexandria. Jones had already realised that he was going to have to enlist the help of others with money if he were ever going to get to the bottom of the mystery. Then, less than a month ago, he had experienced another astonishing revelation. He had learned hieroglyphics specifically to translate the cartouches he had copied from Gordon's journal. He had learned to recognise the royal cartouche of Akhenaten, one of the three in the journal, but the other two had defeated him. And then he had a blinding revelation. The symbols for the Aten, for sun and light, did not mean sunlight after all, but something more down to earth and far more astonishing. This place he was searching for was not just a holy sanctum of a new religion: it was a treasure house – yet a treasure few Egyptologists would ever have imagined possible even in their wildest dreams.

He had not yet told Chaillé-Long because he could not calculate the effect that such a revelation might have on the man, and the actions he might take as a consequence. He was fearful also of word leaking out. Cairo eight years after the war was seething with men of loose purpose drawn by tales of ancient riches to be discovered, who had subverted their passion for war by an obsession with tombs and pharaohs. Until Guerin returned from his dive with word that they were in the right place, his revelation would remain a secret known to him alone, preserved only on a crumpled piece of paper concealed in his belt and in a journal that he presumed by now had disappeared with Charrière beyond knowledge, somewhere on the far side of the world.

Chaillé-Long stood up, and consulted his fob watch. 'He's been down half an hour now,' he said. 'He must be up soon.' Jones stood up as well, scanning the water. He realised that he was now able to see more clearly; looking over the riverbank he could just make out the distant triangles of the pyramids at Giza, caught in the first red glow of dawn.

His heart began to pound. *This was it*.

5

The boat lurched and then trembled again, as if something were bumping along the side. 'What's that infernal knocking?' Chaillé-Long said. The boy ran over to look, and Jones followed his gaze. Something big was floating just under the surface, heaving upwards and bobbing in the current, its form indiscernible beneath the muddy water. Whatever it was had caught the boat and was pulling it out into the current, forcing the captain to push bodily against the tiller to keep the vessel beam-on to the shore. Jones felt the detonator line tighten, but there was still no sign of Guerin's light coming up in the water. The captain shouted at the boy in high-pitched Arabic, gesturing frantically with one free hand at the long wooden pole lying just inside the gunwale. The boy picked it up and lowered the end with the iron hook over the side, holding it upright and walking it along to find the obstruction. The boat veered further into the current, its deck angled down amidships on the port side; the captain was fighting a losing battle with the tiller. He waved wildly with his free hand for Chaillé-Long and Jones to remain where they were on the starboard side to keep the port rail from going under.

The boy stopped, then heaved with all his might. Suddenly the boat lurched upright and the pole angled back to horizontal, the hook caught in a tendril that had pulled up from the main mass of the object, now detached from the boat and floating free. The boy stumbled forward and fell to his knees, trying to free the pole. The captain shouted again in Arabic and Jones saw the danger of the boy being pulled overboard. He leapt on him, still holding the detonator cord, pinned the boy's legs against the deck and grasped the pole. He tried to yank it backwards and forwards to release the hook, but to no avail. As he made one last desperate attempt the object reared up and became visible in an eddy, pitching and rolling as the water swirled around it.

Jones stared in horror, transfixed. The boy had gone white, and the captain had dropped to his knees wild-eyed, sobbing and beseeching Allah. A smell, suppressed by the river while it was underwater, now rose from the object as it rolled on the surface, a smell of colossal, all-encompassing decay. Jones felt sick to the stomach; it was his worst nightmare come true. *It was a crocodile.* Or rather, it was the putrefied, long-dead carcass of a crocodile, its giant skeleton flecked with tendrils of white and grey, just enough matter to have kept it afloat on its final voyage from whatever pool it had inhabited somewhere far upriver.

'*God protect me.*' Jones' breathing quickened, and he grasped his hands round the detonator cord, trying to stop them shaking. *Chaillé-Long must not see.* He flashed back to his state of mind beside the crocodile temple eight years ago. He must not sink into that madness again. He had convinced himself that his obsession with the Leviathan had been delirium brought on by his head wound, something he had snapped out of with the arrival of Kitchener and his camel troops. But suddenly that rationality disappeared, and he felt as if he were being drawn back there again. With all of the fiendish contraptions he had devised, all that his engineering knowledge could spirit up, the dynamite, the trip-wire guns, had he truly killed the sacred crocodile of the pool, a crocodile whose long-dead carcass had now caught up with him? A fear began to grip him, a fear that he knew could become panic, spreading to all of his other dark places, to the fear of confined spaces, of being trapped underground, a fear he had last felt in the gloomy basement rooms of the Cairo museum among the rows of decaying mummies. It was as if the demons of his own underworld were released again, clawing at him and beckoning him down into the portal that lay somewhere beneath them now, the entrance to a world of the dead that lay just below the riverbank.

The detonator cord suddenly yanked him back to his senses. Chaillé-Long was lifting up the underwater lamp, its power virtually expended. Guerin had surfaced on the opposite side of the boat to the carcass, his mask and hood stripped off, panting and wheezing. '*Préparez le plongeur*,' he gasped. 'The charge is laid.' Jones lurched over and gripped the handle of the plunger, winding it hard to generate enough electricity to set off the charge. Something inside him, a voice from his army training long ago, told him that this was wrong, that he should only prepare the plunger the instant before setting it off; they still had to hear from Guerin about what he had found. But the winding focused him, and gave a reason for his shallow breathing. He left the plunger ready and crawled over to the side of the boat. Guerin was fumbling with something in his suit, but looked up at the other two, his eyes feverish and bloodshot. 'I found it. Half an hour of digging, and I exposed the lintel. It bears this inscription.' He heaved up a wooden slate with a hieroglyphic cartouche scratched on it. Jones took it, his hands shaking now with excitement. 'My God,' he said hoarsely. 'Look, Colonel. I was right. It's the royal cartouche of Akhenaten.'

Chaillé-Long raised himself up and stood above the two men, one thumb hitched in his fob pocket, the ivory grip of his pistol clear to see. 'I do believe, gentlemen, we have come up trumps.'

'There's a stone door below the lintel, and it's closed,' Guerin gasped, grimacing in evident pain. 'And the charge is laid against it. But, *mes amis*, I should warn you . . .' He coughed violently, swallowed, and coughed again. 'I should warn you,' he wheezed, 'if the tunnel beyond is not flooded, there will be *un vortex*, and if we blow open the door there may be something of, how do you say, a whirlpool.'

Chaillé-Long looked disdainfully at the captain, who was sitting huddled with the boy beside the tiller, apparently still praying. 'Well, I understand that they are used to whirlpools along this part of the river. A little disturbance might knock some sense into those two. And at any rate,' he said, picking up a distended pig's bladder normally used as a fishing float, 'I for one am prepared for a swim if it comes to it.'

The boat lurched again. Jones could not bring himself to look back over the other side. Guerin reached up with one hand and held the gunwale. 'What was that?'

Chaillé-Long shrugged. 'Some more floating debris in the water, no doubt. Nothing to concern yourself about, my friend.'

Jones knelt over the plunger, protecting the handle from any knocks, and looked at him. 'There's something more I should tell you. About what's down there. I mean what's *really* down there. What Akhenaten built under the pyramids.'

'I know enough,' Chaillé-Long said imperiously, glancing again at his watch. 'We have found what we came for.' The boat seemed to rise slightly and then slide out into the river current, tightening the detonator cord. 'You must detonate that charge now, Jones.'

Guerin looked up. 'Do it, *mon ami*. I'm far enough away to be safe.'

Jones shook his head. 'You know nothing about explosives, Guerin. About underwater shock waves.'

Guerin coughed. A great gob of blood came up, and he retched. He gasped over and over again, bringing up a bubbling red froth each time. 'He's had an embolism,' Jones exclaimed, peering up at Chaillé-Long. 'The shock wave would surely kill him now. We need to get him on board.'

'Depress the plunger, Jones. The boat is pulling the detonator cord and the charge away from the riverbank, and this is our last chance. *Your* last chance.' Chaillé-Long was behind him, his voice cold. Suddenly a huge lurch rocked the boat and he was thrown sideways. As he spun around he saw Chaillé-Long lose his balance, stagger backwards and then fall forward, landing heavily on the plunger. The boat swung into the current, pulling the detonator cord and plunger into the water, leaving Guerin floating in a bloody froth towards the shore. Suddenly the river in front of him erupted in a boiling mushroom of water, sending ripples of shock through the boat and across the river. Seconds later it was followed by a dull boom, and then an extraordinary sound, quite unlike any underwater explosion Jones had ever heard before, seemingly coming from far off under the riverbank. He remembered Guerin's warning, and suddenly realised what it was: an echo, coming from a hollow chamber, a dry passage, running deep under the desert. Whatever lay beyond that portal was no simple chamber, but a long passage, large enough to consume a giant torrent of water if the charge had succeeded in blowing open the stone entrance.

For a moment all was calm. Guerin was floating in the water, unconscious or dead. Chaillé-Long lay sprawled on the deck, groaning and clutching his makeshift pig's bladder float. The captain and his boy were nowhere to be seen. And then, slowly at first but with increased violence, the water in front of him started to swirl round like a giant sinkhole, taking the boat with it. Jones could do nothing but kneel in horror at the gunwale, watching the centre of the swirl as it plummeted deeper and deeper into the vortex, seeing the boat drop below the surface of the river. He saw Guerin's body swirled out of sight, sucked down. And then for a fleeting moment he saw what Guerin had seen, a stone portal, a flashing image of pillars and a hieroglyphic inscription, a dark passage beyond, and then he felt the boat splinter around him and he himself was hurtling forward on a torrent of water, unable to breathe or hear, seeing only blackness beyond.

PART 2

6

Alexandria, Egypt, present day

Jack Howard walked along the old quayside of Alexandria harbour towards Qaitbey, the 15th century fort built on the foundations of the ancient lighthouse that now served as headquarters for Maurice Hiebermeyer's Institute of Archaeology. The sun was beating on the rock, the light shimmering off the waters of the harbour, and for a few moments Jack allowed himself to relish the summer air of the Mediterranean and forget that he was in a country on the brink of war. He cast his mind back ten years to the discovery of a scrap of papyrus in the mummy necropolis in the Faiyum that had led them to the truth behind the Atlantis legend. The Egyptian student who had made the discovery was now Hiebermeyer's wife, and together they had created one of the premier centres in Egypt for the study of archaeology. Jack had a strong sense of déjà vu as he made his way across the worn stones towards the fort; he was going to hear the latest from the mummy necropolis, still an ongoing excavation producing extra-ordinary finds, and he in turn was going to match Maurice with an account of their latest underwater discoveries, hoping for that sparking of ideas and rush of excitement as things fell into place that had marked their collaboration over the years.

But there was a dark side to this day. All of Jack's projects since Atlantis had been threaded together, interlinked by discoveries that had sent him around the world, from Egypt to Greece and Turkey, from India and Central Asia to ancient Herculaneum and across the Atlantic to the frigid waters of Greenland and the jungles of the Yucatan; the loose ends of one project had become the beginnings of another. Yet for the first time today he had felt a looming sense of finality, that what had begun here a decade ago was about to offer up its last, that the extraordinary wellspring of ancient Egypt was about to close down forever. He felt edgy, nervous, and that heightened sense of awareness he experienced while diving was now with him all the time. If there were to be any more discoveries in Egypt, they were going to have to happen in the next days, even the next hours, through a window that was rapidly closing down on all of them.

He stared over the bobbing boats in the harbour at the extraordinary form of the Bibliotheca Alexandrina, the new Library of Alexandria. Just like its predecessor, the famous *mouseion* founded by the Macedonian king Ptolemy in 283 BC, the library seemed fated to suffer from religious extremism; back then it had been Christianity, culminating in the anti-pagan purge by the Roman emperor Theodosius in AD 391 that led to the library's destruction, whereas now it was extremism and the threat of regional war. The reconstructed library had been a noble enterprise at a time when many believed that the Internet and electronic publishing had eclipsed the need for physical repositories of knowledge, and yet the threat of destruction and of Internet sabotage meant that electronic means of data storage were just as vulnerable as the libraries of old. Each epoch seemed destined to build up a critical mass of knowledge, only for it to be largely destroyed and a few precious fragments to survive – buried by chance like the library that Jack had excavated at the Roman site of Herculaneum, or the shreds of papyrus reused as mummy wrappings that Hiebermeyer and his team had unearthed in the desert necropolis.

Jack shaded his eyes against the sun, thinking about the Atlantis papyrus. The story of Atlantis had come down from the 6th century BC Athenian traveller Solon, who had visited the Egyptian temple of Sais, heard it from the High Priest and had then written it down, only for his original papyrus to have been lost and then reused as mummy wrapping. The knowledge memorised by the High Priest had been passed down through generations from earliest times, an oral tradition whose days were numbered with the arrival in Egypt of the Greeks and their new religion. But what if at the height of ancient Egypt, during the New Kingdom of the later second millennium BC, a visionary pharaoh had decided to collate and transcribe all of that ancient knowledge? What if there had been an *earlier* library, somewhere in the heartland of ancient Egypt? Jack stared at the extraordinary discoid shape of the modern Bibliotheca, deliberately designed to look like a sun disk rising out of the horizon to the east. Who would that visionary pharaoh have been? Would it have been Akhenaten, the one who rejected the old religions, the pharaoh who worshipped the sun god, the Aten?

Jack reached into his pocket and took out a military campaign medal from the Victorian period that he had bought from a market stall near the docks where the taxi had dropped him off. It was a Khedive's Star, worn and battered, awarded to an Egyptian soldier who had fought under British command in the 1880s war against the Mahdi in Sudan. Jack thought again of those British officers in the desert who were not only there for war, but whose exploration for ancient sites had so fascinated him. Had they been hunting not just for confirmation of Old Testament history, but for something even greater than that, for a lost repository containing the greatest treasure that a civilisation could offer, the accumulated wisdom and knowledge of the ancient Egyptians?

He grasped the medal until the points of the star hurt his hand, and then thrust it back into his pocket. These thoughts had run through his mind endlessly since he and Costas and Hiebermeyer had been forced to leave Sudan almost two months previously, bringing with them enough evidence from the ancient temple carvings beside the Nile to suggest that Akhenaten's City of Light lay somewhere near modern Cairo and that the pyramids were the key to its entry. He and Costas had been there, on the cusp of an incredible discovery, suspended beneath the Pyramid of Menkaure and seeing where the reflected sunlight shone against something far ahead, beyond a tunnel almost completely blocked by rock fall. Ever since they had been forced to leave the site he had tried not to think of it, knowing that there was no chance of them returning with the tools they would have needed to break their way through. He had gone to the Gulf of Suez intent on moving on, and yet as long as he was in Egypt, as long as there was a glimmer of hope, the image of Akhenaten kept returning to him. Perhaps there was another entrance to the underground complex, closer to the Nile. He needed to look again at the plan that he believed was preserved in the radiating arms of the Aten sun symbol on the plaque from the wreck of the *Beatrice*, and at the known layout of the early dynastic canal system that linked the Pyramids with the Nile. As long as there were still IMU feet on the ground in Egypt, he would pursue it. *He would not give up*.

Ten minutes later he mounted the worn stone steps at the entrance to Qaitbey Fort, passing the red granite blocks from the toppled ancient lighthouse that had been incorporated into the fort when it had been built in 1480. Inside, Hiebermeyer's institute occupied a modern single-storey stone structure set against one wall of the courtyard, with a library, a conservation lab and research facilities for the Egyptian graduate students who were the mainstay of Hiebermeyer's team, funded by a fellowship scheme managed by his wife Aysha. On the opposite side of the courtyard were the foundations of the new museum being funded by IMU's main benefactor, Efram Jacobovich, to complement their existing museum in the ancient harbour at Carthage in Tunisia; the Alexandrian museum would showcase shipwreck finds made by IMU teams off the north coast of Egypt and in the Nile. Like everything else here, like the fellowship scheme, the future of the museum project now hung on a thread, something that Jack knew he was going to have to discuss with Hiebermeyer once they had shared the excitement of their latest discoveries.

Costas came hurrying up the steps behind him, holding out a VHF radio. 'Jack, there's a message from Captain Macalister on *Seaquest*. He wants to talk to you as soon as possible.'

Jack shook his head. 'Not now. I've got to devote all of my attention to Maurice. It's going to be pretty intense in there. Every time I checked the news in the taxi from the airport the situation in Cairo seemed to be deteriorating. This could be Maurice's swansong at the institute. Tell Macalister I'll contact him in an hour.'

'Okay. I'll deal with anything urgent.' Costas stopped to make the call, and Jack turned into the courtyard. On the wall to the left was an IMU poster showing *Seaquest*, the research vessel that was his pride and joy, an image now as iconic from her many expeditions around the world as Captain Cousteau's *Calypso* had been in his youth. For much of the summer she had been in the West Mediterranean off Spain with an IMU team excavating the wreck of the *Beatrice*, the ship that had been taking the sarcophagus of the pharaoh Menkaure to the British Museum when she had foundered in 1824; it was the discovery of an extraordinary plaque within the sarcophagus, not of Menkaure but of Akhenaten, that had propelled Jack on his current quest. But right now he was more concerned with the whereabouts of *Seaquest*'s sister ship *Sea Venture*, which had been carrying out geological research off the volcanic island of Santorini north of Crete. Like

Seaquest she carried a Lynx helicopter, and she had been diverted south towards Egypt ready for an evacuation. Jack had been relieved to see the line of crates on the helipad beside the fort, but it had also made him unexpectedly well up with emotion. If that image brought home the reality of the situation to him, he could hardly imagine how it made Maurice feel. Not for the first time he was thankful for the presence of Aysha, a rock who had kept Maurice anchored through storms in the past and was going to be needed more than ever now.

Costas came up behind him, and together they walked through an open doorway into Hiebermeyer's main operations room. It was a familiar clutter of computer workstations, filing cabinets, books and papers, though the wall by the door was lined with plastic boxes where material had been packed for departure. Hiebermeyer himself was seated with his back to them behind an outsized monitor in the centre of the room. Jack smiled as he saw the tattered khaki shorts, an Africa Korps relic from the Second World War that he had given him years before at the outset of their careers. He was still wearing his leather work boots and was caked from head to foot in dust, having driven in from the desert that morning. The day before, Jack had used the secure IMU channel on the VHF radio to fill him in on their discovery while they had been waiting by the Red Sea for their nitrogen levels to reduce enough to allow them to fly, and there was more to tell him now. But he was determined that Hiebermeyer should have first say; there must have been something exciting for him to have taken a break from the mummy excavation and come all the way here to meet them.

Hiebermeyer turned as they entered. 'Jack. Costas. Good to see you.'

'You too, Maurice.' Hiebermeyer looked exhausted, even more weather-beaten than usual, and Jack noticed that he had lost weight since they had last met. 'What have you got?'

Hiebermeyer gestured at a paused image from Al-Jazeera news on the TV screen above him, showing a reporter in front of the dark shapes of the pyramids on the Giza plateau. 'What we've mainly got is that cleric raving again about blowing up the pyramids, the one who hit the headlines a few years ago when he first threatened to do it. Then, it seemed like a sick joke. Now it looks like reality.'

'Let's forget that for a moment. I want to see what *you've* got.'

Hiebermeyer stared at him, his eyes suddenly gleaming. 'All right, Jack. Prepare to be amazed.'

'Go on.'

He pointed to his computer screen. 'Take a look at this.' He clicked the mouse and an image of an ancient underground chamber appeared, with plastered walls, an array of artefacts in the corners and a mummy casing in the centre, its painted eyes just visible.

Jack peered closely. 'Well, I'll be damned,' he murmured. 'Undisturbed?'

'Completely intact,' Hiebermeyer enthused. 'It's an incredible rarity; there's no evidence of tomb robbing at all. Last night I was the first person in that chamber for more than three thousand years. It's eighteenth dynasty, Jack, I'm sure of it.'

'Eighteenth dynasty,' Costas said. 'Late second millennium

BC? I know most of the necropolis is later than that, from the first millennium BC, like the mummy that produced the Atlantis papyrus.'

Hiebermeyer peered at him. '*Mein Gott*. Costas, we'll make an archaeologist of you yet.'

'No chance of that, my friend. Not as long as you guys have robotic equipment you don't know how to fix. So is this a royal burial?'

Hiebermeyer shook his head. 'Not in the Faiyum Oasis. They're mostly officials, though some of them are pretty high ranking. This one's an army officer, a previously unknown chariot general by the name of Mehnet-Ptah. Actually, it wasn't the mummy casing that got me so excited, but the wall painting. That's really what I wanted you to see.' He clicked the mouse again, changing the image to a close-up of one of the walls, showing flaking coloured plaster. 'What do you make of that?'

Costas leaned over his shoulder and peered closely, and then straightened up. 'Men in skirts. The usual Egyptian thing.'

Hiebermeyer snorted impatiently. 'You mean Egyptian infantry, marching to the right and carrying spears. Now, if I scroll the image along, you can see chariots, just like the ones you've found in the Gulf of Suez, the charioteers holding bows. And now here's another group of charioteers, larger than the first and more elaborately attired.' He paused, looking up. 'Any thoughts?'

Jack stared. The charioteers were also skirted, but wearing sandals, some form of cuirass and distinctive segmented helmets, and they were carrying short thrusting swords with bows slung over their shoulders. Above them was a faded hieroglyphic cartouche and the symbol of a bull's horns. Jack felt a rush of excitement. 'Mercenaries,' he exclaimed. 'But not any old mercenaries. These are *Aegean* mercenaries. Those are bone and tusk helmets like the ones found at Mycenae, and the swords are the same type we found on the Minoan shipwreck we were excavating when you and Aysha discovered the Atlantis papyrus.'

'Perfect,' Hiebermeyer said. 'And they're completely consistent with an eighteenth dynasty date. Before then we'd expect to see Nubian mercenaries, large dark-skinned men from the desert. But by the eighteenth dynasty they'd become too integrated within Egyptian society. Mercenaries have to be outsiders, with no vested interest in the politics, only in it for the loot and the battle. Think of the Varangian bodyguard of the Byzantine emperor in Constantinople, Vikings from Scandinavia. They guarded the emperors over a period of several centuries, but they weren't born and bred in Constantinople. New recruits came from Scandinavia, and returned once they'd finished their service and made their fortunes. I believe that the same happened in Egypt during the eighteenth dynasty with the sea peoples from the north.'

'Mycenaeans?' Costas offered.

'That's what you might think. We know that by the fourteenth century BC the Mycenaeans from mainland Greece had taken over the island of Crete. We think of the Mycenaeans as a warrior society, so you might assume that Aegean mercenaries of this date would be Mycenaean. But the truth is more interesting. *Far* more interesting. In fact, it revolutionises our picture of this period. For a start, the word in that hieroglyphic cartouche, *Hau-nebut*, doesn't specifically denote Mycenaeans, but it's an old Egyptian term for Aegean peoples used from the time when the Minoan civilisation of Crete dominated the Aegean. Why would that term with its strong Minoan connotations be used for these warriors if they were Mycenaeans, who were quite distinct? And the bull's horn symbol specifically denotes Crete, where the symbol is so prominent on the palaces of the Minoans.'

Jack took out his phone and showed Hiebermeyer the screensaver, part of a fragmentary painting showing ducks flying out of a papyrus thicket, impressionistic in shades of blue. 'I've still got this from when we last debated it, Maurice.' He glanced at Costas. 'It's a wall painting from Akhenaten's new city of Amarna. It's a typically Egyptian scene, but very reminiscent in style of the Minoan wall paintings from Crete. Amarna also famously produced a cache of clay tablets that shows the extent of trade with the Aegean during this period. I argued that the link with Crete wasn't just about trade, but that there were cultural influences as well. Akhenaten had turned the old Egyptian religion on its head, and was clearly receptive to outside ideas. Now that I see what Maurice has found, it figures that he might have had Aegean mercenaries too. Akhenaten may have been something of a dreamer but he was practical enough to survive as pharaoh for more than twenty years, so having a strong force of mercenaries who would not be swayed by the factions against him would have made a lot of sense.'

Hiebermeyer swivelled his chair and raised his hands in a gesture of surrender to Jack, and then cracked a grin. 'You and I have debated it for years, and finally I'm forced to concede.

It was a two-way process. Egypt influenced Greece, and now we know it also happened in reverse. And there's even more. In the sixteenth century BC, the first pharaoh of the eighteenth dynasty, Ahmose I, made an astonishing dynastic marriage. A stone stele in the temple of Amun at Thebes describes his wife Ahhotep as "Mistress of the Shores of Hau-nebut". That's the first known use of the word *Hau-nebut*, the term for the Aegean lands, for Crete, that you see in the cartouche here. It goes on to say the following: "Her reputation is high over every foreign land." This leads me to the most astonishing revelation in our necropolis find.'

Costas had been peering again at the image of the tomb painting on Hiebermeyer's screen. He coughed, pointing. 'About those cuirasses. Those breastplates. I mean, *breast-plates*.'

Hiebermeyer swivelled back to the screen, and grinned again. 'I was wondering when you'd notice.'

'Not men in skirts.'

'Not men in skirts.'

'No,' Costas said, shaking his head. 'These are *girl* mercenaries.'

'Good God,' Jack exclaimed, peering. 'You're right.'

'Feast your eyes on this, then.' Hiebermeyer swept the mouse and the next charioteer in the army came into view, an astonishing sight. It was unambiguously a woman, her breasts bare above her cuirass, her head towering above the others. Her long hair was braided down her back and she held swirling snakes above her head. Jack gasped. 'It's the Minoan mother-goddess, the Mistress of the Animals.'

'Not quite, Jack. Look at that cartouche above her head. It's exactly the same as the one for Ahhotep, a century and a half earlier. 'Not "Mistress of the Animals", but "Mistress of the Shores of Hau-nebut".'

Jack's mind raced. 'What are you thinking, Maurice?'

'I'm thinking, forget all that romantic guff about the Minoans being peace-loving idealists. You just didn't survive in the Bronze Age that way. The term "Mistress of the Animals" was made up by Sir Arthur Evans when he excavated Knossos and wanted it to be some kind of paradise, an idealised antidote to the ugly modern world of a hundred years ago. You English can be sentimentalists, Jack. "Mistress of the Shores of Hau-nebut" is undoubtedly a military term, like "Count of the Saxon Shore" for the late Roman defender of Britain. Crete was an island too, and that's where her defences lay. Your Minoan mother-goddess was in truth a Boudicca or a Valkyrie, a warrior queen.'

Jack's mind raced. 'Here's a scenario. The volcano on Thera erupts in the fifteenth century BC, right? Minoan civilisation is devastated, leaving Crete vulnerable to Mycenaean takeover. Shortly before that a Minoan queen marries an Egyptian pharaoh, Ahhotep and Ahmose I. The bloodline of the Minoan rulers passes down not in Crete but through the eighteenth dynasty in Egypt. Maybe that fuels the brilliant mix of genius, military leadership and iconoclasm that makes the New Kingdom stand out so much, peaking with Akhenaten and his wife Nefertiti. Meanwhile, the warrior tradition of Minoan Crete, the *female* warrior tradition, survives the Mycenaean takeover, perhaps in the remote mountain fastnesses of the south. For generations those warriors sell themselves to the highest bidder, led by a woman the Egyptians knew by the old title of their first Minoan queen, Mistress of the Shores of Hau-nebut. How does that sound?'

Hiebermeyer opened his arms. 'That's one small corner of Egyptology conceded. One *small* corner.'

Jack was thinking the unthinkable. *And King Minos was a woman.* He put his hand on Hiebermeyer's shoulder. 'Congratulations, Maurice. Really brilliant. This might just lead to that joint book we've often talked about. Rewriting contact between Egypt and Crete in the late Bronze Age.'

'And putting women on the map,' Costas said, still staring at the charioteer. 'Big time.'

Hiebermeyer turned back to the computer, clicked the mouse and called up the first image, showing the tomb with its contents. 'There's more to be found in there, Jack. A lot more. We've been working against the clock, and I've had to make just about the hardest decision of my life, to shut down the tomb and seal it. There are already too many other parts of the excavation ongoing that need to be finished up. I can't even report the tomb discovery, as that would see the looters descend like vultures as soon as we leave the place. I'm not even sure about the book idea, Jack. What we've just discussed is going to have to remain our own speculation, as it's too controversial to publish without the full excavation and appraisal of that tomb. We all know what happens when a theory like that gets put out prematurely and is ridiculed. It then takes ten times more evidence than is needed to make it stick.'

Hiebermeyer slumped forward, his head in his hands, looking defeated. For a moment Jack felt paralysed, unable to think of anything to say that might help. He had a sudden flashback to their boyhood together at boarding school in England, swapping dreams about the great discoveries they would one day make as archaeologists. Those discoveries had come to pass, more than they could ever have imagined, and yet there still seemed as much to uncover as there ever had been; no single treasure was the culmination of the dream, and every extraordinary revelation spurred them on towards another. It seemed impossible that the perversity of extremism, of human self-destruction, should overtake that dream, and Jack knew that if their friendship meant anything he should do all he could to push Maurice through and see that their shared passion was never extinguished.

Costas put a hand on Hiebermeyer's shoulder. 'Don't kill yourself over it, man. You're doing the best you can. There's light at the end of the tunnel.'

Hiebermeyer grasped his hand for a moment. 'Thanks, Costas. You and Jack have seen it, haven't you? That light, underneath the pyramid. As long as we know it's there, maybe there's hope for us yet.'

Jack took out a memory stick and inserted it into Hiebermeyer's computer. 'I know you have to return to the necropolis as soon as you can, but I want to show you an image from our dive that you haven't seen yet. I'd like Aysha in on this. Is she around?'

Hiebermeyer gestured at the door. 'Outside on the quay, talking to our son on the phone. We sent him away to stay with my mother in Germany. This place has become too dangerous for a five-year-old. She said she'd come back in here when she finishes.'

'I sent him a picture from our dive,' Costas said. 'A selfie of Uncle Costas with a sea snake wrapped round his helmet, and a goofy face.'

'That's good of you, Costas. I really appreciate it. He probably doesn't get too much humour from his dad right now.' He straightened up, and took a deep breath. 'Okay, Jack, what have *you* got?'

7

Jack felt a huge surge of excitement as he saw the photograph on the screen that Costas had taken of him two days before in the depths of the Red Sea, the unmistakable form of a chariot wheel visible in the mass of coral. Hiebermeyer moved the mouse over different points on the image and then zoomed in on the gilded wing of the falcon at the front of the chariot, partly exposed beneath the coral. 'There should be a cartouche above that, a royal cartouche,' he murmured. 'An inscription on the temple of Karnak at Luxor mentions a chariot of Thutmose III made from electrum, and this one must have been from the same stable. With this gilding it can only have been a royal chariot, perhaps lent by the pharaoh to a favoured general.'

'It was our final dive, and we were in the same quandary as you were in the tomb in the mummy necropolis,' Jack said. 'No time to try removing any of that coral.'

Hiebermeyer zoomed out to the original view and sat back in his chair, shaking his head. 'Still, it's an incredible find. You know it was Howard Carter who first reconstructed their appearance, based on the disassembled chariots he found in 1922 when he opened the tomb of Tutankhamun?'

'I know that they first appear in Egypt about the beginning of the New Kingdom, copied from the chariots of the Near East.'

'It was our friend Ahmose I and his Minoan wife Ahhotep, fighting off the Hyksos in the northern marshlands of the Nile Delta, capturing and then copying the weapons of their enemy,' Hiebermeyer replied. 'Judging by the wall painting in the tomb, it may have been Queen Ahhotep's Minoan warriors who took to the chariots most readily. Not what you might expect for a people from a mountainous island.'

Jack shook his head. 'The Minoans were renowned for their naval might, remember? They probably used small vessels like the Liburnians of classical antiquity, designed to dart into range of an enemy flotilla and attack with the bow and the slingshot. The transition to desert warfare was maybe not that much of a leap from a tactical viewpoint. Ships at sea became chariots on land.'

Hiebermeyer put his hands behind his head, staring at the screen. 'Two centuries later at the time of Akhenaten and Tutankhamun the chariot was at the pinnacle of its technology. They were like modern fly-by-wire jet fighters, capable of astonishing speed and agility but inherently unstable. Drive them too fast and the traditional wheeling manoeuvre you just described became impossible, leaving them no choice other than to hurtle directly into an enemy and take their chances.'

Jack looked thoughtfully at the screen. 'Technology so advanced it backfired on them: sheer speed and nimbleness was perhaps their undoing.'

Costas came over from the computer workstation where he had been backing up their Red Sea images. 'Or maybe someone who knew the risks of the technology played with it. The best systems, the best technologies, often have an inherent instability; it's that instability that often makes them capable of great things, like those fly-by-wire planes, but which also leaves them vulnerable to manipulation and sabotage.'

'Go on,' Hiebermeyer said.

'It's something Costas and I discussed on the flight here,' Jack interjected. 'Thinking laterally, that is. What if the pharaoh, Akhenaten – if that's who it was – engineered the whole thing? Think about the backdrop. There's all the modern speculation that he and Moses were more than just master and slave; Sigmund Freud even thought they were two sides of the same coin. Let's imagine they share the revelation of the one god in the desert, and Akhenaten determines to let Moses take his people and establish his own City of Light; for Akhenaten, it might provide assurance that the new religion, the new monotheism, would have a chance of surviving outside Egypt, where he must have guessed that his focus on the Aten might not survive his own lifetime. If Moses was his big hope for the future, for spreading the word, then the pharaoh is hardly going to want to destroy him as he leads his people to Israel, is he? But it might be politically expedient for him to *appear* to do so. Akhenaten knows there's a strong faction against him among the old priesthood, and that he lacks the military credentials of his forebears. Chasing and destroying the Israelites would raise his kudos and hark back to the great victories of earlier pharaohs against the Hyksos and the other peoples of the Middle East. The strength this gave Akhenaten might buy him the time he needed to establish his new religion more firmly, building temples and converting as many people as possible to his beliefs.'

'So you're suggesting he *faked* it,' Hiebermeyer said, staring at him.

Jack leaned forward, nodding. 'Faked the destruction of the Israelites, but not of his own Egyptian army. He would have known that a victory could be made even more glorious by sacrifice. Imagine Akhenaten returning to Amarna with only a few survivors, telling of a great victory, but one where divine intervention caused victor and vanquished alike to plunge into the sea, the basis of the story in the Book of Exodus. Akhenaten's status is enhanced not only by his claim of victory but also by his miraculous survival. Maybe he even lets a favoured general use his golden chariot, the one we found, so that Akhenaten would return without it, something the people would take as evidence of his own role in the battle; pharaohs in the past would never let others take their place. With the Egyptian army gone, the Israelites could escape from Egypt unhindered. There's no reason why Moses and his people should ever be heard of again in Akhenaten's lifetime, as they develop their settlement in a new place of worship that Akhenaten has secured for them in the land of Israel.'

'You're suggesting that Akhenaten was party to the entire exodus?'

'More than that. I'm saying that he *engineered* it. I'm saying that the death ride of the charioteers was a set-up. I'm saying that he and Moses chose the place in advance, that the Israelite encampment was placed dangerously close to an unstable cliff, but that Moses and his people had left it secretly before the attack. To pull it off Akhenaten would have needed some way of egging his men on, of convincing them that they could wheel to safety after trampling over and destroying the encampment and its occupants.'

'Mercenaries,' Hiebermeyer said. 'Those who would do a pharaoh's word without question.'

'*Female* mercenaries,' Jack said. '*Bare-breasted* female mercenaries. What better way to get an army on the move.'

'Like running a rabbit before a pack of racing dogs,' Costas said, sitting down on a chair. 'I love it.'

Hiebermeyer shook his head. 'I'm going to miss these brainstorming sessions, Jack.'

'One thing I wanted to ask,' Costas said. 'About your tomb in the mummy necropolis.'

Hiebermeyer swivelled his chair. 'Go on.'

'The chariot general. Did you get a look at him? I mean, did you see inside his sarcophagus?'

Hiebermeyer pursed his lips, nodding. 'I didn't mention that earlier because I felt like a tomb robber. Thank God none of my team saw me. Just before leaving and sealing up the tomb I took a crowbar and jacked off the coffin lid. As I suspected, it was empty.'

'Huh? I thought the tomb was undisturbed.'

'It was. The empty sarcophagus means that Mehmet-Re died in action, and his body was never recovered. The best his family could do was to go through the motions and hope that the gods would still accept him into the afterlife.'

'The action in the wall painting,' Costas said. 'Could that be the actual battle?'

Hiebermeyer sat back, tapping a pencil on the table. 'I'd assumed it was a generic scene. If a body wasn't recovered that usually meant a catastrophic defeat, one leaving few survivors or eyewitnesses.'

'Sounds like our chariot charge into the Red Sea.'

Hiebermeyer stopped tapping and stared at the screen. 'It's possible. We know that Mehmet-Re was a general and died in battle during Akhenaten's reign. We don't know of any other catastrophic defeat incurred by Akhenaten, certainly none in which such a high-ranking officer died. Assuming that Akhenaten *was* the pharaoh of the Old Testament story of Moses, that chariot charge would fit the bill.'

'And no surprise that there's silence about it in the other sources,' Jack added.

Hiebermeyer nodded again. 'You're only ever going to find evidence buried away like this in tombs. You don't celebrate a catastrophic defeat with inscriptions and relief carvings in the great temples, especially the apparent destruction of the most powerful chariot army in the world by a band of unarmed slaves. If you're going to talk about it at all, it's more likely you give a supernatural explanation. The desert was a feared place and this wouldn't have been the first time an Egyptian army had disappeared into the dust, never to be seen again. The Israelites might not be the only ones who invoked the powers of a deity in their explanation of what happened that day beside the Red Sea.'

'Is there anything else in the tomb that could pin it down?'

Hiebermeyer slumped forward. 'I only had a matter of minutes in there before I had to call in the bulldozer to bury that part of the site. I had my camera with me and photographed everything I could see, and it's just possible that something else will show up in the images of the walls, a hieroglyphic cartouche perhaps. The problem is that much of the wall was heavily mildewed and the painting obscured. The other problem is that apart from Aysha you two are the only people to know about the tomb, and I can't risk giving the images to anyone else in my team to analyse in case word slips out. I might be able to snatch a few moments to glance at them myself over the next few days but I can't promise it. The priority for me now is getting back to finish off the parts of the necropolis that are still under excavation.'

'We hear you,' Jack said.

Another figure walked into the room, a short, compact woman also wearing dusty khaki, her dark hair tied back in a bun. She handed Costas a thick sandwich and offered another one to Jack, who shook his head. Jack knew from glancing at her that now was not the time for niceties, and she walked over and put a hand on Hiebermeyer's shoulder, her expression serious. 'I've seen the pictures you sent from the Red Sea, Jack. What else have you got?

'I wanted you to see this, Aysha, because you were the one who came across that First World War diary entry that led us to the site, and it specifically mentioned what you're about to see.' Jack put a memory stick into the computer and opened up the file containing the images Costas had taken of him in the final moments of the dive. He found what he wanted, and clicked it open.

Hiebermeyer stared at the screen, and then clapped his hands. 'I knew it,' he cried. 'I *knew* when I saw the sketch in that officer's notebook that it was one of those.'

'You can identify that for certain?' Costas asked, his mouth full.

'It's a khepesh-sword,' Hiebermeyer exclaimed. 'Look at that poster on my wall, from the Tutankhamun exhibition that travelled the world a few years ago. You can see one there, almost identical.'

'It's not the most practical-looking weapon, is it?' Costas said, munching on his sandwich and peering at the poster. 'I mean, from a military point of view. That sickle-shaped blade would have been difficult to balance and unwieldy in battle. It's more like an executioner's sword.'

Hiebermeyer nodded. 'Howard Carter thought they were more suited to crushing rather than cutting, but with a razor-sharp edge and the weight of the blade it would have worked well for decapitation. They seem to be Asiatic in origin and arrive in Egypt about the beginning of the New Kingdom, about the same time as chariots, and disappear by the end of the Bronze Age. There's no doubt that these were high-status weapons carried by officers; by army or divisional commanders. It shows that those charioteers were being led by their officers when they rode off that cliff into the sea, and the men were not being forced on some kind of suicide charge by officers who remained behind.'

'Can you date it more closely?' Jack asked.

Hiebermeyer rocked back on his chair, staring at the photograph. 'The closest date we've got for one is the example from Tutankhamun's tomb, about 1320 BC.'

'The son of Akhenaten and Nefertiti?' Costas said.

'Not all would agree, but I believe so,' Hiebermeyer said. 'Whatever their true relationship, they were certainly only a generation apart.'

'Good enough for me,' Costas said. 'And Akhenaten's our man? I mean, are we *sure* he's the pharaoh of the Old Testament, the one who chased the Israelites across the sea?'

Hiebermeyer looked at Jack, who nodded. 'We're not sure, but that's the consensus.'

'Well, looking at those two photos, I'd say those two swords were cast in the same foundry.'

'You may well be right,' Hiebermeyer said. 'But it's not enough evidence to confirm the identification of the pharaoh at the time of the chariot disaster. Egyptologists are used to dealing with very precise data, and our theory won't wash unless we can find archaeological evidence to pin this with absolute certainty to Akhenaten. Did you have time to look closely at the blade of that sword, Jack? Any indication of hieroglyphs?'

'Nothing that I could see.'

'Any other artefacts at the site? Any, at all?'

Costas suddenly shot bolt upright. 'Ah.' He turned to Jack, a guilty look on his face.

'I know that look,' Jack said, narrowing his eyes. 'It means Costas has seen something archaeological but forgotten to tell me, usually because whatever technical thing he was doing at the time was more important. Am I right?'

Costas coughed, spilling crumbs down his shirt, and reached into his shorts pocket. 'Well, not *seen* something, exactly. I *found* something. I'd clean forgotten about it until this moment. Had it in these shorts all the way from the dive boat.'

Jack stared at him. 'You mean you went through security at the airport with some looted antiquity in your pocket, just when we were trying to remain incognito and avoid any confrontation with the Egyptian authorities?'

'Sorry, okay?' Costas took another bite from his sandwich. 'Anyway, I'd also forgotten that my notebook had the full specs for the latest IMU deep-submergence Aquapod on it. That's far worse. I must have had too much nitrogen still circulating in my head. Now it *would* have been a disaster if they'd found that.'

Hiebermeyer stared at him. 'If you hadn't been my son's godfather . . .'

'And an all-round good guy,' Costas said, munching away and handing him the object he had fished out of his pocket. 'You were going to say?'

'*Mein Gott,*' Hiebermeyer whispered, staring at the artefact in his hands, turning it over and letting Jack look. 'It's a fragment of gilding from a wooden panel, thick enough to be gold plate. It must be part of the openwork decoration on that chariot facing. Look at that poster again and you can see a shield decorated that way from the tomb of Tutankhamun, showing the pharaoh smiting a lion and with a small panel on the side containing his two first names.'

'Can you see any detail?' Jack asked.

'Just a moment,' Hiebermeyer murmured, carefully prising

away a layer of marine accretion from the gold and revealing the lower end of a cartouche with symbols inside. 'We're in luck,' he exclaimed, his voice hoarse with excitement. '*Hieroglyphs.*' He turned to Costas, his face flushed. 'As the discoverer and guardian of this priceless artefact, the honour of translating it should be yours.'

'What do you mean? You're the Egyptologist.'

'Have you seen those symbols before? In the Crocodile Temple on the Nile, for example? On the panel inside the sarcophagus of Menkaure in the shipwreck? At Tell-el Amarna?'

Costas stared. 'A reed. That bird. A ball of string. That half-sun symbol.' He looked up. 'Is this our man?'

'Neferkheperure-Waenre Akhenaten, to give him his full name,' Hiebermeyer said triumphantly. 'This cartouche could only have been put on a chariot during his reign. That clinches it. We've not only got the lost chariots from the biblical Exodus, but we've pinned down the pharaoh.'

'Bingo,' Costas said, beaming at Jack.

'What do you mean, bingo?'

'I mean, Costas saves the day again. What would you do without me?' He reached across for the fragment of gilding, and Hiebermeyer gently but firmly pushed his arm away, placing the artefact on a foam pad beside his computer. 'I think you've taken care of that for long enough. I need to get it cleaned up and photographed. When the time's right, we've got what we need for the biggest archaeological press release from Egypt since the time of Howard Carter.'

'When will you do it?' Jack asked.

'It'll have to be just after we've packed our bags and left.

Otherwise I'll have to explain how we raised an artefact from Egyptian waters without a permit, and there will be hell to pay. I'd rather close up shop here before the thugs arrive to do it for me, and then we can leave on a high note.'

'Unless you get some last-minute find from the mummy necropolis.'

'Unless you find a way into Ahkenaten's underground City of Light.'

Aysha put a hand on both men's shoulders. 'Now *that's* what I like to hear. The Jack and Maurice of old. If we're finished here, Jack, I've got something I want to show you.'

Jack looked at her. 'You've done great stuff already for us, Aysha. You should get back to the necropolis with Maurice. This is your country and you need to do whatever's necessary to leave it in your own terms, with your own projects resolved.'

She took a deep, faltering breath. 'I don't feel that Egypt is my country any more. I feel we're on the verge of an exodus just like the one that Moses and the Israelites set out on more than three thousand years ago. We'll be like so many others who have fallen back before this modern-day darkness, like the Somalis, the Afghans, the Syrians, living in exile, a modern-day diaspora. We can't delude ourselves. Egypt will fall, and we have only a few weeks left at most, probably only days. The hours ahead are going to be the most intensive of my life. Part of that is doing what I have to do for you.'

Jack stared back at her. 'Okay, Aysha. Let's hear what you've got to say.'

8

At that moment Jack's phone hummed and he glanced at it. 'It's a text from Rebecca. She's arrived at Tel Aviv airport. Israeli security interrogated her for more than three hours.'

Aysha looked at him. 'You worried, Jack?'

'About my nineteen-year-old daughter flying into a war zone? Of course not.'

Costas coughed. 'What were you doing at that age, Jack? I seem to remember you telling me about Royal Navy diver training, and then a stint with the Royal Marines on some special forces ops in the Arabian Gulf.'

'The Special Boat Section.' Jack said. 'Anyway, I wasn't really with them, I was just trying it out. I'd already decided to go to university instead. Which is more than can be said for Rebecca.'

'Given all the experience we've provided her with on IMU

projects during her school vacations,' Aysha said, 'you can hardly blame her for wanting to bypass that. Anyway, I think she'll do it. I spotted her looking at the prospectus for Cambridge.'

'What's she doing in Israel, anyway?' Costas asked.

'She's been wanting to go there ever since I told her about our hunt six years ago for the tomb beneath the Holy Sepulchre,' Jack said. 'She found out about the big project at the City of David site to sort and wash ancient debris swept off the Al-Aqsa mosque platform when it was built. There are millions of sherds dating back to prehistory, and they're always looking for volunteers.'

Aysha furrowed her brow, looking sceptical. 'Mmm. I remember Rebecca at Troy three years ago volunteering to help us to clean potsherds. As I recall, it lasted about a day. Cleaning potsherds isn't really a Howard thing, is it? Not when there's real excitement around.'

'It did strike me as a bit odd,' Jack said. 'I thought there might have been a boyfriend involved. I think Jeremy was there. I didn't ask because I didn't want to interfere. It's tricky being a dad sometimes.'

Aysha gave him a questioning look. 'Would you ever put a girlfriend above archaeology? And remember, I'm good friends with both Katya and Maria. I know *everything*.'

Jack fidgeted slightly, tapping a pencil on his hand. Katya and Maria were two of his closest colleagues, instrumental in several of his greatest discoveries; Jeremy had been Maria's graduate student in Oxford, an American who was now assistant director of her palaeography institute. 'Katya's always impossible to get hold of, in the middle of nowhere looking for ancient petroglyphs in Kyrgystan, and Maria's always up to her neck in some medieval manuscript in Oxford.'

Aysha peered at him. 'When did Rebecca make the decision to visit Israel?'

'We'd been talking about General Gordon in Khartoum, about how he and the other Royal Engineers survey officers had a fascination with the Holy Land and its archaeology. I'd been telling her my theory that their quest for Akhenaten in the desert of Sudan had been spurred by something they'd found in Israel, in Jerusalem itself, something that had drawn them there repeatedly over the years right up to the time of Gordon's final appointment as Governor-General in Khartoum.'

'And Israel is the one place you haven't visited on your quest.'

'I'd been planning to go there if things in Egypt go belly-up.'

Hiebermeyer looked at him. 'Did you put Rebecca in touch with IMU's Israel representative, Solomon Ben Ezra? Sol and I have been planning a joint Israeli-Egyptian project to evaluate coastal sites at the border, something that seems inconceivable now.'

'I tried that. She wanted to go it alone. But I let him know anyway, so he can keep a discreet eye on her.'

'It had better be pretty discreet,' Costas muttered. 'Otherwise you won't hear the end of it.'

'That's it then,' Aysha said. 'Rebecca hasn't gone to Israel to clean potsherds. She's gone there as part of this project, to make her mark. And she's not the only one working behind the scenes this time; you'd be surprised who else is involved,

Jack, right here in Egypt. That's what I want to talk about now. What do you know of the early caliphs of Cairo?'

Costas raised his hand. 'I know about Malek Abd al-Aziz Othan ben Yusuf, son of Saladin in the twelfth century. He was the one who tried to destroy the Pyramid of Menkaure, who's responsible for all that missing masonry on the southern face above the entrance where Jack and I went in.'

'My worst nightmare,' Hiebermeyer murmured. 'And he didn't even have explosives.'

'Any more takers?' Aysha asked.

'Well, there's Al-Hakim bi-Amr Allah,' Jack said. 'The one that the Druze Christians regard almost as a god. He springs to mind because Rebecca and I talked about how he ordered the destruction of the Holy Sepulchre in Jerusalem in the tenth century.'

'Okay. He's the one I want. Anything more about him?'

Jack thought for a moment. 'Odd behaviour. Took to wandering alone at night in the desert, disappearing for days on end. Murdered, I think?'

'And what do you know about the Cairo Geniza?'

Jack stared at her. 'Arguably the greatest treasure ever found in Egypt, greater even than Howard Carter's discovery of Tutankhamun's tomb.'

Hiebermeyer shot bolt upright. 'You're treading on thin ice there, Jack. *Very* thin ice.'

Jack grinned at him. 'I thought that would get you going. *Intellectually*, I meant. Tut's tomb may have contained the greatest physical treasure, but the Geniza has drawn us into the detail of the past like no other archaeological find except perhaps Pompeii and Herculaneum. And studying it hasn't just been a matter of cataloguing and conservation, but immediately involved some of the greatest scholars of recent times, not just of Jewish religion and literature but also of medieval history and historiography, of the very meaning of history and why we study it.'

Costas peered at Jack. 'You'd better fill me in, Jack.'

'Genizot were the storerooms in synagogues where worn-out sacred writings were deposited. In Jewish tradition any sacred or liturgical writing in Hebrew was considered the word of God and therefore couldn't be thrown away, but the Cairo Geniza was unusual in containing a huge amount of other material related to the medieval Jewish community in Egypt as well. It was found in the Ben Ezra synagogue in Fustat, the Old City of Cairo, the synagogue of the Palestinian Jews. When the Ben Ezra Geniza was opened up in the late nineteenth century, the bulk of it – over two hundred thousand fragments – was shipped to Cambridge under the care of Solomon Schechter, Reader in Rabbinical Studies at the University. I was fortunate to be able to study the archive first hand when I was researching for my doctorate, looking at Jewish involvement in maritime trade in the Indian Ocean.'

Aysha peered at him. 'So you'll know it also contains a huge amount of incidental detail on early medieval Cairo, and not just on Jewish life.'

'"The unconsidered trifles that make up history", as one Geniza scholar put it,' Jack said.

'Including references to the caliphs and to ancient parts of Cairo that have since been demolished or lie buried beneath the modern city.'

'Where are you leading with this, Aysha? Fustat was the

main settlement of Cairo when the Fatimids arrived from Tunisia to take over control of Egypt, and much of the Geniza dates to about the time of Al-Hakim and the two centuries or so that followed. Is that the connection?'

'I don't want to tell you more now, because what we've found is being translated as we speak. You need to see it for yourself at the actual place where it was discovered. Today may well be our last chance. Cairo is still open to us but a midnight curfew has already been imposed and the city will very likely be a no-go zone within days. I've arranged for transport to get us there this evening.'

Jack thought for a moment. 'All right. If you think it'll be a good use of my time here. The clock's ticking.'

'Believe me, it will.'

Hiebermeyer gestured down the corridor. 'Before you go, there's another friend here who wants to see you. A genius-level physicist with a penchant for computer simulation and Egyptology.'

'Uh oh,' Costas said, raising his eyes theatrically. 'Here we go.'

'What on earth is Lanowski doing here?' Jack asked.

'He flew in from *Seaquest* late last night. You know *Seaquest* is still over the wreck of the *Beatrice* off Spain? They were making the final preparations for raising the sarcophagus of Menkaure, but there's been some kind of hitch. He's come to consult Costas.'

Jack nodded. 'I know Captain Macalister's been trying to get in touch with me. Costas took the call before we came in.'

Costas grinned. 'Lanowski comes all the way across the Mediterranean to consult me? We must *really* be friends.'

'You and me both,' Hiebermeyer said. 'His brain is like an analogue of ancient Egypt. Every measurement, angle and coordinate is in there. I can't keep up with him.'

Jack pursed his lips. 'They weren't supposed to raise the sarcophagus without me being there. I don't like being out of the loop.'

Hiebermeyer peered up at him. 'Well, Jack, you *have* been out of the loop. You've been incognito in the Gulf of Suez for the last four days, with instructions that nobody from IMU should try to make contact. The Board of Directors decided to bypass you and authorise the *Seaquest* team to raise the sarcophagus in your absence. It was a way of deflecting attention from everything that's going on in Egypt, from the possibility that the Antiquities people here might rumble your diving escapade and create a huge stink. Better to get the sarcophagus in the public eye before anything like that happened, and to make a huge splash in the media: taken from the Pyramids at Giza in the 1830s, lost in a shipwreck on the way to the British Museum, recovered by IMU. The Board went public about the discovery yesterday and there are now a dozen reporters and film crews on board waiting for the recovery. The press release has even included your promise that if the protection of the sarcophagus can be guaranteed by the Egyptian authorities and overseen by a UNESCO monitoring team, then it goes back to the pyramid. That's what we all agreed from the get-go.'

Costas snorted. 'From the look of what's going on here, it's more likely to be hacked to pieces by the extremists.'

'The new Antiquities Director is aware of that,' Hiebermeyer said. 'He may be a political stooge who cares nothing for archaeology for its own sake, but he's also a pompous egotist who would like nothing better than to be associated with the return of the sarcophagus. He's only been in the job for six months, but he's shutting down foreign excavations across Egypt to keep his xenophobic masters in the new regime happy, but at the same time he's resisting the extremists who want a repeat of the Taliban nightmare in Afghanistan, the desecration of anything they perceive to be non-Islamic. If the extremists get their way, he knows he'll be out of a job and just as dispensable as the monuments that are supposedly in his care.'

'It sounds like a losing battle,' Costas said.

Hiebermeyer looked at them grimly. 'With the press release the Board of Directors have been buying us time, dangling a carrot in front of the Antiquities Director that results in our own projects in Egypt remaining off the hit list for the time being. We have to pray the current director remains in power long enough for us to complete our main excavation at the mummy necropolis.'

'And that scenario could crumble to dust at any time,' Costas muttered. 'Someone from the extremist faction holds a knife to his throat, or the expected coup takes place and the extremists oust the moderates. Then Egypt winds back to year zero and archaeology goes to hell in a hand basket.'

'I couldn't have put it better myself,' Hiebermeyer said.

'Were you in on the decision-making about the sarcophagus?' Jack asked him. 'Did the Board consult you?'

'From the very outset,' Hiebermeyer said. 'They weren't going to go public without my approval.'

Jack took a deep breath. 'Okay. You did the right thing.

You'd think by now I'd have learned to let IMU sail on without my hand always on the helm, but sometimes it throws me. Now, where's Lanowski? If the *Seaquest* team are on hold with the sarcophagus and I can hitch a lift back with him after visiting Cairo, I might even get a look-in at the raising after all.'

Hiebermeyer gestured with his thumb. 'Down the corridor. He's set up his simulation computer in my office.'

'What on earth is he doing with that?' Jack said.

Hiebermeyer gave a tired smile. 'You know Lanowski. He says that when his feet hit Egyptian soil he gets so wired that he can fly through the past and see every detail as if it's laid out in front of him. I told him what you and Costas have been up to in the Gulf of Suez. I've never seen anyone so hyped. He's simulating the Bible.'

Costas coughed. 'Say again?'

'Simulating the Bible.'

'*Simulating the Bible*,' Costas repeated, shaking his head. 'Isn't that flying a little close to the sun? You know, the big guy in the sky?'

'That's Lanowski for you,' Hiebermeyer said. 'Boundaries are there to be crossed.'

'God help us,' Costas muttered.

Aysha stood up, glancing at her watch. 'No more than an hour. Maria's expecting you in the Old City of Cairo at 1900 hours.'

'*Maria*,' Jack exclaimed. 'So that's who you mean about people working behind the scenes. What's she doing here?'

'I was going to mention it before we left, of course,' Aysha said. 'Remember, she's Director of the Institute of

Palaeography at Oxford. Who better to study a new document from the Cairo Geniza?'

'And Jeremy too?'

She shook her head. 'He's just been appointed Assistant Director, so he holds the fort while she's gone. Anyway, he's in London at the British Museum, doing some other research for this project that you don't yet know about.'

Jack put up his hands. 'I surrender. It sounds as if my world really has spun out of my control.'

Costas slapped him on the shoulder. 'It's what friends are all about, Jack. Sometimes you just can't manage it all on your own.'

Jack stood up and put his hands on his hips. 'All right. Lanowski first, then Cairo. And then we'll see what happens. We could be back to *Seaquest* for another dive to a thousand metres in a submersible.'

'I'm good with that,' Costas enthused. '*Very* good.'

Aysha checked her phone. 'I'm going ahead to Cairo. Before you think of planning ahead, wait until you see what Maria and I have to show you. Your quest for Akhenaten's City of Light might not be over just yet, inshallah.'

Jack glanced at Costas. 'Let's move.'

'Roger that.'

9

Jack and Costas made their way along the lower floor of the institute to the director's office, its door slightly ajar. Hiebermeyer preferred the workroom where they had met him so usually lent his office to a visiting scholar, and there was one in there now. Costas had wanted to capture an image of Lanowski hard at work for the IMU Facebook page, and had his phone at the ready as he gently pushed the door open. Lanowski was occupying Hiebermeyer's desk; more accurately, he was perched on it, legs crossed, arms resting on his knees in the lotus position, eyes tightly shut, humming to himself and occasionally uttering a surprised chortle, as if in a state of constant revelation.

Costas took a picture. 'Look, Jack,' he whispered. 'He's gone archaeologist.'

'What do you mean?'

'Ever since we let him take these little sabbaticals out of the lab, he's tried to become one of us. Check out the boots and shorts. He's copying Maurice. Sweet, isn't it?'

Jack scratched his chin, trying to keep a straight face. 'Doesn't really work, does it?' He stared at Lanowski, at the long, lank hair hanging over the little round glasses, the mouth in a half-smile of apparently joyous discovery, seemingly oblivious to them. Lanowski had looked exactly the same since they had poached him twelve years earlier from MIT, to help Costas develop strengthened polymer materials for submersibles casings; since then he had become IMU's all-round genius, with a particular knack for CGI. He was here because a childhood fascination with the mathematics and geometry of ancient Egypt had led him to work closely with Hiebermeyer, a relationship which Jack had been happy to foster and which seemed all the more precious now that the institute was threatened with imminent closure.

Costas coughed, and tapped the door. 'Jacob, what are you doing?' There was no response, and he tried again, louder this time. 'Ground control to Dr Lanowski. Come in.'

'I'm conducting a thought experiment,' Lanowski replied quietly, his eyes still shut. 'Come, take a voyage in my mind.'

'You must be joking,' Costas exclaimed. 'Real life with IMU is enough of a trip as it is.'

'A *thought experiment*,' Jack said.

'Like Einstein,' Lanowski replied. 'He used to spend hours imagining he was sitting on a particle of light flying through the universe.'

'The theory of relativity?' Costas said. 'Are you developing a better one?'

Lanowski suddenly opened his eyes, stared at them and

threw himself off the desk, stumbling towards the computer workstation on the far side of the room. He pulled up the chair and began working the keyboard with one hand, the other hand clicking the mouse. 'I wasn't riding a particle of light,' he said, his eyes darting over the CGI image he was creating. 'I was riding a chariot. To be precise, an ancient Egyptian chariot, at thirty miles an hour on the desert beside the Gulf of Suez, on the twenty-second of March 1343 BC at 0645 hours. The year is a best fit during Akhenaten's reign; the month seems plausible, before the hot season, and the time of day just after dawn is right for an attack.' He glanced at Costas, who had come up alongside and was staring at the screen. 'The only part that's complete guesswork is the day of the month, but to conduct a thought experiment in the past you need a precise day and time.'

Costas nodded thoughtfully. 'I get that.'

Jack came up on the other side. 'I gather Maurice has told you about our discovery.'

Lanowski stopped typing and punched the air. 'I've got it.'

'Got what?' Costas asked.

'Solved the Bible.'

'*Solved the Bible.*'

'Book of Exodus, chapter fourteen: "And the children of Israel went into the midst of the sea upon the dry ground: and the waters were a wall unto them on their right hand, and on their left." That's the King James Version, right? Well, I've checked the original Greek with your old mentor at Cambridge, Professor Dillen, and he thinks it allows for some latitude in translation. I know Aysha's been talking to you about the Cairo Geniza, Jack, because she told me what she has in store for you. Dillen also brought up the Geniza when we talked about the problems of translation. One of the greatest discoveries in the Geniza has been original Hebrew pages of the Ben Sira, the Book of Wisdom from the second century BC previously known only from its Greek translation. He said that seeing those original pages and then comparing the Greek, the Latin and the English versions has made him think again about the huge problem of conveying exact meaning through languages that simply don't have the appropriate words or expressions, resulting in translations that are either inaccurate or too obscure to understand without a mediator. He thinks the original Hebrew of the scriptures was meant to be clear and precise and not to require a priestly interpreter, and that the development of a priestly class was actually a consequence of the written word becoming too baffling in its transmission for people to understand.'

Jack nodded. 'He's been developing that idea since looking at the foundation of organised religion in the early Neolithic, when religion became a tool of control for the first priest-kings. Go on.'

'Your discovery in the Gulf of Suez makes it absolutely certain that this event took place where the sea could only have been parted by a supernatural occurrence, rather than, say, a marsh or lake where the Israelites could have crossed some kind of shallow causeway which was then flooded.'

'That would be fine with most believers,' Costas said. 'God through Moses caused the sea to be parted.'

'Sure. But let's look at the hard evidence. That says to me that those chariots weren't there because Moses parted the sea and they were swallowed up. They were there because someone ordered the charioteers to ride at full speed towards the clifftop which then collapsed as they flew over it, causing them to be submerged in the sea and also to be buried in the resulting landslide.'

'That was our theory too,' Jack said. 'We think the Israelite encampment was right on the edge of the cliff. Go on.'

'It's about thinking laterally, Jack. Or I should say, at right angles. If we assume that the Israelites could never have walked across the seafloor, then they must have gone along the edge. So instead of going east across the sea, they went north up the western shore. The biblical reference to the "wall unto them on their right hand, and on their left", therefore means not walls of water within the sea, but the walls of the sea itself, that is, the western and eastern shores of the Gulf of Suez. Professor Dillen thinks the Greek allows for that. Now take a look at my CGI. I've exaggerated the height of the cliffs for effect, but you can see what I mean. And to cap it all, look at this.'

A close-up satellite image of a beach appeared on the screen. Costas peered at it. 'I recognise those rocks. That's where I had my lunch two days ago between dives.'

'Look closer. With the wide-brimmed hat, sitting with his feet dangling in the water. Almost as if he's on holiday.'

Costas peered again. 'You've got to be kidding me.'

'Yep,' Lanowski beamed. 'I can follow your every move. If you won't let me join in the fun, at least I can watch it and imagine myself there.'

'I thought the Egyptians had cut off Maurice's access to their live-stream satellite imagery, as well as to every other foreign project in the country.'

'This isn't through the institute. It's Landsat, US military. I've got a friend in the CIA who owes me a favour, after I did the maths in his PhD for him.'

'You're a useful man to have around, Jacob,' Jack said.

'Glad you noticed.'

'The new translation makes sense. A *lot* of sense. Anything else?'

'Of course.' He dragged the mouse, and the image zoomed out. 'Aysha told me about her discovery of the First World War diary that led you to that spot, the account of the crates of arms lost overboard and that officer finding the ancient Egyptian sword. Well, she and I read through several previous entries in the diary last night. They showed that the British had developed a ruse in case they were spied on in the desert. Instead of driving the camels with the crates to a point on the cliff directly above the rendezvous point with the dhow, they offloaded them several miles to the south and used a hidden track just below the clifftop, known to local tribesmen, to carry the crates out of view of the desert above. Captain Edmondson, the diarist, was also an archaeologist, and he mentioned how he thought the trackway was probably millennia old, shown by the number of rockslides and mud falls they had to negotiate on the way.'

'And then they came down to that beach where I had lunch,' Costas said. 'Just above the spot where we found the rifles and ammunition underwater, and then the chariots.'

'Right. And just *above* that the Lansat image shows a concavity in the line of the cliff where there's a break in the path. I'm convinced the concavity is evidence of the ancient cliff fall caused by the massed chariot charge, and I'm also convinced that Moses used that path to lead away the Israelites right under the noses of the Egyptians, leaving an empty encampment. The path continues for miles up the coast so would have been a viable escape route. What do you think, Jack? Bingo. Case closed.'

'Well, I'll be damned,' Jack said, staring in fascination at the image. 'I think you might just have earned your pay, Jacob.'

'I'm not the first one to have these ideas. You ever heard of Hiwi al-Bakhi?'

Jack was glued to the screen, but nodded. 'His name means the Bactrian Heretic, a medieval Jewish dissenter from ancient Bactria, modern Afghanistan. He openly criticised the Hebrew Bible for lack of clarity and contradictions, and for representing God as inconsistent and capricious. His writing was another great discovery in the Cairo Geniza.'

'Well, he also tried to debunk the supernatural. For him, the parting of the Red Sea was a matter of the water ebbing and flowing, something he's probably seen in the huge tidal flows on the shores of the Indian Ocean. He wasn't to know that the Gulf of Suez doesn't have much tide nor does it have tidal flats like those he might have seen off India, but I like his way of thinking.'

'A rationalist like you, Jacob.'

'There's something else that's very interesting about Hiwi, Jack. Dillen and I talked about it too. His sect was so intent on cleansing Jewish religion and starting afresh that they wanted to change the Sabbath from Sunday to Wednesday, the day in Genesis when the sun was created. The *sun*, Jack. Does that ring any bells? We thought of Akhenaten and Moses together in the desert, and the revelation of the one god, the Aten.

Akhenaten too was seeking a cleansing of the old religions, a return to a purer notion of deity, a rejection of gods who had become too anthropomorphic and displayed the human traits that Hiwi lamented in the god of the Bible. Maybe we should expect these periodic attempts at cleansing in the history of religion, but maybe too we should be looking for continuity, for a memory preserved even in Hiwi's time of that foundation event in the desert almost two thousand years before. Egypt has had its takeovers, the Greeks, the Romans, the Muslims, and cultural destruction like the loss of the Alexandria library, but it never suffered the utter devastation of so many other regions, the sweeping away of its culture and people. And for the Jewish people their history is all about maintenance of the tradition, isn't it? That's the biggest lesson of the Cairo Geniza, that it's about continuity, not change.'

Jack nodded. 'Even dissent like Hiwi's became part of the Jewish intellectual tradition, one of debate rather than persecution, ensuring that enquiring minds were not stifled in the way they have been in so many other religions.'

Costas looked at Lanoswki. 'I'd no idea you were also something of a rabbi, Jacob. A real multi-tasker.'

' "Happy is the man who meditates on wisdom and occupies himself with understanding." That's from Ben Ezra. My parents were Ukrainian Jews who were smuggled out of Europe just before the Second World War. All of the rest of my family, my grandparents, my uncles and aunts, died in the Holocaust. Both of my grandfathers had been rabbinical scholars and my parents hoped that I'd follow the same route.'

'Is that how you got interested in Egyptology?' Jack asked.

Lanowski nodded. 'I always wanted to know the specific

identity of Pharaoh in the Bible. It annoyed me that he was unnamed, as if he's the one and only pharaoh, but then I realised there was something special about him. Being part of your team in the quest for Akhenaten is fulfilling a childhood dream, Jack. I'm grateful to you.'

'We've got a good way to go yet.'

Lanowski turned to Costas. 'And now about the theory of relativity. Funny you should mention that. As it happens, I do have a niggle with the space-time continuum model. It's, well,' he chuckled, 'wrong.' He suddenly looked deadly serious. 'I mean, *wrong*.' He whipped up his portable blackboard from beside the desk and picked up a piece of chalk, scribbling a formula. 'It's like this.'

Costas immediately took Lanowski's hand and steered the board back down to the floor. 'Not now, Jacob. That's too big even for IMU. Save it for the Nobel Prize committee. Jack has got to go. He's meeting Aysha and Maria in Cairo this evening. And I need to get back on the phone to Macalister on *Seaquest*.'

Lanowski looked crestfallen, and then brightened up. 'Anything comes up out there, you let me know.'

'Come again?'

'Boots on the ground. Jack and Costas stuff.' He pointed meaningfully at his gear. 'You need help, I'm good to go.'

Costas nodded slowly. 'I can see that. Good to go.'

Jack stared at him. 'Thanks for the offer, Jacob. We'll let you know. Meanwhile, get this written up so I can send it to the board along with Costas' photos of the chariots for the press release. It'll make a fantastic mix of hard data and speculation.'

Lanowski looked dumbfounded. 'Where's the speculation, Jack? From where I see it, there's only hard data.'

Jack grinned, and slapped him on the shoulder. 'Of course. Only hard data. Brilliant work, Jacob.'

Just over four hours later Jack jumped out of the institute's Land Rover and hurried after Aysha under the medieval wall into the ancient compound of Fustat, thankful to be in the old part of Cairo away from the din and congestion of the modern city. The drive from Alexandria had been hampered by a seemingly endless succession of police roadblocks and checkpoints; it was already almost nine in the evening, just over three hours to curfew. The Institute of Archaeology logo in Arabic on the Land Rover had eased them through a few sticky checkpoints, but they knew that once the police had been ousted by the extremists then any Western affiliation, in Arabic or otherwise, would become a liability. Earlier, while they had been in Alexandria, Aysha had not wanted to depress Hiebermeyer any further by dwelling on the political situation, but in the Land Rover she had told Jack that she believed a coup in Cairo was now a near certainty. The moderate Islamist regime that had replaced the pro-Western government a few months ago was never going to work, with policies that satisfied nobody; the decision of the new Minister of Culture and his Antiquities Director to shut down foreign excavations had not been enough for the extremists, but had been too much for Western governments which had begun to withdraw financial aid in protest. Increasingly the new regime was being seen as a prop that had been engineered all along by the extremists, a stepping-stone to their own imminent takeover. The regime was filled with petty tyrants such as the new Antiquities Director who had jumped eagerly on the bandwagon without realising that the extremists who had opened the door for them would also be their nemesis in the aftermath of a coup.

Aysha had been concerned as they drove into the city by the absence of gunfire or signs of demonstrations, routine features of Cairo life for months now. The extremist thugs who had battled the pro-democracy demonstrators had seemingly disappeared into the night, leaving the squares festooned with banners but strangely empty of protesters. It had seemed ominous, like a lull before a storm. Reports had come through on the radio of convoys of 'specials', pickup trucks with mounted machine guns, breaking through the border from Sudan, virtually unopposed by the Egyptian police or army. The presence of extremist training camps to the south had been an open secret for some time, and now they were seen for what they were: staging posts for a terrorist invasion of Egypt, taking up where their forebears had been forced to leave off after Kitchener's defeat of the Mahdi army at Omdurman in 1898. Those events of more than a century ago had come back to haunt the world; the slaughter at Omdurman, Kitchener's desecration of the Mahdi's tomb in revenge for the death of General Gordon, had been barely remembered in the West, eclipsed by the horrors of the twentieth century, yet for the extremists they were still as fresh as if they had happened yesterday, the smell of the blood of Omdurman and the sight of the Mahdi's paraded remains embedded in their collective memory and stoking the fires of hate. Jack and Costas had been on the edge of that tidal wave of extremism in Sudan a few months ago, and now Jack knew they had been lucky to get out when they did. If Aysha was right that wave was coming at them again, a matter of days at most before Cairo was overrun, with the Egyptian army officer corps infiltrated by sympathisers and the extremist leaders calling for the mass desertion of conscript soldiers. She was convinced that this evening would be their last chance in Cairo, and that they needed to make the most of the few hours that lay ahead of them now.

Jack followed Aysha into a maze of narrow cobbled alleys and high stone walls, of men in fez caps and galabiyya robes, reminiscent of the Old City of Jerusalem; he remembered that it was to Egypt as well as Spain that many of the Jews who escaped the Roman destruction of Jerusalem in AD 70 had fled, and that there had been other Jews in Alexandria involved in trade with India even before that. A bearded beggar sat at the entrance to the synagogue precinct, and Jack tossed him a few coins. He followed Aysha into the building itself, through the doorway and on to the grey marble floor of the main open space, mottled in pools of white where it was lit up by hanging lamps. Above him on either side, upper-floor balconies ran the length of the building, faced with pillared colonnades of little arches painted in alternating white and red that would not have looked out of place in the court-yard of a Cairo mosque; not for the first time Jack reflected on the inter-meshing of Judaeo-Christian and Muslim culture in the Near East, so at odds with the polarisation created by politics and extremism.

Aysha motioned for him to stay and quickly ran up the stairs to the left-hand gallery, disappearing behind a section at the far end that had been cordoned off with hanging shrouds lit up from within. He could hear low voices, hers and another voice he recognised as Maria's, but he blocked them off for a moment and breathed in deeply, enjoying the smell of old stone and wood after the smog outside, relishing the tranquillity he always found in old churches and mosques and synagogues in the middle of bustling cities, a precious respite from the cloud of uncertainty that hung over Cairo.

He was fascinated to be in the Ben Ezra Synagogue at last, the source of the Cairo Geniza, the greatest collection of medieval documents to be discovered anywhere in recent times. In most synagogues the geniza chambers were cleared out periodically and their contents buried in cemeteries, whereas the geniza in the Ben Ezra Synagogue appeared to contain everything that had been put into it from its inception in the 9th century. When the geniza was first studied it proved to contain not only thousands of pages of sacred writings – biblical, Talmudic, Rabbinical, even fragments of the Qur'an – but also a trove of secular material, documents in Aramaic and Arabic as well as Hebrew that preserved an extraordinary picture of Jewish life in Egypt in the medieval period. When Jack had first pored over those documents as a student at Cambridge he had seen the collection with an archaeologist's eye, much as if he were looking at the evidence of an excavation; the geniza fragments seemed all the more valuable because like Hiebermeyer's papyrus mummy wrappings they were writings that had not been selected by scholars or religious authorities for preservation, and revealed details of day-to-day life that so rarely survive in written records before modern times.

The hanging shroud on the upper floor parted, and Aysha stood at the balustrade of the balcony. 'Okay, Jack. Maria's nearly ready. What are you thinking?'

'I'm thinking how pleased I am that Solomon Schechter over a century ago arranged for the bulk of the archive to go to Cambridge University. I hate to think what the extremists would do to this place.'

'If they were true Muslims, they'd leave it alone. Moses was one of our prophets too, and to Muslims the Jews are People of the Book, those to whom scripture has been divinely revealed. Did you know that the baby Moses was supposedly found at this spot, in the reeds in a tributary of the Nile that ran just behind this place?'

Jack walked towards the stairs. 'Nice story, but it was two thousand-odd years between the Exodus and the re-emergence of the Jewish community in medieval Cairo. It's hard to believe anyone would have remembered the exact spot. Also there's a lot of uncertainty about what was going on in the New Kingdom period where Fustat now lies, whether there was a settlement or perhaps some kind of temple establishment. The site for the story is more likely somewhere north in the marshlands of the Nile Delta, good papyrus country.'

Aysha stood with her hands on her hips. 'What about that famous Jack Howard leap of faith? Maurice says that's your biggest asset.'

'Faith in my instinct, not in every old legend,' Jack said, mounting the stairs and grinning at her. 'Anyway, I'm being Lanowski. Where's the hard data?'

'Well, here's something fascinating for you. You remember the diary of Captain Edwardson, the archaeologist-turned-intelligence officer whose notes led you to the Gulf of Suez? A year before that botched arms shipment he was a newly commissioned second lieutenant in Cairo, working in the same cipher office as his friend T.E. Lawrence, both of them bored out of their minds. Things perked up one day when high command detailed him to act as a discreet escort for a very important visitor who wanted to come incognito to visit the synagogue. Well, the VIP rumbled that Edwardson was following him and when he reached the synagogue let him catch up and invited him inside. The VIP was none other than Lord Kitchener, newly appointed Secretary of State for War, visiting Egypt only months before he went down with the cruiser *Hampshire* in the North Sea. It turns out that there were half a dozen other men waiting in the synagogue, all of them getting on a bit in years. Kitchener told Edwardson that they were all in some way associated with General Gordon of Khartoum, and came together every few years in the synagogue to celebrate his memory. One of the other men present was an American, Colonel Chaillé-Long.'

Jack stopped on the stairs. 'How extraordinary. Gordon's former chief of staff, the explorer of Lake Victoria?'

'By now an elderly man, and a famous author.'

'Of lavishly embellished tales, as I recall. Something of a dandy.'

'And Edwardson mentioned someone else. I've been itching to tell you, Jack, but wanted to wait until we were here. It was a Royal Engineers Colonel well known to you: John Howard.'

Jack stopped in his tracks, staring at her. 'My great-great grandfather? Incredible.' He looked down, thinking hard. 'He'd retired by then, but travelled several times to the Holy Land. He was a friend of Kitchener's and had known Gordon. They were all Royal Engineers together. It makes sense.' He stared back at the floor of the synagogue, suddenly seeing those men standing there in his mind's eye. 'Amazing.'

'They came here to the synagogue because *they* believed in the Moses story. But, being engineers and practical men, they decided to find proof. Apparently, one night almost a quarter of a century earlier, in 1890, they had gathered together here for the first time intent on excavating beneath the synagogue – Chaillé-Long, the then Colonel Kitchener, Captain Howard and a Colonel Wilson, who had died since.'

'That would be Colonel Sir Charles Wilson,' Jack murmured. 'Intelligence chief on the Gordon relief expedition, but before that a surveyor in Palestine who had discovered ancient structures beneath medieval Jerusalem. I prepped Rebecca on him before she went out there, as well as on Gordon and Kitchener. All of them were linked by their archaeological work in Palestine. In 1883 Gordon took a kind of sabbatical there, dispirited by his lack of progress in the Sudan and more interested in seeking proof of the Bible in the archaeology of Jerusalem.'

Aysha nodded enthusiastically. 'Well, they brought surveying equipment and digging tools and went out into the synagogue precinct. They'd been led to the spot by another of the colourful characters in Egypt at the period, Riamo d'Hulst, a self-styled count and subject of Luxembourg who was probably a German deserter from the Franco-Prussian war of 1871 and something of a shape-shifter. In 1890 while the synagogue was being restored and refurbished he took advantage of the construction work to dig around the precinct. Following his lead, the British officers discovered indisputable evidence of a silted up river channel. That doesn't prove the

Moses story, of course, but they did also find the plinth of an ancient structure. According to Edwardson, it contained the worn remains of a hieroglyphic cartouche. Finding something of pharaonic date was enough to convince them that they were at the right spot. Edmondson himself might have been able to decipher the hieroglyphs with his archaeological background but he wasn't able to see the inscription, because the stone block had been removed in secret to England for safekeeping by Lieutenant Howard.'

'By Howard?' Jack exclaimed. 'By my great-great grandfather?'

'Do you remember any Egyptian antiquities on the Howard estate?'

Jack was stunned. *Of course.* 'Yes I do. On the edge of the fireplace in the drawing room. My father found it in a storeroom, and didn't know what to do with it. Egyptian red granite?'

'That's what Edwardson said.'

'Does Maurice know about this?'

'Not yet. He has enough on his plate for the time being.'

'Well, it might just cheer him up. When I first brought him home for the holiday from boarding school, he became obsessed with that thing. He used to spend hours with it, staring at it, sketching it. It was what really spurred him into Egyptology. We thought it was a relic of someone's grand tour in the nineteenth century with no known provenance, the kind of thing that wealthy Europeans brought back to adorn their stately homes. But Maurice constructed all kinds of theories for where it might have come from in Egypt. And of course he translated it.'

'And?'

'It was Akhenaten. The royal cartouche of Akhenaten. The pharaoh of the Old Testament. The pharaoh of the time of Moses.'

The shroud parted, and a slim, dark-haired woman of about forty stepped out, reading glasses dangling from her neck and a pair of conservator's gloves in her hands. 'Evening, Jack. You look a little flushed. Excited to see me?'

Jack stepped forward, kissing her on the cheek. 'I've just had a revelation, Maria. In fact, a really big revelation. Out of the blue.'

'Sounds like Jack Howard,' she said, her Spanish accent giving the words added emphasis. 'You can tell me once we've finished in here.'

Jack nodded towards the shroud. 'This brings it back, doesn't it?' He turned to Aysha. 'Maria and I first met in the coffee room of Cambridge University Library after discovering that we were both there to study the Geniza documents. We haven't looked back, have we, Maria?'

'Or forward,' Aysha added, eyeing him.

Maria put her hand on Jack's shoulder. 'Well, Jack Howard just wouldn't be the man I know and love if he wasn't always disappearing on adventures, would he? But before you disappear yet again, you need to come in here and see what I've got.'

Jack was already staring past her into the gap beyond the shroud, seeing the ladder and hole at the top of the wall that he knew led to the Geniza chamber. 'You lead, Maria. I can't wait.'

10

Jack parted the hanging shroud and followed Maria and Aysha into the enclosed section they had created at the end of the gallery. Within the shroud the air was noticeably warmer, the heat emanating from two portable angle-poise lamps bent low over a wooden table set up in the centre of the space. Two briefcases were open on the floor, and the table was covered with Maria's tools of trade as a palaeographer: protective plastic sheeting for manuscript fragments, tweezers, a magnifying glass, gloves and a laptop, its screen showing a blown-up section of text that Jack recognised as Hebrew by the serifs on top of the letters. Beyond the table the step-ladder that he had seen from outside rose to a rectangular opening in the wall some three metres above them just below the ceiling, an electrical extension cable snaking over the rim into the darkness beyond.

Jack leaned over and stared at a black and white photograph

propped up on the table. 'That's Solomon Schechter,' he said, pointing at the bearded man in a black suit hunched over what looked like a pile of old rags. 'I know the famous picture of him surrounded by the boxes and piles of Geniza fragments in Cambridge University Library, but I haven't seen this one before.'

'That's because Jeremy's just unearthed it,' Maria said. 'He's become quite a sleuth, you know. For a long time it was thought that no photos survived of Schechter's time here in the synagogue in 1896, when the full contents of the Geniza were pulled out of that hole above us and laid in piles all over the floor for him to inspect. In fact, the Scottish twin sisters who had led him here, the widows Agnes Lewis and Margaret Gibson, had brought a box camera with them and took some snaps. Jeremy trawled through all the surviving family he could find in the search for old photo albums and eventually came up trumps. Geniza scholarship has for so long been a man's world, but this photo really reinforces the role of those two women in setting the whole thing in train; it was their search in Egypt for old manuscripts that led them to show fragments from the Geniza to their friend Schechter in Cambridge.'

Jack glanced at her and at Aysha. 'With you two here, it looks as if that role of women in Geniza scholarship has come full circle.'

'There at the beginning, and there at the end,' Maria said. 'I feel as if we're closing one of the most incredible chapters of historical discovery ever.'

Jack peered at the figure in the photo. 'He looked a little overwhelmed.'

'You'd be too, faced with almost two hundred thousand fragments of manuscript. Overwhelmed, but overjoyed. It became his life's work at Cambridge, where as you know the Geniza archive is one of the university's prized collections, studied by scholars of Jewish history from around the world.'

Jack looked at her shrewdly. 'I thought the Geniza chamber had been completely emptied. What exactly are you doing here, Maria?'

She glanced at Aysha. 'Put it this way. One thing I learned years ago from your husband, Aysha, before you'd even met him. When I was a student I worked on one of Maurice's projects in the Valley of the Kings, collecting papyrus debris still lying in a storage chamber that had not only been robbed in antiquity but also cleared out by Howard Carter's team in the lead-up to the discovery of Tut's tomb. That is, never assume that earlier archaeologists have picked up everything.'

'Go on,' Jack said.

'Do you remember our project in England a few years ago at Hereford Cathedral, where Jeremy and I found the Vinland map showing Viking exploration in the Americas? Everyone thought the famous chained library contained all there was to be found in the cathedral, but then we discovered that sealed-up stairwell with its trove of manuscripts.' She reached over and tapped the wall beside the desk below the opening, producing a hollow sound that evidently came from the Geniza chamber beyond. 'It's what Jeremy and I always tell our new students at the institute. Never forget to tap the walls. Sahirah al-Hadeen, one of Aysha's friends who's study-ing the architecture of the synagogue, a graduate student who

139

spent a term with us in Oxford, got into the chamber and did what I just did, on the opposite wall that forms the exterior of the synagogue. As soon as she realised that there was some kind of space beyond, she contacted Aysha and then me.'

'Is she with us now?'

Aysha gave Jack a grim look. 'Earlier this afternoon she was arrested and imprisoned. One of my contacts still employed in the Antiquities service got a message through to Maria just before we arrived; that's what we were talking about while you were waiting below in the synagogue. She's in the Ministry of Culture, which now has a security wing with cells and interrogation rooms where there used to be conservation labs. She was arrested on a trumped-up charge of dealing in antiquities without a licence, because when she was detained they found a fragment of manuscript in her briefcase which she was in fact taking to Alexandria for conservation in the institute, there no longer being any facility in Cairo. But the reality is far worse. Sahirah is from one of the oldest Cairo Jewish families, and the truth is that she's a victim of anti-Semitism. Have you seen the extremists with the black headbands, Jack? They're terrifying. We watched them beat up a man outside the synagogue last night just after I arrived, and it was like those images of SS thugs laying into Jews on the streets of Germany in the 1930s. Did you see the posters plastered all over the precinct wall? Some of them came and did that last night. They're calling for all Jews to leave Egypt or face being asset-stripped and imprisoned. Even the worst of the caliphs didn't go that far.'

'We should be getting her out,' Jack said. 'Not digging around in here.'

Maria put her hand on his arm. 'The best possible thing we can do for her is to finish up here. The manuscript she was carrying when she was arrested was a scrap she managed to reach in the hole she made in the wall of the chamber where she heard the hollow sound. If they torture her and threaten to arrest her family she might reveal where she found it, and the last thing she'd want would be to provide the thugs with an excuse to descend on this place. She'd want us to be here now, getting out everything we can before that happens. It's become personal for me too, Jack. When I lock up here later tonight, this synagogue will be empty and perhaps doomed to destruction, but we don't want it to be as if a thousand years of history were closing down. Removing these last shreds of the Geniza is not an ending, but a thread of continuity. The history represented here has survived darkness before and we must not let these people get their way. That's why, when Sahirah contacted me, I wanted to come out here to help in any way I could, in the eye of yet another storm of ignorance and destruction.'

Jack paused, thinking hard. 'We didn't bring a satellite phone from Alexandria in case we were searched at a checkpoint and had it confiscated, potentially compromising the IMU secure line.' He took out his cell phone, looking at the network indicator. 'What's mobile reception like?'

Aysha shook her head. 'Pretty well non-existent outside Cairo. I can't raise the institute or Maurice, who's in his Land Rover heading towards the Faiyum excavation as we speak. The extremists have been sabotaging the transmitters across the country.'

Jack pocketed his phone. 'Okay. This is what I'm going to

do. First thing tomorrow when I'm back on *Seaquest* I'll get the IMU Board of Directors to rescind our offer to return the sarcophagus of Menkaure to Egypt unless they release Sahirah, immediately. That should put some fire under the Antiquities Director while he still has any power. The return of the sarcophagus was going to be the big event of his probably very short career. We just have to hope that we can still play him before the extremists take over.'

Aysha nodded. 'That might just work, Jack. It's just about the only leverage we've got.'

Jack thought hard for a moment longer. There was nothing else they could do, bar storming the ministry and demanding her release, something that would almost certainly get them arrested or worse. 'All right. Let's see what you've got.'

Maria looked at him. 'We enlarged the hole that Sahirah created as much as we could, but it's still barely big enough to get your arm into. It's a crack in the fabric of the wall that seems to have been overlooked when the synagogue was restored in 1890 and then again a few years ago, probably because the opening that had once existed had become bunged up centuries ago with congealed vellum and other organic matter. Countless generations of mice dragged bits of manuscript into the hole and shredded it to make their nests, so nothing of paper or papyrus has survived beyond a few tiny shreds. But what we do have is some larger pieces of vellum. It seems the mice didn't like something about the vellum, perhaps the gum used to stabilise and dry the gall ink. In time those fragments became glued with mouse droppings to the interior of the hole, actually helping to insulate the nest. When Sahirah showed us the few postage-stamp-sized fragments that she managed to prise out we got really excited, because vellum generally was used for religious texts so there was a chance of it being something really important. After I saw her photos in the email I booked the first flight here.'

Jack pointed at a matte of tissue covering something on the table. 'Have you got a fragment here?'

Maria sat down on the chair and raised the tissue. Beneath it was a piece of vellum about half the size of a standard book page, torn along one edge and filthy. 'Partly the dirt is centuries of mouse droppings and body decay, a kind of congealed stickiness,' she said. 'And partly it's the spread of ambient ink from the lettering, as well as moisture stains that look almost like burning. After I've cleaned this back in the lab and put it under the electron microscope to check the gall ink stability I'll put it in a humidification chamber to give the leather back its suppleness, and then strengthen it with methycellulose and starch paper. But even without cleaning you can still make out the words.'

Jack leaned closer, but then recoiled. 'That's a serious stench,' he said, crinkling his nose. 'I think I need a gas mask.'

Maria gave him a rueful look. 'Nice, isn't it? Nine hundred years of mouse. Solomon Schechter was never the same after the months he spend in here, his health broken. He took to wearing a mask when he studied the manuscripts in Cambridge, but it was probably too late and ultimately that fetid exposure was what killed him.'

'Nine hundred years,' Jack murmured, staring again. 'That makes it early to mid-twelfth century. Have you managed to transcribe it?'

'Take a close look first. What do you see?'

Jack held his breath, stared closely, and then backed off again. 'Hebrew letters, about seventeen lines, broken off at the bottom as if the lower part of the page is missing.' He held his breath again, and peered closely. 'My God. I thought so. It's a palimpsest. I can see older letters floating under the upper text, upside down. I can't make out the words but the letters have Hebrew-style serifs as well.'

Maria nodded. 'At the moment I can't translate the lower text. That's a prize that awaits us back in the lab. I'm hoping against hope for more lines of the Ben Sira, the Book of Wisdom that's probably the greatest single treasure to come out of the Geniza.'

'Lanowski talked about that this afternoon. About the problem of translation and transmission in sacred texts, and the importance of finding the Hebrew originals.'

'I talked it through with him as well on the phone. He's had some startling ideas. He follows many scholars in thinking that Joshua Ben Sira in the second century BC composed the book in Alexandria. But he's taken it one step further and suggested that the great library of Alexandria, newly established at that time, would have allowed Ben Sira ready access to many of the surviving books of wisdom from Pharaonic Egypt, texts that mostly didn't make it through the destruction of the library in late antiquity and are therefore unknown to us. Both he and Professor Dillen think there's enough in what we know of the Ben Sira to suggest a Pharaonic link, though they need more original text to make a case for it. Maybe we've got it here; it's tantalising, but a brick wall at the moment. What I'm really interested in now, what I've got you here for, Jack, is the upper text. Has Aysha prepped you on this?'

'Only that it's something to do with Al-Hakim bi-Amr Allah, the eleventh-century Caliph of Egypt.'

'Okay. Al-Hakim ruled from 996 to 1021. This is a letter written about a hundred and twenty years after his death, by Yehuda Halevi.'

'The Jewish poet?' Jack exclaimed. 'I know that the Geniza contained one of the richest archives of letters from him.'

Maria nodded. 'More than fifty of them. He's one of the most celebrated poets of medieval Judaism. He was Sephardic, from Spain, and had a wide circle of friends there and among the Jewish diaspora around the Mediterranean. He came on a pilgrimage to the Holy Land in 1140, in the last year of his life, arriving in Alexandria in September that year, probably alighting near the site of the ancient lighthouse at the very spot where you left the institute this afternoon. After several months in Cairo he finally left on the eleventh of May 1141 for Jerusalem, where his trail is lost to history. Under the Crusaders neither Jews nor Muslims were allowed into the city, but pilgrims like Halevi were allowed to pray at the Mount of Olives and perhaps he died there after fulfilling his dream. He's another shade from the past you can imagine standing on the floor of the synagogue, Jack. In fact he had quite a lot in common with General Gordon and his circle. Like them Halevi had become convinced that religious fulfilment could only be found in the Holy Land. He lived at the time of the First Crusade, when Baldwin the Third was King of Jerusalem, and also when the Jewish community in Spain was caught between Christianity and Islam.'

'Your own ancestors, I remember?'

Maria nodded. 'They were forced to convert to Christianity and adopt Christian names to avoid the Inquisition, eventually losing their Jewish identity. But I have a huge diaspora of distant cousins who chose to flee, to England, to Holland, to Constantinople, to the New World, even here to Cairo, readopting names like Sarah and Rebecca and Moses and Abraham. Handling this document from the twelfth century gives me a strange feeling, as if that Jewish identity had been lying dormant in my family for all those generations since the conversion, and not been extinguished after all.'

'They say you can never lose it,' Aysha murmured.

'And there's something else. Like those soldiers in the late nineteenth century, Halevi also turns out to have had a fascination with what we would now term archaeology.'

'That's what's in this letter?'

Maria nodded. 'It's a fantastic addition to the archive. His feathery hand is instantly recognisable, and it's incredibly exciting for me to be holding this. It's actually Arabic, but written in Hebrew letters. The Geniza represents a rich fusion of Arabic and Jewish traditions, evidence of a cosmopolitan world far removed from the version of history peddled by the preachers of hate who indoctrinate the extremists. Halevi had been influenced in Spain by Islam just as the Jews had been in Cairo, and had come to believe that Arabic forms of expression could mediate Jewish thought, in poetry and in prose.'

'And he had an eye for the history he saw around him.'

'Correct. And now we're getting to the nub of it. While he was in Cairo for those months in 1140 to 1141 he became good friends with the nagid, the Jewish community leader – a man named Samuel ben Hananiah – and with a wealthy merchant named Halfon ben Netanel. He also corresponded regularly with his intellectual friends back in Spain. He loved Egypt: "This is a wondrous land to see, and I would stay, but my locks are grey," he wrote. He was anxious to get to Jerusalem, but wanted to lap up everything he could about Egypt while he was here. The caliph Al-Hakim comes into the story because the Jews in Spain had a particular fascination with the behaviour of the Muslim potentates of the Near East, at a time when Spanish Jews were looking anxiously over their own shoulders at their own Islamic overlords and wondering what the future might hold. Al-Hakim wasn't exactly flavour of the month; he was reviled among Jews and Christians alike for ordering the destruction of the Holy Sepulchre in Jerusalem in 1021 and, for good measure, the Ben Ezra synagogue here in Cairo as well. But they also saw him as a complex and intriguing man who might be the basis for a lesson in morality. Halevi loved a mystery, and he was especially interested in the questions over Al-Hakim's death. This letter seems to be a draft of something he may never have actually sent off, written to his son-in-law the scholar and historian Abraham Ibn Ezra in Toledo.'

'Can you translate it?'

She clicked the screen, calling up an enhanced photograph image of the text with English words overlaid. Jack leaned over her shoulder and followed as she read:

To my son-in-law Abraham Ibn Ezra and my daughter Ribca, my heart belongs to you, you noble souls, who draw me to you with bonds of love. In my last letter I wrote to you of the Caliph Al-Hakim, and of how my friends the nagid and the merchant Halfon have revealed much that is new to me about his disappearance in the desert, a mystery above all others in this mysterious and beguiling land. I ask you to pass on this letter to my friends the astronomer Ibn Yunus and the mathematician Ibn al-Haytham, as they may be able to sit down with the maps I sent and their measuring instruments and make sense of the story I have been told. Al-Hakim had taken to wandering into the desert alone on his donkey south of Cairo every night, having ordered his retainers and guards to stay at the city gate. Some say he was, in truth, a god; his disappearance was a reversion to his non-human form. Some also say that by persecuting Jews and Christians he was going against Islamic law; yet as caliph he was not accountable to any law, but the law to him. That is surely enough to drive any man to insanity, or to the desert! Perhaps like the pharaoh who sought the Aten in the desert, who made his temple at Fustat, aligned towards the pyramids, he was shedding that impossible burden, and seeking simplicity. When he went to the desert he went not as caliph, but as a man.'

Maria looked up. 'The literal translation of the epithet he uses for Al-Hakim is "sand-traveller", which itself is the literal translation of an ancient Egyptian term known only from hieroglyphs. It's almost as if they were speaking the same language.'

Jack shook his head in amazement. 'Fascinating,' he exclaimed. 'That meshes with my own revelation just now in the synagogue, when I realised that I knew a stone excavated in 1890 from the synagogue precinct contained the hieroglyphic cartouche of none other than Akhenaten. It begins to fit with a wider picture, that the site of medieval Fustat was once connected with the ancient complex of Heliopolis where north-eastern Cairo now stands. Heliopolis was the centre for the worship of the sun god Ra, and a logical place for Akhenaten to build a great temple to the Aten. Maurice told me that blocks from that temple have been identified in the medieval walls of Cairo, and that was my first thought when Aysha told me about the British officers discovering the stone with the cartouche here in 1890. But the account in that officer's diary makes it sound as if it came from an *in situ* ancient structure, not a medieval one, so it fits with what Halevi suggests about a separate pharaonic religious complex here, one aligned to the pyramids rather than to the old cult centre at Heliopolis. Is there more, Maria?'

'A few sentences, before the tear.' She carried on reading:

Now ben Netanel tells me this. His great-grandfather as a boy secretly followed Al-Hakim out into the desert that final night, a dare among the boys of Fustat to see where the caliph was really going. He watched from behind a dune as Al-Hakim hobbled his donkey with a knife, stripped off his clothes and slashed them with the bloody blade, and then stood there naked, raising his arms to the sky. His murder was a ruse. He wanted the world to think that he had died. He had indeed undergone a transmogrification, not from caliph to god, but from caliph to man. He did not die, but he disappeared down a hole in the ground into the underworld, never to be seen again. This is no fable; this is truth.

Jack waited in silence for a moment, coursing with excitement. *The underworld.* Go on,' he urged.

Maria sat back. 'That's it.'

Jack closed his eyes. *That's it?* 'Are you sure?'

Maria glanced at Aysha. 'Well, there *might* be more. Yesterday evening after I got set up here Aysha and I climbed into the chamber and managed to see through the hole with our torches. We were able to prise free this fragment, but we saw another sheet compacted against the stone beyond it that could be the torn lower half of the page. We don't have any extraction tools that wouldn't damage it and probably tear it into shreds. Everything has to be done here the old-fashioned way, with bare hands. And Aysha and I are, well, both a little short on length.'

Jack stared at her. 'You're telling me you got me all the way here because I've got long arms.'

'The longest in Cairo. Probably the longest in Egypt. And fingers used to feeling around in the murk. Diving down holes is your speciality, isn't it?'

Jack shook his head. 'What you need is Little Joey. Costas' miniature robot. His buddy. That's the real reason he's pining to get back to his engineering lab on *Seaquest*, not the problems of raising the sarcophagus of Menkaure.'

'We thought of asking him along too, but didn't think that mouse droppings were really his thing.'

'That's probably wise. Underwater is fine, but holes in the ground full of decayed matter are not what he signed up for.'

'Of course, there's the inevitable curse, as well,' Aysha said. 'The Geniza was said to be guarded by a serpent who bedded down in the manuscripts like a dragon with its treasure.

Anyone who went in was doomed. Look what happened to Solomon Schechter.'

'Snakes,' Jack muttered. 'Definitely not Costas' scene.'

'Then you'll have to go it alone,' Maria said.

Jack stared at the filth on the fragment of vellum. 'I'll need protective clothing. Some kind of respirator.'

Aysha nodded at a large plastic crate beside the ladder. 'We're one step ahead of you. Full biological, chemical and nuclear protection suits liberated from an army depot by a friend of mine.'

Maria glanced at him. 'You good to go?'

Jack looked at his watch, and then up at the hole into the Geniza chamber above him, black and slightly forbidding. 'Okay. There's no time for dithering, or, the gods protect me, for curses. Let's do it.'

11

A light came on, harsh, blinding, and the young woman in the centre of the room turned her head away from it, shutting her eyes tight against the glare. She strained against the bindings that held her hands to the back of the chair, no longer feeling the pain where the rope had cut into her wrists. Even the slight movement of her head had brought back the sickening stench of the room, full of people bound like her who had lain in their own filth for days, and in the filth of others before them who had died or been dragged away for execution. She had only been in here for a few hours, but with their watches removed and no clock she was already beginning to lose track of time; the only break in the sepulchral gloom was when the light cut in, when those who still had the energy moaned and whimpered with fear, when their captors came for another victim.

The first few times it had happened after she had recovered

consciousness she had managed to look around, above the terrified faces and twisted bodies, and had seen the cupboards filled with chemicals and the half-torn posters on the walls, advertising forthcoming exhibitions in the museum. She had been here before; she knew she was in the archaeological conservation labs of the ministry, now used as detention cells by the extremists who had been the driving force behind the new regime. She was only a short walk away from the Old City and the Synagogue where they had snatched her, only a stone's throw from family and friends. Yet she knew she may as well be a world away, beyond rescue. Only a few weeks before these labs had been a hive of activity, filled with colleagues of hers in the archaeological service, and the people around her now had been smartly dressed politicians and civil servants. Those torn posters and soiled clothes might just as well be archaeological relics themselves, of a time before Egypt had begun to fall before the forces of darkness and the people began to stare into the void.

The light shone hot against her face, and she knew it was her turn. A hand pulled her head and jerked it upright, the fingers smelling of khat. A man spoke harshly in English. 'Open your eyes.'

'Turn away the light,' she said hoarsely. 'And speak to me in Arabic.'

'You are a Jew. We will not speak to you in the language of the Prophet.'

'My family has lived in Cairo for two thousand years. Arabic is the language we speak.'

She heard the man talk to another in the distinctive dialect of Sudanese Arabic, and the light moved away. She opened her eyes cautiously, seeing two bearded men in front of her wearing black headbands, both with handguns and one carrying a powerful torch. The closest man waved a tattered piece of paper in front of her face. 'What is this?' he said, still speaking in English.

She squinted at it. 'It's a twelfth-century document from the archive in the Synagogue,' she said. 'I was taking it away for study when I was brought here.'

The man leaned forward and spat a stream of khat juice into the face of a woman on the floor, and then turned back. 'You're a liar. Our informant told us you were stealing holy documents of Islam, and he was right. This is written in Arabic. Even the stupidest of my men can see that. This is a page of the holy Qur'an.'

She looked at him defiantly. 'It's true that there are pages of the Qur'an in the archive. They're one of its greatest treasures. But there are also thousands of other documents in Arabic. If you and your fighters are as holy as you'd like to think you are, then you'd have memorised the Qur'an and you'd see that this is not a holy page. In fact, it's a letter from a wealthy Jewish matriarch to one of her three lovers, encouraging him to keep his Muslim faith because she knows that for him it is the true route to God.'

The man spat again, dropped the fragment of paper and held her by the chin, coming close to her face. 'We know who you work for. You are a spy of the Zionists. We have seen you go into the synagogue with that woman from the Institute of Archaeology in Alexandria.'

She said nothing. The man raised his pistol and cocked it beside her ear. 'Answer one question, and I will make this easy for you. There is a man we want, a so-called archaeologist who spied in my country when he was supposedly hunting for relics, and who is now on the trail of something we want in Egypt.' He let go of her chin, reached into his pocket and pulled out a crumpled page from a magazine, straightening it and holding it in front of her. It showed a picture of two men in diving gear on the side of a boat, one of them tall with greying dark hair and the other shorter and stouter. He pointed with the butt of his pistol at the taller one. 'Where is this man?' he demanded.

She pursed her lips defiantly, saying nothing. He rolled up the page, tossed it aside and then aimed his pistol at the women he had spat on. There was a deafening crack and her head exploded, brains and blood spraying their legs. He turned back to her, held her chin again and brought the pistol close enough that she could smell the smoke. 'I will ask one more time only,' he snarled. 'Where is Jack Howard?'

She continued to say nothing, sitting as upright as she could and staring defiantly ahead. The man waited for a moment longer, raised his pistol and then swung the butt at her head, hitting her and throwing her violently sideways. For a brief moment she saw the fragment of ancient text lying on the floor beside the dead woman, and then she saw a terrifying rushing blackness.

And then nothing.

Twenty minutes after leaving Maria, Jack was crouched at the bottom of the Geniza chamber looking up at the aperture in the wall leading back into the synagogue. The space was cramped, an arm's breadth across each way and some six metres high; it was like being inside a large chimney well in a medieval castle. He watched Maria follow him carefully down the rope ladder they had dropped from the aperture, her white protective suit shimmering in the light from the single bulb they had suspended from the top of the chamber. Jack's own suit felt strangely insubstantial after the countless hours he had spent underwater in a Kevlar-reinforced E-suit, and he had to move and hear the crinkle of the plastic to convince himself he was wearing anything above his own clothes. He shifted the respirator and clear plastic visor to get a more comfortable view, and then looked at his exposed right hand, already smeared with dirt, where he had cut off the glove and sealed the wrist with a rubber band. They had brought mini Maglites with them, but what he was about to do was going to be a matter of touch and feel, with bare fingers essential for the sensitivity needed to prise out what might remain of the ancient vellum letter in the hole in the wall.

Maria landed beside him and looked at the smear on his hand. 'Solomon Schechter called it Genizaschmutz,' she said, her voice slightly muffled by her respirator. 'Dust, insects, decayed manuscripts, flecks of whitewash from the ceiling, desert sand, the residue of all those human hands sweating and smudging as they wrote, and of course mouse goo, stuck together with a gummy ooze from the vellum. It's like pine resin when you get it on your hands, almost impossible to get off.'

Jack looked up at the aperture, lit by the single stark bulb, their route out. 'So this was filled up to the brim with manuscripts?'

'Virtually overflowing. They say the opening is up there so

that the holy words in Hebrew go directly to heaven, like the soul. In reality it was the only practical place they could put the opening, like a giant rubbish bin. Even though the manuscripts were removed over a century ago, I still feel as if I'm diving into a well of history when I come inside here. Aysha is only a few metres away on the other side of this wall, but it's as if we're halfway back to the world of the Geniza, in a kind of shadowy netherland with all of those faces and voices about to spring to life. I've never felt quite like this before in a medieval manuscript repository. In most cases, like the Hereford Library, the manuscripts were part of a scholarly library, so in your mind's eye you walk back into a candlelit scriptorium or a monk's study. Here, you walk back into a bustling Cairo street scene of the eleventh or twelfth century, filled with all the colour and vibrancy that life can offer.'

Jack spied a fleck of lighter coloured material sticking to the wall beside his face and put his forefinger on it, peeling it away with his thumb. It was a tiny piece of paper with a letter on it, a serif just visible. Maria opened up a small plastic box from a pouch on her belt and Jack gently flicked the fragment into it. She closed it, and replaced it carefully in her pocket. 'This is real archaeology, Jack. About creating a huge mosaic from the tiniest of tiny details. That single letter may float through history by itself for ever, or it might just form the crucial piece in a jigsaw puzzle. With the Geniza, you never know.'

'Let's get the job done,' Jack said.

Maria pointed to a hole just above the floor of the chamber on the side opposite the synagogue balcony, leading into the outer wall of the building. It was even smaller than Jack had imagined, barely wide enough to fit his bicep. He eased himself down until he was lying on his right side, his hand poised to reach inside. He paused for a moment, eyeing Maria. 'About that snake,' he said. 'The venomous guardian of the Geniza. If there were mice living in there, then this hole isn't going to have been his lair, is it?'

Maria looked thoughtful. 'The last mouse died in there about five hundred years ago, trapped behind a congealed plug of resinous vellum. The snake could have burrowed its way in there after that. It could be waiting in there for you, Jack.'

'I'm so glad Costas isn't here,' Jack muttered, flexing his fingers.

'There's a great line from Ben Sira, words on a piece of parchment that was floating in that mass of manuscripts where we're sitting now. It goes: "Concealed wisdom and hidden treasure, what's the use of either?" Whatever's in there needs to come out, Jack. I don't think the snake will bite.'

'Okay. I'll trust you.'

'There's something else I wanted to say to you, Jack, while we're here together. Whatever we find in that hole, you're going to want to leave here as soon as possible afterwards and the opportunity will be lost.'

Jack rolled back and looked at her. 'Maybe not the best time, Maria.'

She shook her head impatiently. 'It's not that. It's about scholarship. It's about the exhilaration of discovery. It's about what drives people like Solomon Schechter, like Howard Carter, like you, Jack. At the time when the Geniza was discovered there were many who felt that Jewish scholarship had turned in on itself, like the sophists of late antiquity or medieval Christianity, with too much intellect being wasted on trivia and obscurity, with piety becoming burdensome and negative. The Geniza gave a huge burst of vitality to all of that, almost a cleansing. It allowed people to see afresh not just the fundaments of their religion but also the sheer vitality of the people who had lived by it. It was as if what had gone before was foam on the sea of scholarship, but the uncovering of the Geniza created a tidal wave in the sea itself, one that survived even the darkest days of the Holocaust. It drove some of them to a vision of the world that was not partisan, was not divided into separate communities, but was as cosmopolitan as the world they found in the Geniza, a world where peaceful co-existence across all of the world's great religions might be possible. It was idealism, but idealism based on an astonishing historical revelation. That's what I wanted to say to you, Jack. Every time you make a great discovery it gives that burst of vitality to the world, a rekindling of wonder and excitement. With another dark cloud hanging over us now we need that more than ever. Don't ever give up on the quest.'

Jack stared up at that aperture near the ceiling, utterly still for a moment, feeling his heartbeat slow as it did when he was underwater. 'It's no longer just Jack Howard,' he replied quietly. 'The quest is driven by all of us, by the team.' He rolled back, took a deep breath, and thought again. 'But I know what you're saying. It's the bigger picture, isn't it? Discovery isn't just about the adrenalin rush, the thrill of the chase, the problem solving. It's about consequences, about what you find and how you present it to the world, about enrichment and uplifting, and sometimes, just *sometimes*, about improving the human condition. I'm with you on that, up to the hilt. And I'm humbled that you can think of me alongside scholars like Schechter and Carter. I'd say the same about you, as I would about Aysha and Maurice. And I'm not always the star. Sometimes,' he said, flashing her a smile and raising his right hand, 'I'm just a long arm, aren't I?'

Maria smiled back. 'Time you put it into action.'

Jack bunched his fingers and pushed his hand into the hole, continuing until he was elbow deep. At first he felt only a void, but then his fingers brushed against the edges, against slippery stone and a sticky mass. He tried not to think about what he was touching and pressed in further, reaching the middle of his bicep and already feeling the edges of the hole constricting his arm. 'Still nothing,' he exclaimed, pushing in further. 'I can't feel the end.'

'Another hand's length, no more,' Maria said. 'You can do it.'

He gave another shove, flinching in pain as his shoulder wedged into the hole. 'Okay. I've got to the far end,' he said, his face pressed hard against the chamber wall above the hole. He closed his eyes, imagining what he was feeling, a smooth but undulating surface with edges that curled back from the underlying stone. 'I think I've got the piece of vellum,' he said. 'About twice the size of my hand? I'm prising it away now.' He pulled gently at the edges, carefully forcing his fingers behind, working his way around until only the central part of the vellum remained attached to the masonry. Slowly, with infinite care, he pushed his fingers further behind the flap, feeling it come away millimetre by millimetre until finally it broke free. 'Okay. Got it.' He edged backwards from the wall as he withdrew his hand, pulling out a blackened object that looked like a piece of leather caught in a fire. He handed it to Maria, who peered at it closely and put it in another lidded plastic box. Jack sat upright, his hand blackened with filth. 'Could you see anything?'

'I could, Jack.' Her voice was taut with excitement. 'Maybe twenty lines, and it's in Halevi's hand. The upper tear is exactly consistent with the tear we've got in the other piece. Let's get out of here and see if I can read it.'

Five minutes later they were both outside on the balcony floor stripping off their suits, Jack quickly rubbing off the worst of the dirt from his hand with a pile of wet wipes. Aysha had already taken the box and opened it on the table, and Maria immediately went over and sat in front of it, pulling down one of the angle-poise lamps and putting on a pair of conservator's gloves. She carefully removed the vellum, placing it on a plastic sheet on the table, and picked up her magnifying glass and notebook, jotting down words in translation as she peered at the lines. Jack gave up trying to clean his hand and walked over. 'Can you see more palimpsest?'

'Definitely. It's even clearer than the other piece, but I'm just concentrating on the upper text.' She continued jotting down words, and after about another ten minutes stopped and sat back. She was silent for a moment, and then stripped off her gloves and put the notebook on the table. 'You're going to love this, Jack.'

'Go on.'

'You remember we left off where the boy had been following

Al-Hakim into the desert, and had secretly watched him faking evidence of his own death?'

'Right.'

'Well, this tells what the boy saw next.' She read out from her notebook:

Now, according to my friend ben Netanel, his great grandfather followed the caliph to a place where he disappeared beneath a sand dune, and where the boy hidden above saw a long tunnel leading to brilliant light. He tried to follow, but as he began to enter a stone door came crashing down, quickly to be swallowed by the desert. Before it vanished he saw on the door an ancient inscription of the disk with radiating arms that I have also seen in Fustat, at the place beside the synagogue where Moses was found in the reeds by Pharaoh. They say that the place where Al-Hakim left his donkey and his clothes was near the monastery of Qusayr, and the town of Hulwan, but if the boy indeed saw the pyramids then the place where Al-Hakim disappeared must have been further north, not far south of Fustat where I write to you now from the precinct of the Synagogue of Ben Ezra, surrounded by all of the delights of fruit and wine and beautiful women that this wondrous country has to offer. If you pass this on to my friends the astronomer Ibn Yunus and the mathematician Ibn al-Haytham they may calculate the area within sight of the pyramids close to the Nile where this event took place. I myself would seek out the place in the desert but I must travel while the sailing season is on us to the shores of the Holy Land and to Jerusalem, God protect it. God knows that I have love for both of you, my son Abraham and my daughter Ribca,

*and for my beautiful nieces and nephews, and I will pray
for all of you in sight of the Temple Wall on the Mount of
Olives, inshallah.*

Jack looked at the vellum, his mind reeling. 'Amazing,' he
exclaimed. 'That's exactly what Costas and I saw from under
the Pyramid of Menkaure, only this seems to be from
another entrance in another direction, looking west *towards*
the pyramids. What he's describing is the sun symbol of
Akhenaten, and the one he mentions in Fustat may well have
been associated with the Akhenaten cartouche excavated by
those British officers and taken back to England by my great-
great grandfather.' He took a deep breath, shaking his head.
'It's amazing, though it doesn't necessarily bring us closer to
another entrance that we might get into. The one he's
describing sounds as if it would require a major mechanical
excavation to open up, and could be anywhere within a radius
of several dozen square kilometres, probably beneath the
southern suburbs of Cairo.'

'I'll get one of my Hebrew experts back in Oxford to take
a look at the translation,' Maria said. 'Maybe there's an
alternative nuance to some of those words that might give a
better clue.' She glanced at her watch. 'Meanwhile, I've got
to get on here. There's a cluster of smaller fragments of other
manuscripts from the hole that need to be dealt with. The
clock's ticking.'

'Okay,' Aysha said, pulling out her phone. 'I'm calling our
driver in the Land Rover. He should be outside the main
entrance to Fustat within fifteen minutes.'

Jack turned to Maria. 'How did you guess there might be

something like this in the second part of the letter? The first half left Al-Hakim's fate wide open.'

'Call it instinct. A Jack Howard moment.'

'You have those?'

'*Very* occasionally.' She smiled at him. 'Actually, it was something Jeremy found in his research into the Howard Carter papers. He only gave me the barest details in a text message after I'd boarded the plane yesterday for Cairo, but it seems as if Al-Hakim wasn't the only one to disappear under the desert. And it seems as if there might be a connection with your Royal Engineers officers in the late nineteenth century. Jeremy was expecting his research to be finished by tomorrow and will contact you then.'

Jack glanced at his watch. There was something else he had wanted to do in Cairo, something he had planned since he and Costas had first laid eyes on the relief sculpture of the pharaoh and the Israelites inside the crocodile temple beside the Nile. There, he had seen the pharaoh in two dimensions; now he wanted to see him in three. He turned to Aysha. 'Do we have time to go to the museum? I'd like to see the colossal statue of Akhenaten from Amarna that went with the travelling exhibition around the world a few years ago.'

Aysha looked uncertain. 'It's shut to the public, but I still have a pass. Our driver knows the back routes and could get us to the rear entrance. I'm supposed to return you to Alexandria and then I'm straight off to the Faiyum to join Maurice at the mummy necropolis. But we could squeeze in the extra hour if you really want it.'

'Who knows when I'll be in Egypt again.'

Maria eyed him. 'You'll be back. I've never known Jack Howard walk away from something like this.'

'I'm thinking of visiting Jerusalem next.'

'That's going from the frying pan into the fire, isn't it? There have already been rockets from Syria falling on Haifa.'

Jack shrugged. 'I was there doing research for my doctorate in the week before the first Gulf War, remember? There were no tourists and I had the Holy Sepulchre all to myself. I told Rebecca she should seize the opportunity to explore as much as possible while she's there now, when the place isn't swamped with tour buses.'

Maria looked at him shrewdly. 'If the real reason you're going to Jerusalem is to look out for Rebecca, forget it. She'd never forgive you. You've got to let her plough her own furrow, and then ask you out there herself.'

Jack pulled out his phone and showed her an image. 'That's the tunnel she's about to go down under the City of David. She sent this just after we left Alexandria. She wanted Costas to go too, but I texted her about Lanowski's visit and said Costas might be tied up for a while with some engineering problem on *Seaquest.*'

'When you reply, tell her the trip she and I have planned to Greece is definitely on the cards. I've just had permission for us to visit the monasteries on Mount Athos to look at the manuscript libraries. At last they've agreed to let women in and she and I are going to be the first.'

Jack raised his eyes. 'Fascinating. I've always wanted to have a look in there. Maybe I'll join you.'

'As if, Jack. As Rebecca would put it. This is a strictly

girls-only trip to a once strictly male preserve. It'd look as if we had a chaperon.'

Jack put away his phone, and paused. 'I'll call you in Oxford. We should spend some time together.'

Maria turned back to the vellum. 'How's Katya?'

Jack shrugged. 'Haven't seen her for months.'

She turned to him. 'What's going on there, Jack? She's perfect for you. A palaeolinguistics PhD who can hold her own in a gun battle and runs her own project on the Silk Road in Kyrgyzstan. What is it now, ten years since you first met? She helped you find Atlantis.'

Jack shrugged. 'You helped me find the last Gospel of Christ.'

'What are you doing, Jack? You need to make up your mind.'

'She's with that Kyrgyz guy, Almaty, at the petroglyph site.'

'Well, I guess at least he's on the same continent as her. I know how she feels.'

Jack glanced at Aysha, who gave him a rueful look. 'Time to go, Jack. There's a curfew at midnight and we definitely can't push that.'

Maria glanced at them. 'I'm doing an all-nighter here and then on the early morning flight back to Heathrow. I want to get my Hebrew expert at the institute to look at this and then I'll email you the final translation. And watch out for something from Jeremy. He's working flat out in the British Museum stores looking for more Howard Carter manuscripts, for anything further on the old soldier and his story of lost treasure under the pyramids. Jeremy usually comes up trumps, if you give him time.'

'We may not have a lot of that,' Jack said.

'He was on to the last box of correspondence when I left. With the pyramid a no-go zone, his findings may be the last hope you have of discovering another way underground. Who knows what that guy told Carter.'

'I'll text him when I get back to Alexandria, right after I contact the IMU Board and do all I can to get your friend Sahirah released. Any plans to return the sarcophagus to Egypt are on hold until she walks free. If we are indeed able to raise it tomorrow, that would bring maximum public humiliation to the Antiquities Director. Releasing Sahirah should be a price he is willing to pay to keep face.'

'Tomorrow might be your last chance,' Aysha said. 'The Antiquities Director might not last much longer than that, and whoever takes his place from the extremist junta won't care less about the sarcophagus returning to Egypt. That is, if there's even a Ministry of Culture left. It's already halfway to being an interrogation block.'

Jack gave her a steely look. 'I'm going to insist on her release by midday tomorrow, Egyptian time. If there's no response, I'll be meeting with the IMU security director and assessing all options.'

Maria stood up, arms folded, and looked up at Jack. 'Congratulations on your chariots discovery in the Red Sea, Jack. But it makes me think of lines from Yannai, another poet in the Geniza, on the burning bush in the Book of Exodus. "Omens of fire in the chariot's wind, Pillars of fire in thunder and storm." Take care of yourself, Jack. Don't stretch that envelope too far, otherwise it'll be Rebecca coming to find you, not the other way round.'

Jack looked at her with concern. 'Will you be all right here alone?'

Aysha turned to him. 'That beggar you gave money to at the entrance to the synagogue precinct? He's ex-Egyptian special forces, a cousin of mine, Ahmed. He has a Glock 17 concealed in those rags. He won't let Maria out of his sight until she's sitting on the plane for Heathrow tomorrow morning.'

'Good. I wouldn't want to be coming back here to rescue Maria.'

'You wouldn't need to. I'd be here first.'

Maria paused, and then quickly kissed him on the cheek. 'See you in Oxford when this is over.'

Aysha gave them both a wry smile. 'Inshallah.'

Half an hour later Jack ducked out of the Land Rover into a back street and followed Aysha quickly down a passageway behind the museum. While they had been in the synagogue Cairo had erupted again, the low cloud over the city reflecting the orange glow of fires and the roar of the traffic punctuated by the wail of sirens and bursts of gunfire. Aysha spoke to the two armed guards at the entrance, showed her pass and waited as one of them unlocked the door. Moments later they were in a long ill-lit corridor and then ascending a staircase that came out at the rear of the ground floor exhibits hall. The entire museum seemed sepulchral, with many of the cases shrouded with sheets.

'The last Antiquities Director ordered this, the last *archaeologist*, that is, before he was ousted by the new regime,' Aysha said as they hurried on. 'Everyone here was fearful of a repeat of what had happened to the museums in Iraq and

Afghanistan, and covering the exhibits over at least buys some time, keeping them out of the eye of the extremists who see virtually everything in here as un-Islamic. Here we are, Room Three, the Amarna Room. The one you want is in the far left corner, under the shroud. I'll wait here in case a guard comes by and I have to explain what we're doing. You've got ten minutes, maximum.'

She switched on the light and Jack left her pacing the entrance to the room. The air smelled musty, tomb-like, and Jack had the chilling sensation of being at the end of an era, that the mummies and sculptures and other priceless artefacts celebrated the world over were about to be entombed again, swallowed into the ground or smashed to pieces within the ruins of this place. He passed the famous unfinished sculpture of Nefertiti, her beautiful face looming out of the darkness, and then he saw her again in a relief sculpture, no longer so beautiful with the same elongated profile and bulbous features as her husband. He stopped at the far corner in front of a shrouded form that towered over the rest of the room, and carefully pulled off the sheet. The sculpture rose above him just as he had remembered it in the travelling exhibition in London, only here the features were even more deeply accentuated by the shadows. It was a representation utterly unlike that of any other pharaoh from Ancient Egypt, with the extended chin, the thick, half-smiling lips, and the bulbous eyes, as if it were from another place and another time altogether.

He had not known for certain why he had wanted to see this statue again, but now he realised. Before she had left for Jerusalem Rebecca had talked to him about Baldwin the

Fourth, the Crusader King who had ruled the city with his Frankish barons in the 12th century, soon after the Geniza poet Halevi had met his end there. Together they had watched the Peter Weir film *Kingdom of Heaven* in which Baldwin is portrayed in a golden mask, concealing the leprosy that had ravaged his face and was eventually to kill him. Jack had remembered the wooden Burundi face masks with their hooded eyes that he had seen in Sudan, ceremonial masks with a history that may have extended back thousands of years to the time when the pharaohs had tried to conquer the desert. It was there that Akhenaten had experienced his revelation of the Aten, had cast off his priestly role and pushed aside the old religion. Had the tribesmen seen his extraordinary features, and created their masks in his image? Or had he seen *their* masks, the masks of those who lived under the radiance of the Aten, and had he and Nefertiti adopted them for their own, symbols of their own allegiance to the new religion? How else to explain the transformation of Nefertiti in the sculptures? Instead of signs of illness, as many had suspected, was Akhenaten instead portraying himself like the Burundi, seeking the anonymity that a mask gave him in the light of God?

He looked up one last time at the sculpture. He did not know whether he had just experienced a blinding revelation, or whether the idea of the mask just pushed Akhenaten further back into mystery. It was as if the pharaoh himself were playing games with him, tempting him to take one step further into the unknown, then showing him that the trail was an illusion. It seemed to reflect everything that had happened over the last few months, of tottering on a knife-edge between success and failure, between unlocking a mystery that Jack knew lay somewhere beneath their feet and having to walk away with that ambiguity in Akhenaten's face, that mask over reality, seared into his mind.

His phone hummed. It was a text from Costas. He quickly read it, and suddenly coursed with excitement. The dive from *Seaquest* to raise the sarcophagus was on for tomorrow afternoon. The IMU Embraer jet was due at Alexandria at dawn tomorrow, and the Lynx helicopter was already waiting at Seville airport in Spain to transfer them to the ship. Rebecca would understand his trip to Jerusalem being postponed, and Maria had been right; it would have been wrong for him to jump on the first plane to Tel Aviv after receiving her text, as if he had been waiting on tenterhooks for a chance to watch out for her. And she was used to the last-minute change in priorities that often took place when Jack was following too many leads at once.

As he put away his phone he smelled the Geniza on his hand. He remembered Maria at the bottom of the chamber, eyes ablaze, voicing her passion for the project, for Jack to hold on to his vision of what might lie ahead. He felt a sudden upwelling of emotion, and swallowed hard. After reading the letter of Yehudi Halevi he had begun to understand what it was that had overwhelmed Solomon Schechter and the other Geniza scholars, not so much the sheer quantity of material but the humanity it represented, preserved with breathtaking immediacy. It had been as if Halevi had been writing the letter to him, brimming with curiosity and a fascination with the world around him that struck right to the core of Jack's being. He felt revitalised, more determined than ever to pursue his own quest. He remembered those last lines of Halevi, the extraordinary account of the tunnel, and he felt a burning excitement. But meanwhile he had another priority, to do all he could to secure the release of the Egyptian student who had been the first to make the discovery. The sarcophagus might only give him a small amount of leverage, but he would use it to his utmost. He needed to make contact with the outside world as soon as possible.

He turned and walked quickly back to the entrance to the room. Aysha already had her finger on the light switch. 'Seen what you wanted to see?'

'I've seen it.'

'Right. Twenty minutes to midnight curfew. We need to get out of here.'

PART 3

PART 3

12

Off Spain, in the West Mediterranean

Jack sat back in the passenger seat of the Lynx helicopter, glanced at the helmeted figure of Costas asleep in the seat opposite and stared out at the shimmering blue of the sea below. At Valencia Airport he had turned down the pilot's offer to take over the controls, relishing instead the half-hour of down time before they hit the bustle of *Seaquest* and all the demands of the day ahead. Jack knew that he would be walking off the helipad into a teleconference to discuss the imprisoned Egyptian girl, and Costas would be straight down into the engineering lab to make sure all of the equipment was as ready as it could be for the dive that afternoon. The sound of snoring came through his headphones, and Jack turned just in time to see the grizzled face loll forward in his shoulder straps. He leaned over and pushed him gently upright, and Costas opened his eyes and looked blearily about. 'We there yet?'

'Not yet, but you were taking a slow nosedive for the floor.'

'Dive,' Costas mumbled. 'Need to adjust the dynamo in the ADSA submersible stabiliser system. I knew I'd forgotten something on my checklist. Always think better when I'm asleep. Can't believe I won't have Lanowski to help me.'

'His talents were needed in Alexandria stripping Hiebermeyer's computers and making sure his database was secure. You'll just have to wing it.'

Costas crinkled his nose where Jack's hand had been and leaned towards him, sniffing like a dog. 'What's that smell? That *terrible* smell?'

Jack looked at the fingers of his right hand, seeing the dark stains from the resin and remembering the Geniza chamber. 'Ah, yes. Couldn't scrub it off.' He sniffed the tips of his fingers. 'That, my friend, is a thousand years of mouse.'

'Huh?'

'An ancient archive. A hole in the wall. With Maria.'

'That sounds just like a date with Jack. Really romantic. You're talking about the synagogue in Cairo?'

'I'll fill you in when I can show you my pictures. It was a fantastic discovery, a clue that pushes us one step closer to getting under the desert again. You'd have loved it. There was a sacred snake, guarding the archive.'

'No way.'

'Only kidding. Well, nearly only kidding. Anyway, Maria thinks the curse was lifted long ago.'

Costas looked aghast. 'What curse? What snake?' He looked

back into the cargo compartment at their bags. 'You haven't brought anything with you, have you?'

Jack grinned. 'Just something for you to dream about. I'll wake you when we're there.'

'Huh? Oh, yeah. Okay.' Costas slumped against the window, and seconds later Jack heard the low rumble again. He glanced at the text message he had received from Maria when he and Costas had landed in the Embraer from Egypt an hour and a half before. All it said was *Thanks for last night*. He smiled at the irony of it. 'Last night' meant a dusty chamber in an old synagogue poring over a medieval manuscript, with barely a farewell embrace.

He stared out at the shimmering expanse of the sea, his lifeblood since he had first donned a wetsuit more than thirty years before. He thought back to Rebecca's mother Elizabeth, to a relationship that had ended even before Rebecca was born, when they had both been graduate students together; she too had been an archaeologist but had been forced by threats and intimidation back into the world of her *camorra* background in Naples, to give archaeological legitimacy to their tomb robbing and antiquities dealing. When she found out she was pregnant she decided not to tell Jack, not to allow her family to get their tentacles around him as well and destroy his dream, and she had struggled to bring Rebecca up alone and carve out a legitimate position for herself in the antiquities service. When Rebecca herself was threatened, used as a pawn to try to get Elizabeth back into the criminal fold, she sent her secretly to close friends in New York State to be brought up and educated, while she remained in Naples to do enough of what was asked of her to keep them from acting on their threats to hunt out Rebecca and bring her back into the family.

Jack had only seen her once again, when he had gone to Naples to explore the Villa of the Papyri at Herculaneum, and in their brief conversation she had broken down and told him everything, revealing the existence of their daughter and her wish that he take care of Rebecca if anything should happen. She had witnessed one drug deal too many, had made some distant cousin jittery that she would go to the police, and a few days later her body was found by the seashore with a bullet through the back of her head. That had been more than five years ago, and Jack still felt the numbness, a heartache that he knew would always be behind everything he and Rebecca did together, behind her own drive to make a mark on the world and show the strength that her mother had shown to bring her up against the odds.

Jack knew that his seeming ambivalence towards Maria and Katya was not a consequence of juggling between the two, or of a greater love in the past that he had been unable to shake off, or of the sense of responsibility that had channelled so much of his emotional reserve towards Rebecca after her mother's death. Rebecca had told him that he was like the great sea captains of old, brilliant at sea but directionless on land, most at home navigating his life with the prize always just beyond the horizon and the voyage towards it at the mercy of the elements and chance. Perhaps his relationships with women had become an analogue of that. Yet he knew it did not have to be so. He had seen it work with Hiebermeyer and Aysha; he remembered Maria's parting words in Cairo, and resolved that this time, when it was all over, he would take that step that he so often baulked at, and actually give her a call.

A rocky headland came into view, the limestone reduced to the jagged, sun-bleached form characteristic of the northern Mediterranean shore, and his heart leapt as he saw *Seaquest* in the bay beyond. He knew that the pilot would need to hold off before getting permission for landing, and he had been relishing the chance to inspect her properly from the air for the first time since her refit in Falmouth earlier that year. On the stern she was flying the Spanish flag, a courtesy to the country that had agreed to allow the search within their territorial waters, and below that the IMU flag bearing the anchor on a unicorn, the crest of Jack's seafaring ancestors and a recognition of the donated land from the Howard estate that formed the main IMU base beside the Fal Estuary in Cornwall. She was the second IMU vessel to bear the name, the first having been lost almost ten years before to a battle with a warlord in the eastern Black Sea during their search for Atlantis. The second *Seaquest* and her sister ship *Sea Venture* were multi-role scientific research vessels, in keeping with IMU's expanded brief over the last decade not only to be at the forefront of archaeological exploration but also to spearhead other aspects of oceanographic research. Like the Royal Navy's latest Echo-class vessels she was equipped for full hydrographic survey, including multi-beam echo-sounders, a side scan sonar and sub-bottom profiler, as well as an integrated navigation system of bow and azimuth thrusters and propellers within a swivelling pod that allowed her to hold a precise position over the seabed in all but the worst weather conditions. Her defensive capability was also closely based on the Echo-class vessels, with a retractable twin 20 mm Oerlikon pod set below her foredeck and two 7.62 mm general purpose machine guns, an essential provision given the fate of her predecessor and namesake and the threat of piracy when she was conducting operations in unpoliced international waters.

In other respects *Seaquest* and *Sea Venture* formed a unique class with many features designed from the bottom up by Jack and his team. At a little over 6,000 tons and 120 metres in length they were larger than her naval counterparts, with a top speed of 25 knots and a range of up to 12,000 nautical miles that made them capable of extended deep-ocean voyages. Behind the bridge lay an extended accommodation block for up to thirty researchers and technicians, including state-of-the-art labs for the conservation and analysis of finds and below that an engineering facility custom-designed by Costas for the maintenance of the ship's remote- and autonomous-operated vehicles and manned submersibles. The submersibles hangar opened out on to a unique internal docking facility on either side of the propeller shaft towards the stern, allowing divers and vehicles to enter and exit safely even in extreme weather conditions.

The Lynx banked low, its rotor kicking up a halo of spray as it held position some five hundred metres off the ship's port side, allowing Jack to see her more closely. Behind the accommodation block lay the helipad and the aft operations deck, the focus of most activity when they were working on a site. Jack cast a critical eye over the equipment visible in the stern. The main purpose of the refit had been to install an upgraded derrick for raising and lowering Zodiacs and submersibles, and he could see it extended over the starboard side, the cradle they had made for the sarcophagus sitting on the deck beside it. The derrick had passed its sea trials off Cornwall with flying colours but it was having its first proper outing here. Jack remembered years before watching the Tudor warship *Mary Rose* being raised from the Solent, and the terrifying moment as the hull surfaced and the cradle slipped. That had also been in the glare of the world's media, and he knew that Captain Macalister would be putting the derrick through every possible safety check to try to ensure that there was no brush with disaster this time round.

Jack watched a group of technicians in IMU overalls and safety helmets begin to release the derrick from its deck restraints and roll out the winch. IMU's greatest assets were not equipment but personnel, and he knew he had the best. Over the years he had assembled a crack team, a mix of old friends and fresh talent, many of them bridging the divide between commercial and military experience and the strong focus on scholarship and research that drove all of Jack's projects forward. Unlike treasure hunters, their jobs were not on the line every time they embarked on a new quest, counting the cost hour by hour, holding out for prize money that rarely came; IMU operations were financed entirely from an endowment that released Jack from ever having to raise funds or satisfy investors. It had been a dream of his from the time when he ran student expeditions from a battered old van and an ex-navy inflatable, a dream realised when one of his most stalwart expedition divers, Efram Jacobovich, had ridden the wave of the software boom that was making huge fortunes when they had been students. Fifteen years later he backed

Jack's budding institute with an operating budget far larger than that of any other oceanographic institute in the world. Jack still had to answer to a Board of Directors, but with their criteria being scientific merit and feasibility rather than financial profit he was in a unique position among undersea explorers able to mount multi-million dollar projects. Above all, he was freed from ever having to consider selling artefacts; all of their finds went on museum display or as part of the cycle of travelling exhibits that had brought their discoveries to audiences around the world. It was one commitment that Jack shared with Colonel Vyse, the British officer who had extracted the sarcophagus from the pyramid and despatched it on its ill-fated voyage to the British Museum in 1838; Jack was determined that it should go to the best possible place for display as well as for its own security, and if that meant reneging on their offer to return it to Egypt, then so be it.

Beyond the rotor downdraught the sea was millpond-calm, and it took an effort to imagine the storm winds on that December day in 1838 and the abyss that lay beneath. Since their find of the chariots in the Red Sea and touching the manuscript fragments from the Geniza in Cairo, biblical phrases had been running through Jack's mind, snatches of verse he had remembered from chapel at boarding school. *And darkness lay on the face of the deep.* Far below them, unimaginably deep, in the place that creation had forgotten, lay the wreck of *Beatrice,* the ancient sarcophagus in its hull standing stark above the silt like the tomb of a long-forgotten sea-god. That was temptation enough for any archaeologist, but it was not just the sarcophagus itself that had brought Jack back here. It was what Colonel Vyse had packed inside, a surprise for the museum, perhaps a sweetener to persuade the trustees to continue to sponsor his excavations; it was something that he himself had not recorded and was lost to history until that dive when Jack and Costas had brought it back to light.

When Jack had swept the silt from the plaque he had been astonished to see the sun-symbol of Akhenaten, a pharaoh who had lived over a thousand years after the mummy of Menkaure had been sealed within the sarcophagus. It was only after they had found a second Akhenaten plaque in the desert, one with a depiction showing the pyramids, that Jack had made sense of it, realising that Akhenaten had taken over the pyramid as a portal into the underground complex beneath the Giza plateau that he and Costas had glimpsed for a few precious moments three months ago far below the burial chamber. Inside that chamber, perhaps mounted above the portal, Colonel Vyse had unwittingly found a clue to what might have been the most extraordinary discovery ever made in Egyptology; his decision not to mention the plaque and its loss in the wreck – perhaps to avoid criticism for not having recorded it – was to keep the world in ignorance until now. Jack had been clutching at straws since then, desperately hoping for clues to another entrance into the complex, a discovery he might make before Egypt shut down on him entirely. Coming back to the wreck was part of that trail; the plaque had been missing a section from one side, and he was hoping against hope that the lost fragment would be buried in the silt nearby.

The pilot's voice came through his headphones. 'Jack, we're holding off for another fifteen minutes or so while a helo ahead of us delivers a film crew. As soon as they've cleared the helipad, we're good to go.'

'Roger that, Charlie,' Jack replied. 'I'll use the time to get up to speed on the site. I don't think I'm going to get much chance for that once I'm on board. And our colleague could always use a little more beauty sleep.'

'Roger that,' the pilot said. 'I'll advise you.'

A noise like a snorting water buffalo came through the intercom, and Jack pushed Costas up again and wedged him beside the window. He took out his iPad, attached the keyboard and propped it on his knees, opening a ghostly image of the sarcophagus as he and Costas had first seen it from the submersible three months before. There was no indication that any other antiquities had been on board the ship, and the decision had been made not to excavate the site any further than was required to clear a large enough space to feed the cushioned winch cables beneath the sarcophagus preparatory to lifting it. He touched the screen and opened up the image that had brought them to this spot in the first place, a previously unknown watercolour that had appeared in an auction a few months earlier showing *Beatrice* in the harbour of Smyrna in Turkey; on the back had been a pencilled note made years later by the captain of the ship, George Wichelo – a man thought to have died in the wreck – giving its location in this bay a few nautical miles north of Valencia, resolving a mystery that had led undersea explorers on numerous false trails over the years in the hunt for the fabled lost sarcophagus.

The artist had accurately shown *Beatrice* as a brig, with foremast and mainmast and the boom for a spanker over the stern. Despite being on the cusp of the Victorian era, only a generation away from the transformation to steam power, *Beatrice* was indistinguishable in appearance from her forbears of the Napoleonic Wars period; she still bore the chequer-board 'Nelson pattern' of gun ports that merchantmen in the Mediterranean retained against Barbary pirates from North Africa, still a threat in the early 1830s when the painting had been made. He tapped the screen again and brought up a 3-D visualisation of the wreck that Lanowski had completed a few days before, based on weeks of survey using a high-precision multi-beam sonar array mounted on a remote-operated vehicle flown a few metres above the seabed. The programme allowed a virtual fly-around of the site, and he swept his fingers across the screen, getting as many angles as possible. The wreckage had been rendered in metallic grey to distinguish it from the sediment in which it had been partly buried; he could clearly see the lines of protruding frames and the regular mounds that were all that was left of her iron deck knees, the results of a refit that provided the only concession to modernity in a hull otherwise built in time-honoured fashion using timbers and copper nails. The sarcophagus and the ship's sixteen guns had been rendered in white, highlighting the elements with the greatest inert weight that might have affected the ship's freeboard and stability. In a way that he had not appreciated on the seabed, the visualisation showed how all of the starboard guns had shifted to the port side and how the sarcophagus was also off-centre, as if straining on the cordage that must once have held it in place.

There was little doubt in Jack's mind what had caused the wreck. Lanoswki's simulation had shown that even with extra compensating ballast she would have been dangerously unstable with the sarcophagus laden on deck, three tons of granite that would have unbalanced a ship of little more than 200 tons deadweight. He closed his eyes for a moment and tried to imagine the sea as it must have looked on that winter's day when the ship had come to grief in the bay. Her last known ports-of-call had been Valetta in Malta and then Leghorn, modern Livorno, far up the Italian coast. At that time of year Wichelo may have encountered strong north-easterlies all the way from Alexandria, and have decided to claw his way up the western shore of Italy rather than attempting to sail due west from Malta with the risk of being blown into the North African shore and any awaiting corsairs. From Leghorn it would have been plain sailing with a north-easterly mistral behind him across the Gulf of Lyons, an exhilarating run when all went well, with the hope of rounding the southern coast of Spain into the Strait of Gibraltar. For some reason, perhaps because the wind became a gale, perhaps because the recent refit had given the vessel more leeway than the captain had been used to, perhaps because the lading of his cargo had made the ship less manoeuvrable – probably a combination of all these factors – his course and the coast of Spain converged just north of Valencia. Had they rounded the next headland, they might have made Valencia; as it was, the bay where they came to grief offered no shelter and only a jagged rocky shore dropping off to great depth, offering little hope of grounding the ship or saving its cargo.

The sarcophagus had been lashed down and wedged with beams but would still have been vulnerable to a sudden roll; the captain would have done his best to avoid broaching to –

coming beam-on to the waves – knowing that a roll could cause the sarcophagus to strain against its lashings and break free. Although the ship's guns were only lightweight six- and nine-pounders, they still weighed over half a ton apiece and must have been part of the problem in her final moments, the eight guns on her starboard side breaking free of their carriages and crashing to port as the ship heeled over, adding to the displaced weight of the sarcophagus and making recovery impossible. But then as the port gunwale became submerged she took on such a weight of water so quickly that she came upright again as she sank, keeping the sarcophagus from tumbling overboard and providing enough cushioning in the hull structure to protect it from damage when the ship hit the sea floor.

The sudden swamping had been fortunate for the preservation of the sarcophagus, but less so for the crew. As always Jack reflected on the human cost, on the terror of those final moments. It probably took only seconds for the ship to sink, taking with it anyone below decks and sucking down the others in the vortex. It was a minor miracle that anyone should have survived, and more so that it should have been Captain Wichelo himself, a man assumed to have gone down with the ship but whose pencilled note years later on the back of the watercolour had shown otherwise. Jack felt certain that his survival was an accident of fate; there would have been no time for anyone deliberately to abandon ship. He remembered the time he had spent in the crow's nest of a cadet training ship when he had learned to sail, and imagined that Wichelo might have scrambled up to the maintop in the search for a safe anchorage and then been thrown clear when the ship heeled over and the masts dipped into the waves.

Wichelo's disappearance after coming ashore was not difficult to fathom. He was an experienced captain who had taken *Beatrice* many times across the Atlantic and through the Mediterranean, who must have looked death in the face before; he would have been bound by the immemorial custom of the sea that a captain is always the last to leave his ship. That custom was so deeply embedded in the seafarers' code that even a hint of suspicion among friends and colleagues that he had put his own life before others might have been too much for him to bear. He might also have been doing a favour to his beneficiaries, knowing that the insurance claim would stand a better chance of succeeding if he were not there to give evidence of unsafe lading that as an honest man he might have been unable to conceal. He would have known that he had taken a risk in accepting the cargo, and that the price of failure was absolute.

Jack imagined the scene with Colonel Vyse on the docks at Alexandria, a stone's throw from Qaitbey Fortress and the place where the Geniza poet Halevi had landed from Spain in the 12th century. Wichelo would have been a good captain for Vyse to approach, one with an established reputation who perhaps had taken antiquities before for clients to England; Vyse might have been less concerned with the suitability of the ship itself for his particular cargo, his blunderings in the pyramid suggesting that he lacked a good eye for the logistics of transport. But he was a wealthy man who would have offered Wichelo a handsome remuneration, perhaps enough to secure a comfortable retirement capped by the small fame of being the man who had brought the centrepiece of the

British Museum's collection safely from Egypt. If Wichelo had declined, there would have been others eager to accept. He would have known that his ship was not ideal and that the summer sailing season was coming to an end, but he was swayed by the rewards. It was always a precarious business being a ship's captain, with the lion's share of the glory if a venture succeeded but a quick fall to ignominy if things went wrong.

Jack touched the screen to bring up Lanowski's second CGI, an animation that he had not wanted to see until he had worked it through in his own mind. He smiled as he saw the ghostly image of the ship, exact in every particular of a brig's standing and running rigging; the attention to detail was just like Lanowski. He had shown Wichelo gambling on a full spread of canvas, with the rudder hard over to port in an attempt to steer parallel with the coast. As the bay loomed the topsails were furled and the ship suddenly broached on to the waves, heeling over and swamping. As if in X-ray through the hull he could see the sarcophagus shift and the starboard guns break free and tumble to port, and then the ship submerging, coming upright again and hitting the seabed almost a thousand metres below in a cloud of silt before sliding to a rest.

Jack stared at the screen. 'Bingo,' he said quietly. He now felt fully prepped for what lay ahead. He took the iPad apart and slotted it into his backpack, and then brought his mind back to the present and to Captain Macalister on *Seaquest*, a man as embedded in nautical tradition as Wichelo had been. As captain he had final say on all operations carried out on board, not just navigation but also diving and exploration.

Since finding the wreck three months previously the work to map and evaluate the site had been in the hands of a highly experienced project director, and Jack had no intention of taking over; his role with Costas was to be on the seabed to secure the cradle and look for anything that might be revealed as the sarcophagus was lifted free. Jack knew the pressure that Macalister would now be under, with the countdown into its final phase and the focus on safety for the equipment operators as well as for the divers in the water.

He watched the other helicopter rise from the ship, swoop low over the bay and then disappear beyond the rocky shoreline. He thought back to Egypt, to Hiebermeyer and his desperate race against time to complete the necropolis excavation before the forces of darkness descended. At least here they were working in full cooperation with the Spanish authorities, and the only political dimension was one created by IMU itself, to use the raising of the sarcophagus as leverage with the Egyptian authorities both to allow Hiebermeyer to finish his work and to secure the release of the student in Cairo. With primetime media across the world prepped for the event this afternoon, and with the return of the sarcophagus to Egypt hard-wired into the story, the pressure on the Antiquities Director in Cairo would be considerable. That had been their gamble in letting in the film crews, but with the additional situation with the girl it had seemed a gamble worth taking. He drummed his fingers against the side of the seat. *If* the weather held. *If* the new derrick cooperated. *If* there was no other glitch. He shut his eyes, mouthing the words that had become his mantra: *Lucky Jack*.

The pilot came over the intercom. 'Jack, we're going in now.'

'Roger that.'

Costas suddenly shot awake, blinking hard, his face beaming with excitement. 'I've got it, Jack. *I've got it*. I know how to fix Little Joey. And I'm starving. Take us home, Charlie.'

13

Twenty minutes later Jack opened the door of the conference room on *Seaquest* to a blaze of camera flashes and shouted greetings. He held up a hand, smiling, and scanned the room. He counted at least twenty-five journalists, some of them familiar faces who had followed his projects for years, others big-name foreign correspondents who had been attracted not only by the drama of the sarcophagus but also by the political dimension of its return to Egypt. There was a large contingent of Spanish reporters, and as Jack made his way behind the table at the head of the room he quickly shook hands with the two representatives of the Spanish Ministry of Culture who were sitting there. Beside them was James Macalister, a short, dapper man with a white beard, immaculate in his uniform with the braid of a captain on his shoulders. Space had been left for Jack between Costas and the project manager, and as he sat down Macalister leaned back and spoke to him. 'We've done the background on the *Beatrice* and the sarcophagus, and run through the logistics. You're here just for a quick meet and greet.' Jack nodded, and Macalister stood up, addressing the room.

'All of you will be familiar with Jack Howard, who has just arrived on board *Seaquest* with Dr Kazantzakis. They'll be on the seabed supervising the raising of the sarcophagus, and you'll be getting broadcast-quality live feed from them. There'll be plenty of opportunities after that for interviews. Right now this is just a chance to say hello.'

A woman in the front row raised her hand, waving it in the air. 'What were you doing in Egypt, Jack? You were spotted at the airport at Sharm el–Sheikh.'

Jack groaned inwardly, but kept his cool. The journalist who had asked the question was one of his most ardent fans, but also a blunt instrument as far as the politics were concerned. She was one of the main reasons why he preferred to avoid any kind of press conference before a project was over, but he knew that to try to deny his presence would only stoke up her interest further. 'Just checking out the dive resorts. Dr Kazantzakis tells me that with IMU it's all work, no play, so I was looking into doing something about it.'

There was a titter of amusement from the others, but the woman persisted. 'We had a round robin in the office guessing what mystery Jack Howard would be trying to solve in the Red Sea. The best we could come up with was the biblical Exodus, the story of Pharaoh's lost chariot army.'

Jack looked at her unblinkingly, and smiled broadly. 'Now that *would* be a find. If I ever make it, you'll be the first to know. Meanwhile, I'm delighted that you're all here for this afternoon's show. Captain Macalister and his team have been working around the clock to get everything ready. I'm looking forward to spending time with you later.'

Macalister held up his hand. 'That's it. There will be another briefing here with the project manager at 1430 hours, and then all going to plan you will be allowed on to the starboard bridge wing with your cameras to film the recovery. Meanwhile, you are required to remain in this room or your quarters, with the deck strictly out-of-bounds for your own safety. Thank you for your attention.'

Jack and Costas quickly got up and followed Macalister out of the room, past the two security men stationed there to enforce the captain's instructions. Macalister turned to Jack. 'That was close.'

'Let's hope we can keep this operation on track to give them what they're expecting. I won't answer any more questions from journalists about Egypt until everything is resolved there.'

Macalister pushed open the door to his day cabin and ushered them in. The room was already occupied by IMU's security chief, Ben Kershaw, a former Royal Marine who had also worked for MI6, the British secret intelligence service. He was standing at the window with a satellite phone, but lowered it as the others entered, quickly shook hands with Jack and Costas and then sat down with them at the conference table at one end of the room. Jack poured himself a glass of water and leaned forward, his eyes steely. 'Okay, Ben. Tell us what you've got.'

'I followed our plan not to involve diplomatic channels except as a last resort. I used personal contacts from my intelligence days in Egypt. I now know exactly where she's being held, in the lower ground floor of the Ministry of Culture building in Cairo where the conservation labs have been converted into interrogation chambers.'

'Archaeology meets the modern world,' Costas said grimly.

'Our plan was to go to the Antiquities Director to see if he could exert leverage to get the girl released. I couldn't get any response, and then Professor Dillen intervened. As chair of the IMU Board of Directors he was in on this from the start.'

Jack took a sip of coffee. 'I know why. About ten years ago Ibn Afar tried to obtain an archaeological qualification in Britain, when he had his eye on the top job in the Egyptian ministry. He showed up in Cambridge thinking he could bribe his way into a Master's degree by promising future excavation permits to anyone who helped him. Dillen was the only one who didn't dismiss him outright, sitting down and explaining how things work in the West and arranging for him to start off as a volunteer at the British Museum. That didn't last long, predictably, but I know that once he was back in Egypt working his way up the greasy pole he often contacted Dillen to ask for references and endorsement, seeing him as a kind of patron.'

'They had a phone conversation this morning,' Ben said. 'Dillen told him that the offer to return the sarcophagus to Egypt still stood, and that Ibn Hafr would have all the limelight. But he also told him that there would be no movement until the girl was released. Dillen and I had already agreed that we should give him a two-day ultimatum. With the sarcophagus being raised today, Ibn Afr was told that the press would be clamouring to know its destination and that the Spanish authorities would reinstate their claim to ownership if it looked as if there was uncertainty. Of course, we all know that the Spanish government, UNESCO and IMU will no longer condone the plan to return the sarcophagus to Egypt given the present political circumstances, but Ibn Afr is in Cairo cocooned from reality and won't necessarily guess that. But he's wily enough to know a veiled threat when he sees one. If he fails to come up with the goods, three days from now he suffers international humiliation and opprobrium when it's revealed that the decision to return the sarcophagus has been revoked and his name is linked with the arrest of the girl.'

'So what was his response?' Jack said, finishing his drink.

Ben leaned forward, his hands clasped together, staring at Jack. 'There's a trial due in two days' time. She'll be in the dock with a hundred or so others. The accusation is read out, they are convicted and sentenced to death.'

'A *death* sentence?' Jack exclaimed. 'That's outrageous. For being accused of stealing a scrap of medieval manuscript?'

'Ibn Hafr says that he'll try his best to get her off. My intelligence source says that as things stand he will probably succeed. Antiquities theft was of more concern to the old regime than to the extremists, and they're more interested in cases of apostasy or adultery. If there are actually going to be executions, those will be the ones to go first. My source says that Ibn Hafr will make a big show of the difficulty and how he's putting himself on the line, and that we should go along with that; it's all part of the game. But we should hold him absolutely to the deadline, which stands at 1030 hours two days from now.'

'To the second,' Jack said coldly.

'There's one big *if* in all this,' Costas interjected. '*If* things stay as they are. If there's a meltdown and the extremists take over in two days' time, then we've lost her.'

'She won't be the only one,' Ben said. 'If there's a takeover, the hundreds awaiting execution now will be joined by thousands more. My source is expecting a complete purge of government ministries.'

Costas shook his head. 'Roll on the dark ages.'

'We have to try to be optimistic,' Jack said. 'Egypt isn't like Iraq or Afghanistan, brutalised by dictatorship or decades of war. We're talking about a civilised and decent people who will not allow themselves to be taken to the cage without a fight.'

Macalister looked grim. 'Not so easy when your oppressors are psychopaths who have been building up a head of steam for over a hundred years.'

'There's always the military option,' Ben said.

Jack stared at him. 'Are you suggesting that we invade like the British did in 1882, and again in 1956? With the right force you might push the extremists out of Cairo, but then you'd be likely to create an insurgent war like the one the coalition fought in Iraq, with the same cocktail of terrorism, suicide bombings, and an enemy who disappears and rematerialises as soon as you think you've scored a success. The civilian population would soon become too weakened and demoralised to resist. And any Western intervention in Egypt now would be seen by hardliners elsewhere as tantamount to an alliance with Israel. Any radicalised regime not yet in open conflict with Israel would soon join in. We'd be stoking up World War Three.'

Ben leaned over the table, looking at him intently. 'You know the other military option, Jack. You've been in special forces.'

'You mean targeted assassinations?' Jack pursed his lips. 'I was involved in two ops against leadership targets in the Middle East. I was just a ferryman, a temporary naval officer who happened to be good at driving Zodiacs. One op was a success, the other an abort. But if you want to hear about the tit-for-tat consequences of those ops, go no further than Engineer Lieutenant-Commander Kazantzakis of the US Navy Reserve, who won his Navy Cross rescuing seamen blown into the water from his ship in a copycat attack of the terrorist assault on USS *Cole*, provoked by a similar US special forces assassination attempt.'

Costas looked at Ben. 'I was at the debrief with the SEAL team who did the op. That was back before 9/11, and the conclusion even then with targeted assassinations was that you cut off one head and another one grows in its place. Since then the bad guys have become very good at creating the infrastructure to absorb punishment. Kill one Taliban commander, five others are there to take his place. The extremists in Egypt must have a tight command structure, but they've been very careful not to publicise their leadership. Assassination is only useful if the target is a known quantity and a big name.'

Jack tapped his pencil on the table. 'Which brings us back to archaeology, and to the people of Egypt. Archaeology is the greatest weapon we have against extremism. Egypt more than any other country in the world has become dependent on archaeology for its livelihood. From the lowliest camel driver on the Giza plateau to the hotel owners and the tour guides, archaeology provides the lifeblood of the nation. That's what we've got to marshal in this battle. It could be the first time that archaeology, the place of archaeology in the modern world and people's lives, provides the critical groundswell for a popular uprising. Right now, that's what we're in this game for. We're talking about saving people's lives.'

Ben nodded. 'Let's hope it happens in time for a frightened girl and her family in Cairo.'

Jack stared bleakly around the table. He knew what Aysha would say: inshallah. He took a deep breath. 'Okay. We're done here. Thanks for everything, Ben. Keep me in the loop.'

Costas stood up. 'I can finally get to the engineering lab. No time for Little Joey, but I want to run some final diagnostics on the gimbal in the submersible. There's something I need to adjust. And I haven't had a go with the new derrick yet.'

Macalister glanced at his watch. 'Meet on deck at 1500 hours, dive at 1530. Let's try to keep to the schedule.'

Jack pushed his chair back. 'Roger that. On deck one hour from now. Enough time for me to get some shut-eye. See you then.'

Ten minutes later Jack closed the door of his cabin and lay back on his bunk, suddenly realising how tired he was. His cabin was just below the bridge, its portholes looking out over the foredeck and to starboard. He glanced around at his most treasured belongings, at the cases of old books, at the battered old chest first taken to sea by an ancestor of his on an East Indiaman three hundred years before, at the artefacts and pictures that covered the walls. More so than anywhere else, more than his rooms in the old Howard estate in Cornwall, his cabin on *Seaquest* was where he felt most at home, anchored by familiarity; this was where he dreamed of new discoveries, and yet it was also where the reality when he wakened and felt the tremor of the ship's engines was more hard-edged and exciting than anything he could imagine.

He stared at the wall opposite, at the hanging brass gauntlet from India in the shape of a tiger and above that a painting Rebecca had made of the Jewish menorah from the temple in Jerusalem, the lost ancient treasure that had taken him on a quest halfway around the world when she was just a child. He was now only a flight away from seeing her, and yet when he closed his eyes it was not her he saw but the immediate task ahead of him, the inky darkness a thousand metres below and the extraordinary scene that he and Costas had seen three months before when they had discovered the wreck of the *Beatrice* and the ancient sarcophagus. He tried to relax, thinking of nothing but the sensation of being underwater, but his mind kept returning to the nagging question that had driven him to return here. Was the missing fragment of the plaque of Akhenaten still inside the sarcophagus? Did it contain the clue that he so desperately wanted, the final piece in the jigsaw puzzle that would justify a return to Egypt and their unfinished quest beneath the pyramid?

'Dr Howard. Time to go.'

Jack opened his eyes and sat bolt upright, staring at the

chronometer beside his bed. He had been out for almost half an hour. He stood up, took a swig of water from a bottle on his desk and then the coffee proffered by the crewman, quickly drinking half the cup. 'What's the state of play?'

'Costas is already in the water.'

'What? In the sub? He's supposed to wait for me.'

'He wanted to get it submerged to check the gimbal, to make sure it'll keep the sub trim and level. He realised that the only way he could do it was to have it in the water for a shallow-water trial. All going well, he should be finished and on the surface by the time you get on deck.'

Jack drained the rest of the coffee and handed back the mug. 'Thanks. Two minutes to change into my overalls and I'm there.' The crewman ducked away down the corridor and Jack stripped off his outer clothes, pulling on the orange IMU overalls that had been hanging behind his door. They were more comfortable in the confined space of the bathysphere, and cooler if the heat ramped up. He had to steel himself to spending the next few hours cooped up inside a metal and Perspex ball barely big enough to fit the two of them crouched down, something that preyed on a lingering claustrophobia he had battled since a near-death experience diving in a mineshaft when he had been a boy. He splashed some water on his face, wiped it on his sleeve and stooped out of the door into the passageway. He kept his own personal demon at bay by focusing his mind on the objective. This was not just about the plaque, about his burning personal quest. It was also about ensuring that the sarcophagus was successfully winched to the surface, a huge achievement in itself but also a carrot to dangle in front of the egomaniacal tyrant in charge of the

Egyptian antiquities service who might thus be persuaded to save a young woman from an appalling fate.

Jack slid on his hands down the rails of the stairway to the main deck level, swung open the hatch and stood in the full glare of the sunlight on the foredeck below the bridge, cursing himself for having forgotten his sunglasses. In front of him the new red derrick was swung off to starboard, its cable taut where the submersible was held over the side of the ship. Jack grabbed a hard-hat from the bin beside the hatch and went over to the rail, looking down and seeing the submersible awash in the azure blue of the Mediterranean. Out of the water it was an ungainly beast, like some giant insect, a mass of cylinders and piping and manipulator arms, the pressurised bathysphere with its double-lock chamber suspended beneath the yellow carapace that contained the batteries and electronics. In the water it was another story entirely: the vectored-thrust propellers allowed an extraordinary precision of movement and position-holding, perfect for archaeological work and the task ahead of them almost a thousand metres below on the seabed this afternoon.

Macalister came alongside him, and they both watched as the submersible rose higher and Costas came into view through the Perspex viewing dome. Jack glanced at his watch. The journalists would be having their second briefing now, and soon afterwards be expecting to set up their cameras. Before that the submersible would have to be raised out of the water and placed on its cradle on the deck in order for Jack to get inside, and then winched out again. If this was going to be in full view of the world's media, they needed everything to run as smoothly as possible and not to allow filming until they were in the water again and certain that everything was good to go.

Macalister pressed the earphone he was wearing and bent down to listen more clearly, and then straightened up, gave a thumbs-up and made a whirling motion with his hand, looking back at the derrick operator. He turned to Jack. 'That was Costas, and he's ready to come up. He said it was crucial to trial it, and the issue's resolved.'

'You mean he got itchy feet, and just couldn't resist taking it for a joyride.'

Macalister grinned, and signalled again to the derrick operator. The cable creaked, and the motor screeched. There was a sudden lurch, and the cable began paying out rapidly from the derrick, coiling in the sea around the submersible. Jack glanced back in alarm and saw the derrick operator frantically pulling the emergency handbrake. He looked at the submersible. At least it was buoyant, not dependent on the winch to keep it afloat. But as he watched the top of the submersible dipped beneath the waves, and then was submerged. Jack's heart began to pound. *Something was wrong.*

'It's the cable,' Macalister shouted. 'The coils have fallen on top of the submersible, weighing it down.'

Jack stared at the cable. At least fifty metres had been paid out. If the weight of the cable forced the submersible down to ten metres depth, then the volume of air in its ballast tanks would be halved and it would sink of its own accord, coming to a halt only when it reached the maximum extent of the cable. Jack grabbed another intercom headset from its stand, tossed off his hard-hat and put it on. 'Costas, do you read me?'

'Loud and clear.'

'Blow the ballast tanks. There's a malfunction in the derrick and about fifty metres of coiled cable has dropped on to you.'

'No can do, Jack. Something's jamming the valve.'

Jack stared at the wavering form of the submersible just beneath the surface. He could just see where a coil of cable had caught around the manifold linking together the rack of compressed air cylinders on one side. The submersible suddenly sank deeper and the coil disengaged, swirling round with the rest of the cable in the water below the derrick. 'Okay,' Jack said. 'A coil of cable was caught around it. Try now.'

'Still no good. The drag from the cable must have somehow closed the external valve.'

Jack turned back to the derrick operator. 'Can you hold it?' he shouted.

The man gave a thumbs-up, his other hand still on the brake. 'I should be able to hold it once it reaches the maximum extent already paid out, that's fifty-seven metres from the top of the derrick. But I can't guarantee for how long. After that, it's a one-thousand metre payout.'

Jack turned back to the water. The submersible was nearly out of sight now, sinking more rapidly, the cable unwinding and straightening out above it. Two men with tool kits rushed up to the derrick and removed the panel over the electronic controls, trying to isolate the problem, and beside Jack the two safety divers were quickly finishing kitting up. Jack cupped his hand over the mike so that Costas could hear against the noise. 'You're going to come to a halt at about fifty metres depth. The divers should be able to free the valve.

Failing that you can do an emergency egress through the double-lock chamber and they'll escort you to the surface. You copy that?'

'Copy, Jack. But there's another problem. It's also cut off my breathing air. The carbon dioxide levels in the bathysphere are already in the red. I've only got a few minutes before blackout.'

Jack stared at the two safety divers, his mind racing through the options. They had just zipped up their E-suits and were donning air cylinders. The cable suddenly became taut, and the derrick jolted. 'Okay,' he said into the mike. 'The divers are less than a minute away from entry. Do you copy?'

There was a pause, and Costas' voice when it came through sounded distant. 'Copy that. I'm on the way out, Jack. My legs and arms are tingling.'

Jack stared at the cable, watching the water shimmer off it. In the space of a few minutes a routine equipment check had turned into a deadly crisis. He felt his breathing and heart rate slow, as if he were making time itself slow down, stretching out the seconds so that he could run through all of the options. The divers only had the compressed air tanks they used for shallow-water safety checks and maintenance; it would take too long now to rig them up with mixed gas or rebreathers. With compressed air they were limited to fifty metres, maybe twenty metres beyond that in an extreme emergency, but no more. If the cable ran free again and the submersible plummeted beyond that depth there was only one option left for rescue, one that he would never allow another member of his team to take.

And then it happened. The derrick screeched and the cable

began to feed out again. Jack ripped off the headphones and glanced back to the derrick operator, seeing where the others had leapt forward to help him try to hold the brake, their tools cast aside. The cable was falling fast, dropping the submersible far beyond air-diving depth now. Jack turned, feeling as if he were in slow motion, his vision tunnelled, his metabolism slowed as if he were already in dive-response, his system anticipating what his brain was telling it and doing all it could to maximise his chances of survival. He blew on his nose to clear his ears, keeping his nose pinched, and with his other hand scooped up the weight-belt of one of the divers, holding it tight and bounding to the edge of the deck beside the cable. He was barely conscious of those around him, of Macalister's shocked face, of the two divers too stunned to move, of voices behind yelling at him not to do it.

He stared into the abyss. All that he thought of was the darkness, and Costas.

He breathed fast, gulping in the air, took a final deep lungful, and jumped.

14

Jack just had time to cross his ankles and arms to present minimal resistance before he hit the water, his right hand pinching his nose ready to equalise the pressure in his ears and sinuses and his other hand wrapped around the diver's weight belt he had grabbed just before leaving the deck. He knew that the cable from the derrick to the submersible was only a few metres away, and that with the dead weight of the belt he would plummet directly on target without having to angle sideways. In the seconds it took him to leave the deck his mind had flashed through the physiology of free diving: the possibility of middle ear and sinus rupture if he failed to equalise, the inevitability of lung barotrauma and blood shift into the capillaries as his chest cavity was squeezed, and yet also the reflexive response of the body to being under water, the reduction of metabolic rate that could allow him to remain conscious for the crucial few extra seconds he might need to reach the submersible and open the air-tank manifold to give Costas a chance of survival.

Below him lay almost a thousand metres of water to the wreck of the *Beatrice*. At that depth without a pressure suit his organs would be crushed, but he would have been dead a long time before that. With every ten metres of depth from the surface his lungs would halve in volume, so that at fifty metres the air that had filled his lungs would occupy only one fifth of that volume, at a hundred metres one-tenth. By a hundred and fifty metres, lung barotrauma was a near certainty; the constricting volume of his chest cavity would cause the membranes to rupture and he would begin to drown in his own blood. By then, perhaps two minutes or two and a half minutes into the dive, he would be reaching the limit of his breath-holding endurance. At that point he would either give way and breathe in water, or black out because the increased carbon dioxide level in his body would trigger unconsciousness; either way meant death. All that he knew for certain was that the maximum free-diving depth ever achieved had been a little over 250 metres, less than a quarter of the depth of the water below him now and representing almost superhuman physiological endurance. If the submersible had dropped any deeper than that before he reached it there could only be one possible outcome, for him as well as for Costas.

He was instinctively prepared for a shock of cold but as he sliced into the water he felt the warmth of the Mediterranean envelop him. He knew that the cold would come, a rapid, numbing cold as he passed through the thermocline, and that the oxygen saturation in his brain was inducing a mild sense of euphoria, something that would wear off quickly as the oxygen was depleted. As he felt himself plummet he concentrated on equalising his ears, his eyes shut tight. To open them in the pellucid water would be to reveal the enormity of the darkness beneath him, something that would make even the strongest diver baulk. He would only do so once he had passed the point of no return, once he knew that baleout was impossible. Less than ten seconds after entering he passed the first big thermocline, at this time of year at a depth of about thirty-five metres. Even if he dropped the weights he knew that without fins he would stand no chance of returning to the surface now. The cold increased his sense of speed, his skin more sensitised to the water rushing past. Equalising became easier as the pressure differential decreased, each halving of the air spaces in his body every ten metres now involving smaller and smaller volumes of gas. He was deeper than he had ever free-dived before, eighty, perhaps ninety metres, far beyond the safe depth for compressed-air diving, well into the death zone where the chances of sudden unconsciousness increased dramatically with every metre of descent.

He felt a searing pain in his lungs, as if a clamp were compressing his chest from all sides, tightening with every second that passed. Even if there had been air to breathe he felt that his chest could never bear the expansion. The cold was shocking now, as cold as the Arctic Ocean, further paralysing him. He knew he had little time, maybe half a minute, no more. He opened his eyes. For a few seconds he was distracted from the agony in his body as he concentrated on trying to see. He looked down, blinking against the blur. Directly below him it was pitch dark, an absolute darkness like he had never seen before. He had the sense that he was sinking into it, that he had plummeted below the final gloom of natural light. He knew that meant he was at least 120 metres deep, probably closer to 150 metres. For an instant the pain seemed to leave him and he felt himself holding Rebecca tight, a memory of a moment when he had felt that his life had been most worthwhile, of utter contentment. He forced himself out of it, back to reality. He needed to remain focused for his final seconds, even if it meant excruciating pain. *Costas*.

And then he saw it. A few metres below him a suffused glow appeared, the emergency lighting of the submersible. He hit the cable and slid down it, the metal cutting into his exposed forearm, and crashed into the carapace of the submersible like an astronaut out of control on a spacewalk. He let go of the weight belt, which spun a crazy dance into the depths, disappearing out of sight below. He saw the recumbent form of Costas watching him through the viewing port of the bathysphere, his face distorted by the thick Perspex. He pulled himself over to the manifold linking the air cylinders together and found the wheel that opened the valve, seeing where it had been bent over by the cable falling on it. He pulled it anticlockwise. *Nothing*. He tried again, using every fibre of his being, every ounce of energy he had left. Still nothing. He suddenly felt the overwhelming urge to breathe, and began gagging, each reflex sending a jolt of pain through his lungs. He caught sight again of the face in the porthole. *He could not give up now*. He heaved one last time, and suddenly it gave way, cracking open. He spun the wheel round several times and pulled himself frantically down to the wheel that opened the double-lock chamber, spinning that too, feeling the hatch open inwards and pulling himself inside, pushing it shut and slamming his hand down on the handle that opened the valve to fill it with air.

A deafening hiss filled his ears and the water in the chamber became a raging maelstrom, lit up by the orange glow of the emergency lighting. Seconds later his head was above water, and he was gasping, taking in huge lungfuls of air, shuddering as the oxygen coursed through him. He coughed hard and saw a fine mist of red, evidence of some respiratory tissue damage but not enough to indicate major barotrauma. He saw blood drip from his nose, and tipped his head up. He glanced at his watch; it had been a little over four minutes since he had last looked at it on the deck of the ship just before jumping. The depth gauge on the casing of the chamber showed 275 metres, and was increasing rapidly. In the course of tangling with the submersible he had dropped through the threshold of possibility for free diving; another ten metres and he would probably have been gone. He had been lucky.

The chamber emptied of water, the hissing stopped and the hatch from the bathysphere clanged open, Costas' head appearing through it. 'Jack. Good of you to drop in.'

Jack coughed again, his voice hoarse, distant sounding. 'Don't mention it.'

'You okay?'

Jack tipped forward, a finger pressed against his nose. 'Could use a tissue.'

Costas fumbled in the pocket of his overalls, leaned in and passed over a scrunched ball of white. Jack took it, holding it cautiously. 'Pre-used?'

'Tried and tested.'

Jack wet it, tore off a chunk and shoved it up his nostril, holding it there and cautiously tipping forward again to see that the bleeding had been stemmed. His breathing had nearly returned to normal, and he edged forward, noticing for the first time the gash like a deep rope burn on his left forearm where he had slid down the cable. Costas handed him a towel, a fleece and a pair of tracksuit bottoms. 'My spare clothes. A little short and a little wide, but who's looking. Once we get into the bathysphere we'll dig out the first-aid kit for that arm.'

'You okay?'

'I was nearly gone, Jack. Seeing stars.' He jerked his head at the emergency oxygen bottle attached to the casing beside him. 'Couldn't risk using that because the air cut-off meant there was a pressure build-up inside the bathysphere, enough to make pure oxygen toxic. But it's back to normal now.'

Jack rubbed the towel on his hair, feeling the ache in his head from the cold. 'What's our status?'

'We're going to the bottom, Jack. When you opened the valve it filled the bathysphere, and we've got enough air for at least six hours. But there's still a problem with the pipes to the ballast tanks. Right now I just have to concentrate on maintaining life support and keeping the sub stable and upright. Once we get within fifty metres of the seabed I'll activate the vertical water thrusters to soften the landing. If the vectored thrusters work as well they might give us enough power to hop around like a big bug on the seabed but not to rise more than a few metres without draining the battery.'

'How close will we be to the sarcophagus?'

'We should be dead on target.'

'Comms?'

'Dead as a Dodo. The fibre-optic cable was severed. We have no way of communicating with the surface.'

'But they could still brake the cable before we hit the seabed.'

Costas shook his head. 'Too much of it has been paid out. The weight of that amount of cable as well as the dead weight of the submersible will be too much by now for them to be able to halt the fall. The only way of repairing the winch will be to let the cable uncoil completely after having secured the upper end with the old derrick, and then attempt to repair the fault in the winch machinery. I was never happy with that new derrick, Jack. Too many corners were cut to get this show ready in time for the media, who now look as if they might not get a show at all. But we've got the best people topside including the engineer from the shipyard who installed it, and with any luck we'll be back on track soon. The biggest danger is the cable spooling off entirely and falling on us, two tons of metal dropping a thousand metres at about fifty metres a second, like a gigantic whip. If that happens, this submersible will become the second sarcophagus down there.'

'Meanwhile they'll be sending down an ROV.'

'It'll be on its way as we speak. My guys in the engineering lab will be on to it.'

'Okay.' Jack eased out of his wet clothes, realising that he was shivering uncontrollably. He had hardly noticed it in the euphoria of survival but now he felt the cold ache all over his skin, adding to the residual pain he felt in his chest. He towelled himself down as well as he could, pulled on Costas' clothes and followed him through the hatch into the bathysphere, sliding down in the co-pilot's seat beside Costas. He leaned back, closing his eyes for a moment. 'I never thought I'd be happy to be in a confined space, but this is that time.'

'Seat belts on, Jack. Brace yourself.'

Jack strapped himself in and watched Costas activate the thrusters. The three portholes in front of them showed pitch black, the external lights still off. The depth gauge showed 820 metres, then 840. The thrusters came to life, slowing the submersible down and forcing Jack up in the seat against his belt. Costas activated the multi-beam sonar and a high-definition image appeared on the screen in front of them as it swept the seabed some eighty metres below, revealing undulating sediment and then the familiar outline of the shipwreck, the scatter of guns clearly visible and the sarcophagus standing stark in the centre where the pit had been dug around it preparatory to lifting. Costas flicked on the external strobe array, revealing a shimmer of reflected particles through the portholes, and then he took the joystick in his right hand while keeping his left on the water-jet throttles. 'Easy does it,' he muttered to himself. 'I need to pull us a fraction off the vertical of the cable, to avoid landing right on top of the sarcophagus. The vectored thrusters aren't responding, but I should be able to do it by reducing the flow through the port-side vertical thrusters while keeping the starboard ones on full throttle.'

Jack could feel the vibration of the water jets on one side of the submersible, and watched the altitude gauge, measuring their height above seabed. At twenty-two metres he could see a hint of something through the forward viewing port, and suddenly he was seeing the shipwreck, the dull green of brass guns covered with verdigris poking out of the sediment. Above the breech of one of them he could see the distinctive heart-shaped bale mark of the East India Company, a little detail he had not noticed before when he had studied photos of the wreck, opening up a small unexplained byway in the history of the ship that sent a frisson of excitement through him. And then with a soft explosion of sediment they came to a halt, 934 metres beneath *Seaquest* and the surface of the Mediterranean.

'The eagle has landed,' Costas said, releasing the controls.

The veil of sediment dropped and the white form of the sarcophagus came into view only a few metres in front of the strobe array. Jack could clearly make out the architectural style of the carving, a geometric pattern that made the sarcophagus one of the greatest exemplars of sculpture from the Egyptian Old Kingdom, at the time of the building of the pyramids. For almost two hundred years the only image that the world had seen of the sarcophagus had been a woodcut in Colonel Vyse's account of his excavations, showing the sarcophagus inside the burial chamber of the Pyramid of Menkaure. Now it was in front of them, looking almost as if it had been designed to be in this place, unaffected by the forces of nature that were steadily eroding and crumbling the wreck around it.

Costas tried the controls again. 'It's gone dead. I can't move it. That coil must have caused more damage than I thought.'

'So we're not going anywhere. No big bug hopping on the seabed.'

Costas shook his head, and lay back, stretching. 'All we can do now is wait.' He reached down into a paper bag on his side. 'Brought lunch with me. Didn't have time topside. Sandwich?'

Jack felt as drained as he had ever felt, bone-tired and aching all over, and he knew that when they surfaced the medicos on *Seaquest* would want to give him a thorough road-check. But meanwhile he was famished, and the idea of a picnic with his best friend trapped inside a submersible almost a kilometre deep in the abyss did not seem such a bad plan at all. He took the sandwich, and they ate together, occasionally swigging from a water bottle that Costas had placed between them. As Jack sat there munching, staring at one of the greatest archaeological discoveries they had ever made, he knew there was nowhere at this moment that he would rather be.

It felt good to be alive.

Twenty minutes later Jack finished wrapping a bandage around his forearm and stared out of the front viewing port at the sarcophagus. Inside it, he knew, lay the plaque they had discovered on their dive to the wreck three months previously, something that Colonel Vyse must have found inside the pyramid and included as an added extra for the British Museum when he consigned his cargo to the *Beatrice* that day in Alexandria harbour in 1837. It was not the plaque they had seen that had spurred Jack to come back here, as they had been able to record all of the surviving carving three months earlier, but rather the hope that they might find the fragment a metre or so across that had been missing from one corner, the sharp edges suggesting that the break had been recent rather than ancient and might have taken place during the wrecking. The plaque had shown the Aten sun-symbol super-imposed on a plan of the pyramids at the Giza plateau, with the orb of the Aten in front of the Pyramid of Menkaure and the radiating lines extending eastwards towards the site of modern-day Cairo and the Nile. There was a chance, just a chance, that the missing fragment might show the intersection of the thickest radiating line with the river at a point just south of modern Cairo, the clue that Jack needed to the location of another entrance into the underground complex that he and Costas had seen from beneath the pyramid.

Jack glanced across at Costas, who was absorbed in a mass of wiring that he had disengaged from the upper casing of the bathysphere, and tapped the viewing port. 'Come and look at this. Tell me that I'm seeing things.'

Costas grunted, left a pair of miniature pliers dangling from a wire and slid over beside Jack. 'What are you looking at?'

'About two metres in front of us, at eleven o'clock, nearly abutting the sarcophagus. Just visible sticking out of the silt.'

Costas pressed his face against the middle of the glass. 'Doesn't look like ship structure or fittings. Looks like it might be stone.'

'That's what I thought. It's off-white, like marble.'

'The missing fragment of the plaque?'

'Any chance of getting the manipulator arm to work?'

Costas jerked his head back towards the dangling mass of wires. 'Not a chance, Jack. We've got life support, that's all. Somehow, when that coil hit the sub it short-circuited the main electronics board. It's more than I can fix down here.'

Jack stared at the few centimetres of white stone visible in the silt. *So near, yet so far.* It was close enough that he felt he could almost reach out and grab it, yet he may as well be trying to touch ice on Mars. He took a deep breath, feeling the ache in his lungs. He would have to wait and see where they stood with the excavation, whether the back-up submersible or remote-operated vehicle could examine his find, something that would take precious time he could ill afford if he were to return to Egypt before the country went into meltdown.

A swirl of sediment filled his view, and in the distortion through the left side of the port he saw a commotion on the seafloor. Apart from a few diaphanous fish he had seen little sign of life in the desolation outside, and he peered with some curiosity, expecting something larger. Suddenly an eye appeared only inches away, staring directly at him, luminous, blinking, the size of a baseball. He jumped back, startled, and then saw the flexible metallic neck. 'Costas, we've got a friend.'

Costas slid back alongside him. 'Joey!' he exclaimed excitedly, putting his hand against the Perspex. 'I *knew* he'd come. Good boy.'

The eye retracted, looking down, and a manipulator arm came into view, pivoted at the elbow and wrist and with five metallic digits just like a human hand. Behind it Jack could see the yellow carapace covering the batteries and electric motor that powered the water jets and array of tools that Costas and his team had built into it, all of it operated from the surface via a fibre-optic cable that was just visible trailing off above. The forefinger of the hand pointed down at a tablet-sized LCD screen on the front of the ROV just below the manipulator arm, and Jack could just make out letters appearing on it, distorted through the Perspex cone of the viewing port. Costas pressed his face against the centre of the cone where there was the least distortion and after a minute or so rolled over and turned back to Jack.

'Joey's inspected the manifold, and everything looks okay. They can't reconnect our communications cable so it's going to have to be done the old-fashioned way, with written messages. The problem with the derrick was an electronic switch override which the engineer has replaced. They're currently re-coiling the cable on the spool and expect to be ready to retrieve us in about twenty minutes. The recompression chamber is prepped and the medical team are waiting. You're supposed to breathe pure oxygen.'

'I'm fine,' Jack said. 'Tell them there's no evidence of barotrauma.'

'You know what the medicos are like. And Joey's watching.'

Jack grunted, pulled the oxygen mask from the emergency bottle beside his seat, cracked the valve and pressed it against his mouth and nose. 'Okay?' he said, his voice muffled.

Costas turned back to read the screen. 'Meanwhile, Joey's going to carry on snaking the hawser under the sarcophagus, the job we were meant to be doing. Now that they know we're safe and sound, they're going to carry on with the plan. As soon as we're back on deck the cable will be dropped again for Joey to attach to the hawser. Fortunately the media people haven't yet been allowed out so they'll have no idea what's happened, other than a small delay. They'll be told that the decision was made to use the ROV rather than the manned submersible because Joey's manipulator arm was better up to the task than the arms on the submersible. Which happens to be true.'

Jack stared out of the viewing port beside him at the white form of the sarcophagus. The fragment of stone protruding from the silt was only about a metre from Joey. He sidled over to the main port beside Costas, and pointed exaggeratedly at it. The eye looked at him and cocked sideways, and the hand twisted around with the palm up, as if questioning. Jack dropped the oxygen mask, picked up a pencil and notepad and quickly scribbled on it, pressing the pad up against the window. The eye slowly scanned the paper, and Jack turned to Costas. 'If we've got twenty minutes, that might be just enough time for Joey to see whether that slab is the missing fragment.'

The screen on the ROV began scrolling out letters again, and Costas pressed his face against the Perspex to read it. 'The ROV operator is under strict orders from Captain Macalister to focus on the task at hand. In no circumstances is he to let Dr Howard divert him to dig a hole somewhere else.'

'You try. Doesn't Joey have a mind of his own?'

Costas scribbled on the pad and pressed it against the window. Joey read, flexed his hand, looked up and around as if to check that he was not being watched, and then backed off slowly. 'I think I got a result,' Costas said. 'I told him he wouldn't get a treat unless he obeyed you.'

'You mean the ROV operator, or Joey?'

Costas grinned, and they both stared out of the port. As Joey turned towards the sarcophagus they could see his entire form. Unlike the box-shape of most ROVs, Joey had a tapering body and an extended tail that flexed as he swam, providing improved hydrodynamics and stability while working on the seabed. With his second manipulator arm now extended he looked like an outsized prehistoric scorpion, angling gracefully through the water and coming to a halt just above the protruding stone. The eye extended ever further on its mount, snaking round and down and peering at the slab from every angle.

'Okay,' Jack murmured. 'That's the one. Go for it, Joey.'

The left arm reached under the carapace and drew out a tube like a vacuum-cleaner hose, placing the end near the slab. Seconds later a jet of silt blew out behind the tail and the surface of the slab was revealed, the pump sucking away sediment until all four sides had been uncovered. Joey backed away, and Jack pressed his face against the cone, staring.

'That's it,' he said excitedly. 'I can see the fracture line. This *must* be the missing piece of the plaque.'

'I can't see any carving,' Costas said. 'It must be upside-down.'

'Can Joey shift it?'

'If I tell him to.' Joey had remained in position as the silt settled, and then looked back to them, his eye rolling sideways as if questioning. Costas pointed at the slab and made a turning motion with his hands, repeating it. Joey raised his finger upwards, and slowly shook his eye. Costas glared at him, jabbing his finger at the slab. 'Come on, Marcus,' he muttered. 'I know it's him. He's my best ROV operator, usually. He always gives Joey that bit more personality. Now he needs to make him into a free thinker.'

Joey looked back at the slab, then at the submersible, then back at the slab again. He suddenly jetted forward, settling again on the seabed just in front of the slab.

'Good boy,' Costas murmured. '*Good* boy.'

Stabilising legs drove down from each corner of the carapace into the sediment. The second manipulator arm came into play, and Joey hooked both hands under the exposed edge of the slab. He heaved upwards, shuddering, a fine sheen of sediment rising with each vibration. The slab slowly rose to vertical, and then Joey retracted one arm, pulled out the vacuum pipe and sucked away the sediment from it. They saw the flash of a camera, and then Joey gently lowered the slab back to the seabed, released it in a puff of silt and jetted back towards the submersible. He came to a halt, raised both hands as if in a gesture of uncertainty and pointed with one of them at the screen below. It showed the surface of the slab, dazzling white with the flash, at first sight devoid of any features of interest.

Jack stared, his heart suddenly racing. 'That's it,' he exclaimed, pointing. The ROV moved closer, and the image came more sharply into view. A line furrowed into the rock extended from the fracture to the centre of the slab, where it joined another, wider line extending to either side roughly at right angles, creating something akin to a T-shape. 'The first line is the extension of the radiate line from the Aten symbol. The second line is the River Nile. I believe the first line shows the course of a man-made tunnel, and this map reveals where it intersects with the Nile.'

'You think that's a way in?'

'I've got to get this to Lanowski. He can try to match it to modern coordinates. This is fantastic. It might be the best break we've had.'

Joey's screen flashed with another message, and Costas pressed his face again the viewing port, reading it. He gave Joey a diver's okay sign and then turned to Jack. 'Everything's now fixed topside and they're going to begin lifting us in about two minutes. The plan for raising the sarcophagus is still on schedule. Joey's going to rig up the sarcophagus for raising, and the media can get live-stream video from his camera. Once we're topside they'll drop the cable and Joey can hook it on. Macalister says that our little glitch served a useful purpose in ironing out a problem with the derrick winch, and that assuming our ascent is successful the engineers now have complete confidence in using it to raise the sarcophagus.'

'Glad to know our little jaunt has been of some use.'

Costas punched a finger at the viewing port. '*That's* where it's been of use. Getting Joey to perform exactly the kind of task I envisaged for him. He's the one who should have come down here to do this job in the first place.'

Jack waved the piece of note paper with a sketch he had made of the depiction on the plaque fragment. 'Nothing beats the Mark One human eyeball. Joey might never have found this without us to guide him.'

Costas was barely listening, watching Joey uncoil the hawser strap from a basket beneath the ROV that he would feed beneath the sarcophagus. 'You think Joey's impressive, you should see *Little* Joey. Almost thinks intuitively.'

'I remember his predecessor. Got stuck inside a volcano.'

Costas looked suddenly crestfallen. 'Don't remind me. But

all of his technology has gone into the new one, and more. He's truly pocket-sized.'

They strapped themselves back into the seats, and Jack gazed one last time at the sarcophagus *in situ*, Joey alongside. 'That's how I want to remember it,' he said. 'I'm glad I won't be here to see it being raised. Do you remember seeing the Egyptian sculptures raised from the harbour of Alexandria, where they'd fallen when the ancient lighthouse collapsed? They seem diminished on land, like rusty old cannon raised from shipwrecks. Some artefacts are just better left on the seabed, where they have much more power and meaning. If I had my way, the sarcophagus would go to the British Museum just as Colonel Vyse intended, only in a way he could never have envisaged, not as an actual artefact but as a virtual exhibit. The HD multi-beam sonar scan and terrain-mapper could produce a CG model of the wreck in incredible detail, and we've got enough imagery to simulate a real-time submersible dive to the site. Leaving the actual sarcophagus here on the seabed would mean that you retain the power and mystique of an object in the darkness of the abyss, in a place where no human could survive. That's what would really fire up people's imaginations, not being able to inspect the finer points of Old Kingdom architectonic sculpture close up.'

'We're caught in a political game, Jack. Ownership was always going to be an issue with an artefact like this, and where there are conflicting claims of ownership the winner is always going to want to trumpet their prize. And now there's the added factor of the leverage it might give us in Egypt with the antiquities people.'

'That's the one plus for me. But I still feel uncomfortable

playing the media game and seeing archaeology used as a pawn like this.'

'Chances are you won't even see it being raised. The instant we're on deck, you'll be whisked off to the sickbay for a complete check-up and then will probably have a spell in the recompression chamber. After that my guess is you'll be out of here as soon as the medicos allow you to fly, if not sooner. Heading towards the Holy Land.'

Jack stared for a moment at the sarcophagus, his mind back on the Cairo Geniza and the Jewish poet Judah Halevi, on the extraordinary letter he and Maria had read only the evening before in Cairo. Halevi too had travelled from Spain to the land of the Old Testament, certain that after a lifetime of searching, the answers to his questions lay there; that revelation for him could only come in the land of the Israelites. Jack had begun to feel the same too, now even more strongly with the discovery of the missing fragment of the plaque, that he was being driven back to the only place where he could find his own personal redemption, the resolution to a quest that had come close to costing him everything.

Costas nudged him. 'By the way, thanks.'

Jack stared at him, his mind already focused on Jerusalem, on seeing Rebecca again. 'Huh?'

'For the rescue. Thanks.'

'Oh, yeah. No problem. You would have done the same for me.'

Costas tapped the casing. 'Yeah. Probably. Wouldn't have been able to live with myself afterwards. Would have hated to lose a good submersible like this.'

He grinned at Jack, and then made a whirling motion at

Joey and gave a thumbs up. The eye peered closely at them, cocked sideways, and then the manipulator arm pivoted upwards on its elbow and the hand extended palm-outwards towards them, as if blowing them a kiss.

'Now that *was* weird,' Jack said.

The submersible shuddered, and they both lay back and braced themselves. They felt it rise and swing sideways, free of the seabed. After a few seconds hanging motionless Jack saw the depth readout slowly but surely begin to reduce, metre by metre. As they rose above the cloud of silt created by their departure he looked out of the viewing port beside him and saw Joey bustling around the sarcophagus, feeding the hawser beneath it and then jetting over to the other side to pull it through, a pool of light in the darkness that became smaller and smaller until it was no more than a smudge of yellow, and then was gone entirely. All Jack could see was blackness, the utter void of the abyss, as if the wreck of the *Beatrice* and their extraordinary discovery had been no more than a phantasm of the night, as quickly dispelled as it had been conjured up.

He shut his eyes and was instantly, dreamlessly asleep.

15

Larnaka, Cyprus

'Jeremy! Good to see you. We haven't got much time.'

Jack stood up and extended a hand as the tall young man loped through the airport concourse towards him, wearing a T-shirt and khaki trousers and carrying a compact backpack. He shook Jack's hand, sat down at the coffee table and quickly opened the rear of his pack, taking out his computer. He glanced at the people milling around the terminal. 'Is there anywhere more private?'

Jack shook his head. 'This is as good as it gets. Rule number one of travelling incognito is to be part of the crowd, not apart from it.'

'You worried about being spotted?'

'The last thing I want is for one of my journalist fans to tweet about how they've just seen me in Cyprus checking in to a flight to Israel, only two days after the world saw me off Spain raising the sarcophagus. Reminding the extremists in Egypt that we also have a research presence in Israel might be the final card that brings everything crashing down around Maurice. We're walking on a knife-edge as it is and don't want to provoke the Egyptian regime any further.'

'I heard that the medicos on *Seaquest* wanted you to wait three days for observation before flying.'

'That was just precautionary. I didn't breathe any compressed gas at depth so there was no problem with excess nitrogen. I had some soft-tissue rupture in my sinuses and air passages but no lung collapse. Even the twenty-four hours I agreed to stay was pushing it. The Israelis banned incoming private and commercial aircraft other than El-Al three hours ago, meaning the Embraer had to put me off here in Cyprus. The latest threat of all-out terrorist attack from the extremists in Syria means that they're probably on the cusp of halting incoming flights altogether, cutting me off from seeing Rebecca. And then to cap it all I've just had a text from Aysha saying that Maurice and the rest of his workers are on their way back to Alexandria from the Faiyum this afternoon. That can only mean one thing – that they've been booted out. Events could be coming to a head very quickly.'

'At least the delay gave me the chance to come out and see you.'

'We could have Skyped.'

'Not when you see what I've got to show you. When I saw the image you sent us yesterday of the plaque, I knew you'd want everything I could fire at you.' He glanced up at the departures board in front of them. 'We've got forty-five minutes to final boarding. That should be exactly enough time.' He flipped open the computer and began typing. Jack took a deep breath, trying to forget his frustration over the lost day, and watched Jeremy. He had grown a thick black beard but still looked as boyish as he had done eight years before when he had joined Maria as a graduate student in her palaeography institute in Oxford. It was hard to believe that he now had a doctorate as well as a prestigious research fellowship from his Oxford college under his belt, and had just returned from a six-month sabbatical at Cornell University, his alma mater, where he had turned down a faculty position in order to remain as assistant director of Maria's institute. For IMU he had become an invaluable complement to Maria where ancient writing and textual analysis was concerned, and for Jack no small part of his role had been the friendship he had developed with Rebecca since she had joined her first IMU project while she was still at high school.

Jeremy stopped tapping and looked at Jack. 'You ready?"

'Fire away. About Howard Carter.'

'Right. After what Maria told me about the Halevi letter from the Geniza, you'll see how this fits. Carter was born in London in 1874, the son of a painter; he went out to Egypt at the age of seventeen as a draughtsman. Within a year he was working under Sir Flinders Petrie at the excavation of El-Amarna, Akhenaten's capital, and by the age of twenty-seven he was Inspector-General of Monuments for Upper Egypt. But then he resigned after a dispute, spent four years as a painter and antiquities dealer, and only gradually got back into archaeology proper, eventually finding patronage from Lord Carnaervon to begin his exploration of the Valley of the

Kings. In 1924 he chanced on the tomb of a little-known boy pharaoh, and the rest is history.'

'So somewhere along the way he heard the story of the mad Sufi claiming to be an English soldier in the Old City of Cairo. Aysha told me about the article she'd found.'

Jeremy nodded. 'It was in an issue of the Cairo *Weekly Gazette* from 1904. The *Gazette* was less a newspaper than a social and entertainment journal for the British community in Cairo, with a travel section mainly aimed at ladies disposed to explore Old Cairo while their husbands were away doing frightfully important things like drinking gin in their club. One of the columns was a whimsical offering by an anonymous lady who described how the Sufi had become something of a tourist attraction. He evidently played up to the ladies, who were fascinated by him. It was hot and steamy, and they were bored and frustrated. I think there might have been a bit of the Rasputin effect.'

'But none of them believed his story.'

'They might not have done, but somebody else did. What Maurice remembered when Aysha found that article was Howard Carter's journal from his so-called lost years, between his resignation as Inspector-General in 1903 and the beginning of his exploration in the Valley of the Kings some ten years later. Because that period has less bearing on the lead-up to the discovery of Tut's tomb it hasn't received as much attention from biographers, so some of his papers from that time haven't been thoroughly studied. But trust Maurice to have done so while he was researching some of Carter's manuscripts held in the Bodleian Library in Oxford when he was a student.'

'I remember him going there,' Jack said. 'He was trying to trace the whereabouts of a sculpted head of Akhenaten that had been sold in Egypt before the First World War, and he remembered Carter's period as an antiquities dealer. Back then the distinction between archaeologist and antiquities dealer was less clearly defined, with some eminent scholars being both. Carter was forced into it as he had no private means and felt his career as an archaeologist was over.'

'It took a lot of ferreting about but eventually I found the diary that Maurice had seen for 1908,' Jeremy said. 'It makes for fascinating reading, and is a spotlight on the period. It shows that Carter really had his nose to the ground, like any good dealer. Cairo was awash with antiquities at the time, with mummies falling off the back of camels brought in by hopeful Bedouin from the desert and every street urchin hawking a pocketful of scarabs and little bronzes. Carter had his trusted network of informants, including former Egyptian employees of his in the antiquities service who had also fallen on hard times, unable to find legitimate work because Carter himself had been blacklisted. It was a world of patronage and corruption, with some senior officials up to their neck in it.'

'*Plus ça change*,' Jack murmured. 'So he came across the Sufi and his tall tales of treasure?'

'Actually, he'd come across him a lot earlier than 1904,' Jeremy enthused. 'And this is what makes the story that bit more plausible, because there is a consistency between the accounts. When Carter first arrived in Egypt as an impressionable teenager in 1891 he threw himself into Cairo, lapping up all the history and mystique he could find. It was then that he first saw the man, begging outside the Ben Ezra synagogue. He wasn't yet the mad mystic of the *Weekly Gazette* seventeen years later, but simply one of innumerable beggars on the streets of Cairo, filthy and emaciated. Carter tried practising his beginner's Arabic on the man, who became frustrated and replied in English. He swore Carter to secrecy and showed him a battered Royal Engineers cap badge. It was only a few years after the failed Nile expedition and the human detritus of war was also very visible in Cairo at the time. Destitute and maimed veterans of the Egyptian army, as well as miscreant British soldiers, were scraping a living however they could in the backstreets of the city, some of them mentally unbalanced by their experiences fighting the dervishes. But the Mahdist threat from Sudan was still very real and Kitchener's promise to avenge the death of General Gordon rung in everyone's ears, so to be fingered as a deserter risked the harshest penalty. Howard seems to have kept to his word, though, and the man, a former sapper called Jones, began to tell him an incredible story, of being trapped underground for months on end. But just as he was planning to return to hear more Carter was whisked off to Amarna by Petrie, and it was only in 1904 with the downturn in his fortunes that he came back to look for the man.'

'Who by then was the mad mystic.'

'Self-styled, with appearance to match: bald with a skull-cap, a huge grey beard, sun-blackened skin. He lived by selling gullible European ladies restorative balms he claimed to have been given by Osiris himself, during an underground journey to the afterlife. He was evidently quite a character, theatrical with a deep booming voice, speaking a strangely accented English as well as Urdu and Arabic, and local children flocked to hear his tales. He'd become something of a celebrity.'

'Urdu is plausible for an ex-soldier who might have served in India, and he could have accented the English to disguise his true origins,' Jack said.

'Carter noted that the man he met in 1891 was lucid enough when he was in full flow, but physically weak and fearful of being caught. He said he had been a corporal in the Royal Engineers and had been with the river expedition to relieve General Gordon in Khartoum in 1884, but after a particularly savage battle had been knocked unconscious and lost track of time and place. After a long period of wandering and a terrifying encounter with a crocodile he found himself in Cairo, where his extraordinary underground adventure took place. He had clung to Carter in desperation as he told the story, clearly tottering on the edge of sanity, babbling about the crocodile and mummies. It was the Royal Engineers cap badge that convinced Carter that there might be some element of truth in his story.'

'Royal Engineers,' Jack muttered, thinking hard. 'How extraordinary. He must have gone up with the river expedition past the crocodile temple, the one that Costas and I discovered on the Nile. And the battle can only have been Kirkeban, the one major encounter with the Mahdi army for the river column. The expedition pretty well disintegrated after that, so it's plausible that a man left for dead on the battlefield or lost in the river might have ended up that way.'

Jeremy positioned the computer screen so that Jack could see it. 'I know all this because Howard summarised it in his diary entry for the day in 1904 when he rediscovered Jones.

He wrote an account of what Jones told him next. I've scanned it so you can read it in its entirety.'

Jack stared at the screen. It showed a single notebook page of handwriting, neat and legible. He began to read:

13 October, 1904. Visited the souk outside the synagogue today to seek Jones, about whom I wrote in my entry yesterday. I feel that with the passage of years I can use his name without fear of compromising his safety, as surely by now his desertion from the army would be beyond retribution, if indeed his story were to be believed. Having searched all the usual places and nearly giving him up for dead, a reasonable conclusion after all these years, I spied the man I described yesterday, and, after observing him discreetly, watching him dispense who-knows-what concoction to a gaggle of credulous Belgians, I approached him; he immediately recognised me and we renewed our acquaintance. I reminded him of his unfinished story and after some egging he took me in hand and led me to the back corner of the courtyard where the rabbi allows him to sleep, and brings him food and water.

Here is what he told me. One night some three years after the death of Gordon, he and an American, whom I surmised to be none other than the estimable Charles Chaillé-Long, former officer in Gordon's service and now distinguished author and lawyer (about whose subsequent career I did not apprise Jones, not wishing to divert him from his story, or render him too amazed), along with a Frenchman, an inventor of a submarine diving apparatus, went to a place on the Nile where Jones knew from an ancient carving found in the desert that there lay an underground entrance, below a ruined fort some few miles south of the present city boundary; and in dynamiting it open they were sucked in from their boat and Jones yet again suffered a knock to the head, waking up some indeterminable time later, without Chaillé-Long or the Frenchman, both of whom he gave up for dead, but with the remains of the boat washed all round him, in a kind of darkness suffused by a distant brilliant light.

At this point I had to hold Jones in my hands to keep him talking. His eyes widened and he spoke feverishly, in the grip of a barely suppressed terror. He talked of deep pools of water, and again of a blinding light. He said that he ate some kind of slimy fish, and, to my considerable consternation, the flesh of long-dead bodies, bodies that he described as if they were ancient mummies. After an inordinate time and much hopeless terror he came to a great chamber with many lidded jars on shelves, tall jars, hundreds of them, filled with papyrus. In that chamber he saw many great treasures, gold and amulets and crystal, and he then told me he had made a long-dead friend, who had pointed him the way out. I felt that Jones had strayed into fiction and delirium, and knew this must be the case when he showed me a ring he had taken from the hand of his supposed friend, clearly not pharaonic or even ancient but a signet from the caliphate, a Fatimid ring of a type I have sold before (a particularly fine one, I have to say, of Al-Hakim I am certain, for which I considered offering him a generous price; but then I saw from the fervour in his eyes that this was not a ring he would be parted from, and indeed that this was a man beyond the draw of mammon). He told me that he had come up from this place under the west bank of Cairo, but that the tunnel had collapsed behind him and could never be found, as the spot had been filled in and floored over.

I thanked Jones for his story, but will not, I think, return to press him for more. I considered writing to Mr Chaillé-Long, but cannot afford to be made a laughing stock if the story should prove false, so decided against it; my cachet is low enough in Egypt as it is. Of submarine diving apparatus I know precious little, but might surmise that Jones had come across such an inventor in his career as a sapper, and thus found a place for him in his story. Jones did also mention an officer of engineers, a Main or Mayne, and a check of the Army List in my club library indeed reveals a Major Mayne in 1884, a not uncommon surname and perhaps, indeed, a former officer of his, though the name had disappeared from the list by the following year; perhaps he too was a victim of that benighted campaign, and, in any event, being in all likelihood long dead, is not a lead to pursue. Cairo to me sometimes seems a miasma of make-believe, of stories of tombs and treasures too numerous for all of the ancient dynasties of Egypt many times over, and though I think there is something in Jones' story, some kernel of truth, it is not one to which I will be returning unless I am stripped of all other possibilities, unless the Valley of the Kings is to be shut to me forever. Oh, for just a small pharaoh's tomb of my own . . .

Jack stopped reading, his mind reeling. For Howard Carter the Fatimid ring had pushed the story beyond credulity, yet it was precisely the detail that nailed it for Jack. He stared at

Jeremy. 'It's the ring, isn't it? That's the clincher.'

'Now you know why I was so excited when Maria showed me the Halevi letter. Carter nails it for us by identifying the caliph as Al-Hakim and the ring as a signet, worn only by the caliph and his immediate family. Corporal Jones must have stumbled across his body. What he meant by his new friend pointing the way out is a little mystifying, but Jones may not have been entirely grounded at that point. He'd been underground for weeks, probably months, and may have been hallucinating. Do you remember Wilson in the Tom Hanks film *Castaway*? People alone in desperate situations make friends out of the most unlikely objects, and a skeleton at least has a semblance of humanity.'

Jack's eyes were ablaze. 'The other breakthrough is Carter's reference to the ruined fort on the banks of the Nile, giving us a modern waymarker to another entrance to the underground complex. If those ruins can be pinpointed, then there's a chance, a *small* chance, that we might be able to find the entrance under the river that swallowed up Jones and the French diver, and an even smaller chance that we might get in.'

Jeremy grinned at him. 'A small chance is still a chance, isn't it?'

'Damn right it is.' Jack pulled the satellite phone out of his bag and pressed the key for the secure IMU line, waiting for the connection. He turned to Jeremy. 'Can you email that scan to Lanoswki, Costas and Aysha?'

Jeremy typed quickly and tapped a key. 'Done.' He shut down the computer and slipped it in his bag. 'We've got to go. Our flight's boarding.'

Jack peered at him. 'What do you mean, *our* flight?'

'You didn't think I'd come all the way out to Cyprus just to see you and then return, did you? I'm coming to see Rebecca too.'

'Does she know?'

'Remember, I didn't even know myself that I was coming until this morning. I sent her a text from Heathrow but haven't had a reply. The last I heard from her yesterday was that she was going underground.'

'That would be Temple Mount,' Jack said, pursing his lips. 'I hope she hasn't pushed the boundaries. That place is a tinderbox at the best of times. David Ben-Gurion is due to meet me at Tel-Aviv Airport and take me straight there.'

'IMU's Israel representative?'

Jack nodded. 'I'm glad you're coming with me, Jeremy. Rebecca's got something she really wants to show me, but it looks as if I'm going to be doing a quick turnaround. I may not have more than a few hours in Jerusalem.'

Jeremy looked at him shrewdly. 'Back to Egypt?'

Jack nodded. 'David's a reserve captain in the Israeli navy. With any luck he'll be able to get a reconnaissance flight to divert out to *Sea Venture* for a paradrop, and then it's a short flight by helicopter to Alexandria.'

'Sounds like a return to special forces days, Jack.'

'The real test is going to be Cairo. It was bad enough when we left, but by tomorrow it could be in the grips of an extremist coup. Somehow we've got to get through that if we're going to get to this ruined fort beside the Nile south of the city.'

'By "we" you mean you and Costas.'

Jack looked nonplussed. 'Of course. If he's up to it.'

'You need to access some satellite imagery to look for the site of that fort.'

'Lanowski will be on to it the moment he reads that email.'

The satellite phone flashed green to indicate a link, and Jack quickly tapped in a number and raised it. After a few moments a familiar voice answered.

'Jack?'

'Costas? How soon can you be in Alexandria?'

'The Embraer is due to touch down on its return flight to Valencia in two hours and can be refuelled for Heraklion in Crete immediately. From there I'll take the Lynx to *Sea Venture* two hundred miles due south. Twenty hours from now, maybe a little more.'

'Sounds like you've got it all mapped out.'

'I've learned to be one step ahead of the game, Jack. I knew we were going back even before we left Egypt.'

'Equipment?'

'I'll get everything together on *Sea Venture*. E-suits, re-breathers, underwater scooters. I'll need to score some extra oxygen off the equipment storeman on *Sea Venture*; we're always somehow in short supply with them. But I'll manage. No worries, Jack. You just do what you have to do with your daughter.'

'Bring my Beretta, Costas. You know where it is.'

'Roger that. And I'll be visiting the armoury on *Sea Venture*.'

'Rendezvous Alexandria, twenty-four hours from now?'

'You got it. Over and out.'

Jack quickly replaced the phone in his bag and got up just as the announcement came on for final boarding. He strode alongside Jeremy to the departure gate, his mind filled with what he had read. *A great chamber with many lidded jars on shelves, tall jars, hundreds of them, filled with papyrus.* He was on a knife-edge still, but coursing with excitement. All going well, a little over a day from now he would know whether the soldier's story was the key to one of the greatest archaeological discoveries ever made. He glanced at his watch, wishing the hours forward. He could hardly wait to tell Rebecca.

16

Jerusalem, Israel

Jack had arranged to meet Rebecca outside the Jaffa Gate into the Old City of Jerusalem and he saw her there now, under the shade of the ancient wall chatting to two Israeli soldiers who were guarding the entrance. In the last year since turning nineteen she had grown into a self-confident young woman, her slender limbs and height coming from Jack but her dark hair and complexion reflecting her mother's Italian background. She was wearing khaki trousers, a T-shirt and robust hiking boots, and had on a small backpack. Jack knew that she had spotted him but had not wanted to attract attention, so was waiting for him to come to her. He quickly led Jeremy across the busy street and the pedestrian square and reached her, nodding at the soldiers and giving her a kiss on the cheek. She embraced Jeremy and turned back to Jack. 'Good trip?'

'We were met at Tel Aviv Airport by a friend of mine who dropped us off just up the hill.'

'I watched the live-stream of the sarcophagus being raised on CNN on my iPhone. It seemed to go without a hitch.'

Jack nodded. 'It was a relief to get it on deck. Now the politics begins.'

She peered at him. 'Uncle Costas sent me a text just before you arrived at the airport. Said he'd thanked you, but had forgotten to say he owes you. Usually, when he sends me a message like that to pass on to you it means that something bad did happen, but the unspoken hallowed code means you can't thank each other directly because if you do so then the next time it won't work out so well. Am I right? And what about that bandage on your arm?'

Jack cleared his throat. 'Okay. There was a small hitch, but everything worked out fine in the end and we're all in one piece. I'll tell you about it later. The crucial thing is that we found the missing fragment of the plaque that was inside the sarcophagus, and it seems to give us a location for getting into the underground complex from the Nile.'

'So you're definitely going back to Egypt?'

'The friend who dropped us here is going to pick me up again in the early evening and take me to the coast south of Tel Aviv, where I'm taking a ride on an Israeli naval reconnaissance plane out to *Sea Venture*.'

'You doing a paradrop?'

'Yep.'

'You *promised* me. Do you remember? Almost two years ago.'

'I said I only dropped out of planes when it was absolutely

necessary, and not for the thrills. Anyway, you're your own boss now. You can arrange it with the IMU training director.'

'*Yes,*' she exclaimed, putting an arm around Jeremy. 'We can do it together, Jeremy. Our first proper holiday, just the two of us.'

Jeremy looked more than usually studious, and stroked his beard. 'Not really my scene. Diving, yes, maybe, but jumping out of planes, no. I was thinking we could spend a week back in Naples with your mother's family, giving me a chance to get up to speed with the conservation work on the scrolls from the Villa of the Papyri at Herculaneum. Some amazing new texts are being revealed. You could help piece them together.'

Rebecca looked aghast, and pushed him away. 'I'm talking *holiday*, Jeremy, not work.'

Jack cracked a grin. 'Remember what Maria has in store for you. She asked me to tell you that the trip to look at the monasteries on Mount Athos is all fixed.'

'You been seeing Maria, Dad?'

'In Cairo. She came out to look at some new manuscript finds in the Ben Ezra Synagogue.'

'I know about the Geniza. You mean you've been seeing her at the bottom of a hole in a wall.'

'Something like that.'

She shook her head. 'You're the one who needs a holiday with Maria, not me, Dad.'

Jack smiled at her. Ten years of schooling in New York had given Rebecca not only her distinctive accent but also a candour that he found refreshing, even if it sometimes presented him with awkward truths. He glanced at the Jaffa

Gate, at the medieval crenellations and stonework that seemed to rise unperturbed above the tides of humanity that swept beneath it, the countless pilgrims and warriors, merchants and prophets who had come to Jerusalem in its long history. The last time he had stood at this spot had been more than twenty years before on the eve of the first Gulf War, when Jerusalem had been devoid of tourists and the air-raid sirens were sounding. Standing here then, with his khaki bag slung over his shoulder and his camera poised, he had felt like a diver about to plunge into the unknown, and he felt that same frisson now; the crisis that again loomed over Israel and the Near East gave the same sense of danger to the place. He turned to Rebecca. 'Okay. I've told you about my latest find. Now it's your turn to show us yours.'

Ten minutes later Jack hurried with Jeremy through a maze of alleyways and narrow streets in the Coptic quarter of Jerusalem, trying to keep up with Rebecca as she led them deeper into the city. Apart from army and police patrols and local men who eyed them as they passed there were few people to be seen, the usual bustle of activity reduced to the minimum as people stayed indoors with the threat of missile attack. Rebecca stopped at a poky hole-in-the-wall street vendor, greeted the woman behind the counter like an old friend and waited while she squeezed her a fresh orange juice, taking a bread roll as well. 'Breakfast,' Rebecca said apologetically. 'Didn't have time earlier.'

Jack shook his head when she offered to buy him one. 'You came here to volunteer for the Temple Mount archaeological project. How's pot-washing going?'

She finished the roll, and wiped her mouth. 'Yeah. Good.'

'Really?'

'It was fun. For about ten minutes.' She gave Jack a glum look. 'They've got twenty tonnes of the stuff, Dad. I did a quick calculation as I was sitting in front of my first tray. With each sherd averaging five centimetres across, that means fifty million sherds.'

'Each one a precious link to history. And one day one of them might just provide a clue to something bigger.'

'I know. I get that. It's kind of a privilege. And it is special to a lot of the volunteers who've never done archaeology before. But I've been spoiled, haven't I? I was digging at Troy at the age of fourteen, and hunting for Ghengis Khan's tomb in Lake Issyk-Gul in Kyrgystan the year after that. Anyway, I've been finding my own links to history.'

'I'd guessed you might be.'

She swerved into an alleyway lined with dingy metalworking shops, swerved again into a smaller alley with men squatting along the side, smoking and talking in low voices, and then came to a halt in front of a decaying wooden doorway in the shadows beneath a balcony. The man squatting in the alley beside the entrance nodded at her, peered suspiciously at Jack and Jeremy and then unlocked the door, pushing it open.

'That's my friend Abdul,' Rebecca said quietly, leading them into a gloomy passageway. 'He's the one who showed me the way to the tunnel entrance.'

'What tunnel?' Jack said.

'Patience, Dad. Here first.'

They reached another door, and Rebecca knocked. A small boy opened it, grinning broadly when he saw Rebecca. He ushered them in, and then locked and bolted the door behind them. The room looked like a living room, with shoes lined up beside the door, a table covered with school books and papers, and the typical furnishings of a well-appointed Arab household. The boy went over to the far wall and pushed aside an ungainly looking wooden bureau, the base sliding easily on rollers. Behind it lay another door, and the boy beckoned them through. The space beyond was dark, with only a crack of light visible at the far end. He flicked on a light switch, led them to a door with a lit space beyond and ushered them in.

Jack had already guessed where they were going from the smell. It was the same smell he remembered from the storerooms of the Cairo Museum, and the Geniza chamber: the smell of ancient artefacts and decay, of millennia-old dust and the organic matter that built up in long-sealed tombs. It was as if he were entering an Aladdin's Cave of antiquities, with artefacts of every description filling every available space: pottery vessels of every type and period, oil lamps, metalwork, bronze armour and weapons, much of it intact and in spectacular condition. It was as if all of the top museums of the world had been shorn of their best exhibits of Near Eastern and biblical antiquities, and yet Jack knew that none of this material had ever seen the light of day in a museum, that it had all been spirited out of tombs and dark places unknown to archaeologists and destined for the international black market in antiquities.

A small wizened man appeared, white-bearded and wearing a robe and a tatty red fez. His bloodshot eyes lit up when he saw Rebecca, and he took her hands and clasped them between his own, shaking them. He let her go and clicked his fingers at the boy, who went off the way they had come. He turned to the other two, and his eyes alighted on Jack. 'So, you must be the famous *Jack Howard*,' he said, rolling the words slowly, his English thickly accented. 'You think you know what happened to the Temple menorah, eh? Well, I know where the rest of the treasure lies. Maybe you give a little, I give a little, and I will tell you.' He laughed, a low cackle. 'You have a fine figure of a daughter, eh? She has the makings of a tomb raider. I think nobody messes with her.'

Jack looked at him coldly. 'Nobody messes with her,' he repeated.

The man peered at Jack, and then waved an arm in the air dismissively. 'Yes, yes, we know all about that. She has a bodyguard, yes, your man Ben-Gurion? We could have made him disappear, but we are all friends, yes? You are in the business of antiquities, Jack Howard, and I am a businessman too, and we can help each other. It has been this way in Jerusalem for more than a thousand years, ever since my ancestors began selling pieces of the holy cross to the Crusaders.'

Rebecca turned and glared at Jack. 'You had me *followed*?'

Jack continued to hold the man's gaze. 'Precisely for this reason.'

The boy returned with a tray of little glasses of tea, which he offered around. Jack took one, dropping a sugar cube into it and sipped the strong liquid. He replaced it on the tray. 'So, I take it you are an antiquities dealer?'

The man opened his arms expansively. 'I am Abdullah al-Harasi. My shop is one of the best known along the Via

Dolorosa. I am licensed by the antiquities authority and everything I sell in my shop comes with an export permit. Every day I sell to tourists: coins, lamps, little pottery vessels, mementoes of antiquity that bring them closer to whichever prophet or messiah they hold dear, inshallah. I sell to them, that is, when there is not another war looming. Business has been difficult these last months.'

'And this is your storeroom?' Jack said.

Abdullah opened his arms wider. 'This is where I keep my prize items, for select customers.'

Jack knew that those words were a thinly veiled code for artefact excavated illegally, and sold to those who could get antiquities out of the country without a licence. He hoped that Rebecca had not got herself in too deep. The uninitiated could easily be seduced into an agreement over a glass of tea, and if some kind of deal had been struck it might be difficult to extract themselves without things getting ugly. The antiquities black market was a murky underworld that only those experienced in its ways could negotiate without coming to serious grief. Even David's surveillance team could not prevent what might go on behind closed doors. For a moment Jack felt culpable, responsible. His decision to let Rebecca come to Jerusalem at this time might have been more fallout from his quest in Sudan and Egypt, preoccupying him when better judgement might have prevailed.

Rebecca finished her tea and replaced it. 'Abdullah brought me here after I'd visited the antiquities dealers asking if anyone had Egyptian antiquities that might have been found in Jerusalem.'

Abdullah reached under the table next to him, taking out a

square object about twice the width of his hand. 'By good fortune I had just what she wanted, eh?' He held the object up so that Jack and Jeremy could see. It was like a miniature icon, an ancient frame of hardwood surrounding a plaque of beaten gold about ten centimetres across. Abdullah held it under the bare light bulb that lit up the room. To his astonishment Jack saw the Aten sun-symbol in the upper right corner, the radiating arms with upturned hands extending from it.

'Akhenaten,' he murmured, moving for a better view. 'It can only be Akhenaten.'

'There's a hieroglyphic cartouche below,' Rebecca said. 'And you can see partial clusters of hieroglyphs on the left-hand side, showing that this plaque was actually cut out of a larger sheet of gold, a decorative cover for a curved surface.'

Jack's mind was racing. He had seen something like this before, only a few days ago. And the hieroglyphs in the complete cartouche were identical to those that Hiebermeyer had found in the tomb of the general in the mummy necropolis, on the wall painting recounting his achievements: a sheaf of corn, two half circles, two birds. 'That's the Egyptian word for the Israelites,' he exclaimed. 'This is incredible.'

'Turn it over, Abdullah,' Rebecca said.

He did so, and on the back Jack saw an inscription in black ink, like a museum acquisition label. He immediately felt a cold shiver down his spine. If this was a stolen antiquity from a museum, then they were in even deeper waters. He peered at it, and read it out. 'Jerusalem, 27 April 1864, CRW, RE.'

'This was once a possession of General Gordon of Khartoum,' Abdullah said.

Jack looked at him in disbelief. '*Gordon of Khartoum*? How do you know?'

'Because my great-grandfather got it from him.'

Jack stared at the letters again, racking his brain. *Of course.* 'CRW. That's Charles Richard Wilson, surely. RE means Royal Engineers. Wilson was employed by the Survey of Palestine, in the 1860s. He surveyed extensively in Jerusalem, and had an abiding interest in archaeology.'

'Later General Sir Charles Wilson,' Rebecca said. 'I worked that out too, and I looked him up. He was intelligence chief during the campaign to rescue Gordon from Khartoum in 1884, and a close personal friend of Gordon himself.'

'Yes, yes, yes,' Abdullah said, holding up one hand and counting off the names. 'Wilson. Warren. Gordon. Kitchener. All of them British officers who came to Palestine to map the land for Queen Victoria, but who became obsessed with antiquities and the ancient past. Men little different from you and me, Jack Howard.' He turned the artefact over in his hands, eyeing Jack. 'You wish to purchase this? For your museum? It did not come to my family cheap. But for you, a bargain price.'

Jack raised his hands. 'Not this time.'

Abdullah considered it again, and then handed it to him. 'Accept this as my gift. In hopes of future business, inshallah. If you ever wish to sell the artefacts from your shipwreck finds, I offer myself as your agent. My clients include the richest Russian oligarchs, those of Jewish background who now have interests in Israel and who can ship antiquities unseen back to the mother country. You could be a rich man, Jack Howard. You could reclaim the Howard family fortunes. Think of your daughter's education. Of her future.'

Jack placed the object firmly back in Abdullah's hands. 'I'm grateful for your offer and your hospitality. But you know my position.'

'Ah, yes. Archaeology versus treasure hunting. Artefacts consigned out of sight from an excavation to a museum store, or artefacts made available for anyone to own and enjoy. But there is a bridge, my friend, and we can meet in the middle.'

'You know I can't be associated with an unprovenanced artefact acquired from an antiquities dealer. All of our museum exhibits are finds from our own excavations.'

'We could photograph it,' Jeremy said.

Abdullah wagged a finger, suddenly looking less amiable. 'No photography.'

Jack turned to Rebecca. 'Do you have anything more you want me to see?'

She narrowed her eyes at him. 'Maybe. But you might not think it's safe for me. Without a minder.'

Abdullah cackled, twisting his hands in the air. 'Fathers, daughters, eh? I have four of them. Two are doctors, one is a police colonel and one is in my business. One day the women will rule Jerusalem, eh? It is the men who have made such a mess of this place over the last two thousand years. Men of the Roman army, of the jihad, of the Crusades; the British, the Zionists, and the fundamentalists today. Look at the Al-Aqsa Mosque. The authorities prevent Jews from worshipping at their holiest site, the platform of the temple. Jews must crowd against the edges, praying at the Western Wall, digging tunnels into the rock to get as close as they can, but no further. If women were in charge they would be more accommodating, eh? As accommodating as you and I could be in our business, Jack Howard. Think of my offer. You know how to contact me. Inshallah.'

'Thank you for helping my daughter.'

Abdullah waved his hand dismissively. 'Go now. Follow your daughter. She has a good nose for treasure. My son will show you out.'

Ten minutes later they were again hurrying through the labyrinth of the Old City, along streets and alleys that Jack recognised as leading towards the Western Wall and the site of the Temple Mount archaeological project. Rebecca slowed down and gave him a piercing look. 'I still can't believe you had me followed.'

'David Ben-Gurion's team is the best there is, all ex-Israeli special forces surveillance experts, several of them Palestinian Arabs who know how to blend in.'

'Not very well if Abdullah knew about your guy.'

'David would have wanted them to see him. Abdullah can puff himself up like a caliph, but he knows perfectly well that with any hint of trouble David could shut down his entire business. He's only allowed to carry on because there's a delicate balance to be maintained, with the authorities standing back from business activities that they know are shady but have been part of the culture of this place for hundreds of years. And what Abdullah didn't know is that three of the Arabs squatting in the street outside were David's men. David had guessed where you'd be taking me from his earlier surveillance and had provided me with a phone with an emergency beacon. If I'd activated it, the response would have been instantaneous.'

Rebecca looked away. 'I just wish you'd told me.'

'That would have defeated the purpose, wouldn't it? You would have tried to shake him. That's probably what I would have done at your age.'

'The difference between us is that my mother was from one of the oldest Camorra families in Naples. I know how to handle myself with these kinds of people. Remember how my mother died? They thought she was about to shop them to the police, and she suddenly became one family member too many. I know about boundaries and what happens if you cross them.'

Jeremy coughed. 'It's a pity we don't have photos of that artefact.'

Rebecca sighed, dug in her trousers pocket, pulled out her phone and held it up so they could see, scrolling through a series of images that showed the golden sheet from numerous angles in close up. 'You didn't think I was going to leave without that, did you? As Abdullah said, he's the father of four daughters, and I know how to tug on those strings. During my previous visit I told him I felt faint and asked for a glass of water. His son wasn't at his beck and call as he was at school and Abdullah left me alone in the storeroom for a few minutes.'

Jeremy gave Jack a rueful glance. 'Nice one, Rebecca.'

She held the phone up to Jack. 'Well? What do you really think?'

Jack's mind had been in a tumult since they had left Abdullah's lair. 'The last time I saw anything like that was on the floor of the Red Sea with Costas five days ago.'

'You're certain it's genuine?' Jeremy asked.

Jack nodded. 'Absolutely. And more than that, I'm sure that Maurice would confirm that it comes from the golden facing of an Egyptian war chariot. After our find in the Red Sea, I spent enough time looking at the chariot fragments and depictions with Maurice to be certain of it.'

'Any theories?'

'About how a piece of a chariot of Akhenaten mentioning the Israelites ends up in Jerusalem?' Jack ducked sideways under an awning to avoid a passing army patrol, and the other two stopped beside him. 'Well, it's most likely to have been contemporary, brought here at the time of Akhenaten's reign or soon afterwards. Maurice told me that a pharaoh's cartouche and any other identifying features were often beaten out of armour and other military embellishments after his death, to be replaced by those of his successor. The one way you might expect an artefact like this to survive is on the battlefield, as a consequence of an Egyptian defeat where the spoils were picked up by the victor. Akhenaten wasn't a great campaigning pharaoh and in fact we know of only one major set-piece encounter, though it is one that can be counted as a resounding defeat, perhaps the worst disaster an Egyptian army ever suffered.'

'The loss of the chariot army in the Red Sea,' Jeremy said.

'It's the only plausible scenario.'

'But if the Israelites had already fled from their clifftop encampment, how do you account for the recovery of this object?'

'Somebody stayed behind to watch,' Jack said. 'Moses would have wanted confirmation that the deed was done, that his people could continue their trek north-east towards the Holy

Land without the risk of further Egyptian attack. We know there must have been Israelite eyewitnesses because of the account of the destruction of the chariot army in the Book of Exodus, something we now know is based closely on fact. Lanowski's study of the Landsat imagery suggests that there could have been an old path leading down to the beach that Costas and I explored between our dives, immediately below the point where the chariot army had careered off the cliff and brought down a landslide with it. Imagine a couple of Israelite spies making their way down among the carnage afterwards, finding a decorated wrecked chariot in the shallows, maybe that of a general, recognising a hieroglyphic reference to the Israelites and wrenching that off to take back to Moses as evidence, an artefact that might later have been treasured as one of the small number of objects brought from Egypt to the Holy Land.'

'Where it remained secretly buried somewhere until Wilson got his hands on it,' Jeremy said.

Jack turned to Rebecca. 'Did he tell you anything more about its source?'

Rebecca shook her head. 'One of Mamma's uncles told me that in the antiquities black market asking any kind of question about artefact origins is a big taboo, and will see you ending up like she did with a bullet in the back of your head. But I believe Abdullah's story. I've studied Gordon's *Reflections in Palestine*. He spent the best part of a year here in 1883, carrying out some very exacting exploration in and around Jerusalem but also undergoing something of a religious epiphany. He'd resigned from his governorship in the Sudan in a state of dismay about the lack of government support for his initiatives to help the people there, and he never suspected that he'd be invited back the following year or end up where history has immortalised him. He was a close friend of Wilson, of Warren, of the young Kitchener and the other British engineer officers who had worked on the survey of Palestine, and I believe that this artefact might have been one of a number that he collected from them to take back to Jerusalem as part of his attempt to unlock the mysteries of this place, a project he could immerse himself in after his perceived failure in Sudan. I believe that following his abrupt recall to Sudan he may have entrusted them to someone here, and that after his death with nobody to claim them they were dispersed and sold. This one ended up in the hands of Abdullah's great-grandfather, also an antiquities dealer.'

'Then how come he still has it?' Jeremy said. 'It's a long time for a dealer to sit on something that would have considerable value, even as gold bullion.'

'That happens,' Rebecca replied. 'In Naples artefacts are sometimes cached away for years, even decades, waiting for the right time for a sale, for the right person or an upturn in the market.'

'Abdullah may have been waiting for something more,' Jack said pensively, looking at Rebecca. 'He may have been waiting to dangle it in front of someone who might be tempted to go where he was unable to go, to find the place where Wilson had actually discovered the artefact and to see what else might lie there.'

Rebecca suddenly seemed distracted, and looked back down the alley. 'Are we still being followed?'

Jack nodded. 'By David's men, and probably Abdullah's.

Everyone's always watching everyone else here. It's a place you can't disappear into, unless you really know where you're going.'

'Underground,' Rebecca said. 'That's where you need to go. Everything's just under the surface here: war, the truth behind religion, the reality of history. Jerusalem's riddled with natural caves and man-made tunnels, a honeycomb beneath your feet almost everywhere you step. Some archaeologists I've spoken to say there's nothing more to be found here, that every last fissure has been scraped clean by treasure hunters over the centuries. Others believe that the ban by the mosque author- ities on exploration beneath Temple Mount has concealed untold treasures, the sacred relics of the temple and much else besides.'

'The stuff Abdullah really wants to get his hands on,' Jeremy said.

'Abdullah was being disingenuous when he lamented the ban. For him, the possibility of undiscovered treasure boosts the mystique of the place, and keeps his customers coming back for more. Buy a coin or an oil lamp from Jerusalem and you buy into that dream. And there may be a blanket ban on official exploration beneath the Temple Mount, but those who supply him with antiquities operate outside the law and will always be trying to find a way in. Once they've got there it would be a free-for-all, but with Abdullah poised to stake the biggest claim.'

Jack peered at Rebecca. 'And he's canny enough to know that someone like you might be able to go to places along the temple precinct that would be denied to his people, and that you might be able to unlock vaults that would make him richer than his wildest dreams. That's what those Russian oligarchs really want, the real treasure, not pots and coins, and they'd compete with each other to own it. Abdullah truly would become the new caliph of the Jerusalem underworld, and you would have been his unwitting pawn.'

'But I've used him, not the other way round. Let's move. We've only got a few hours until you have to leave.'

They came out in front of the Western Wall precinct, the midday sun after the gloom of the alleyways reflecting blindingly off the white surface of the rock and making Jack squint and shade his eyes. A pair of Israeli Air Force F-16s shrieked overhead, banking right in the direction of the southern border with Gaza and Egypt. The police and army presence was stronger than he had ever seen it before, and the worshippers were limited to a few groups of Hasidic Jewish men with black hats and long hair, bobbing and praying in front of the wall. Jack found himself hoping that the 12th century poet Joshua Halevi of the Geniza letter had got here, that he had broken the Crusader ban on Jews entering the city and had touched the wall before he died, finding the spiritual revelation that had eluded him in his life in Spain. The wall itself seemed impermeable, as if the shaped masonry were a natural extension of the bedrock, and Jack had to remind himself that like the mosque above it the wall was an accretion on a rock that had a far older history of human occupation than either of the two religions that claimed it.

Rebecca veered to the left, heading back towards the city and the conjunction between the Western Wall and the medieval structures that abutted it. Jack followed and caught up with her. 'Isn't the Temple Mount excavation to the right, at the City of David site?'

Rebecca waved her hand dismissively, and flashed him a smile. 'Been there, done that. I've got a new project.'

Jack stared at the wall ahead. He remembered what Rebecca had said: *underground*. He had an ominous feeling, but one tinged with excitement. He had guessed where she might be taking them. Any political storm that he might have provoked by transgressing on forbidden territory in Egypt and Sudan would be nothing compared to the one Rebecca might be risking now.

They came to a halt in front of a stone archway, and Jeremy walked up alongside. 'Any hints, Rebecca? Any special equipment needed?'

She hitched up her rucksack, kicked back on the heel of one boot and stared determinedly at a man-sized crack in the wall in front of them. 'All I can say is, you haven't seen anything yet. Follow me.'

17

Jack squeezed sideways through the crack in the masonry and came out on a boardwalk that ran the interior length of the wall, at least twenty metres in either direction. They were inside a cavernous enclosed space between the outer medieval wall they had just penetrated and a continuation of the Western Wall of the Temple Mount; its huge blocks were visible some ten metres in front of Jack and disappeared to the left under accretions of later structure. On the ground in front of the wall was the exposed rock that formed the edge of Temple Mount, an area previously covered over with paving slabs of Roman appearance that were now stacked around the edges. Pockets of the rocky ground were under excavation, with hard-hatted archaeologists visible where the dolomite had been cut in prehistory to form tombs and underground dwellings. Rebecca beckoned Jack and Jeremy forward along the walkway to a table covered with files and cameras where a bearded man with a skullcap was working at a laptop. He smiled when he saw Rebecca, and then sprang to his feet when he saw Jack following. Rebecca quickly kissed his cheeks and took his hand. 'Shalom, Danny. My friend, Dr Jeremy Haverstock, and my father.'

Danny shook their hands, and spoke quietly to Jack. 'It's an honour to meet you. Let me know if I can help in any way.' He watched them as they each took hard-hats and torches from the table and Rebecca led them along the final length of the boardwalk. She turned to Jack. 'Danny's the assistant director, in charge for today. I told him I wanted some time alone with you in my excavation and he agreed not to broadcast your presence. It's a good thing the director's not around as he'd have been all over you, the rest of the team would have been clamouring to meet you and we'd never have got anywhere.'

The boardwalk ended where the outer wall and Western Wall began to converge, and the area of exposed bedrock reduced in width to less than five metres. They were a good twenty metres from the nearest excavator and well beyond the temporary lighting that had been set up over the main area. Rebecca led them out of sight behind a rocky knoll and then down an ancient rock-cut staircase some fifteen steps into the gloom. They passed several burial niches, rectilinear recesses cut into the rock, turned a corner in the passageway and came to a halt in front of a hole in the lower side wall only a little wider than Jack's body. Rebecca sat down and poked her legs inside, and then switched on the headlamp on her helmet. 'Okay,' she said. 'Here goes.'

She disappeared down the hole, followed by Jeremy, and

Jack eased himself behind, holding the rim of the rock with his fingers and feeling for the floor with his feet. 'Another six inches, Dad,' Rebecca called up, her voice resonating in the chamber. Jack let himself slide down, twisting sideways to prevent his spine from being scraped, and landed in a low crouch. He looked around, his headlamp beam joining the other two, and could see immediately that they were inside an ancient rock-cut tomb, the walls showing some erosion from rainwater percolation but overall in a good state of preservation. One wall was partly covered by a hanging sheet and still had large sections of its plaster facing intact; a foldable plastic chair lay in front, an array of cleaning tools and brushes set alongside as well as a bucket half-filled with debris. The opposite wall from the entrance tunnel, in the direction of the Western Wall, was not rock-cut but instead was made up of a precarious-looking jumble of rubble, more like a rock fall than a deliberate construction.

Jack looked at Rebecca. 'Okay. Fill us in.'

Rebecca nodded, kneeling beside the rubble wall. 'When I saw those initials on that artefact in Abdullah's storeroom and identified them as Charles Wilson, I immediately thought of Wilson's Arch, the feature abutting the Western Wall that was above us when we came into this place. It's named after Wilson because he uncovered it in 1867, and if he was working there then this seemed a good place to begin my search for places underground where he might have found that artefact, places dating to the later second millennium BC. By good fortune the Israelis have been carrying out extensive excavations and clearance as far as they can along the length of the Temple precinct at this point, so my next step was to get myself on the excavation team.'

Jack cleared his throat. 'Let me see, that would normally take a degree in archaeology, probably a Master's, a track record of several years and impeccable references, not to speak of several months coming up the hard way washing potsherds and pushing wheelbarrows.'

'Not if you're Jack Howard's daughter. Not if you've been seen on our films excavating at Troy and at Herculaneum. Two days after being accepted on the team I had my own special hole in the ground, one that I'd selected myself.'

'And how did you manage that?'

'I took a page out of Uncle Hiemy's book. Maurice once told me that the best way to get to grips with an excavation is to go there at night when nobody else is around. So I sweet-talked my friend Doron the nightwatchman into letting me stay here one evening, and I spent the entire night searching every cavern and tunnel I could find in this place. I was looking for somewhere near the arch that looked as if it might once have led deeper into the rock, actually beneath the Western Wall. I finally broke my way into this tomb. That far wall of rubble was plastered over, but the plaster looked to me to be relatively recent, within the last couple of hundred years rather than ancient. It *might* have been put there by an excavator in the nineteenth century to seal up a discovery. That was nearly good enough for me to have a go breaking through, but I wanted some more definitive indication that this might have been Wilson's hole. So I looked carefully around, and I found this.'

She reached up to a ledge and took down an old smoke-blackened tobacco pipe. She passed it over to Jack, who turned it over in his hands. 'Intriguing,' he said. 'Probably Victorian, pretty high-quality ebony. The kind of thing British officers smoked.'

'Take a look at the initials on the bowl.'

Jack turned the pipe over, wiping away the dust. 'Well, I'll be damned,' he exclaimed. 'CRW. It's Charles Richard Wilson.'

'That's what clinched it for me,' Rebecca said, her voice taut with pent-up excitement. 'I can just see him sitting here after he'd plastered up that hole, contemplating his golden find and the explorations he'd just undertaken beneath the Temple Mount. Smoking a pipe would have been a very British thing to do. Later he realises he's left it inside on that ledge, but by then he's sealed up the entrance to the tomb as well and decides not to bother trying to retrieve it. He was probably having to act covertly as well, wary of men like Abdullah's great-grandfather and the other tomb robbers and shady characters trying to dig under Temple Mount at that time. He'd found something he'd wanted to conceal, and he was successful in doing that. What I found in there hadn't been disturbed since he left it.'

'So how did you make this tomb your own?' Jeremy asked.

'I rediscovered it – so to speak – the next day, after I'd asked to explore this corner of the excavation site, an area that hadn't yet been cleared. The night before I'd also discovered this.' She leaned over and carefully lifted the hanging sheet, revealing the remains of an ancient plastered wall with fragments of red fresco adhering to it. 'This was once a painted tomb, probably late prehistoric. I played up the fact that wall paintings were my speciality. The excavation director had seen me on TV helping Professor Dillen uncover the painting of the lyre-player at Troy. I insisted that if I were to take this on I'd need to do it alone and without disturbance because of the fragility of the fresco, and he agreed. I even insisted that there should be no electrical extension here as the light might damage the painting. As a result I was able to break through Wilson's plaster and rubble fill without being seen, to get beyond and then to rebuild the rubble after returning.'

'And you're going to take us through there again?' Jeremy asked.

She turned to the rubble face, put her hand on a protruding rock and glanced at them. 'Stay back.' They shifted to the rear of the tomb, and Rebecca gingerly pulled at the stone. Nothing happened, and she tried again, this time more forcibly. Suddenly the entire wall shimmered and collapsed in a grinding roar, narrowly missing Rebecca as she leapt back in a cloud of dust. They all put their shirts to their mouths until the dust settled, and then stared at the black hole left in the wall where the rubble had been. Rebecca looked apologetically at them, her face white with dust. 'Whoops.'

A voice called down. 'Rebecca. Are you all right?'

'Fine, Danny,' Rebecca shouted back. 'Just spilled my bucket.' She turned to Jack, whispering. 'That wasn't supposed to happen. I thought I'd balanced the rocks so they'd fall inwards.' She scrambled over the rubble, coughing in the dust, and peered through the hole in the wall. 'Okay. Everything looks stable beyond here. Headlamps to maximum.'

Jack replaced Wilson's pipe on the shelf and brought up the rear, crawling forward behind Jeremy and bending to avoid a jagged rock sticking down from above. Any of his old discomfort about enclosed spaces was eclipsed by his concern that Rebecca might be taking them on a reckless adventure, but he was committed now and there was little sense in trying to hold her back unless the way ahead was clearly too dangerous. He came out at the beginning of a tunnel where Rebecca and Jeremy were crouched. 'What about the entrance?' he said to Rebecca. 'We could be followed.'

'The site director is away until tomorrow, and none of the other excavation team comes down my hole without being invited. It would take too long and be too noisy to rebuild that barrier, and we'd only have to take it down again when we go out. But Danny will see to it that we're undisturbed. And we don't need to be in here for more than twenty minutes.'

Jeremy aimed his torch high, revealing an immense block of masonry above their heads. 'Are we where I think we are?'

Rebecca nodded, her eyes ablaze. 'Directly beneath the Western Wall of Temple Mount.' She pointed back the way they had come. 'That way is present-day Jerusalem. This way, we're crawling into three-thousand-year-old history.'

'That way, we're legal,' Jack said. 'This way, we're transgressing the strictest religious laws on the planet.'

Rebecca peered at him. 'I've never known laws of *any* description put off Jack Howard.'

He paused for a moment, giving Rebecca a long appraising stare, and then nodded. 'Okay. Just this time. We'll talk about boundaries later. You lead.'

Five minutes later they came out of the tunnel into a cavern at least five metres across, their headlamp beams dancing across the walls. Jack had noticed that the tunnel was scored with the marks of picks, whereas the cavern walls were irregular in shape, with cracks and fissures that rose out of sight, and showing no obvious signs of being hewn by human hands.

'It's a natural cave,' Rebecca said, echoing his thoughts. 'The rock beneath Jerusalem is riddled with them, where water has eroded away layers of softer rock within the dolomite. I read everything I could about the geology and archaeology of underground Jerusalem in the weeks before I came out here. But this one's unusually large and well-proportioned, the kind of place that could have served as a refuge for several dozen people or as a storeroom. The first thing I noticed was how smooth that outcrop of dolomite is in the centre, like the sacred omphalos you showed me inside the Diktaean Cave in Crete. You can see that many hands must have worn it smooth, and that it has enough of a flat surface for objects to be placed on it.'

'It must be an altar,' Jeremy said.

Rebecca nodded excitedly. 'That's what I thought. And if you look around you can see apertures and fissures in the walls that could have served as niches for displaying sacred objects. But what really made my heart leap was seeing a patch of the wall that had been plastered over, with plaster of exactly the same colour and composition as the plaster Wilson used to seal the rubble wall that he put in place in the tomb after he left this place for the last time.'

'Can you be certain he was here?' Jeremy asked.

Rebecca nodded vehemently. 'This is where he found that piece of golden chariot decoration. I'm absolutely sure of it. I think he dug around in here and that's all he found, perhaps concealed in one of those niches. But I've no doubt that three thousand years ago there were more – many more – artefacts of similar age and origin, all of them of sacred significance to the people who stored them here. This was their holy of holies.'

'What about the plaster?' Jack asked. 'What did that conceal?'

She beckoned them over to the far side of the chamber, lighting up a polished section of wall about a metre wide and half a metre high. Jack could see that it was covered with several dozen lines of written inscription, the letters alphabetic but spidery and difficult to discern. 'Fantastic,' he exclaimed. 'I've seen something similar to this before, in the Istanbul Archaeological Museum, taken from Jerusalem when the Ottomans ruled Palestine. It was found in the Siloam Tunnel near the Gihon Spring.'

'Look closer, Dad.'

Jack made his way past the altar stone, and as he did so he saw something else on the stone, faint lines and symbols that appeared to underlie the inscription. He stared, hardly believing what he was seeing. 'My God, Rebecca. Now I get it.'

'It's the Aten sun-symbol, the radiating arms,' Jeremy exclaimed, coming alongside.

'And the symbols at the bottom are hieroglyphic cartouches,' Rebecca said. 'You can barely make them out, but I'm sure they're identical to the groupings of symbols Aysha showed me, one for Akhenaten and the other for Israelites.'

'Of course,' Jack murmured, looking around. '*Of course*.'

Jeremy peered closely at the words of the inscription. 'It's Palaeo-Hebrew,' he said. 'That puts it before the Babylonian period, before Nebuchadnezzar conquered Jerusalem and destroyed the first temple in the early seventh century BC. I think I recognise some of the words, but I haven't done Old Hebrew since I was an undergraduate. I'd need some time and some reference material.'

'Don't worry, Jeremy. I'm one step ahead of you.' Rebecca turned to Jack. 'I brought Danny in on this. When I found the inscription all I recognised for certain was that sun-symbol and the hieroglyphs, and I knew I was going to need someone else to translate it. Danny's got a PhD from Chicago in Near Eastern archaeology and he's also a reserve captain in the Israeli Army intelligence corps. He knows perfectly well the need to keep this discovery absolutely secret until the time is right. He's the reason I've felt confident that nobody else would follow us down here, and he'll see that the entry tunnel from the tomb is completely sealed up after we leave.'

'Go on,' Jack said.

She pulled out her phone and opened up a paragraph of text. 'First, the date. You've probably guessed it, but this inscription is much older than the Babylonian period. The Siloam tunnel inscription is thought to date to the eighth century BC, but Danny thinks that ours might be even earlier, nineth or even tenth century BC, right at the beginning of the Iron Age and the inception of Hebrew script. The sun-symbol and the hieroglyphs are part of an *earlier* inscription. Danny studied the wear and patination on the inscribed lines and reckons it could be two to three centuries earlier than the Palaeo-Hebrew writing, putting it close to the time of Akhenaten and the Exodus.'

'It's like a palimpsest,' Jack said. 'Like Joshua Halevi's letter that Maria and I found in the Geniza, written on a reused piece of vellum that preserved a shadow of the original text. Only here no attempt was made to erase the earlier inscription.'

Rebecca nodded. 'The Siloam inscription was made to commemorate the joining up of two tunnels, part of a complex dug to improve access to the spring. As you'll see, this inscription served a similar purpose; the tunnel we came in through was a later cutting into this chamber, and continues on ahead of us to the east where it joins a natural fissure that must have been the original entrance from the surface when this was a holy place. The foreman of the tunnel gang may have chosen this slab simply because there's no other suitable flat surface inside this chamber, so it was ready-made for a new inscription. The sun-symbol and the hieroglyphs already there would probably have meant nothing to him, though as you'll see there was a memory of the earlier significance of this place.'

Jeremy stared at the inscription. 'I can see it now. There are numbers, cubits. And I recognise the word for water.'

'Here's Danny's translation.' Rebecca read out from her screen:

This is the way the tunnel was joined. As the men were wielding their pickaxes, each towards the other, and while there were yet three cubits to the breach, the foreman could see through an opening to the cavern ahead, and beyond it another tunnel. On the day of the breach, the men struck hard, pickaxe beside pickaxe, and broke through. Down below the water flowed from the spring to the pool, a distance of one thousand cubits. In the cavern, one hundred and fifty

cubits was the height of the rock above the men. I,
Yeshua-hamin, foreman, made this with my team. In
the days of the king Abdu-Heba this was the place
occupied by the prophet, when he came from Egypt.

There was a stunned silence. 'Incredible,' Jack said. 'Are we really talking about Moses?'

'That's what Danny thinks the word he translates as "prophet" would have meant to people at the time.'

'Abdu-Heba,' Jeremy murmured. 'Wasn't he the king of Jerusalem at the time of the Amarna letters?'

'*Precisely,*' Rebecca said, her eyes lit with fervour. 'The Amarna letters were cuneiform tablets found in Akhenaten's capital that included an archive of correspondence from foreign rulers swearing allegiance to the pharaoh, and at least six of them are from Jerusalem. Listen to this one.' She read from her screen.

To the Pharaoh, my Lord, say: thus Abdu-Heba, your
servant. At the two feet of my Lord, the Pharaoh,
seven times and seven times more I fall. Behold, the
Pharaoh has set his name in mât urusalim, the Land of
Jerusalem, for ever.

Rebecca looked up. 'That's Amarna Letter number 287, lines 60–64. The others are in a similar vein, obsequious, almost fawning, as if the pharaoh had threatened him. But why should the pharaoh have done so, to the extent that Abdu-Heba felt the need to swear allegiance over and over again?'

Jeremy looked at her. 'The land of Canaan was a battleground for the Egyptians and the Assyrians and the Hittites, with citadels like Jerusalem acting as pawns for one side or another. Alliances with the big powers were the name of the game for a king like Abdu-Heba.'

'That may be true for the New Kingdom period in general,' Rebecca replied pensively. 'But I've been listening to everything you guys have been saying about Akhenaten over the last couple of months. He bucks the trend. He's *not* a bellicose pharaoh. He makes a half-hearted attempt to suppress a tribal rebellion in the southern desert, and waves his hand in the direction of Assyria. His only fixed battle that we know of is his disastrous chariot charge against the Israelite encampment beside the Red Sea. Ramses the Great he definitely is not. So why pick on a relatively minor settlement in the Jordan Valley and insist that its ruler swear undying allegiance to him, over and over again?'

'Because he was securing a safe haven for Moses and the Israelites,' Jack said quietly.

'You've got it,' Rebecca said, putting away her phone. 'And this is where they came, to a natural cave just outside the walls of Bronze Age Jerusalem, a place where they could establish their first primitive altar and store their sacred artefacts. A place that was rapidly superseded once their new religion swept through the population of Jerusalem and they built the first temple atop this site, all those cubits above us, the memory of the cave lasting long enough for the foreman of that excavation team a couple of hundred years later to know its significance, but which was then sealed up and lost to history until a British officer broke his way into it more than two and a half thousand years later.'

Jack gazed around, breathing in the dust of ages, savouring the history. *Moses had been here*. He put his hand on Rebecca's shoulder. 'Congratulations. This is a phenomenal discovery. A game-changer. And you've really put your heart and soul into this one.'

She stared at him, her eyes passionate. 'This isn't about clues, Dad. You've already got what you need for the next stage of your quest. This is about the point of it all. After finding this, after sitting here beside that altar, I began to understand what drove men like Wilson and Gordon to keep coming back to Jerusalem, and to seek Akhenaten in the desert. I thought back two years ago to your extraordinary discovery of the birthplace of the gods beside the Black Sea, of the first stone temples erected at the dawn of civilisation. Then, the shamanism and superstitions of the hunter-gatherers were discarded, and people looked to a new spirituality. But in time that optimism was clouded by the power games of priests and priest-kings, and then one pharaoh had the courage to do away with it all and try to start afresh. I don't think the revelation of the one god came to Akhenaten out of the blue; I think he was yearning for it. It allowed him to be human again, to discard the sham of deified kings and priests. This place, the vision it represents, the presence of the prophet who would perpetuate their shared revelation, would have represented a sea-change in his world. And now three thousand years later we are again at a turning point. That's why I wanted you to see this, Dad. Just like those Victorian soldiers fighting the Mahdi, you're about to go into a pit of darkness where religion has again been enlisted to justify bestiality and war. Bringing you here was to remind you that there can be hope, that another spiritual awakening is possible, another cleansing. That's what I believe Wilson and Gordon and the others caught up in their war felt too, and what they so desperately hoped to find.'

Her eyes were red-rimmed, and she wiped them, looking away. Jack felt an unexpected upwelling of emotion. Hiebermeyer was not the only one whose guard had been eroded by the events of the past weeks and months, and Jack realised that he had been on edge for too long, that his body and mind craved the resolution that now lay ahead of him one way or another in the coming days. He thought of Rebecca's mother, of the passion of her convictions that had attracted so many to her, and for a split-second he seemed to see Elizabeth standing in the shadows behind Rebecca, the same fervour in her eyes, egging her daughter on. He blinked, and the image was gone, and Jack felt a sudden yawning emptiness he had not allowed himself to feel in the years since her death. He swallowed hard, and nearly said something to Rebecca, but chose not to; there would be a better time. He glanced at his watch and put his hand back on her shoulder. 'Time for me to go.'

Jeremy aimed his headlamp beyond the inscription, towards the blocked-up entrance where the tunnel continued under Temple Mount. 'Any thoughts about what lies beyond there?'

Rebecca wiped her eyes again, and gazed along his beam. 'Danny and I think it's blocked up. I mean *seriously* blocked up, not just rubble and plaster but actual shaped masonry, huge slabs of stone barring the way. To get through it would require pneumatic drills and explosives and that would rock the foundations of the mosque, a very big no-no.'

'Must be something pretty significant for it to have been blocked up like that.'

'Danny's done some basic geometry and reckons it leads directly under the central part of the temple site.'

'Where you might expect there to be a repository,' Jack said.

'A treasure chamber,' Jeremy added.

Jack looked at Rebecca. 'This one's all yours. For the future.'

Rebecca gave him a wry look. 'I'm not really sure about being an archaeologist. Too much dust and dead old stuff.'

Jack raised his eyes, and grinned at Jeremy. 'Right.'

Rebecca suddenly looked serious, and held Jack's arm. 'Aysha sent me a text yesterday about the Egyptian girl, Sahirah. Jeremy and I took her around when she came to England last year to study with Maria.' She pulled out her phone and showed Jack a photo taken in front of the lions in Trafalgar Square, with Rebecca on the left and beside her an attractive, well-dressed girl with a computer bag slung over her shoulder. Jack had never met Sahirah, and this was the first time he had seen a picture of her. He stared at the dark eyes and Egyptian features, imprinting them in his memory. It was like looking at the exquisitely lifelike portraits that Hiebermeyer had found painted on mummy coffins from the Hellenistic and Roman periods, images that gave sudden humanity to the distant past. Sahirah's face was like a beacon of light in the darkness that was enveloping Egypt, a darkness that Jack knew would soon be streaked with fire and running with blood.

Rebecca put away the phone. 'You will get her out, won't you, Dad?'

Jack looked at her, silent for a moment. He thought of Sahirah's parents, of her father, of the anguish they must be going through seeing their daughter trapped in a tide of history that must seem to them unstoppable. He gave Rebecca a steely look. 'That's really why I'm going back to Egypt. And Aysha is doing everything she can.'

He gave her a quick embrace and shook hands with Jeremy. 'My advice is that you photograph every square inch of this place and leave as soon as you can. If I don't see Danny on the way out, give him my warmest regards and an invitation to IMU to discuss the future of your find. He'll know that if word of this discovery under the Mosque leaks out the extremists of both sides will be at each other's throats. It sounds as if he'll be able to wrap things up for you here. David's men will be waiting outside the Western Wall to take you away to a safe house, and after that you'll be put on a flight out of Tel Aviv back to London. Under no circumstances should you make contact with Abdullah the antiquities dealer or his men, who will also be somewhere outside waiting to induce you back into his lair. As far as they know we've just been visiting the Israeli excavation.'

'Don't worry, Dad. I'm on to it.' Rebecca took out her DSLR, set the controls and began photographing, while Jeremy knelt down and began sketching the inscription. Jack began to make his way out through the tunnel, but then thought for a moment and turned back. 'And Rebecca.'

She glanced back at him, camera poised over the altar. 'What is it?'

'Look after Jeremy.' He flashed her a smile, and turned back to the tunnel. A few minutes later he was out of the tomb and walking quickly past the Israeli excavators towards the shafts of sunlight coming through the entrance from the Western Wall. He saw Danny on a photo gantry above the excavation and gave him a quick wave. His mind was already on the task ahead, on the trip from the coast of Israel to *Sea Venture* and then to Alexandria, back to the brewing firestorm that he hoped against hope had not yet ignited, that would still allow him and Costas the time they needed to complete their quest.

He strode out into the dazzling light of the afternoon, and immediately spotted David and two of his men waiting beside a car on the far side of the square.

This was it.

PART 4

18

Alexandria, Egypt

Jack stepped out on to the helipad beside Qaitbey Fort a little over six hours after leaving Rebecca in Jerusalem. The paradrop from the Israeli Air Force Hercules had gone without a hitch, and minutes after being picked up from the Mediterranean by a Zodiac from *Sea Venture* he had been strapped into the Lynx helicopter for the eighty-mile flight due south to Alexandria. The city was still under its elected administration but now close to anarchy, and they had decided to fly in at night under the radar screen in order to minimise the chances of interference from any Egyptian police or coastal surveillance units that might remain functional. As Jack ducked away from the rotor downdraught he saw a small stack of crates beside the edge of the helipad. He knew from the pilot that they contained the final batch of material from the institute, that the next scheduled flight of the helicopter out of here would be its last, carrying Hiebermeyer and Aysha with their last precious records from Egypt to safety.

Across the harbour the first glow of dawn silhouetted the disk shape of the Bibliotheca Alexandrina, and the streaks of pastel red lit up the water and the bobbing rows of fishing boats moored across the basin. It seemed a timeless scene, yet Jack knew it was an illusion. He walked through the fort entrance into the courtyard and saw Costas, who had preceded him from *Sea Venture* by several hours and was crouched over several large kitbags. He gestured for Jack to come over.

'Everything's ready. Two E-suits, two oxygen rebreather backpacks with double cylinders, giving us about five hours endurance. We also have the first two prototypes of my new UPD-4 underwater propulsion device, able to go under-water or skim along the surface. It's the only way we're going to get three kilometres underground from the river edge to the pyramid plateau, assuming we can even get through the tunnel entrance.'

'Has Lanowski got us some coordinates?'

'He's inside waiting to tell us.'

'And the kitbags?'

Costas jerked his head towards the harbour. 'Aysha's uncle Mohammed has a motorised felluca. He and his son are coming any time now to take the bags and stow them out of sight. He's going to take us up the Nile past Cairo to our insert point. We'll be travelling in daylight, but that means we'll be less conspicuous among the other daytime traffic on the river than we would be at night. It'll give us a chance to get some rest before the night ahead.'

'What's our departure time?'

'He wants to leave at 0800. That's two hours from now. The Lynx is scheduled to leave later in the morning to give Maurice and Aysha a chance to do a final shutdown on this place, but that might be ramped forward if things hot up.'

'Is that likely?'

'There's been shooting and explosions through the night. Mostly it's been gangs of local men taking on the extremists who have been embedded here and making their presence known over the past few days. But there are additional gunmen poised to take over in the event of a coup. I've just spoken to Ben on the satellite phone and the latest intel is that there's a forward camp just inside the Libyan border comprising several hundred men with pickup trucks, almost certainly tasked to take Alexandria. They'll be joined by much larger groups heading up from Sudan towards Cairo. The Egyptian military has been so extensively infiltrated by extremist sympathisers that it's no longer an effective defensive force for the government. Once the gunmen arrive, all resistance will crumble and this place will go over to the dark side. It could happen at any time.'

'Did Ben say anything about the situation with the girl in Cairo?'

'He hasn't been able to raise the Antiquities Director or his intel contact in Cairo. The deadline for a response is 1230 hours this morning, Egyptian time. It doesn't look promising, Jack, but we have to hold on until then. I know that Aysha's got another option.'

Jack grunted. 'Okay. Let's hear what Lanowski has to say.'

Costas took a swaddled package from the top of one of the

kitbags and handed it to Jack. 'Three extra magazines loaded personally by me, and the Beretta stripped and oiled. I've got a Glock and a few other goodies from *Sea Venture*. If we're caught out we can't surrender to these people, Jack. By the time the coup's in full swing they won't be taking any prisoners.'

Jack strapped on the holster, took out the Beretta, ejected and then replaced the magazine, pulled the slide to the rear and released it to chamber a round, and then replaced it in the holster. 'Okay,' he said. 'Let's move.'

Fifteen minutes later they stood with Aysha and Hiebermeyer behind Lanowski, who was sitting in front of the last remaining computer console in the operations room. Everything else was bare, the books and files and posters gone, and all that remained beside the computer on the desk was an open briefcase and a satellite phone. Jack leaned over and stared at the image of the radiating Aten symbol from the plaque that Lanowski had just opened up on the screen, showing the additional fragment with the line running to a point where the depiction showed the River Nile. 'We've got a little over an hour before the felucca is ready,' he said. 'I want everything you've got on those Nile coordinates, but before that I want a full operational briefing, everything we know about the archaeology under that plateau. This is the last chance we've got.'

Hiebermeyer unrolled a map from the briefcase showing the Giza plateau, the Nile and the southern Cairo suburbs in between. 'All right, Jack. During the 1980s an international company was hired to construct a new sewage system under the Giza suburb, to the south of old Cairo abutting the pyramid plateau. It was an unparalleled opportunity for archaeology, promising the kind of revelations we've seen in Athens with construction work in advance of the Olympics or in Istanbul with the new Bosporus tunnel terminus. But the need to get those sewers done was truly desperate and corners were cut. We got a tantalising glimpse of what might lie beneath, nothing more. I was a student at the time and managed to join the archaeological team monitoring the work.'

'Unofficially, as I recall,' Jack said. 'Your supervisor wanted you to finish your doctorate, but you wanted a finger in everything going on in Egypt. The Antiquities Director at the time point-blank refused you a permit. Had your best interests at heart.'

'Not the way I saw it at the time,' Hiebermeyer said, shaking his head in frustration. 'If I'd had another couple of hours out there we might be a lot closer to our objective right now. I was appalled at how the investigation was shut down as soon as the construction work was finished and all of the holes backfilled. Today it's all completely buried beneath the suburb that now laps the Giza plateau itself. But the night guard at the most interesting site was a friend of mine and he let me inside on the final night before it was filled in. What I found was fascinating, though of course I couldn't tell anyone about it as I was there illegally. At the time I had bigger fish to fry, or so I thought, and I set it aside in my mind. But it suddenly makes sense and is *huge*. Jacob?'

Lanowski tapped a key, and an aerial photo of the Giza plateau appeared on the screen, showing the three pyramids and the Sphinx, the mass of lesser structures and excavated foundations in front of the Great Pyramid and in the foreground the sprawling buildings of the modern suburb. Lanowski tapped again and the scene transformed into an isometric computer-generated image with a reconstructed overlay showing the plateau with the ancient structures intact. The modern suburb had disappeared, replaced by regular cultivated fields, and suddenly the jumble of ruins in front of the pyramids made sense, with rectilinear buildings, courtyards and linked causeways. The most striking addition on the edge of the floodplain in front of the pyramids was a large man-made basin and complex of canals, one of them leading to an irregular waterway about a kilometre east of the plateau that was clearly a branch of the Nile.

'Give us a rundown, Maurice,' Costas said.

'Okay. You've got the three pyramids, Khufu, Khafre, Menkaure, largest to smallest, north to south. They're on the edge of a plateau called the Mokkatam formation, a limestone ridge that rises at this point about fifty metres above the modern suburb. To the east of the plateau is the ancient floodplain of the Nile, to the west the open desert. The limestone is easily quarried and easily tunnelled. The plateau to the east of the Pyramid of Menkaure is completely free of ancient structures, leaving the raised plateau in front bare over almost a square kilometre until you drop down into the floodplain.'

'You mean where we would have been looking when we were suspended beneath the pyramid, facing east?' Costas asked. 'Where we were looking down the blocked-up tunnel?'

Hieberemeyer nodded. 'First, let's look at what we can

see above ground. This image shows the plateau as it might have looked during the New Kingdom, about the time of Akhenaten, over a thousand years after the pyramids were built. Originally each pyramid would have been fronted by a mortuary temple, and then a further temple – really a kind of entrance portico – on the floodplain below, the two joined by a causeway. But by the time of the New Kingdom the mortuary complexes for the Pyramids of Menkaure and Khafre had been removed and everything was focused on the structures associated with the Great Pyramid. By then, of course, the use of these structures as mortuary temples, to prepare the bodies of the pharaohs for the afterlife, was ancient history, and I mean *really* ancient history. People tend to think of Pharaonic Egypt as a continuum where everything can be lumped together, whereas in fact we're dealing with a timespan between the construction of the pyramids and the time of Akhenaten similar to that between, say, the end of the Roman period and the present day. In such a huge expanse of time we should expect monuments to change in meaning and function.'

Jack nodded. 'So what began as communities of priests perpetuating the memory of the three individual pharaohs – Khufu, Khafre and Menkaure – becomes a unified cult of the ancient pharaohs, centring on the one complex associated with the Great Pyramid. The other temples become redundant.'

'And more than that,' Hiebemeyer enthused. 'The entire *cult* could have become redundant.' He paused, standing back. 'What is it that fascinates us most about the pyramids? It's not so much the dead pharaohs, but the engineering marvel and the geometry of the alignments, the relationships in particular to the sun. Egyptians of the New Kingdom would have been as awestruck by these ancient monuments as we are today, and would have been well aware of the celestial alignments. More than that, they would have celebrated them. It's my belief that the cult of the pharaohs would have been largely subsumed by a cult of the Sun, of Ra and the other sun gods, a transition that could have taken place already by the beginning of the New Kingdom.'

'And that brings us to Akhenaten,' Costas murmured. 'And to how it was that plaques showing the Aten sun symbol could have been placed inside the burial chamber of Menkaure, something that would have been impossible while his cult was still alive.'

Hiebermeyer nodded, pointing at the screen. 'Let's look at these structures in front of the Great Pyramid first. This is was what was revealed during the sewer construction. What was *officially* revealed, that is. First, a mass of mud-brick buildings that was undoubtedly part of the town that sprang up to house the workers and then the priests who maintained the cult. Second, the remains of a huge mud-brick wall, the so-called palace. Third, the massive basalt revetment of the man-made harbour abutting the valley temple, joined to the Nile by canals wide enough to float barges with stone blocks up to the harbour and later for the ceremonial final boat journey of the dead pharaoh from the Nile to the mortuary temple.'

Costas pointed at a sinuous channel shown to the east of the harbour. 'You mean here?'

'That's the Bar el-Libeini, the projected line of a channel of the Nile in Old Kingdom times. Since then it's silted up and the main channel of the river has progressively migrated east, except in a few places where it has remained in more or less its ancient position. The man-made canals have also been lost, but they would have been huge engineering feats in their own right.'

'What all this shows,' Jack said thoughtfully, 'is that the construction of some kind of passage between the Nile and the Giza plateau, an underground passage, would have been perfectly feasible, that our idea that those radiating lines on the Aten symbol might map out its course is within the realm of possibility.'

'More than that, Jack. It's a dead certainty.'

'Go on.'

Hiebermeyer took a deep breath, steadying his excitement. 'I've listed the *official* discoveries. Well, now for the unofficial ones.' He reached under the computer table, felt around for a moment, and then pulled out a book-sized slab of highly polished granite, the end of a hieroglyphic cartouche deeply cut in its surface. He placed it carefully on the table beside him, and swept his hand across the surface. 'This has been my guilty secret for all these years. I've been waiting for the right time to reveal it, and this is it. I've got nothing to lose.'

Costas peered at it. 'There's that bird, the Egyptian buzzard. And the mouth, the face and the half-sun. The rest I don't recognise.'

Hiebemeyer's voice was taut with excitement, and his hand was trembling as he traced out the hieroglyphs. 'I found this that night in the trench beside the huge mud-brick wall. This is why I said the *so-called* palace; it's because it wasn't a palace. There are three certain words here. One is *secrets*. Another is *writing*. Another is *storeroom*, or *repository*. The only other person I've shown this to is Aysha, who happens to be my best hieroglyphics expert. She's certain it means *storeroom of written secrets*.'

There was a stunned silence. 'My God,' Jack whispered. 'A *library*.'

Hiebermeyer stared at Jack, his face flushed. 'I always objected to the word *palace*. A closer approximation would be monastery, a place where priests lived and worked. And just like medieval monasteries, the priestly colleges of ancient Egypt would have been repositories of knowledge. Do you remember the Temple of Sais in the Nile Delta, where Solon the Greek heard the Atlantis story? By that stage, half a millennium after Akhenaten, the old knowledge had become fragmented, parcelled among many temples, jealously guarded by the priests and only passed down by word of mouth. The first Macedonian King of Egypt, Ptolemy the First, tried to rectify that with his establishment of the great library at Alexandria, though by then much of the old knowledge had died after the closure of the last of the ancient temples. But I believe that he was inspired by a memory of a great centralised repository, a great library, that had existed far back in the glory days of the pharaohs, in the New Kingdom at the time of Akhenaten and his son Tutankhamun.'

'And where better than at Giza,' Jack murmured. 'The great centre for the worship of the sun-god during the New Kingdom, and before that of the earliest pharaohs. A place of continuous occupation by a priestly caste for over two thousand years, priests who could safeguard a repository of knowledge through the centuries.'

'And if this was a library, it could have been the earliest library on this scale anywhere,' Hiebermeyer exclaimed. 'That mud-brick wall dates back to the Old Kingdom, to soon after the construction of the Great Pyramid, about 2500 BC. That's over a thousand years before the heyday of the New Kingdom, before Akhenaten. Imagine what such a repository might have contained: all of the knowledge passed down from Egyptian prehistory, from the time of the first hieroglyphic texts of the previous millennium as well as the oldest writings of Mesopotamia. And we're not just talking about funerary texts, sacred mantras, Books of the Dead and all the familiar religious tracts, but about material that predates and transcends all of that: the earliest sagas and histories, accounts of exploration and discovery, lost medicinal knowledge. Ptolemy's library at Alexandria would only have been a pale shadow of that.'

'But like Ptolemy's library it could have acted as a magnet for other collections, an accumulator,' Jack said, his mind racing. 'I'm thinking about something else, Maurice, about the Minoan Queen of Egypt in the fifteenth century BC, about your theory of her legacy in the bloodline that led to Akhenaten and the other great New Kingdom pharaohs. Maybe the Minoan legacy in Egypt wasn't just about a dynasty and a mercenary army of amazons. Maybe it was far more profound than that, a legacy of preserved knowledge that passed to Egypt after the volcano of Thera destroyed Cretan civilisation and the priests fled over the sea to the south from their ruined palaces.'

Hiebermeyer nodded. 'Palaces, but not palaces. People have wondered about the function of the Minoan palaces ever since they were discovered, about the complexes of store-rooms, about the labyrinth.'

Jack closed his eyes for a moment. 'Imagine what that might contain.'

'But then it was all lost,' Costas said.

Hiebermeyer tapped the screen where the image showed the empty limestone plateau in front of the Pyramid of Menkaure. 'Maybe. Or maybe it's still there. Maybe it went *underground*.'

Jack stared, his mind racing. *Of course.* 'Ahkenaten's City of Light,' he exclaimed. 'It's exactly what Akhenaten would do. He's a pharaoh who's created a whole new religion, who has built himself a new capital at Amarna, who has dedicated massive new temples at Luxor and Heliopolis. Re-founding the library at Giza, removing it to a more secure location from that old mud-brick complex, bringing it under the aegis of his new cult centre to the Aten and putting it underground would be completely in keeping with his vision. Jacob, can we see your plan again?'

Lanowski tapped a key, and the image transformed to the Aten symbol from the plaques with the pyramids behind, transposed on the actual topography of the plateau. 'It fits exactly,' Jack said. 'The central sun symbol falls exactly on the plateau in front of the Pyramid of Menkaure, the place from which the rays emanate. That's got to be it.' He glanced at Costas. 'That must be what we saw down the tunnel under the pyramid.'

Costas nodded. 'Lit up by sunlight coming through those

air shafts in the pyramid, reflected off polished basalt mirrors that magnified it somewhere deep beneath the plateau.'

'Okay,' Jack said. 'Now for the egress point of that tunnel on the Nile.'

Lanowski reeled off a twelve-figure set of coordinates. 'That pinpoints it to within twenty metres. I simply superimposed the image of the plaque on a modern map, maintaining the exact alignments of the pyramids.'

Costas peered at the map dubiously. 'You really think it can be that accurate?'

Hiebermeyer and Lanowski both turned and stared at him. Jack put a hand on his shoulder, grinning. 'You want to watch what you say. We're outnumbered by Egyptologists here.'

'I think,' said Lanowski slowly, eyeing Costas, 'given that the ancient Egyptians were able to align a pyramid with geometrical precision, if they really intended this to be a map then we can trust them.'

Costas raised his hands. 'I was only asking. Mea culpa.'

Lanowski tapped a key and a satellite image of Lower Egypt came into view, the Nile Delta and Cairo clearly visible above the belt of green that marked the course of the river through the desert. He tapped repeatedly, coming closer and closer to a point on the Nile to the south of Cairo. 'Google Maps is still down for Egypt, but I kept open the link to Landsat that my friend at Langley sent me when I was researching the Red Sea chariots site. Take a look at this. My coordinates come out almost exactly on this ruined structure half-fallen into the Nile. Aysha?'

'My research shows that it's early nineteenth century, thought to have been built by Napoleon's forces when they took Egypt,' she said. 'It would have been a ruin by the time Corporal Jones and Chaillé-Long and the French diver undertook their foray in 1892. There's nothing else like it on that stretch of the west bank of the Nile, and no doubt this is the fort they saw and that Howard Carter mentioned in his diary entry. The entrance to Akhenaten's tunnel should lie somewhere very close to that spot.'

'Bingo,' Lanowski said quietly.

Jack put a hand on his shoulder, his excitement mounting. 'Good work, Jacob. Now let's do some geomorphology on this. We need to be thinking about the water level.'

'I'm already there,' Lanowski replied, his eyes gleaming. 'Obviously, there's the issue of changes in the course of the Nile over three thousand years. But this is one of those places where the position of the bank has been almost static, as we can infer from the discovery of the tunnel entrance apparently below the modern bank of the river.'

'It might not have been chance,' Costas said thoughtfully. 'Akhenaten's engineers must have known their river intimately. If they were going to build a tunnel entrance, they'd have chosen somewhere stable.' He glanced at Jacob. 'After all, these were the guys who built the pyramids. You said it.'

Lanowski turned to Costas, his face suffused with pleasure. '*Very* good, Costas. You're learning.'

'What about the river level?' Jack asked.

'The latest sedimentological research suggests that the New Kingdom floodplain was lower than has generally been believed, though of course we have to factor in the annual flooding and lowering of the Nile that's now controlled by the Aswan Dam. My calculations suggest that a tunnel built into the bedrock at that point could have been dry for part of the year, and partly flooded for the remaining months when it might have been navigable.'

'You mean an underground canal,' Jack said. 'Something that would have allowed barges to be poled or wall-walked right up to the pyramid plateau.'

'Exactly. We've already seen a precedent for it in the canals and artificial harbours dug for each of the pyramids when they were constructed, only they were above ground.'

'But our tunnel doesn't lead to a mortuary temple,' Hiebermeyer added.

'What about the present water level?' Jack asked.

'My model suggests that the tunnel will be completely submerged, though it may well rise once it reaches the plateau and connect with passageways and chambers that have always been above the water level and remain dry today. Ground-penetrating radar survey in the past has revealed nothing like this under the plateau in front of the Pyramid of Menkaure, but that may only reflect the limitations of the technology. It would be possible for the roof of chambers to be many metres deep, beyond the range of the radar, but for the chambers still to be above the water table. And there's no doubt that they exist. You and Costas saw through to some kind of space when you were under the pyramid.'

'I just hope you can break through from the Nile,' Lanowski said. 'When that French diver blew his way in over a hundred years ago he may have caused a rock slide.'

'We can't know that until we get there,' Jack said, squinting at Costas. 'And my colleague usually has a few bits and pieces up his sleeve.'

'C5,' Costas said. 'A diver's best friend. I liberated a few slabs from *Sea Venture*'s armaments store.'

Hiebermeyer was still staring at the screen. 'Do you really think you can make it? I mean, more than three kilometres through that tunnel, completely underwater?'

Costas nodded. 'Physically, yes. As long as the tunnel's clear beyond the entrance, as long as our scooters work and as long as our rebreathers hold out.'

'But?'

'I can't help thinking of those who have gone before us. The only ones we know about were the Caliph Al-Hakim and Corporal Jones, the first apparently dead somewhere down there and the other one seriously unhinged by the experience. And our first foray under the pyramid was hardly auspicious. We saw the light once, but maybe that's all the pharaoh will allow us.'

Lanowski glanced at him. 'You're in the wrong movie, Costas. This isn't the one with the curses, the flesh-eating scarabs and the zombie mummies. Akhenaten ditched all the old religion, remember. He was above all that.'

Costas gave him a wry look. 'Yeah, and this is the one with the extremist fanatics, the public executions and impending Armageddon. I think I'd take swarms of locusts and come-alive mummies over that given the choice.'

Aysha's phone hummed, and she took it out of her pocket. 'We've got reception back. It won't last, so let me check on the latest.' She tapped it, waited and then stared at the image that came up on the screen, before scrolling quickly down. 'You need to see this, all of you. It's on the news, now. Our time may be tighter than we thought.'

19

Aysha propped her phone on the computer so they could all see the screen, and Hiebermeyer sat forward gripping the armrests of his chair, his knuckles white with tension. 'It's from Al-Jazeera, their Arabic service,' Aysha said. 'It's live.'

Jack leaned over and stared. Above the footer with breaking news was a scene that looked like the aftermath of a terrorist attack, the foreground filled with flashing lights and emergency vehicles in front of a high perimeter fence. The headline said 'Giza, live'. The camera zoomed in beyond the fence to the looming forms of the three pyramids. Suddenly there was a white flash in front of the smaller of the pyramids, and then another. 'That looks like white phosphorus, probably grenades,' he murmured. 'Phosphorus won't bring anything down, but if they use it on the pyramids it'll blacken the stone and make them seem as if they're on fire.'

'It's a portent of what's to come,' Hiebermeyer muttered.

'Next time they'll pack the burial chambers with high explosive.'

'Isn't that our pyramid?' Costas said. 'The Pyramid of Menkaure?'

Hiebermeyer nodded. 'The one that Saladin's son tried to dismantle in 1196, so they're taking up where he left off. Look what the new report says. They've been chanting "Saladin, Saladin". They may be threatening to do this to the smaller pyramid now, but next time it'll be the Great Pyramid.'

Aysha switched on the loudspeaker and listened intently to the report, in Arabic. 'Apparently it's the same militant cleric who's been threatening this ever since the Taliban blew up the Bamiyan Buddhas in Afghanistan in 2001,' she said, switching the sound off again. 'It seems that his thugs managed to break their way through the perimeter fence about an hour ago in a convoy of pickup trucks, and are in an armed standoff with the police at the entrance to the plateau. The police have no interest in a firefight and, anyway, their senior officers have been infiltrated by the extremists, just like the army. As for our beloved Antiquities Director, Al-Jazeera has managed to track him down at home halfway through packing to leave. He was a political nobody before the current regime came into power and I expect right now he's bitterly regretting having accepted the position. With the media spotlight on him he's been forced to return to the ministry in Cairo, where I don't imagine he'll last long.'

'I've read the Qur'an right through,' Lanowski said, shaking his head. 'There's nothing in there about ordering the destruction of monuments or statues just because they pre-date Mohammed.'

'The glory of Allah shines through everything from creation to the present day, including all of the marvels of ancient Egypt,' Aysha said quietly. 'To suggest that it does not do so for history before Mohammed is wrong. These people are the enemy of true Muslims.'

The TV camera refocused to show the shady figures in front of the trucks that were parked in a line just inside the entrance to the Giza plateau. 'Take a look at the gunmen,' Costas said. 'They're all wearing black headbands.'

'They call themselves the new followers of the Mahdi,' Aysha said. 'Al Jazeera says they've been training in secret camps in Sudan and Somalia for months now. Many are veterans of Iraq and Afghanistan, with close ties to the extremists now operating in Syria against Israel. For the first time since the rise of the Taliban in Afghanistan, since Yemen and Somalia, we're looking at an extremist group about to stage a coup to take over a country. They've been planning this for over a century, ever since Lord Kitchener desecrated the Mahdi's tomb outside Khartoum after he'd defeated the dervish army at the Battle of Omdurman. Intelligence analysts at the time knew that Omdurman was a hollow victory, and now it's come back to haunt us.'

'And archaeology is being used as the tinder-box,' Jack said.

Hiebermeyer shook his head. 'Not just as a tinderbox. Look at what's happening. The West proved powerless to prevent the destruction of the Bamiyan Buddhas, and now we watch helplessly while the greatest antiquities of Egypt are threatened. The forces behind this are about to pull off an extraordinary publicity stunt. How better to show the weakness of the West? Archaeology, the West's fascination with ancient Egypt, is about to become a pawn in the hands of the extremists. What we are seeing is a gesture of contempt, not only to the West but also to the people of Egypt who have made archaeology their livelihood and the basis for their sense of national identity. A little over two centuries after Napoleon arrived with his team of cartographers and scholars, Egyptology is about to be extinguished.'

Lanowski put a hand on Hiebermeyer's shoulder. 'Not for you it won't be. Not for any of us here, nor for the millions around the world who follow your work. You've got a lifetime ahead of you putting together everything you've got out of Egypt. There will be books, films. The whole incredible story of Akhenaten, for a start, when we finally get to the bottom of it. *I'll* be there with you.'

Aysha put a finger to her lips and gestured towards Hiebermeyer, who had turned away from them. She leaned down and whispered to him, kissing his forehead and brushing his cheek. As she did so the image on her phone changed from the pyramids to another view, the headline reading 'Cairo Museum under threat'. The live streaming showed the museum behind a line of bonfires; in front of them men in black headbands were chanting and praying.

Hiebermeyer turned, took a deep breath and stared at it. '*Mein Gott*,' he said. 'It truly begins.' He got up and turned around, his face drained.

'Jacob was right,' said Jack. 'You may have to hang up your trowel for a while, but now is the time for ideas. After all, a few days ago, after your find of that carving in the tomb in the mummy necropolis, you handed me the best proof I could want that the Egyptian New Kingdom came about as a result of influence from Minoan Crete.'

Hiebermeyer suddenly bristled. 'I did *what*? I said nothing of the sort. A gaggle of bare-breasted Minoan amazons cavorting around in chariots in the desert does not amount to cultural influence.'

'Prove it. And prove to me that the Egyptians travelled further than the Greeks, in the Mediterranean, around Africa, even across the Atlantic. Go out and find the sites. That is, if they exist.'

'Oh, they exist.' Hiebermeyer was positively glaring at him now. 'You *know* they exist. I'll prove it to you. Just wait for it.'

Jack gripped his shoulder. 'That's the Maurice I know.'

Lanowski scuffed the floor with his feet and raised his hand, coughing.

'What is it, Jacob?' Costas asked cautiously.

'Permission to join the team,' he said.

'You're already part of the team,' Jack said. 'And a highly valued member. You've proved it yet again today.'

'No, I mean the real team. The *expedition*. You and Costas.'

'Come again?'

'You're going to need someone else topside. Mohammed and his son will have their work cut out for them managing the felucca. I've already been out with them in the harbour and seen what it's like. You'll need someone else to manage GPS position-finding, and to help with equipment. And Mohammed's English isn't that great. I speak pretty reasonable Arabic.'

'You speak Arabic,' Costas murmured. '*Of course* you speak Arabic. I should have guessed.'

Jack eyed him. 'There's a big risk factor. You know that.'

Lanowski raised his arms in the air, looking exasperated. 'The last big risk I took was when I turned down a tenured professorship at MIT for what amounted to a technician's job at IMU. My friends thought I'd finally flipped. All hope of the Nobel Prize went out the window. What attracted me to IMU was the chance to combine my, well, genius with hands-on archaeology, something I'd dreamed about since first being fascinated by Egyptology as a kid. And I've been part of this project from the get-go. And show me a Jack Howard project that doesn't involve big risks. *Real* risks.'

Jack glanced at Costas, who cracked a smile. 'I guess we could use the odd genius.'

Jack pursed his lips. 'You'd be our man on the felucca. Shore excursions are strictly off-limits. Okay?'

Lanowski punched the air. 'Thank you, Jack. You won't regret it.'

'One question,' Costas said, putting up his hand. 'About *our* shore excursion. Assuming we make it out alive, how do we get picked up?'

Lanowski took a black object the size of small alarm clock out of his pocket. 'Obviously you'll be on your own under-ground, and the mobile network around Cairo will probably be completely dead by then. You'll have a satellite phone, but the most reliable device is going to be this little gizmo.'

Costas peered at it. 'A beacon?'

'You got it. Switch this on anywhere and your GPS coordinates will be transmitted instantly via satellite to *Sea Venture*.'

Costas looked uncertain. 'Our people won't risk flying in a helicopter to pick us up on land. One thing the extremists have learned from Iraq and Afghanistan is how easy it is to shoot down helicopters. You can see shoulder-launched SAMs among those trucks in the Al-Jazeera report, some of them looking very like Stingers.'

Aysha looked at him. 'Our plan is for you to get out the way you got in. Mohammed and his son, and now Jacob too, will be waiting on the Nile in the felucca. Wherever you egress, your plan should be to make your way to the nearest point on the riverbank and activate the beacon. *Sea Venture* will pass on your GPS coordinates via satellite phone to Jacob. After they pick you up the felucca will sail north of the Nile Delta far enough out to sea for the Lynx to extract you without danger of attack.'

'We may well have to go through Cairo to get back to the river,' Costas said.

'That's a risk you'll have to take. There are still going to be Westerners there: journalists, some diplomats, the usual vultures who show up during a coup thinking they'll be in pole position to score lucrative deals with a new regime. But the first target for the extremists is likely to be members of the existing government, many of them Muslims. They might even want Western journalists there to report on it. It's afterwards when there are gangs of blood-crazed gunmen roaming the streets that you'd be in the most trouble. We'll just have to hope that they're still preoccupied with the purge when you arrive. You'll never succeed in being inconspicuous, so you need to look self-confident, assertive. I take it you'd strip off your E-suits to the clothes you've got on now. And I may be on the ground to help.'

Jack stared at her. 'What do you mean, on the ground?'

She gave him a steely look. 'It's about Sahirah, the Egyptian girl. The deadline Ben set on *Seaquest* for a response from the antiquities director is only a few hours away. We've just seen on the newscast that he's more concerned with saving his own skin right now. But something else has happened, Jack. One of the extremists who now effectively runs the judiciary saw that Sahirah had been arrested in connection with a visit to a synagogue. As a result he's had the charge against her changed from the lesser one of antiquities theft to the worst crime of all in their books, apostasy. She won't be given a chance to deny it. And even if the Antiquities Director were to intervene, there would almost certainly be no clemency.'

Jack pursed his lips. 'I take it you have a contingency plan.'

'Do you remember the beggar outside the synagogue, when we went in to see Maria? I told you that he was in fact my cousin Ahmed, the former Egyptian special forces soldier. What you weren't to know is that he's also Sahirah's boyfriend. He and several of his former army friends think that in the confusion of the coup they'll be able to get into the ministry building and find her. I'm going to Cairo to meet up with them.'

'You mean they're planning to shoot her out,' Jack said.

'There may be no other choice.'

'Good people are going to get killed.'

'It's going to be a bloodbath anyway, Jack. All we can do is try to save a few lives.'

'What's our rendezvous point in the city to meet up with you?'

'The synagogue. If you have to come through Cairo and

can't safely get to the river, make your way there and activate the beacon. I'll be in satellite phone contact with *Sea Venture* as well. I can help to guide you.'

Jack looked at Lanowski. 'Make sure you keep that beacon safe.'

'I've got two of them. One for me, the other for you.'

Costas peered closely. 'Why didn't you tell me about this, Jacob? I tell you about everything I'm working on.'

Lanowski looked hesitant. 'Well, it was going to be a birthday surprise for you. For today. Rebecca told me.'

Jack looked at Costas. 'For today? Today is your birthday?'

The building vibrated from an explosion somewhere near the harbour, the detonation followed by the ripping sound of machine-gun fire. Costas jerked his head towards the door, his face grim. 'I don't think today is one for any kind of celebration.'

Jack pointed to the fragment of ancient masonry beside the computer, the find that Hiebermeyer had made years before in the sewage pipe excavation beside the pyramids. 'Don't forget that, Maurice,' he said. 'If Costas and I get nowhere tonight, those hieroglyphs could be the only real proof we have for what lies under the plateau.'

'Maurice and I have got everything,' Aysha said. 'The First World War diary I found in the museum archives, the Geniza letter of Halevi, all of the images and data from the mummy necropolis, everything.'

Jack reached out and shook Hiebermeyer's hand. 'Do you remember our old school motto? "Quit ye like men, be strong." We use to joke about it, but now is one of those times.'

Hiebermeyer tapped his head. 'It's all up here, Jack. I'm taking Egypt with me. I won't let it go.'

The phone hummed, and Aysha picked it up, reading a text. 'That was my sister near Tantur, about eighty kilometres south of Alexandria. She says she's just seen a convoy of trucks with gunmen racing up the highway. If Cairo falls, Alexandria won't be far behind.'

Jack looked at his watch. 'Okay. Time for us to go.'

Aysha nodded. 'Mohamed has food and drink and sleeping bags on the felucca. All you need to do now is visit the washroom and say your prayers.'

Jack looked around the room. 'Anything more we can do?'

'Everything's on *Sea Venture* except what you can see here and the crates on the helipad.'

'Institute staff?'

'Anyone who wanted to leave has been airlifted out, with their families. They'll get refugee status in the UK.'

Jack turned to Costas, making a twirling motion with one hand. 'We need to get the Lynx fired up.'

Costas unclipped the VHF radio from his belt, and started walking to the door. 'I'm on it.'

Jack turned to Hiebermeyer. 'We'll help you get this remaining stuff to the helipad. It's 0730 hours already, and Mohammed's probably loaded up and waiting. We can get going early and give him a little leeway.' He turned to Lanowski, who had shouldered a small rucksack and picked up a crate of books from the floor. 'Jacob? You still on for this?'

Lanowski stared at him, his face pale but determined. 'Roger that, Jack. I'm good to go.'

★ ★ ★

Forty minutes later Jack was crouched between the thwarts of the felucca, staring in horror at the scene that was unfolding around them. The explosion they had heard while they were in the operations room had been the first of a succession every few minutes along the harbour front, all of them car bombs. After the third one Hiebermeyer had decided to bring forward his plans and evacuate the institute immediately; Aysha had left quickly with their driver for Cairo, shorn of anything associating her with a foreign institute and dressed in a burkha with a face veil. A few minutes later Mohammed and his son had finished loading the felucca and poled it away from the quayside, Jack and Lanowski sitting in the bows and Costas helping the boy to fire up the diesel engine. As it coughed to life the noise was drowned out by the Lynx, which raised a dust storm around the fort as the pilot held it poised for departure. Jack had watched as Hiebermeyer ran out of the fort with his briefcase and rucksack, ducked down on the helipad while the crewman loaded the last of the crates, and then took the outstretched arms and jumped on board himself. He had turned for a last glimpse of Egypt as the helicopter rose, angled sharply and clattered off over the Mediterranean, soon leaving Alexandria and Egyptian airspace far behind and disappearing from view over the northern horizon.

For Jack it should have been a scene of almost unbearable poignancy, watching his friend in his trusty old shorts and boots, still streaked with dirt from his last excavation, leave his beloved Egypt perhaps for the last time. But any reflection was instantly cut short by a cacophony of gunfire and engine revving coming along the highway from the west, the first of the trucks screeching on to the quay mere minutes after the Lynx had taken off. One of them disgorged half a dozen gunmen who raced up to the fort, firing their Kalashnikovs into the air, one of them waving the black flag of the extremists. Within minutes they had entered the fort and raised the flag on a pole above the ramparts. Qaitbay Fort suddenly looked as it had been intended, a stronghold of medieval Islam, all indication of its use over the past few years as an archaeological institute obliterated.

Two trucks raced up to the fort and this time let off a cluster of handcuffed prisoners, all of them Egyptian women in Western dress, the gunmen rifle-butting them into the courtyard. Seconds later there was an ear-splitting clatter of gunfire and the gunmen reappeared, leaving one man at the entrance and piling back into the trucks. Jack turned away, feeling numb, glad only that Maurice and Aysha had not witnessed what had just happened. As the felucca chugged out into the basin towards the sea he steeled himself for more to come, keeping his eyes glued on the gunmen at the fort. Suddenly the air was rent by another explosion, deeper and more resonant than the others, and then a rushing noise and the sound of shattering glass. 'My God,' Costas exclaimed. 'They've torched the library.'

Jack spun around, staring at the far side of the harbour. A gas truck had been driven into the foyer of the Bibliotheca and exploded, its wrecked form lying upside down on the road in front. The huge disk shape of the Bibliotheca was wreathed in flame, like a burning sun rising from the eastern horizon. Jack cold barely breathe, his mind reeling. It was as if he had been transported back fifteen hundred years to an event that seemed fossilised in history, too awful to comprehend. But this was real and happening before his eyes. For the second time in two millennia the great library of Alexandria had been destroyed by religious extremists, by those who believed that knowledge was offensive to their god. Jack could hear the screams of people streaming out of the building, and bursts of gunfire from the trucks that had ranged up beside the wreck of the tanker, their machine guns trained on the steps and raking them every time another person appeared. It was not just the books that were anathema to the extremists; it was those who had read them as well. In that instant the frailty of civilisation seemed laid bare, the foundations of wisdom as fragile as those of morality, with those who espoused it as vulnerable as the women who a few minutes before had paid for their freedom of expression with their lives.

Another burst of automatic fire rang out from near the fort, and Jack spun around. A truck with a gunman on the roof was hurtling along the edge of the harbour to the point closest to the felucca, no more than a hundred yards distant. It screeched to a halt, the gunman vaulted out of the rear and he began to taunt a fisherman who was gathering up his net on the quay, prodding him with the barrel of his Kalashnikov. The fisherman backed away, his hands in the air, gesticulating towards his family in a small car beside them. The gunman raised his rifle and shot him in the head, watched his body jerk back and fall into the harbour and then ran along the quay looking for others. Mohammed gestured frantically at Jack and Costas to get down. They dropped into the scuppers and crawled forward to where Lanowski was already lying under the deck in the bow of the boat, absorbed in checking the battery in one of the beacons. Jack looked back and saw Mohammed unfurl and raise a black flag in the stern, and then slowly swing the tiller to take them further out into the basin towards the entrance. With any luck there would be more interesting and easier targets for the gunmen than a felucca setting out to sea, especially one that appeared to be sporting the flag of the extremists.

Jack drew himself up further into the crawl space in the bows of the felucca, wedging his feet beside one of their kitbags and pushing a sleeping bag forward as a makeshift pillow. He felt the bulge of the Beretta in the holster on his chest, and shifted slightly to make sure the grip was accessible in case it was needed. He could make out Lanowski and Costas lying in the gloom beside him, their faces etched with the reality of what they were undertaking. They all knew there was no going back now. Even if they had decided to abort, Jack would never have risked calling back the Lynx to a place that was crawling with trigger-happy gunmen who almost certainly had SAMs in their trucks. The only way ahead was the one they had mapped out, from one burning cauldron to another, but with a plausible exit strategy. They would stick to their plan.

He shifted again, trying to find a more comfortable position, and shut his eyes. He tried to forget what he had just seen, and to think instead of those who had gone before him down the Nile in search of fabulous discoveries, of the sand-travellers of the past, those who breathed in the dust of the desert and felt the brush of the wind that blew from the pyramids. He thought of what could lie beneath, of sealed chambers full of treasures, of rows of pottery jars brimming with papyri that might contain all of the lost wisdom of the ancient world.

The chug of the engine increased to a throb, and he felt the bows rise. He opened his eyes and peered through a crack in the planking, seeing the end of the quay and hearing the slap of the waves as they passed into open water. The engine began to vibrate badly, seeming to jar every bone in his body, and each slap of the waves felt like a body blow. The movement of the boat had released a rancid smell of fish from the scuppers, and wafts of diesel smoke erupted every few seconds from a hole in the engine. The great triangular sail would remain furled until they had traversed the coast and veered south into the Nile, where a good following wind might allow them to ease off on the engine.

He rolled over again and looked at Costas. He was splayed out on top of the kitbags, his mouth open and snoring, oblivious to everything around him, rocking to and fro with every shudder of the boat.

Jack swallowed hard. He was beginning to regret devouring the food that Mohammed had offered him on the quayside. He stared at the planks above him, wishing he could be outside and focusing on the horizon, and glanced at his watch. They had ten hours to go until they passed Cairo.

It was going to be a long day.

20

It was dark by the time the felucca passed through the northern suburbs of Cairo, the lingering heat of the day tempered by a torrential downpour that had left a mist over the banks of the river. Earlier they had used the boat's huge triangular lateen sail to make their way with the wind against the current, but with the city looming ahead Mohammed and his son had furled the sail and lowered the mast to make the boat less conspicuous and had fired up the old diesel engine again. As they chugged past vessels heading north Mohammed had exchanged a few words with their captains and learned that everyone who could was leaving Cairo by whatever means possible, by river or road or on foot, with groups of people even striking out across the desert with all they could carry to find a place to hide and wait out the worst of what was happening in the city.

There had been a tense half hour as they passed the centre

of the city and the walled enclosure of Fustat, Old Cairo, near the Ben Ezra synagogue where Jack and Maria had explored the Geniza chamber only four days previously. Jack had tried to make out the medieval walls in the gloom and the mist, remembering that this was the place where he and Costas were due to rendezvous with Aysha before dawn and to find the felucca for their return journey up the Nile to the sea. Between now and then they should finally have answered the question that had been eating at Jack for months now, ever since they had returned from their explorations in Sudan, since he and Costas had seen the shaft of light beneath the Pyramid of Menkaure. He glanced at Costas' recumbent form beneath the foredeck of the boat, next to the spot where Jack had just spent several of the most uncomfortable hours of his life hidden from sight during the long daylight passage down the Nile. At least one of them would have had a good rest.

They had begun to pass amorphous shapes floating in the river that Jack knew must be bodies, but until now the city had been ominously quiet, with only the odd gunshot and distant scream. Then just before they reached Fustat there had been the call to prayer, the muezzins and recordings from the minarets joining in the familiar cadences that seemed to undulate over the city, reaching a crescendo and then stopping suddenly. It had been more than a call to prayer; it had been a signal for the extremists. Seconds later the city erupted in gunfire and a cacophony of shrieking and yelling, rising from all directions and echoing across the river. A long burst of automatic fire came at them from the east bank, the muzzle flashing like a distant jet of flame in the night, the bullets zipping overhead and several of them slapping into the side of the boat. Mohammed kept his nerve, staying in the central channel of the river, and the gunman soon turned his attention elsewhere, firing short bursts into groups of people who were running and tripping along the embankment.

Jack knew that people were dying now, by the scores if not the hundreds, and that before the night was out the river would run red with blood. As the glow of fires began to redden the night he cast his mind back to the descriptions of Khartoum in Sudan a hundred and thirty years before, the first city on the Nile to fall to the extremists. Those who were watching from the river then must have seen similar sights. Despite all of the advances in technology, in weaponry and in communications, when it came to the razing of a city and the destruction of its inhabitants, little had changed through history. It was reduced to the same individual acts of savagery and horror that were little different from the time when the forces of jihad had first swept west across Africa almost fifteen hundred years before, or when the Crusaders had done the same in the name of their own faith.

Jack huddled down again out of sight beneath the thwarts, watching the river through a slit in the planks, and soon the glow of Cairo was enveloped in darkness and the sounds of gunfire receded into the night. He knew they must be nearing their destination, the ruined Napoleonic fort on the west bank of the river that Lanowski had identified as the point where the tunnel from the pyramid entered the Nile. He could see the screen of Lanowki's computer now in the space in the bows opposite his own makeshift bed, and a few moments later Lanowski emerged with his GPS receiver, his long lank hair coming out from under a woollen Jacques

Cousteau hat and his face daubed black. Jack smiled to himself despite the grim scenes of the past hour. Lanowski had come into his own as IMU's newest field operative, and was clearly relishing it. He made his way up to Mohammed, exchanged a few words in Arabic and then came back to Jack, crouching down and showing him the GPS readout and its convergence with the programmed position for the fort. 'We're less than a kilometre away,' he said quietly. 'Time to wake Costas?'

Jack nodded. 'We've got to get our equipment ready. We can't afford to linger once we get there.'

'Roger that. Mohammed's apprehensive about his return journey through the city. He thinks it's only a matter of time before the gunmen find the police river launches and begin joyriding. He wants to be at his rendezvous point north of Cairo before that happens.'

Costas blearily raised himself, banged his head on the deck above him and then fell back, easing himself out of the space feet first. He turned around and pulled out the two gear bags that had made up his bed, and then cracked opened a water bottle and drained it. 'What's our ETA?' he asked gruffly.

'About twenty minutes,' Lanowski said. 'Time to saddle up.'

'Saddle up?' Costas rubbed his eyes. 'Since when are we cowboys?'

'It's what you said in that film. In the TV special about Atlantis. I watched it a couple of times to get the lingo.'

'Oh, yeah. Okay. We're cowboys.' Costas swayed slightly. 'I need some coffee.'

As if on cue Mohammed's son appeared with a tray of glasses of strong tea, and they each took one. Costas pulled out a bag of fat sandwiches and offered them around, taking a huge bite from one himself.

'Always the sandwiches,' Lanowski said keenly. 'Always New York deli. That's in the film too.'

'Yeah, well, life imitates art.' He swallowed and peered at Lanowski. 'What's with the commando paint?'

'You should see your faces. They'd stand out like beacons to anyone watching from the shore.'

Costas grunted, swallowed his last mouthful, wiped his hands and crouched down, pulling his E-suit from his bag. 'You help Jack on with his, and then you can zip me up. I've got a few additional bits and pieces I need to clip on.'

'A shame you lost your old boiler suit in that volcano.'

'Yeah.' Costas looked disconsolate for a moment. 'It melted. I've kept the shreds of it in my cabin on *Seaquest*. It was great to wear that over my E-suit. I haven't worked out how to carry tools properly since then.'

Lanowski ducked down and pulled a package out of his own bag, handing it to Costas. 'I hope you don't mind. I took a look at that old one in your cabin to get the size.' He tore open the plastic, and an immaculate blue boiler suit complete with outsized leg and arm pockets came tumbling out.

Costas stared. 'Hey, Jacob. *You're the man.*' He took the suit, holding it out appreciatively. 'It's even the correct pattern, 1954 US Navy submariner issue. Where the hell did you find this?'

Lanowski shrugged. 'Ebay, of course. You can find everything on Ebay. I reckoned you were likely to ditch this one with your E-suit at the end of this mission, so I ordered two. There's another one hanging up behind the door in your cabin.'

Costas looked at Jack, jerking a thumb at Lanowski. 'This guy's good. *Really* good. We should have him on all our dives.'

Lanowski glanced at his GPS receiver. 'Time to saddle up. I mean it this time.'

Costas grinned, and slapped him on the shoulder. 'Roger that.'

Twenty minutes later Jack was floating beside Costas on the starboard side of the felucca, the buoyancy in his E-suit holding him upright with his head and shoulders out of the water. Between them were the aquajets they planned to use to extend their exploration reach underwater, compact propeller-driven units capable of 2.5 horsepower with a battery life of up to three hours. The E-suit was an all-environment, Kevlar-reinforced protective shell developed at IMU and refined over the last ten years, providing a dry interior with temperature control but giving the diver the agility of a wetsuit. Critical to its performance was the streamlined console on the back containing a breathing unit of choice, in this case a semi-closed-circuit oxygen rebreather ideal for maximising bottom-time in the shallow depths they were likely to encounter. The upper part of the console contained a computer that regulated oxygen output, monitored the diver's physiology and contained a two-way communication unit, all of it feeding into the helmet with a pivoting visor that was clamped on top of the E-suit. In a refinement since the early days the helmet was now a closer fit to the head with a flexible neck made of the same material as the E-suit, allowing the diver to move almost without restriction. Jack loved the E-suit for the freedom it gave him, and for the adaptability that allowed them to use it in every conceivable environment, from the Arctic to the superheated water above an underwater volcano, to the dive they were about to carry out now into the murky depths of the Nile, searching for an ancient tunnel under the desert and what might lie beyond.

Lanowski's head reappeared over the gunwale, staring down at them. He had prepared a comprehensive equipment checklist on his computer, something that Jack and Costas usually winged, and had just finished running through it with them. Jack could feel the bulge under his E-suit where his Beretta was holstered, and the slight discomfort of the shirt and lightweight jacket, casual trousers and leather shoes he was wearing under the suit, ready for him to walk out of it into the streets of Cairo. They had run carefully through every scenario, assessing the best plan of action. Everything depended on them finding the tunnel, being able to get into it and then finding an egress point; if there was no tunnel below they would abort the mission here and now, and if there was no egress point further along the tunnel they would hope to return to this point, stash their suits in the ruins of the fort and make their way along the riverbank to the north. As Jack floated there, seeing nothing below, everything seemed to hang in the balance; the yawning uncertainty seemed to eclipse all of the hours and days of speculation, the endless juggling of scenarios and possibilities that had filled his mind since finding this spot had become a reality.

Lanowski looked at Costas. 'Double-check the two radio beacons.'

'Roger that. One to be activated when we exit, the other when we reach the Nile.'

'And the marker buoy?'

Costas patted the front pocket of the boiler suit he had donned on top of his E-suit. 'Roger that. We release it here as soon as we know we can get inside the tunnel.'

'Is your GPS activated?'

'Roger. The in-helmet display will navigate to the precise fix you calculated for the tunnel.'

'Mohammed wants to stand off as soon as possible in the centre of the river. He's the world's most level guy as you could see from how cool he was going through Cairo, but he's got twitchy. His son told me that this part of the river has a bad reputation among the felucca captains. They think it's spooked. Apparently there are whirlpools and some of them think they're caused by river monsters. Probably nothing to worry about, just giant Nile carp inflated by rumour into monsters.'

'That's bad enough,' Costas grumbled. 'Those things have been known to pull fishermen under.'

'Or it could be crocodiles.'

'Or *what*?'

'Crocodiles,' Lanowski said distractedly, looking at his list again. 'Apparently, they sometimes get this far. Mostly only small ones these days, but some big carcasses still get washed down. Sometimes they're not carcasses. Sometimes they're alive and snapping.'

Costas groaned again. 'That's great. I thought we'd left all of that behind at the crocodile temple in Sudan. Why didn't someone tell me?'

'You'd still have volunteered,' Jack said. 'You'd never have let me do this alone.'

Mohammed appeared beside Lanowski, looking anxious. 'Okay, boys,' Lanowski said. 'You've got to go. See you back on board in a few hours, inshallah.'

'Thanks, Jacob. Look after yourself. No shore expeditions, remember?' Jack turned to Costas. 'Good to go?'

Costas made a diver's okay signal. 'Good to go.' They both shut their visors, and Jack felt the slight increase in pressure as the helmet sealed and the rebreather came online. A second later the in-helmet screen display activated to the left and right of his main viewport, a low-light readout that could show up to thirty variables, from carbon dioxide levels to pulse rate. He tapped the computer control inside the index finger of his left glove and reduced the display to the minimum, showing depth in metres, compass orientation and external water temperature. He raised his right arm in an okay signal to Lanowski and Mohammed, then turned and did a thumbs-down signal to Costas and descended two metres, bleeding off air manually from his suit and waiting for the automated buoyancy system to compensate. He pulled down the aquajet after him and waited while its computer altered the trim in the small ballast tanks on either side of the unit, an automated process that self-adjusted with depth to ensure that the scooter remained neutrally buoyant.

He switched on his helmet light but was dazzled by the reflection of particles in the water that reduced the visibility to almost zero. He switched it off and was again in blackness, the moonless night meaning that no light filtered down from the surface. As he stared out he remembered the lines that Jeremy had read from Howard Carter's diary, the account that Carter had heard from Corporal Jones of what went on here that night in 1892 when Colonel Chaillé-Long and the French diver had accompanied Jones to this very spot. He could well imagine the trepidation of the diver as he went down with his home-made gear, yet also his excitement at seeing that the valve and cylinder worked and at what he might discover on the riverbed below. What had happened then was a mystery. All Jack knew for certain was that somewhere down there must lie the remains of that diver, and of the boat that had been sucked down by the same vortex that had taken Jones into an underworld that had sent him spiralling further on his own descent into madness.

Costas tapped him on the shoulder, and Jack could just make out the glow of the readout inside his helmet a few inches away. 'Jack, testing intercom. Over.'

'Reduce the squelch level about twenty per cent.'

'How's that?'

'Good. Visibility's about as bad as I've ever seen. We're going to have to rely on the virtual terrain mapper.'

'Mine's already on. It's a revelation, Jack.'

Jack tapped his finger and a green isometric lattice appeared in front of his visor, gradually filling with detail as the multi-beam sonar built into the top of his helmet mapped out the riverbed in front. The display provided a continuously adjusted virtual image, with a time-lapse of about half a second as new data streamed in. Jack was constantly amazed by the clarity of the images it produced, and this time was no exception. It was as if they were suspended in mid-air above a sharply angled scree-slope some twenty metres from top to bottom. To the left the slope was covered with debris from the 19th century fort, the building whose ruined form on the shore had been their waymarker, the feature described by Corporal Jones to Howard Carter. To the right was a more regular shape about ten metres below the surface, an overhanging ledge about five metres across with another jumble of material below it, much of it larger, more regular blocks. The red tracking lines showing the GPS fix converged on his screen directly in front of the ledge. Jack's heart began to pound. *This could be it.*

Costas dropped below, his aquajet held in front. 'I'm activating my helmet camera and the recording function on the terrain mapper. That means everything we see will be recorded on the memory chip.'

'Check,' Jack said. 'I've done the same.'

Jack felt something bump his fins, and a spectral form seemed to undulate across his terrain-mapper, filling the entire lower half of the screen and swaying from side to side, caught like a series of stills in a time-lapse. 'Did you see that?' he exclaimed. 'I could swear something swam by. It seemed to be all tail.'

'No, I did *not* see it,' Costas said, his voice quavering. 'I *definitely* did not see it. What I saw was a glitch in the mapper. This is reality, not a nightmare.'

'Whatever it was, it's gone now,' Jack said. 'A serpent off to join the party, heading to the hell of Cairo.'

'It never existed, Jack. You've just got a touch of Mohammed's river fever.'

Jack held his aquajet by the handles on either side of the encased propeller housing, released the safety lock with his thumbs and pulled the trigger, feeling the backflow of water course down his body. The jet had a deflector so that at full throttle it dropped just below the diver, keeping the flow of water from the propeller clear and unobstructed. Costas came alongside and they both gunned the jets forward, quickly coming to within a few metres of the GPS fix and then releasing the triggers. Jack stared at the image on his terrain-mapper, taking in the detail. It was astonishingly clear, as if he were looking at a wall of masonry on land with the naked eye. He remembered Lanowski's model showing how the scour effect of the Nile at this point could have kept the submerged bank free from loose sediment, a phenomenon also manifest in the whirlpools and eddies that made Mohammed and his fellow felucca captains so apprehensive. And there was no doubt about it now. The block in front of him that had looked like a ledge was fixed into the bank, part of a larger structure rather than fallen masonry; it was clearly a lintel, a huge block that must have weighed ten tons or more. Below it on either side he could just make out two massive upright blocks, and between them a jumble of stone that had fallen in from the sides.

Jack did a double take, not entirely believing what he was seeing, swinging from left to right and back again to recreate the image on his terrain-mapper, and exactly the same features came into view. He was absolutely convinced of it now. It was an entranceway, an ancient portal beneath the Nile. Its depth put it exactly on Lanowski's prediction for the level of the Nile at low water in the second millennium BC, allowing a partly flooded channel to act as an underground canal beneath the desert, wide enough to take barges that could have been walked or poled along. He clicked on his headlamp, and as he came within inches of the lintel he began to make out the stone beyond the reflected haze of particles in the water, unmistakably the fine-grained red granite favoured by the New Kingdom pharaohs as a prestige building material. He stared more closely. He realised that he was not just looking at a smoothed surface of granite. *He was looking at hieroglyphs.* He switched back to the terrain-mapper, and suddenly there it was, the cartouche that had become etched in his mind over the last months, from the crocodile temple in Sudan, from the plaque they had found with the sarcophagus on the wreck, from Rebecca's underground find in Jerusalem. He put out his hand, tracing his finger over the bird at the beginning and the sheaf of grain at the end. He stared for a moment longer, mouthing the word. *Akhenaten*.

Costas' voice came through the intercom. 'Jack, we've got a problem.'

'I've just found the hieroglyphs. We're bang on target.'

'I mean down below the lintel,' Costas said. 'I think I can see what happened back in 1892.'

Jack dropped a few metres below the overhanging block to where the terrain-mapper showed Costas' form above the pile of blocks between the uprights of the portal. In front of him he could see where the blocks filled the entrance, with cracks leading to deeper spaces beyond. Costas' voice came on again. 'I think the diver blew open the stone doors that once sealed off this entrance, and in the process caused the rock fall that's blocked it up again for us. But there's one spot where I think we might get through, directly in front of me now, where my terrain-mapper shows a block that could be dislodged. With a little assistance.'

'Explosives?'

'C5. Always be prepared.'

'I was wondering about that bulge in the front of your boiler suit.'

'It's our only option. We've got to try it.'

'Remember what happened in 1892,' Jack said. 'We don't want to create an explosive vortex and see our felucca sucked in.'

'I think that happened because the stone door was watertight and there was an air space in the tunnel beyond, so that when the doors blew the water poured in and created a whirlpool that must have pulled down their boat. My guess is that our diver was using some kind of waterproofed dynamite and probably didn't really know what he was doing, using too much of it and creating a hole so large that the flow of water pushed those slabs open too quickly and created a lethal vortex. C5 is a far better explosive and much easier to position for maximum effectiveness with small quantities. I think I've got just about the right amount for the job.'

'Risk factor?'

'An underwater shock wave, but that should be mitigated by the pressure resistance of our E-suits.'

'Okay. Let's do it.'

Costas drew a package out the bulge in the front of his boiler suit, swam forward and pushed it into the crack, working it further in for a few minutes and then pushing himself back out. 'Okay. I've separated it into three charges, with individual detonators. They're manual, and I've set the delay for two minutes. You good with that?'

'Roger. Go ahead.'

Costas finned into the crack again, and then pushed himself out. 'Fire in the hole. Swim hard right.' Jack followed him along the face of the riverbank, coming to a halt behind a rock that protruded between them and the likely blast radius. 'Okay,' Costas said. 'Now.' Three nearly simultaneous detonations shook the water, causing the rock to shift slightly and a pressure wave to pass through Jack's body. Costas immediately swam back, and Jack followed. On his terrain-mapper he could see the jerky image of rocks tumbling down to the base of the slope, and ahead of them a hole about a metre and a half across had opened up where the charges had been set. Costas poked his head through, and then withdrew, detaching the marker buoy from the front of his suit and holding it out. 'It's clear. There's open water beyond, presumably the tunnel. You good to go?'

Jack stared through, seeing only darkness. Releasing the buoy was the signal for Mohammed to leave, though it still left them the option of egressing this way if the tunnel beyond proved to be blocked. They should ideally do a recce before releasing the buoy, but he knew that by now Mohammed would be desperate to get back through Cairo before the river became a no-go zone. He turned to Costas. 'Do it.'

Costas released the buoy, and a few seconds later Jack heard the throb of the boat's diesel engine firing up. Mohammed must have been waiting with his hand poised over the starter. Costas immediately swam through the crack, and Jack followed, both pushing their aquajets in front of them. As they passed through the haze of silt created by the explosion, the external water temperature dropped by over ten degrees and the visibility opened up, the water no longer clouded by river sediment. They panned their headlamps around and an extraordinary scene came into view. They had passed through a monumental entranceway, and ahead of them a tunnel with smoothed walls about five metres in diameter extended into the darkness as far as Jack could see. Below them the cascade of rock created by the explosion in 1892 lay over the hull of a wooden boat, so shattered that it was barely recognisable. Jack remembered Corporal Jones' account of that night. Chaillé-Long had clearly survived the sinking, somehow avoiding being sucked under and making his way to the riverbank, but the boat's captain and any crew must have died almost instantly. Jones' survival was little short of a miracle, sucked through and riding the wave far down the tunnel, something that must have contributed to the haunted state of the man Howard Carter had met months later dazed and begging on the streets of Old Cairo.

Jack adjusted his headlamp beam and saw something metallic pinned under one side of the wreckage. 'My God,' he exclaimed, his heart pounding. *It was the diver.* With some trepidation he finned closer, brushing the silt from the man's visor. The glass was corroded and opaque, but inside it he could see the amorphous fatty remains of a human face, the eye sockets filled with white matter. He realised that the rest of the man's body must be in the same condition, held in place by the canvas suit and the straps of his equipment. He gently pushed the head to one side to look at the valve arrangement of the breathing apparatus. He glanced back at Costas. 'You need to see this.'

Costas was preoccupied with his aquajet. 'What is it?' he said.

'I've just met our French diver.'

'What do you mean, just met him?'

'He's fully intact. I mean his equipment. What's inside is pretty well-preserved, too. Adiposed.'

'I don't want to see, Jack. I really don't. That's what we'll look like a hundred years from now if we don't get out of this place.'

'Fascinating equipment. Looks like a fully developed demand valve, fifty years before the Cousteau-Gagnan device.'

'1892,' Costas replied, still preoccupied. 'France was the hotbed of diving invention, with Rouquaytol having developed compressed air cylinders and Denayrouze a reduction valve. It always amazes me that it took so long to mate them effectively and develop a proper automatic demand valve.'

'Imagine the military applications in the arms race leading up to the First World War.'

'That's probably why it never saw the light of day. It was probably his only working example and he'd kept it secret. It was a highly competitive world.'

'You need to see it.'

'I'll look at your pictures. After I've had several stiff drinks. Meanwhile we have a problem. My aquajet's gone dead.'

The water suddenly shimmered, and out of instinct Jack powered forward into the tunnel. There was a dull rumble and he was slammed by a violent surge in the water, tumbling him over on to his back. He quickly righted himself, checking his readout for any damage to his equipment, and looked back. He had guessed what had happened, and his fears were confirmed. The corpse had disappeared beneath a massive fall of rock and debris. Through the swirl of sediment that now filled the water he could just make out their entry point, now completely blocked. He saw Costas recovering himself and finning back a few strokes, scanning the rockfall with his terrain mapper. 'Houston, we've got a problem,' he announced. 'My aquajet is now the least of our worries.'

Jack looked back to where he had been examining the diver. 'There is some more bad news. My aquajet's crushed under the rock. The propellor's sheared off.'

'We can both use mine, though it will double the drain on the battery. That is, if it starts. I think the shock wave of our explosion knocked it offline. I'm rebooting it now.'

Jack closed his eyes for a moment, and then looked back through the settling silt at the jumble of rock where the entrance had been. 'No more C5,' Jack said.

'No more C5,' Costas repeated. 'But you'd need a cruise missile to open up that entrance now.'

'What's your predicted oxygen timeout?'

'Two hours and fifty-five minutes, at my current breathing rate.'

Jack turned and stared down the tunnel. Two hours and fifty-five minutes, and at least five kilometres until the beginning of the Giza plateau, the point where the tunnel might rise above the waterline. There was no way they could make that distance, or even half of it, without the aquajet. The passage down the tunnel had been the biggest gamble of their plan, and the odds were now stacked dramatically against them. If Costas' aquajet failed to start, or if it ran out part-way along the tunnel, they would be doomed to an inevitable agonising countdown, able only to swim forward in desperation until exhaustion overtook them and their oxygen ran out. Jack stared into the constricting walls of the tunnel, at the black hole ahead. For the first time he felt a tightness in his chest, a pinprick of fear. They might not get out of here alive.

He swam over and grasped the right handle of the aquajet, and watched as Costas' finger hovered over the trigger in front of the left handle. Everything now depended on what happened next. For a moment they hung there motionless, side by side, the aquajet held in front of them, aimed down a tunnel that right now seemed more forbidding than any they had ever dived down before, with their survival even if they made it to the surface threatened by the apocalypse of biblical proportions that was now engulfing Egypt.

Costas pulled the trigger. Nothing happened. He pulled again, *Still nothing.* Jack stopped breathing. Costas held down the emergency start switch on top of the aquajet, and pulled the trigger again. Suddenly it whirred to life, and Costas gunned it a few times, moving them forward. He put it in neutral, and held it firmly in front. 'You ready for this?' he said. 'Prepare for the ride of your life.'

Jack took a deep breath. 'Time to go.'

21

Forty minutes later Costas eased off on the throttle of the aquajet and they slowed down to swimming speed, allowing Jack to relax his grip on the handle and focus more on the tunnel around them. The most telling feature so far had been a line of foot-sized indents carved into the side walls at intervals of about a metre, running the entire length of the tunnel from the outset. Jack had recognised them not from ancient parallels but from the Black Country in England, where he had once explored an underground canal from the time of the Industrial Revolution and seen where the barge-men had lain down and walked their vessels along the walls of the canal. The same had happened here, three thousand years earlier, only the Egyptians with their engineering exactitude had provided their bargemen with secure footing along the entire length of the canal. For Jack it was confirmation that this was indeed a passageway for boats to make their way between the Nile and the Giza plateau, with the Nile at low water lapping just below the level of the footings. The tunnel could have accommodated vessels up to three metres in beam and one and a half metres in draft, large enough for the type of river barges that plied the surface canals to the pyramids during their construction, hauled by teams of oxen and slaves plodding along the towpath just like those English canal boats of the 19th century that Jack had examined.

Costas reduced the speed by a further setting and Jack felt the wake wash forward, his legs dropping with the reduced momentum. He could see nothing but the receding darkness of the tunnel ahead, and he felt a niggle of unease again. 'Do we have a problem?'

'I'm trying to reduce the drain on the battery. We're not at critical yet, but it's showing the orange warning light.'

'What do you make our position?'

'In the absence of GPS reception down here we can only go by dead-reckoning. The tunnel has maintained a straight course almost exactly due west, bearing towards the southern end of the Giza complex in front of the Pyramid of Menkaure, just as Lanowski mapped it. And the aquajet's computer calculates a lapsed distance of four point three kilometres. That puts us a kilometre or so from the point where Lanowski thought the tunnel could break above the water level.'

'If the tunnel links to the complex we saw from beneath the pyramid, then it has to rise above water level,' Jack replied. 'The intensity of light we saw reflected through that shaft in the pyramid could only have come from mirrors set up in dry spaces, as refraction through water couldn't have produced anything so bright.'

'We have to hope that the other radiating arms on that map represent tunnels that are above water too. Otherwise we're dependent on finding an exit from the main complex, and if that means the shaft we saw from beneath the pyramid then we're going nowhere. The shaft had been filled with masonry so that the aperture for the light was a slit less than half a metre high. There's no way we're getting through that.'

'While you were in never-never land today on the felucca, Lanowski and I worked up a best-fit CGI for what might lie ahead of us. The plaque from the shipwreck, the one that shows the Aten symbol superimposed on the Giza plateau and the desert, had a total of eight arms radiating south-east to north-east towards the Nile, all of them extending out from the sun symbol that we imagine represents the central complex below the plateau. Our tunnel is the second arm from the bottom, the one running nearest to due east. We guessed that two of the other arms might also represent actual tunnels or canals, and not just be symbolic depictions. One of them must be the above-ground canal used during the months of the year when the Nile was in full spate, when the tunnel we're in would have been completely submerged and unusable. We think the above-water channel may well have been the canal already in existence from the time of the pyramid construction, adapted and perhaps strengthened by Akhenaten's engineers.'

'You mean the canal from the Nile to the artificial harbour that was dug in front of the pyramid, beside the mortuary temple.'

'Right', Jack replied. 'Each of the pyramids originally had one. All trace of the above-water canal from the Pyramid of

Menkaure has been lost beneath the southern suburbs of Cairo, but we think it's likely to be the next radiating line of the Aten symbol to the north of us, at an arc of thirty degrees from our tunnel and reaching the Nile about two kilometres north of our entry point. But it's the line above that one that interests us most. When Lanowski superimposed the depiction from the plaque on the modern map, keeping to the exact alignment of the pyramids, not only did our line end up exactly at the Napoleonic fort but the line two up from that, the one I'm talking about, abutted the river directly opposite Fustat, Old Cairo.'

'Which didn't exist in antiquity,' Costas said.

'Not as we see it now. But knowing about the masonry block with the Akhenaten cartouche found in 1892 by those Royal Engineers officers beside the synagogue confirms what Maurice has long suspected, that the other blocks of that date found in the medieval walls of Fustat were not all reused from Akhenaten's great temple at Heliopolis, to the north-east of Fustat, but included material from a structure whose remains lie beneath the boundaries of medieval Fustat itself. If you extend the Aten line across the river it points almost exactly to the site of the synagogue.'

'So you think all of these features from Akhenaten's building programme were interconnected – the Heliopolis temple, the structure under the synagogue and this complex in front of the pyramids.'

'The Egyptians were really into alignments, right? It's the kind of thing you can do in the desert over long distances, by line of sight. Maurice thinks that this was intimately tied up with worship of the sun, and that the Aten symbol with its very precise radiating lines suggests a particular fascination for Akhenaten himself. Maybe the passion for geometry that shows in the planning of his capital at Amarna should lead us to look for the same kind of grandiose conception here. With polished stone surfaces you can make the rays of the sun link together distant places, something that we might see in microcosm in the mirrors that we know must direct the light beneath the plateau. But Lanowski and I concluded that the line leading to Fustat may well represent another real tunnel, one likely to be above the flood level of the Nile so that it could be used all year round. The tunnel we're in now and the above-water canal were used mainly for barging in building materials and other goods, at low water and high water respectively. The tunnel from Fustat might have been some kind of processional way, for priests and even the pharaoh himself.'

'Whoah.' Costas put the aquajet in neutral and pointed to the wall on his side. A flight of narrow rock-cut steps led upwards to an aperture in the ceiling. 'That's exactly what I've been expecting,' he said. 'While you had your head down earlier as we were going at full throttle I saw several small dark openings in the ceiling that must once have been ventilation shafts, long ago blocked by sand and rockfall. This one looks more like a service entrance, something you'd expect partway along a tunnel of this length.' He released the handle of the aquajet and rose to the ceiling, poking his head into the hole. 'No good for us. It's completely filled with a jumble of rock.'

'You sure?'

'I wouldn't even want to try. Pulling out one of those rocks might create an instant rockfall and bury us.'

Jack stared at the steps, his mind racing. 'I'm thinking of our eleventh century caliph Al-Hakim. He disappears somewhere around this part of the desert, and then eight hundred years later Corporal Jones reappears after his own little adventure in this place wearing the ring that Howard Carter recognised as the signet of the caliph. Maybe Al-Hakim stumbled across this entrance, literally falling through it. I'm imagining him coming back here again and again, night after night, exploring ever further into the tunnel, able to do so because the Nile was at low water when he was out here. And then one night he finds something inside, something revelational, that makes him determined that his next visit will be his last one, that leads him to walk away from his day-job once and for all. So he leaves his bloody clothes elsewhere in the desert to suggest that he's been robbed and murdered, exactly the fate that those around him would have expected for a not very popular caliph wandering alone in the desert at night, and then he comes down here and finds a way of sealing himself inside by triggering a rockfall.'

'If he did that, he might have caused us another problem I've just spotted.'

'What do you mean?'

'Take a look ahead.'

Jack turned away from the steps and stared down the tunnel. He finned forward, and out of the darkness his beam began to reflect off irregular rock, quickly revealed as a fallen jumble that blocked the tunnel. It had been their unspoken fear from the outset. Costas powered ahead, leaving Jack with the aquajet, and came to a halt at the top of the pile where there was a visible crack between the rocks. Costas reached in his arms and pulled, dislodging a block and sliding it out under him. 'Watch out,' he exclaimed. The block slid down the pile to the floor, and was followed by several more as he dug his way deeper in. After a few minutes he pulled himself in entirely and disappeared, and then his headlamp beam reversed and shone back at Jack, momentarily dazzling him. 'Okay,' Costas said. 'If I can get through, then you should have no problem. But I can't take out anything more. Everything in the jumble below those blocks that I shifted is way too big even to budge.'

Jack swam up to the crack, leaving the aquajet to be pulled through afterwards, and eased his way into the hole. Costas was considerably bulkier than he was but surprisingly agile, and with his greater length Jack found it difficult to angle himself through the final part of the gap that Costas had created. Finally he was through, and he immediately turned round to retrieve the aquajet, reinserting himself in the crack and reaching for it. He caught hold of one of the handles and pulled it as far as he could, but it quickly became jammed. He pushed himself out and turned to Costas, who was hovering alongside. 'I can't get the aquajet through. There's absolutely no way. It's the shield around the propeller.'

Costas pulled himself in the hole to have a look, and he grunted and cursed as he tried every angle. He pushed himself out, breathing noisily. 'It was nearly out of juice anyway. It was probably only going to give us another five hundred metres or so.'

'We have another problem. I only noticed it when we slowed down.'

'You mean my leak?'

'It must have been caused by that rock fall that sealed us in at the entrance. There's a dent in your pack and a stream of bubbles from the manifold. I'd have to take the cover off to take a look.'

'Don't even try. It might just make it worse. My helmet display told me about it when it happened, but there was nothing I could do about it and I didn't see any point in mentioning it. With the aquajet online I calculated that I should still be able to make the likely length of the tunnel with oxygen to spare.'

'And now?'

'Twenty-five minutes of oxygen left. Almost a kilometre of tunnel. We're going to be buddy-breathing.'

Jack focused on their training. One of the safety features of the IMU rebreather was an inlet on the manifold that allowed a hose to be attached from another rebreather so that the oxygen supply could be shared. He stared at the manifold, looking for the outlet. He suddenly felt cold in the pit of his stomach. *It was gone.* He looked quickly around, but he knew he was not going to find it here. There was no way he could attach his hose into Costas' rebreather now, no way they could share gas. He dropped down alongside Costas, looking at him. 'We're not buddy-breathing. The inlet for the hose is gone. It must have been struck during the rockfall and popped off.'

Costas looked back at him, his face drawn. 'I've got my portable emergency bottle, and I can use yours. That's a further ten minutes each.'

'That means having to take off your helmet. Tell me when your carbon dioxide level reaches critical. I won't be able to help you if you've blacked out.'

'Roger that. Let's move.'

Costas powered ahead again, trailing bubbles behind him. Jack followed, watching his own oxygen consumption rise as he began to exert himself for the first time since entering the tunnel, finning hard to keep up. Suddenly everything they had talked about, the prospect of what might lie ahead, was blanked out of his mind, and all he could think about was the next few minutes. It felt horribly like the final countdown of a condemned man. He remembered four days earlier seeing Costas semi-conscious in the submersible as he reached it on his free-dive, and the huge relief when he had opened up the jammed air valve and seen his revived face at the door of the double-lock chamber. This time there could be no quick solution, no instant reprieve. Once the emergency air had run out there would be nothing Jack could do except watch Costas drown. If that happened his own life as he knew it would be over. Every second now counted.

After fifteen minutes Costas slowed down, his breathing hard and fast. 'Okay, Jack. Ten minutes of oxygen left on my readout.'

'Roger that. Less than five hundred metres to go now.' As they swam forward the tunnel ahead seemed to be surrounded by a golden glow, a ring of shining yellow that separated itself in the centre of the tunnel as they came closer. It was a huge torque of gold, shimmering in their headlamps, each arm ending at the top in a finial in the shape of a serpent's head. On either side of it the tunnel opened out and split into two parallel channels, separated by a row of rock-cut columns that extended from the golden ring as far as they could see. 'This is what we want,' Jack said, desperately hoping he was right.

'This is the beginning of a dock complex that would have allowed barges to arrive on one side while others waited on the opposite side for departure, ready to head back towards the Nile. The wharf can't be far ahead.'

'Snakes, Jack. I just can't get away from them. You remember the Red Sea?'

'I remember the image of those sea snakes you sent Maurice's boy. That made his day.'

'The sonar can see further ahead than our eyes, and I don't see anything yet.' Costas swam through the ring, and Jack followed him, brushing against the gold. If it was solid it was far larger than any golden object ever recovered in Egypt, an extraordinary testament to the wealth and vision of the pharaoh who had built this place. He followed Costas into the left-hand passage, still seeing nothing ahead to suggest a surface to the water. A few minutes on, Costas stopped finning and sank slowly to the floor of the tunnel. 'I've reached critical, Jack. I'm beginning to feel like I did in the submersible. A little dizzy and out of breath. I need you to get my helmet off now.'

Jack sank down beside him and saw Costas' blue-tinged lips through the visor, his eyes dulled. He unclipped the emergency air unit from the thigh pocket on Costas' right leg, a miniature cylinder about fifteen centimetres long with a mouthpiece in the middle, and twisted it to crack open the valve, pressing the purge button to test it and seeing a blast of bubbles. He put it in Costas' hand and then placed his own hands on the locking levers on either side of his helmet. 'The water's twelve degrees. You ready?'

Costas' voice sounded distant. 'You know, Jack, I could really do with one of those sandwiches now. Promise me you'll have them if I go. I can't bear to think of them wasted.'

'We'll have them together. A picnic on the beach. You ready?'

'I meant to say, Jack. About everything. You know. '

'I know. Me too. Keep focused.'

'Camera. Keep my camera. And my headlamp.'

Jack unlocked and snapped the unit off the top of Costas' helmet, and wrapped the straps around his wrist. 'Done.'

'Now, Jack. *Now.*'

Jack quickly snapped open the locking clamps, twisted the helmet and lifted it off, pushing it out of the way behind the backpack. Costas had shut his eyes tight against the shock of the water, but immediately put in the mouthpiece and took a breath. He reached down and took his spare mask out of his other thigh pocket, pressed it to his face, pulled the strap over the back of his head and cleared it, giving Jack the diver's okay signal as he did so. Jack remembered that they could no longer talk, that all he could do if the terrain-mapper showed signs of the surface ahead would be to gesture. He unclipped the straps of Costas' backpack and pushed it off, freeing him of the helmet and all encumbrances, and then took out his own emergency air and cracked it open, holding it ready to hand to Costas when the first one ran out. He had no idea what he would do then, when there was nothing more, when Costas began to breathe in water and convulse. He had seen it enough times to know that drowning was not the easy death that people imagined, but tormenting, horrible, like a slow hanging, the victim conscious for a few moments of terrible pain and sometimes taking minutes to die. He forced himself ahead, powering after Costas. All he could do now was hope.

A little over five minutes later Costas put up his right hand, still finning hard, and Jack put his emergency air into it. Costas sucked the last of his own, spat it out and put Jack's in, taking a deep breath and powering on ahead. At this rate of breathing he had only six, maybe seven minutes left. Still there was nothing on the terrain-mapper. Jack hardly dared glance at the timer on the readout inside his helmet. Five more minutes had gone. There could be less than two minutes left. His heart began to pound, his mouth dry. *This was not happening*.

And then he saw it. Fifty, maybe sixty metres ahead, the tunnel seemed to slope up. A few moments later he was absolutely sure of it. He finned as hard as he could, drawing parallel with Costas and turning to him, gesturing forward with a sloping motion with one hand and opening all five fingers of the other to show the distance. Then he realised that he was no longer seeing exhaust bubbles; Costas had taken his last breath. He spat out the mouthpiece and put his head down, swimming as fast as he could. They were so close now that Jack readied himself to pull Costas along if he became unconscious, knowing that there might be a glimmer of hope that he could be saved if he could pull him to the surface in time.

Then, miraculously, he saw the unmistakable glimmer of surface water in his beam, and seconds later they exploded through, Costas gasping and coughing, floating on his back and breathing heavily. Jack panned his beam around, seeing a slope leading up to some kind of entranceway, and beside them a wharf that surrounded the end of the channel, evidently the ancient dock. He glanced at the external sensor array to check the air quality, and then unlocked and wrenched off his helmet, relishing the cool air on his face and taking a few deep breaths. He turned to Costas. 'You okay?'

Costas was still floating on his back, his arms and legs outstretched. 'Okay,' he said, his breathing becoming normal. 'But hungry. *Really* hungry.'

Jack sniffed the air tentatively. 'Extraordinary smell,' he said.

Costas heaved himself over and hauled himself partway up the slope. 'That, my friend, is the smell of ancient Egypt. And from where I am, it smells good. *Very* good.'

'Interesting,' Jack said, peering back inside his helmet. 'My readout shows a slightly lower than normal oxygen content.'

'We only know of one open ventilation point, the shaft under the pyramid where the light got through. And we don't know yet whether that links to this tunnel.'

'I smell jasmine, thyme, acacia. Almost a hint of incense, and a definite odour of organic decay.'

'Must be something recent,' Costas said, struggling out of his fins. 'Rats, maybe. This is a good place for rats.'

'Rats and little fish in the canal. That's what Jones survived on. When he wasn't eating mummies.'

'No way. You don't know that.'

'That's what Howard Carter's diary entry said. After weeks down here Jones was desperate, and opened up some coffins. It must have been like eating desiccated old wasps' nests. With eyes and teeth.'

'Don't, Jack. Just as I was about to have lunch.'

'It's midnight. And we didn't bring a picnic.'

Costas patted the bulge in the front of his boiler suit. 'Oh yes we did.'

'You didn't *really* bring sandwiches.'

'What do you think I was doing while I was waiting for you to come from Jerusalem? Took over the entire galley on *Sea Venture*. Brought my own ingredients, airfreighted out from my favourite deli in Manhattan. The one I always tell you I'm going to take you to one day. Gino's, where you can get a haircut and a shave while you wait. You'd think you'd gone to heaven.'

'Okay,' Jack said, grinning and helping Costas to his feet. 'We'll have lunch. But let's find a way out of this place first, right? Otherwise we might be rationing your very special sandwiches over a very long time, and looking for alternative food sources. Okay?'

A little fish flapped out of the water where it lapped at the edge, slimy looking and with bulging eyes, the only other living thing they had seen since leaving the Nile. Costas contemplated it with a distasteful look on his face, and then edged it back in with his foot. 'I don't like the sound of that at all,' he said. 'Not *at all*.'

'You need more rest?'

Costas shook his head, checking the waist strap on his boiler suit and easing the constriction of the E-suit on his neck. 'Let's get this show on the road.'

Jack stared up the slope. 'Roger that.'

22

Jack eased off his rebreather backpack and laid it with his helmet on the sloping floor, having first removed the head-lamp console and handed Costas back his. There were still over two hours of breathing time left in his cylinder, but with Costas on empty and no way of buddy-breathing he was not going to carry on alone if they came to another underwater passage; after what had just nearly happened to Costas and Jack's reaction to it, they were either getting out of here together or not at all. They both unwound the straps from the back of the lamp consoles and put them on their heads, first checking that the integrated miniature video cameras were still recording. With the backpack air-conditioning unit removed the E-suits might become uncomfortably warm, but at the moment that was better than being chilled and the Kevlar would afford protection against bumps and scrapes along the way. Whatever lay in store now, Jack knew it was unlikely to be an easy walk through, and being in a breathable environment did not mean that an escape tunnel out towards Cairo somewhere ahead was still anything more than a shaky hypothesis.

Costas detached the hose from the hydration pack on the left side of his E-suit and took a deep draw on it, patting his boiler suit as he did so to check that everything was there and still in place. He paused for a moment and then delved deep into the front pocket, removed a watertight bag, unzipped it and took a huge bite from the sandwich inside, munching noisily and swallowing as he replaced the bag. 'It was going to be my dying thought, and now it's my kiss of life. Thank you, Gino.' He took another mouthful of water and then stowed the tube, panning his headlamp beam over the top of the ramp. 'You think that's the way to go?'

'We don't have any choice,' Jack replied. 'There's an identical ramp at the end of the channel parallel to us, just visible through the columns, but it joins up to the single passageway ahead. My guess is that it will lead first to some kind of boat stowage facility, probably linked to the artificial harbour that we know was associated with the Old Kingdom mortuary temple. The space we saw lit up from beneath the pyramid three months ago lies somewhere between the edge of the pyramid and the harbour site, and we have to hope there will be some kind of entrance to it ahead.'

Costas nodded, heaving himself upright. 'If it had been daytime, we might have seen reflected light coming through those shafts leading from the pyramid. I assume that's what allowed the caliph Al-Hakim and then Corporal Jones to see their way around this place. As it is, there isn't even a moon tonight.'

Jack stared ahead, reciting. '"Omens of fire in the chariot's wind, pillars of fire in thunder and storm."'

'Come again?'

'Something I remembered when I mentioned our chariot discovery in the Red Sea to you a few minutes ago. When I told Maria about our discovery she quoted those lines to me, from another of the medieval Geniza poets, Yannai. His imagery comes from the Book of Exodus.'

'The burning bush, the mountain on fire,' Costas replied. 'I had to learn all that stuff backwards when I was a boy. I used to think ancient Egypt was a vision of hell.'

'It's not just ancient Egypt now. You should have seen Cairo when we came through it this evening on the felucca.'

'Are you thinking of the pyramids? That CNN footage we saw in Alexandria?'

Jack nodded. 'You're right that we won't be seeing sunlight down here. But we may see another kind of light reflected in those mirrors. Akhenaten's City of Light won't be illuminated by the rays of the Aten, but it might be lit up by something he would have thought unimaginable, by fires that may as well be drawn straight from the biblical image of hell. The reflection from a burning pyramid is not a waymarker any archaeologist would wish to follow, but if it is there it might be all we've got to go on. Let's move.'

The ramp sloped up at an angle of about thirty degrees until it reached a platform some five metres above the level of the water. From there it became a rectilinear tunnel about four metres across and three metres high, wide enough for the two of them to proceed side by side. Jack paused to adjust the angle of his camera while Costas carried on ahead, his beam reflecting off the polished veneer of granite that lined the lower part of the walls. About ten metres ahead Costas stopped and peered closely at the side of the tunnel, then he pressed his hands against it.

'Jack, this is interesting. It's been plastered over. It's—'

There was a sudden bellow and the sound of collapsing masonry, and Costas was gone. Jack stared aghast and quickly made his way forward. Where Costas had been standing was a jagged hole about the size of a small door. He approached it and leaned forward into the chamber that had been revealed. That air inside was dry, aromatic, and made his eyes smart. He blinked hard, coughed and then saw Costas' headlamp beam coming from somewhere below, apparently stationary and at an odd angle. For an instant Jack had a yawning feeling of fear. They had basic medical kits inside their E-suits but nothing to treat major trauma other than blood coagulants and shell dressings. If Costas was seriously injured, there was little he could do for him and no way of calling in help.

He pulled himself carefully through the hole, and peered below, his heart pounding. 'Costas, are you all right? Talk to me.'

There was no response, and Jack held his breath. Then the beam from below shifted slightly, and he heard a grunt and a mumbled curse. 'Fascinating,' Costas said. His voice sounded impossibly distant, as if coming from deep inside a chasm.

'What's fascinating? Are you all right?'

'Never seen anything quite like it. Sewn joinery, each timber individually shaped. Amazing technology.'

Jack stared out beyond Costas and gasped as he realised

what he was looking at. It was a huge rock-cut chamber, at least ten metres across, the size of a giant water cistern. At the bottom was a mass of timber, disarticulated and carefully laid out. Costas' beam was coming from beneath a section of stacked planking close to the corner of the chamber beneath him, and Jack watched as he began to extricate himself. He looked up, shading his eyes against Jack's beam, his face white with plaster dust. 'What do you make of it, Jack? A nautical archaeologist's dream, or what?'

'It's fantastic,' Jack enthused. 'The chamber must have been airtight before you broke through, preserving all of those timbers like that. There's another of these boat pits still unopened in front of the Great Pyramid, known as a result of archaeologists pushing a fibre-optic camera down into it. Unless I'm mistaken, you've just fallen into the dismantled funerary barge of the Pharaoh Menkaure, the boat that took his body down the canal from the river to the harbour and the funerary temple. And you're right, the joinery is sewn planking. Actually an incredibly robust technique that could produce a hull well up to sea travel, though this is a ceremonial riverboat. You can make out the raking stem and stern timbers, the oars, the fine woodwork of the deck house. Amazing.'

Costas made his way across to the far side of the chamber as Jack was talking, carefully avoiding causing more damage to the timbers. Jack could see that he was heading towards another aperture in the wall, and he watched him crouch down and crawl in, until only his feet were visible. There was another sound of collapsing masonry, a small cloud of dust and then silence, followed by violent coughing. A few moments later his face reappeared, and he beckoned. 'Jack, you really need to see this.'

Jack stepped through the jagged hole and peered over the side. It was about three metres to the chamber floor, and he did not want to risk a broken limb. He stared across. 'Is it *really* good?'

'Really good, Jack. You're not leaving without seeing this. Trust me.'

'All right. I'm on my way.' He found a lip of rock, jammed his fingers into it and swung out over the edge, lowering himself until he was hanging above the floor. He looked for a landing point and then let himself go, falling into the dust and narrowly missing the edge of the pile of planks. He got up, flexed his legs and then stepped over the wood towards Costas, who had backed out of the hole to give Jack space to get through.

'It's another chamber,' Costas said. 'At least twice as big as this one. Prepare to be amazed.'

Jack ducked down and crawled in, trying not to scrape his back against the top of the hole. His headlamp beam caught timbers, the joinery visible; they were clearly more boat elements. He pulled himself out and squatted on the floor of the chamber, moving aside to let Costas follow, and aimed his beam upwards for a better view.

An astonishing sight met his eyes. Instead of dismembered timbers it was an intact vessel, the flush planks of its bows only inches from his face. He reached out and touched it, feeling a frisson of excitement. The timbers were covered with pitch, and as Jack eased forward he knocked a pot on the floor that contained a congealed black mass, presumably the source of the material. He shifted to the left, and saw a pile of planks and a bronze adze beside a section of the hull that was evidently being repaired, the edges of the timbers showing where they had been sewn together with some form of cord as well as joined with wooden mortise and tenon joints. Jack stood up carefully, raising himself until his head was just above the gunwale, and panned his beam over the entire vessel.

'See what I mean?' Costas said, standing beside him. 'Looks like old Menkaure took a whole fleet with him to the afterlife.'

Jack shook his head. 'This isn't Menkaure. This vessel is characteristically Late Bronze Age, dating more than a thousand years later. And it's not a river barge. This is a full-blown seagoing ship.'

'No kidding.' Costas stood on a stone block beside Jack, allowing him to see in at Jack's level. 'My God. I see what you mean. Deck house at the back rather than the centre, wide beam, deck planking. And that's a mast, stepped down, and stern steering oars. A cargo ship?'

'Do you remember first seeing the timbers of our Minoan wreck off the north coast of Crete ten years ago, where we were excavating when Maurice found the Atlantis papyrus? It's taken most of the last decade to conserve and record the timbers, but I reviewed the final report just before coming out here. This boat is astonishingly similar, in almost every detail. This isn't an Egyptian ship. It's a Minoan ship, or at least one built to Aegean specifications or by a Minoan shipwright.'

'How do you know the date?'

'See the row of empty jars in the hold?'

Costas peered over. 'Aha. Early amphoras. Like on our Minoan wreck.'

'Canaanite jars,' Jack said. 'Second half of the second millennium BC, fifteenth, maybe fourteenth century BC. And I can see a so-called pilgrim flask beside the deck house, a typical Aegean pottery oil container you see on Egyptian wall paintings depicting trade with Aegean merchants.'

Costas stepped off the block and eased his way around Jack, coming to the prow of the hull. 'Take a look at this. It's got an evil eye.'

Jack dropped down and moved alongside Costas, then stepped back against the wall for a better view. 'Well, I'll be damned,' he exclaimed. 'That clinches it. Fantastic.'

'Talk to me, Jack.'

'Look closely. That's not an evil eye. It's the Aten, the sun-symbol. If you look really closely you can see it's even got the radiating lines, etched into the planks.'

'Akhenaten?'

'It could only be. It's the first certain evidence we've had of him since that hieroglyphic cartouche at the entrance to the tunnel on the Nile.'

'What's the Aegean connection?'

'You remember Maurice showing us the Aegean mercenaries he identified on the tomb painting from the mummy necropolis?'

'Who could forget it. The bare-breasted amazons.'

'Well, I think that dynastic marriage in the fifteenth century BC with a Minoan queen brought the Egyptians more than just a ready army of mercenaries. One of the few technologies the Egyptians lacked was seagoing ships, apart from vessels used on the Red Sea that look more like strengthened river craft.'

'Was this a war harbour?' Costas suggested. 'A secret naval base?'

'I don't think so,' Jack murmured. 'Not exactly. These aren't warships; they're not galleys. They're also not deep-bellied merchantmen. They're more like passenger transport vessels, definitely designed for deep-sea sailing with room for plenty of provisions.'

'Ships of exploration?' Costas suggested.

Jack stared, his mind racing. *It was possible*. 'This boat looks as if it was abandoned hastily in the middle of a refit, with tools still left lying around.'

Costas had moved out of sight beyond the prow. 'Take a look around the corner, Jack. There's an empty berth, and in front of it a ramp leading down to where we think the artificial harbour must have abutted this part of the plateau, the exit now completely sealed in.'

Jack followed him through and stared at the open space, at the wooden formers that looked as if they had been hastily cast aside. He shook his head, astonished. 'One pharaoh goes in dead, another one comes out alive.'

'What are you saying?'

'Just another hypothesis. A best-fit scenario. We know that Menkaure came here dead, probably already embalmed, ready for the rituals of the mortuary temple and then interment in his sarcophagus in the pyramid. What we don't know yet for sure is how this place figured in Akhenaten's journey over a thousand years later. Nobody has ever conclusively identified his tomb or his mummy. One possibility is that he may be buried here, and that was what all this underground construction was really all about, but my instinct says no. I see this, whatever he built here under the plateau, his City of Light, as something that he saw through to completion, and then sealed up before departing.'

'Maybe he mocked it up for any suspicious observers as if he were constructing a funerary complex, a pretty normal thing for a pharaoh to do, when in reality he was planning to do a runner,' Costas suggested. 'Maybe that was his final opt-out. Come up here as if dead, in a funerary barge like the pharaohs of old, but instead of going to the afterlife he leaves very much alive, on a vessel equipped for a long sea voyage.'

'It's possible. The ship that's still here was abandoned in the middle of refitting, as if it too had been intended for departure but there was no time to make both vessels ready. Akhenaten must have known his life was in danger, a man like the caliph Al-Hakim who had done beneficent things, had perhaps endowed some kind of library or seminary at this spot, but who had made mortal enemies in the old priesthood for his desecration of their temples and banning of their rituals. Maybe departure was his only option once he had achieved his ambitions and seen the Israelites safely resettled in Canaan.'

'Have you voiced this idea to Maurice?'

'He says that for a man who founded a new religion, created a new capital city and seems to have engineered the destruction of his entire chariot army to let the Israelites escape, anything is possible. Akhenaten was ancient Egypt's wild card.'

'Just as long as he took Nefertiti with him too.'

Jack looked at the ship again, making sure his camera took

in as much as it could of the astonishing sights around him; it was as if they had walked into an ancient Egyptian shipyard while the workers were out on a lunch break. He turned back to Costas. 'Okay. *Definitely* worth it. Where do we go from here?'

Costas jerked his head back the way they had come. 'The passageway from the wharf carried on beyond the point where I broke through into these chambers. There might once have been entrances from these sheds into a complex under the plateau, but if so they've been sealed up. We could spend hours sounding out the plaster on the walls and not find them. Every entrance seems to have been sealed up, as if this whole place had been mothballed. That might fit in with your theory.'

Jack followed Costas back through the ship chambers and clambered up the jumble of fallen masonry where they had entered, heaving Costas up on his shoulders and then straining as he took Costas' outstretched arm and hauled himself into the passageway. He suddenly felt exhausted and woozy, as if he had experienced a rapid loss of blood pressure, and he leaned against the wall of the passageway, taking a drink from his hydration pack. He realised that he had not drunk anything since they had passed through Cairo, and he made a mental note to keep hydrated. He pushed off and followed, his unsteadiness having passed. Ahead beyond the western limit of the boat chambers he could see Costas' beam waver, and then stop. As he neared he could see that the passageway had ended, carrying on only as an aperture at head level about half a metre high and a metre wide that extended into the darkness as far as their beams could penetrate. He remembered three months before, staring down a similar slit from under the pyramid, looking in exactly the opposite direction to their position now. Somewhere between the two was the space that had been lit up so brilliantly by the light that had come down through the pyramid. He refused to think that that was the end of the road, that what they had seen was no more than a reflection from further tunnels and ventilation shafts. What they had found already had been extraordinary, but there had to be more, a central hub to the radiating passageways indicated on the plaque, something set further back under the plateau directly ahead of them now.

'Are you thinking what I'm thinking?' Costas said.

'I'm thinking that if there's another chamber ahead, it must have been accessible from this tunnel if it was used to bring in building materials and workers. But maybe once the work was completed this tunnel was shut off except for this aperture, with the entrance to the chamber then becoming the hypothetical processional way that we think might be represented by that other arm of the Aten heading towards Fustat.'

'You mean our hypothetical egress tunnel.' Costas crouched down at the corner of the tunnel, peering closely at the gaps where the slabs of granite abutted each other. 'You're right, Jack. Under the veneer I can see the edges of blocks of masonry. The Egyptians were past masters at this, weren't they? Creating burial chambers and then devising ingenious ways of blocking them off to deter tomb robbers. Look at all those obstructions that Colonel Vyse had to blow his way through to reach the sarcophagus in the Pyramid of Menkaure. Somebody was doing the same kind of thing here.'

'Only I don't think what lies beyond here was a burial chamber.'

'Maybe not. But I have a horrible feeling that there's one right here.'

'What do you mean?'

'Beside the floor, Jack. Look down to where I am. There's a really bad smell coming from it.'

Jack followed Costas' gaze and knelt in front of an irregular hole that looked as if it had been punched through a plastered space between two slabs of granite. He saw something, reached in and gingerly pulled it out, holding it under his beam. It was a human hand, a very old human hand, mummified and nearly skeletal. He held it out to Costas. 'Ever wanted to shake hands with a mummy?'

'I knew it. We weren't going to go underground in Egypt without finding mummies. No way.'

'I think we might just have found Corporal Jones' larder.' Jack carefully replaced the hand, took a deep breath and poked his head partway into the hole, panning his beam around and revealing a carved-out annex the size of a small bedroom. It was a charnel house, filled with a mass of disarticulated mummies and mummy parts, bedded down in a great mass of feathery material that looked like pieces of mummy wrapping and shredded human skin. He looked for anything diagnostic, and then saw a fragment of wooden coffin casing, its edges gnawed away but part of the painting and hieroglyphs on the surface just visible. He pulled his head out and sat back against the wall of the tunnel, gasping for breath, his eyes smarting from the dust.

'Well?' Costas said. 'Is there a passageway?'

Jack shook his head, and coughed. 'What we've got in there,' he said, 'is a giant rat's nest.'

'Not caused by Corporal Jones after all?'

Jack nodded, coughing again. 'Him too. I'm sure of it. I think he took his cue from the rats. They must have gnawed out a small entrance from this passage, and Jones in his desperate hunt for food must have seen it and enlarged it. There's more damage in there than rats could cause, and more bits missing. Originally that chamber was stuffed full of intact mummies, but they're not from the time of Akhenaten. The one fragment of decorated coffin I saw was definitely Old Kingdom, almost certainly from the time of Menkaure. What I think we've got here is a secondary burial, mummies probably of viziers and minor officials involved in the construction of the pyramid, cleared out of their tombs by Akhenaten's workmen to make way for something bigger. It makes sense that the original tombs should have been under the plateau in front of the pyramid, and if they were removed and maybe extended to make a larger chamber then that's a promising sign.'

'If we could get through.' Costas eased himself up, looking back distastefully at the hole where the withered nails of the hand were poking out. Jack followed suit, and they both peered down the aperture at the end of the tunnel.

'It could be done,' Jack said after a moment. 'Al-Hakim and Jones must have crawled down there, as we haven't seen any way ahead other than this.'

'I know what would have drawn them on,' Costas said. 'I think this was a light shaft, like the one under the pyramid. Even at night if there was a moon they would have seen some light ahead, enough to tempt them to try their luck at getting through. After all, by this stage if they were trapped down here they wouldn't have had anything to lose.' He glanced back again at the hand. 'Other than Jones, leaving his mummy larder behind.'

'Do we risk it, or double-check for entrances elsewhere?'

'We could do a recce.'

'What do you mean?'

A chirping sound came from the bulge in the front of Costas' boiler suit, and then it moved. Jack jumped back, startled, but then he relaxed slightly, shaking his head. 'You brought along a little friend, didn't you?'

Costas unzipped the top of his boiler suit and a little mechanical eye on a stalk peered out, followed by two miniature robotic hands that slowly reached up and grasped the edges of the suit. 'I couldn't leave Little Joey behind, could I?' Costas said, gently stroking the neck behind the eye. 'Not after Big Joey had all the fun at the wreck site.'

'I worry about you sometimes. Aysha thinks you'd be a great dad, to living, sentient human beings.'

Little Joey seemed to bristle, and cocked his eye at Jack. 'Careful what you say,' Costas said. 'He's very sensitive.' He reached in and took the robot out, placing it on the ledge at the beginning of the aperture and then pulled out a radio control unit and strap-on virtual goggles. 'He's programmed to be reactive to his environment, and because of what we tend to do I've made him fully sensitised to tunnels and the kind of archaeological features we've encountered in the past. He's like a robotic tomb raider. I'll send him down that tunnel now and he'll stop and report back anything unusual.'

'How does he do that?'

'He'll tell us. You'll see.' Costas reached under the tail of the robot and activated a switch. Like its larger counterpart, Little Joey was shaped like a scorpion, with four legs on either side, the single eye on its stalk and two flexible arms, only it was no bigger than a large rat. Costas lifted it and aimed it down the tunnel, but it leapt up, assumed its original sideways position, looked back at Costas and then leapt round again, aiming itself down the tunnel. 'He's very independent,' Costas said, shaking his head. 'Doesn't like to be shown what to do. Always has to try it himself first.'

'Just like children,' Jack said thoughtfully. 'That's what you'd discover if you had them. Like a certain teenager we know.'

Little Joey suddenly scurried off down the aperture, his lights showing as pinpricks in the darkness, and came to a halt perhaps ten metres ahead.

'Dead end?' Jack asked.

Costas hunched over the radio. 'It means he's seen something, but we won't know until I've booted the system up and he can react. Once that's done I'll be able to put on the goggles and see what he sees. It'll take a few minutes.' Costas stood back, took a deep breath and wiped the back of his hand over his face, blinking hard.

'You okay?' Jack said.

'Beginning to feel the effect. Nothing serious, yet.'

'What do you mean?'

'Some basic science, Jack. Those extremists at the pyramid were spraying it with some kind of fuel, right? We saw those tanker trucks on the CNN report. It must have been a pretty well-planned operation.'

'They've been threatening it for years. Nothing about this coup is spur of the moment. They're taking up where the Mahdi left off in 1885.'

'Well, spraying fuel and igniting it is how you get a stone building to look as if it's burning. The biblical burning bush is thought to have been based on something similar in appearance, where in some conditions the gas exuding from certain desert species could be ignited to give the appearance of a bush wreathed in flame, but not actually burning. Some of that fuel is likely to have entered the pyramid through the shafts that were used to bring light to this underground complex. The fuel will be burnt out long before it reaches us, but that's not the problem. The problem is what I experienced first hand during that terrorist strike on my destroyer in the Gulf, when I was trapped by fire below decks in the engine room before I managed to escape and help with the rescue.'

'Fire consumes oxygen,' Jack murmured. 'I think I see what you're getting at.'

'You remember the low oxygen readout you noticed after we surfaced? Ever since then when I've exerted myself I've felt a little lightheaded. I put it down to the residual effect of carbon dioxide build-up during my final minutes on the rebreather, but this is a better explanation.'

Jack nodded. 'That's reassuring. I felt it a few minutes ago. I nearly blacked out.'

'Reassuring, but not. They'll be jetting fuel continuously at the pyramid to maintain the spectacle, and that means more fuel getting down those shafts. With the outer surface of the pyramid wreathed in fire, the only way the burning fuel inside can feed its flames is by sucking up the oxygen from inside the pyramid, from the shaft, from the burial chamber, from the well we went down three months ago, and ultimately from every connected part of this underground complex. Slowly, but surely, we're being starved of oxygen.'

'How long, do you think?'

'Two or three hours, probably. Maybe less.'

'Well, we weren't planning on lingering. If we're in here much longer than that we'll never make our rendezvous with the felucca before dawn.'

'At least it means if we do get stuck down here we won't be around long enough to have to eat mummies.'

Jack gave Costas a wan look. 'I for one do not intend to suffocate because of some deranged extremist.'

'Amen to that. Let's just hope Little Joey can save the day.'

They were interrupted by a chirping sound from down the aperture. Jack angled his headlamp beam and peered down. The robot was shaking and waving its arms, the eye looking back at them and then at the wall in front. 'Something seems to be wrong,' he said. 'Looks like a malfunction.'

Costas stared incredulously at Jack. 'Malfunction? Little Joey? No way. He's just excited. It means he really has found something. It shows that the system is coming online.' He picked up the mask, trying it on and then removing it. 'About a minute more, and then I can actually *be* Little Joey, real time. Lanowski calls it a mind-meld.'

Jack continued staring at the chirping and chattering apparition that was caught in his beam. 'Is he really agitated? I mean, you must have programmed this.'

'It's like a smoke alarm. He's programmed to respond if he finds what I've asked him to look for. But he really *has* been acting like a wilful teenager recently. You think you've got problems with Rebecca. I left Lanowski alone with him in the engineering lab for half an hour a few weeks ago, and he hasn't been the same since.'

'It's stopped,' Jack said.

Costas put on the mask. 'Eureka,' he murmured, manipulating the controls. 'I'm looking through his eye, Jack. The shaft goes off to the right and there it is, a very suffused red glow.'

Jack's heart began to pound with excitement. 'Can you get up to it?'

'I'm getting there now. About a metre to go. Okay. Looking out over a big room, circular, maybe twenty metres across. Recesses around the edge, filled with jars. Holy cow. *Holy cow.*'

Jack could barely contain himself. He wanted to be there, to be where Costas was. Jars like that were exactly what Jones had described to Howard Carter. 'What is it? What can you see?'

Costas seemed to be transfixed, his hand motionless on the control lever and his mouth wide open. He slowly let go of the control and took off the mask, his eyes staring into space, and then turned to Jack. 'You remember those first ever pictures of King Tut's tomb? You're not going to believe what I've just seen.'

23

Jack pushed ahead with his feet through the shaft, using his elbows and hands to pull himself along, inching towards the halogen beam from Little Joey some five metres away where the shaft angled sharply to the right. The image he had seen from the robot's camera confirmed beyond doubt what lay around the corner, yet Jack refused to register it until he saw it with his own eyes. He could hear Costas grunting and cursing where he had climbed in behind from the tunnel, his frame barely fitting into the shaft. They knew that they must be following in the path of Corporal Jones, and almost certainly the caliph Al-Hakim before that, taking the only passage left open when the ship sheds and the entrance tunnel had been blocked up in antiquity, crawling along a shaft that was part of the extraordinary network cut through the rock to reflect sunlight into the underground complex.

Jack paused, his breathing fast and shallow, remembering

that the oxygen level would by now be seriously depleted, that he was not in the first stages of a panic attack. The turn in the shaft was only a few metres ahead, and he watched as Little Joey used a miniature air jet to blow dust from a black basalt slab angled at forty-five degrees in the corner of the shaft, polished to a glassy sheen and clearly intended as a mirror. Jack shut his eyes until the dust settled and then he saw it, the same extraordinary image they had seen through Little Joey's eye a few minutes before, a glow of red as if he were looking through a slit into a furnace. His heart began to pound with excitement. He had dreamed of this for months, and now, incredibly, it was just within his reach, something that had seemed virtually impossible only a few days before.

Moments later he was round the corner pulling himself to the edge of the aperture overlooking the chamber. Little Joey clattered ahead and perched on the rim, chirping and shaking. The shaft had widened enough to allow Costas to heave himself alongside, his E-suit smeared with grime. As they panned their lights ahead an astonishing scene met their eyes. They were on the edge of a huge circular space, perhaps twenty metres across and eight metres high where it rose to an apex. On the floor below the apex was an elevated dais capped by a rectangular altar or sarcophagus, its top above their line of vision. From the dais radiating outwards on the floor were raised ridges terminating in carved hands, the unmistakable sign of the Aten, the sun-symbol of Akhenaten. One of the arms pointed directly to the shaft they had come through and another to a second shaft visible to the left, coming from the direction of the pyramid. Costas gestured at it, his voice hushed.

'That shaft must be the one we were looking through three months ago from beneath the pyramid. You can see the light from the fire shining through and reflecting off basalt mirrors around the walls. In daylight the reflection back would be dazzling, exactly as we saw it.'

'The light of the Aten, concentrated on this one spot,' Jack said. 'It's an incredible feat of precision, ancient Egyptian engineering at its best. Maurice would love it.'

Costas pointed to the opposite wall of the chamber. 'That's what we want to see, Jack. One of the arms, the longest one, is pointing to an open tunnel. Another one's pointing to the wall just to the right of us that must lead to the ship sheds. You can see an area of plaster, clearly different from the polished rock veneer, and I bet that's where the entrance remains sealed up. The entrance to the open tunnel looks as if it was once plastered over as well, and was broken into relatively recently.'

'Corporal Jones?' Jack suggested.

'He was a sapper, right? He would have had an eye for constructional detail. He would have been looking for a way out, just as we are. That is, when he wasn't living in a twilight world of his own, crawling around here like the undead looking for tasty snacks. This place would have been pretty eerie at night with only moonlight reflecting through, enough to unhinge someone already halfway there and weak with hunger. It's spooky enough in this light.'

'What's your take on the orientation of that open tunnel?'

'It's heading towards Cairo. It almost certainly corresponds to that line on the plan leading to Fustat. And it's clearly above water level, a dry channel. It could be our ticket out.'

'If it's not blocked by rockfalls.'

'Only one way to find out.'

'I need some time in here, Costas. We need to get as much as we can on video.'

'Thirty minutes, maximum. I can actually feel the air being sucked up that shaft by the fires on the pyramid. If we leave it longer than that we won't have the energy to get far enough down that tunnel to get out, and then we end up in a terminal countdown.'

Little Joey chirped and sighed, almost an electronic moan, and the eye peered dolefully at Costas. 'I know,' he said, stroking its neck. 'Good boy. *Very* good boy.' He pressed something beneath the carapace, and Little Joey jumped slightly, and then settled down and purred. 'I can't give him a biscuit, but I can give him an electronic buzz. It means he'll go to sleep happy. He might be holding the fort here for some time.'

Jack slithered round until his feet were hanging over the edge, and slowly lowered himself to the floor. 'Okay,' he said. 'Thirty minutes. Keep your camera rolling.'

'Roger that.'

As Jack hit the floor he felt for his head camera, making sure it was at the right angle to catch everything he saw. He knew what he wanted to look at. It was what had set his pulse racing when he had heard Jeremy read Howard Carter's account of what Corporal Jones had seen, and then a few minutes ago when he had looked at the video image relayed from Little Joey. It was what had been sitting in Hiebermeyer's desk for all those years since he had found it in the excavation beside the plateau, the hieroglyphs that hinted at the truth behind Akhenaten's City of Light. Jack glanced around the chamber. Akhenaten's treasure was not to be another Tutankhamun's tomb, not another trove of gold and jewels and precious artefacts. It was the greatest treasure of all. *It was a treasure in words.*

Costas dropped behind him and they slowly proceeded along the wall. At intervals of about five metres the rock had been carved into alcoves like the burial niches he had seen in Jerusalem with Rebecca, only here they were not designed for bodies. Each niche was filled with dozens of tall pottery jars, more than a metre high, almost all of them lidded and sealed with a mass of black resinous material. Those that were not lidded had been smashed open, their contents strewn over the floor, visible in front of three of the twelve alcoves that Jack had counted around the chamber. He squatted in front of the first and picked up a handful of material strewn among the pottery sherds, fragments of papyrus that crumbled to dust as he touched them. Costas thrust his hand deep into the base of one of the smashed jars still remaining in the alcove and came up with a handful of the same material. 'My best guess?' he said, letting it drop between his fingers. 'Corporal Jones, looking for food. He gave up at the third alcove once he realised that the contents were inedible.'

'What was inside,' Jack murmured, staring at the shreds in his hands, 'was papyrus scrolls. This place is a library.' He got up and did some swift arithmetic. 'If there are twelve alcoves containing thirty jars each, and each jar contains four or five scrolls, that's the best part of two thousand scrolls. That's way more than you'd expect for a collection of religious tracts and Books of the Dead.'

'Check out the pots,' Costas said. 'They've all got symbols on them painted in black. The pots in each alcove have the same principal symbol, but then above that each pot has a unique additional symbol. From my memory of Lanowski's attempt to teach me hieroglyphics, those upper symbols are numbers. So this must be some kind of cataloguing system.'

Jack brushed the dust from the symbols on one pot and then moved to the next alcove, doing the same. 'You're right. Each alcove has an individual hieroglyph: a sheaf of corn in the first, a seated bird in this one, a half-moon in the next one along. I think they're signifiers like our letters of the alphabet, part of the cataloguing system.'

'Sheaf of corn means religion, squatting bird mean science, half-moon means medicine?' Costas said. 'Something like that?'

Jack nodded, suddenly overwhelmed by the enormity of what they were confronting. 'Imagine what those could contain.'

'You know we can't risk opening them, Jack. We have nowhere to take them, and they might just crumble to dust on contact with the air. Our job now is to see to it that this place remains secret until we can get back here with the biggest manuscript conservation team Maria and Jeremy have ever assembled. Meanwhile our clock is ticking. I'm going to check out that dais in the centre.'

Jack turned back to the pots, putting his hand on one of them, struggling to contain his emotions. Costas was right, of course. It would be grossly irresponsible to tamper with them now. If there were huge secrets of science and medicine, the cures to diseases, then they could be lost in an instant; far better to leave them here in the hope that a return would be possible. But it went against his grain as an archaeologist not to at least see some writing, to record it with their cameras. Not to do so, to leave empty-handed, would be to leave something unsatisfied in his soul, a need for something tangible to make all of the effort seem worthwhile.

Costas' voice came from the dais. 'It looks as if you might have been wrong about Akhenaten leaving here alive. Looks like we might just have solved the mystery of his burial place.'

Jack turned and mounted the steps, gasping in astonishment at the sight in front of him. In the middle of the chamber with the ridges in the floor radiating from it stood a huge sarcophagus in gold, larger even than the outer sarcophagus that had surrounded the mummy of Tutankhamun. The head was that of a man with a slightly upturned nose and almond eyes, reminiscent of Tutankhamun, his braided beard and headdress decorated with strips of faience and his eyes surrounded with inlays of niello to represent the lines of kohl. It was a face unfamiliar and yet familiar, the father of the pharaoh who had accidentally become the most famous in history and yet whose achievements were puny by comparison, cut off by death before he had even reached manhood. Jack knew who it was even before he had gazed down over the figure's torso, over the crossed arms carrying the jewel-studded staff and ankh symbol, to the circular representation of the Aten with radiating arms that clinched the identity beyond any doubt. *Akhenaten*.

Costas was peering closely at edge of the sarcophagus near

the feet. 'Fascinating,' he said. 'The lid was originally sealed over with sheet gold, but then someone's been around and scored it, cutting through to the crack between the sarcophagus and the lid. It's been pushed slightly off centre.'

Jack knelt down beside him, staring. 'Corporal Jones again?'

'Maybe when he got hungry,' Costas suggested. 'Before he found those other mummies.'

Jack heaved on the lid, suddenly feeling woozy as he did so, his heart pounding and his chest tight. He knew they were more than halfway through Costas' predicted countdown before the oxygen level becoming critical. He pushed again, creating a crack just large enough for him to aim his beam inside. He panned it round, and then looked again. 'I think Jones would have been disappointed. There's nothing inside.'

'Ancient tomb robbers?'

Jack shook his head. 'There's no evidence I can see for robbers ever having got inside this chamber. When it was sealed up, that was it for over two thousand years. Ancient robbers would always leave the worthless debris behind, the mummy wrapping and bones, and they'd never have left without hacking off those parts of the sarcophagus that look like solid gold – the hand, the ears, the beard. No, this was empty from the outset.'

'Well, if Akhenaten could pull the wool over the Egyptians' eyes over the real cause of the loss of an entire chariot army in the Red Sea, then I guess he could fake his own death.'

Jack stared at the face on the sarcophagus. It was Akhenaten as nobody had seen him before: not the elongated, misshapen pharaoh with the mask-like visage, exaggerating his otherness, but instead Akhenaten the man, a fitting consort to the

Nefertiti whose face had transfixed Jack a week before in the Cairo Museum. This was Akhenaten not as the world would know him but as he wished to be seen in the place of his greatest legacy, presiding not as a pharaoh but as a man over a treasure far greater than any of the riches that filled the tombs of his ancestors.

'Jack, take a look at what I've just found. These definitely aren't ancient.'

Costas had followed one of the ridges to the edge of the chamber between the alcoves filled with jars, and was squatting down. Jack walked over and joined him. On a ledge in front of the wall were two tarnished medals, their ribbons faded and dirty but laid out as if they had been carefully arranged. Jack recognised them immediately as Victorian campaign medals. One was silver, showing the Sphinx with the word Egypt above and the date 1882 below, its ribbon made up of three blue and two white stripes. The other was a five-pointed bronze star with the Sphinx and the three pyramids in the centre, also inscribed Egypt and 1882 but with the year in Arabic in the Muslim calendar at the foot and surmounted by a star and crescent. Jack carefully picked up the silver medal, wiping the rim and inspecting it closely. 'Well, I'll be damned,' he said quietly. 'It's our friend, 3453 Corporal R. Jones, Royal Engineers. We meet at last.'

Costas picked up the star. 'How did he get these, if he'd basically deserted?'

'Look at the date, 1882,' Jack replied. 'After Jeremy found that account in Howard Carter's diary he looked up Jones' service record in the National Archives. It lists him as missing in action after the Battle of Kirkeban in February 1885, presumed killed. But it also shows that he'd first arrived in Egypt from India in 1882, as part of the expeditionary force sent to support the Khedive against an army uprising but that soon became embroiled in the war against the Mahdi. So Jones had already had these two medals, the Egypt Medal and the Khedive's Star.'

Costas examined the star, fingering the crescent on the clasp. 'Ironic that British soldiers for years to come would have worn the symbol of Islam and the caliphate on their chests, after having fought a war that many would have seen as a latter-day crusade against the jihad.'

Jack put the Egypt Medal back, carefully laying the ribbon as he had found it. 'That's history for you. Never quite what it seems. Officially the British were fighting for the Khedive of Egypt and the Ottoman Empire, the largest Islamic state the world has ever seen. And some among the officers were sympathetic to aspects of Islam, particularly those who had spent years in the Arab world. Gordon and the Mahdi would have been an interesting meeting of minds, philosophically not that far apart.'

'Well, it's pretty clear where Jones was coming from,' Costas said, pointing to the wall just to the right of the shelf with the medals. 'Take a look at that.'

Jack shifted round and stared. The lower part of the wall was covered in an inscription, written in the neat, precise hand taught to all Victorian schoolchildren, with the subject matter that was often their sole source of simile and metaphor. Jack slowly read it out: '"Yea, though I walk through the valley of the shadow of death, I will fear no evil; for thou art with me; thy rod and thy staff they comfort me."'

'"I will dwell in the house of the Lord for ever,"' Costas murmured. 'The twenty-third Psalm. He must have been awestruck by the appearance of the pharaoh, by the crossed rod and staff on the sarcophagus. Those medals with their images of the sphinx and the pyramids must have seemed like offerings to him, meant for this place.'

Jack took a few steps further towards the open tunnel heading in the direction of Cairo, stepping over fragments of plaster that Jones must have dug out of the wall over the days it probably took him to open it up. Beneath the plaster he saw something else, a skeletal form. He stared at it and then gestured to Costas. 'I think we might just have solved another mystery.'

Costas came over, and then stopped abruptly. 'I see bones. Don't tell me. Not Jones' final mummy feast.'

Jack shook his head. 'This is the skeleton of someone who has lain down to die, or been placed in this position. Look at what he's holding. It's a little Arab dagger, beautifully engraved on the blade and embellished with gold. I think this is where Jones got his souvenir, that ring.'

'Caliph Al-Hakim bi-Amr Allah,' Costas murmured. 'We knew he'd be in here somewhere. Do you think he was trying to escape, too? Do you think Jones found his body, and then laid him out like this?'

Jack stared at the skeleton. 'The medieval accounts suggest that he went alone at night into the desert on many occasions before disappearing for good, clearly faking his own death. I think after finding that entrance we passed in the tunnel, the partly collapsed ventilation shaft, and exploring this place, he eventually found the light shaft we came through and got into this chamber. Maybe seeing the sarcophagus did it for him, and he decided next time to come in here for good, never to go back.'

Costas sifted the dust on top of the bones. 'Maybe he had delusions of grandeur. He could have been the one who tried to open the sarcophagus, not Jones. Look at the way he's lying, with his arms crossed like that. Maybe he wanted to lie down inside the sarcophagus, to be Akhenaten.'

'Being a caliph was not that much different from being a pharaoh,' Jack murmured. 'And Akhenaten isn't the only ruler in history to want to get away from it all.'

Costas peered down where he had been sifting. 'Look at this, Jack. He's got something in his hands. It's a small wooden frame containing a piece of papyrus, with text in hieroglyphs.'

Jack knelt down and peered at it, feeling a sudden rush of satisfaction. *He had found his piece of text.* 'I don't know what it is,' he said. 'But it must have some special significance to have been framed like that. Let's make sure we both have detailed images.'

Costas followed after him, leaning over the hieroglyphs, panning his camera slowly over the papyrus. 'Okay,' he said. 'That's done.'

Jack gestured at the open tunnel in front of them. 'Our time is nearly up.'

Costas nodded. 'There's one thing left to do. Little Joey.'

'You can't take him with us.'

'I know. I've been dreading this. But I *can* switch him off. I can't have him going mad in here like Jones.'

He made his way back to the shaft, and Jack turned to the

nearest alcove, putting his hand on one of the sealed jars. Costas came back and stood beside him. 'Think of yourself as a caretaker of knowledge, Jack, just like those priests of Akhenaten who sealed this place up after he'd left. They were protecting it against Akhenaten's enemies of the old religion who might have destroyed it, and now we're protecting it against the modern-day forces of darkness. Akhenaten must have ordered this place to be sealed up in the hope that it would be discovered and revealed some time in the distant future, when the time was right. He left clues in those plaques that have taken all of our combined intelligence and even a little bit of genius to work out. It's almost as if he anticipated a time like ours when exploration like this would be possible, when people would be driven to seek the truth about the past. But the time's not yet right, Jack. Akhenaten would not have wanted his legacy to be consumed by the fires that are raging above. Maybe the time will come in our lifetimes, or maybe this will be our legacy to pass on to Rebecca and her generation. But right now we've got the present to deal with. There's a girl in Cairo who needs to be rescued, and a lot of people depending on us. It's time to go.'

Jack pushed off from the jar, took one last look around and put his hand on Costas' shoulder. 'Roger that. We move.'

Almost half an hour later Costas stopped jogging and bent down, his hand on his knees, panting hard. 'We must be getting close to an exit, Jack,' he said, his face streaming with sweat. 'It's getting warmer. And I can smell it.'

Jack stopped beside him, wiping the sweat off his own forehead, and breathed deeply. He realised that he felt stronger, revitalised. Costas was right: they must be close to a source of fresh air. And the smell was unmistakable, a cloying tang of burning, a sharp reminder of what lay in store for them outside. They must be at least three kilometres beyond the Giza plateau by now, but the fire on the pyramids would send heat and the reek of burning fuel far over the desert, a smell that by now would be commingling with the reek and ash of fire from Cairo itself.

They began jogging again, and after a few minutes came to a rockfall that completely blocked the tunnel ahead. Costas crawled up the slope, pulling aside blocks of stone, working feverishly until he reached the top. A cascade of sand came down, and a new kind of light appeared, not the suffused red glow from the tunnel but a flickering, darker red, bathing Costas' face in a luminous glow. He disappeared upwards and then reappeared, sliding down the sand until he was back beside Jack.

'Okay. We ditch our E-suits here. Keep your hydration pack, and give me your camera microchip. We're in the desert, maybe a kilometre away from the edge of the southern suburbs, and I can see a road to the west with abandoned vehicles. We might get lucky and find something still with gas.'

Jack unzipped the front of his E-suit, ducked his head and shoulders through and quickly pulled the rest off, straightening his jacket and trousers and then removing his head strap and dismembering the camera. He watched as Costas took out one of the satellite beacons, activated it, and then pointed up. 'We'll have to block this entrance.'

'No problem. A shove of one rock up above and the whole

thing will come tumbling down, followed by about ten tons of sand. Nobody walking by would ever guess.'

'What does it look like topside?'

Costas kicked off the feet of his E-suit, took out the Glock from its holster, checked it and gave Jack a grim look. 'You know those medieval images of hell? They always have it underground. Well, they got it wrong. Prepare yourself for just about the worst thing you've ever seen.'

24

Jack stared in horror at the western horizon. The Pyramid of Menkaure was engulfed in flames, lighting up the Giza plateau like a vision of hell. Those who had been threatening it had finally got their way, picking up where the son of Saladin had left off in the 12th century, only with powers of destruction that no medieval caliph could ever have envisaged. Jack felt the anger well up inside him, a rage against those who had orchestrated this. They claimed to be acting in the name of the one god, but in truth they represented no god. He looked down at the form that had followed him out of the tunnel entrance. He and Costas had just carried out one of the most extraordinary dives of their lives, and had uncovered the greatest treasure that any civilisation could offer. He glanced at the flames again, this time feeling only a cold determination. He would not let the forces of darkness destroy the truth of history. He turned back and helped

Costas to his feet. 'This place is about to implode. If we don't get out of here nobody will ever know what we've found. Let's move.'

A little over an hour later they crouched behind a wall just outside Fustat, the Old City of Cairo, a stone's throw from the Ben Ezra Synagogue. After leaving the tunnel they had jogged in the darkness along a dusty track towards the lights of the city, both of them soon drenched in sweat in the humid air of the night. The smell of burning had been all around them, an acrid, cloying smell that became worse as they entered the outer sprawl of the city, making them cough and slow down. Partway along they had found an abandoned car with the key still in the ignition and had sped along a highway towards the Nile, leaving it once they had found a motorboat which they used to cross the river to the eastern shore beside Fustat. The journey had been an eerie one, with hardly any other cars on the roads and only a few people to be seen, the rest probably cowering in their houses or caught up in what was going on in the city centre. As they had come closer the noise had become louder – chanting and wailing, shrieks and screams, long bursts of gunfire, and above it a constant call from the minarets around the city, their recordings put on a continuous loop by the extremist junta who must by now have swept aside the last residues of legitimate government in Egypt.

Jack tried to ignore the noise as he stared along the alleyway ahead towards the entrance into Fustat, watching for gunmen and gauging the best time to enter. He took out his Beretta from the holster beneath his jacket, pulled back the slider partway to confirm that a round was chambered, and put it back in its holster. With the two extra magazines he had forty-five rounds, hardly enough to put a pinprick in the side of the coup but giving him the option of self-defence if it came to it. He watched Costas check his Glock, and then pull out the second transmitter beacon, placing it behind the wall where it would be concealed from view but the satellite signal would be unimpeded. 'Okay, he said quietly. 'It's activated. That means *Sea Venture* will know we're here.'

'Mohammed won't be able to get his felucca this far south,' Jack said. 'You can see that the river ahead of us is jammed with burning feluccas, and chances are the gunmen have got hold of the police patrol vessels and are raking any boat they see. We'll have to rely on Aysha to get us out through the city to a rendezvous point further to the north.'

'That's could be like walking through the fires of hell,' Costas said.

'We haven't got any choice.' Jack checked his watch. 'It's three fifteen a.m. There's about two hours of night left. We're going to be far better off trying to do this under cover of darkness than waiting for the day, and we need to get to the rendezvous point at the synagogue. Let's move.'

They got up and walked quickly to the entrance through the medieval wall into Fustat, ducking inside and coming within sight of the synagogue precinct. There were more people now in the streets, clustered fearfully in doorways and dark alleys, and the gunshots were close enough in the still air to sound like sharp hammer blows, but still there were no gunmen to be seen. Jack stared at the synagogue, and pursed his lips. 'Aysha should have had our first beacon signal relayed to her by now, but I don't see her there. It was always going to be a gamble, and maybe we just ran out of luck. All I can see is that Sufi sitting in front of the wall.'

A truck filled with jeering gunmen suddenly lurched into view on the cobbled street, roaring past them in low gear and disappearing down another dark alley. Jack had flattened himself against the wall, and he felt his heart pounding. They had been in full view of the gunmen, but had been ignored. 'I think they've got other fish to fry,' he said, standing forward again and looking around. 'Most of the noise is coming from the direction they were heading, where the alley opens out in front of a big mosque.'

'My God,' Costas whispered, his eyes glued on the synagogue. 'The mystic. It's Lanowski. Only we would recognise him. I mean, *instantly* recognise him. He's in double disguise, disguised as Corporal Jones disguised as a mad mystic. Genius, or mad.'

'I told him to stay with the felucca,' Jack muttered. 'Something must have happened.' He turned to Costas, straightening his shirt and patting his hair. 'We're going to have to walk in the open now. We've got no choice, and we need to be confident about it. There are still going to be reporters and diehards of the expat community here, and we need to look like them, as if we know what we're doing.'

Jack felt himself beginning to sweat again in the tepid air. He took out the hydration pack that he had kept from his E-suit and offered it to Costas, who shook his head. 'Still got some in my own,' he said. They both drank the remainder of the water pouches and discarded them. Jack peered at Costas. 'Still got the camera microchips?'

'They're zipped into my side pocket.'

Jack looked down, forcing himself to accept reality. 'If it

comes to it, you have to promise me that you'll destroy them, right? If the bad guys get hold of those images and work out where we came from then the world really will never know what we found. Maurice was right. There are going to be terrible scenes of destruction across Egypt, not only what we've already seen happening at Giza but also at Luxor, at the Valley of the Kings, scenes to make even the destruction of the Bamiyan Buddhas pale by comparison. The world had better get ready to weep.'

Costas straightened his jacket. 'Let's do it.'

They stepped out into the street and walked towards the Sufi, stopping close enough to be heard. 'Jacob,' Costas said quietly. 'We see you.'

'Walk towards the alley where that truck went,' Lanowski replied, without moving or looking at them. 'It might attract attention for me to join you, a Sufi with two Westerners, so I'll be shadowing you. I had to come here to warn you that Aysha's been delayed, but that she will find us if we head slowly west. You're conspicuous enough for her to see, Jack, because of your height.'

'Be careful, Jacob,' Jack said. 'We'll be going into a death zone.'

'I've seen it, Jack. I had to walk through it when Mohammed let me off from the felucca. Prepare yourselves for the worst. Now get moving. With any luck we'll meet again at the felucca within the hour and be out of here.'

Jack glanced to left and right, and then hurried ahead as Lanowski had instructed, leading Costas through a dark cobbled alley about two hundred metres long and out into another square. This one was packed full of people, large milling groups with black-hooded gunmen sauntering among them, occasionally raising their Kalashnikovs into the air and firing a deafening blast. Jack held Costas back, unsure what to do. Ahead of them a cluster of women dressed in burkhas stood on the pavement, swaying and ululating, their heads covered except for a slit for their eyes. One of the women was frantically stripping off her tights beneath her burkha, the others closing in around her protectively. A gunman spotted her and rushed in, pulling her out screaming and sobbing, and dragged her towards an open area where three other women in Western dress lay sprawled in the dust surrounded by men with Kalashnikovs. Beside them an acacia tree in the middle of a small garden had been hacked down to a man-sized stump, and a few yards in front of it boys with wheelbarrows were dumping building debris brought from a structure they could hear being demolished somewhere beyond. One of the men slung his rifle, picked up a brick and hurled it with huge force at the stump. Jack stared at the scene, feeling a cold dread. 'My God,' he said hoarsely. 'It's a stoning ground. They're going to force those other women to stone those three to death.'

Another woman in a burkha came alongside. 'Don't do anything, for God's sake,' she said in a low voice. 'If you try to intervene, you will be shot and I will be the next one to be put against that post.'

Jack stared at her. '*Aysha*.'

She said nothing, but steered them around a corner into another dark alley, quickly looking round. 'Follow me,' she said urgently. 'We haven't got much time.'

'What's going on?' Jack asked, hurrying after her.

'You've been incredibly lucky. About an hour ago the junta issued a fatwa against all Westerners except accredited journalists. Evidently the news hadn't quite reached the gunmen who've seen you so far. Apparently it still matters to the junta for the world to see what they're doing, though that won't last long. Here, take these.' She steered them down the passageway, handing them each a ziplock bag. 'Passports, press documentation. Take out the cards and hang them around your necks. You're CNN journalists. The Cairo bureau chief is an old friend of mine and he's issued bogus accreditation to help some friends get out. These are the last two cards he had.'

'They'll rumble that soon enough if Cairo is suddenly swarming with CNN journalists.'

'Hopefully we'll be out of here by then. When I came to Cairo two days ago I had to ditch the institute's Land Rover in the northern suburbs, as it was too dangerous for me to be seen in it. The way to Alexandria is clogged with people fleeing the city. I'll be coming out with you by river, from a rendezvous point I agreed with my uncle, about half a mile north of here.'

'Mobile phone networks? WiFi?'

'Everything's down. The only contact with the outside world is by satellite phone, and I couldn't risk being caught with one. They're searching everyone. I was lucky to get here with those documents.'

'What's the situation with Sahirah?' Jack said.

Aysha looked grim. 'She's still being held in the Ministry of Culture. They cleared out all of the remaining staff yesterday. There have been mass trials and convictions of government people through the night. A lot of good people are going to die, Jack; a lot of good friends. Once they've dealt with that, they'll turn their attention to Sahirah and any other prisoners still alive in the interrogation rooms.'

'Your cousin Ahmed, the ex-special forces man and his team?'

Aysha nodded. 'It's out of our hands now, Jack. If they can spring her, they'll do it. If not, they'll die trying.'

'What about Lanowski?' Costas said, jerking his head to the shuffling mystic following them a discreet distance behind.

'He volunteered to be your point of contact at the synagogue after I'd heard about the impending crackdown and knew I was going to be delayed getting those documents. I could only get two CNN passes. But he's the least of my worries; he blends in just fine.'

'You won't believe what we found,' Costas said.

'Don't tell me. I don't what to hear anything, just in case I'm interrogated.'

They came to the end of the alley and peered into another, much larger square, with a columned structure in the centre. The square seemed a maelstrom of activity, with eruptions of shouting, the sound of falling masonry and bursts of automatic gunfire, and lines of black-clad men with Kalashnikovs encircling the perimeter.

'That's the mosque of Amr ibn al-As,' Aysha said. 'It's the oldest mosque in Cairo, founded in AD 642. The extremists have taken it over as their spiritual focus. The original mosque where Amr ibn al-As pitched his tent was made of palm trunks and leaves, and they're planning to recreate that. The present mosque is made of reused columns and blocks from ancient Egyptian sites which they regard as non-Islamic. And beyond that they've created an execution ground. The gunmen have already begun dragging people there from the Government buildings, the Ministry of Culture first. They seem to have the greatest contempt for the Antiquities Service.'

'It's a cold calculation,' Jack said. 'They've used the moderate regime as a stepping stone over the last months, sweet-talking men like our beloved Antiquities Director and promising him big rewards, but now that the coup has happened it's a different story. They want moderates to see that only a strict regime is possible and that any who fail to follow them will pay the price.'

Aysha peered out at the square. 'You're going to see some terrible sights, but you must keep your cool. Do not, I repeat, *do not* try to intervene.'

'You mean we're going through *that*?' Costas said, sounding horrified.

'You're reporters, right? Reporters don't slink around in back alleys. They go to where the action is. You're going to walk right past that crowd and then on towards Salah Salem Street beyond. I'll make my own way and rendezvous with you there.'

'Won't you be safer sticking with us?' Costas said.

She shook her head, replacing her veil so that her face was concealed except the slit for her eyes. 'From now on any Egyptian seen helping reporters is going to be targeted, especially a woman. They'll assume I'm using you as a means of escape.'

An ear-piercing shriek rent the air behind them, followed by the sound of women wailing. There was another shriek, abruptly cut short by a burst of gunfire. Jack remembered the face of the young woman he had seen sprawled on the ground. That girl had a father and a mother somewhere; she could have been Rebecca, anyone. Aysha saw him staring, and touched his arm. 'I call on all Muslims in Egypt and all of other faiths to defeat this evil and bring an end to it,' she said. 'In Egypt the people will prevail.'

'Amen to that,' Costas said.

A call to prayer suddenly rent the air, crackling out from loudspeakers mounted on a truck that was slowly circling the square.

'Okay,' Aysha whispered. 'Walk out now. Don't even look at me as I leave.'

She was gone, and without thinking Jack did as she instructed, Costas following close behind. Lanowski was nowhere to be seen, but Jack could not afford to track him now. Everyone in the square was kneeling towards the east and praying, following the instructions of the recording from the vehicle. Two of the gunmen saw them and jumped upright, but backed off when Jack walked brazenly forward and thrust the press ID at them. About fifty yards further on they passed the place where the facade of the mosque was being hacked down and the boys had been picking up rubble to take to the stoning ground. Abruptly the prayer ended and the vehicle sped off, and everyone jumped to their feet. Jack kept pressing on, veering sideways to avoid a crowd of people and the gaze of more gunmen whose eyes were following them.

He reached the north-west corner of the perimeter wall around the mosque, about halfway to the street exit that Aysha had indicated. He took a deep breath as he and Costas rounded the corner. They had walked into an open space about fifty yards across surrounded on three sides by dense throngs of men and on the other by the perimeter wall of the mosque. By skirting the wall they had walked straight into the gaze of the onlookers, but they were not the main focus of attention. In the centre he caught sight of a line of kneeling men, and then he saw the flash of a sword. He forced himself to look forward, to focus on getting through. He remembered the image of the burning pyramid; he had thought that was as bad as it could get, but now he realised that it was merely a grim portend. Already another line of men were being led out, kicked and rifle-butted by the gunmen, as the swordsman walked back to his starting point, his blade dripping with blood. Jack reached the onlookers and forced an opening with Costas following close behind. From his height he could see above the throng to where a further group was being escorted from a street into the square, providing the executioner with a continuous line of victims, the women among them forcibly separated and led in a separate group towards the stoning ground. Many of the men were well dressed but already dishevelled and bloody, some of them pleading and praying as soon as they began to realise what was about to happen to them.

Jack suddenly remembered what Aysha had said: the Ministry of Culture. *That was who these people were.* Then his heart lurched. The Ministry of Culture included the Antiquities Service. He pressed through the throng, staring at them. He was sure that he recognised some of the faces, inspectors and dirt archaeologists who had been the mainstay of Egyptian archaeology for years, friends and colleagues who had worked alongside Hiebermeyer at the mummy necropolis, at their excavation of the Roman port on the Red Sea, at the crocodile temple site beside the Nile in Sudan. Jack was suddenly conscious of his own visibility, hoping that none of them would see him. He felt as if he were betraying them, but there was nothing he could do. To be recognised now for who he was would be the death-knell for him and for Costas. He forced himself to think of what they were doing, taking away a last hope for Egyptology and the achievements of those people, something that might just give the world a legacy of Egypt other than the images of medieval horror they were witnessing now.

They were nearly through, but the swaying momentum of the crowd was forcing them close to the line of prisoners. Jack pressed against the crowd to push away from them, but to no avail. There was another eruption of yelling and chants from behind them, and the line of prisoners shuffled forward. He tried to keep his head down, focusing his mind solely on the open street ahead, moving towards the line of gunmen who formed a cordon around the outer perimeter of the crowd, his Press ID held forward.

For a fleeting moment he made eye contact with one of the prisoners. It was an overweight man, balding, dishevelled, his hands tied behind his back, with gunmen holding him on either side. Jack's mind froze. He had only met the man once, an imperious audience of a few minutes in the ministry after he and Hiebermeyer had been made to wait for hours. *It was the Antiquities Director.* Jack pushed past, holding his breath. There were only a few yards to go before they were out of the throng and on the street. There was still a chance he had not been recognised. He pressed on, pulling Costas close behind him.

Suddenly, there was a commotion in the line behind him and he heard a shrieking voice, the high-pitched voice he remembered from the audience in the ministry. Jack knew enough Arabic to understand what he was saying. 'It is Jack Howard, the archaeologist *Jack Howard*. He is a blasphemer, a destroyer of sacred works. Arrest him!'

Jack glanced over his shoulder and saw the man struggling to point towards him, his eyes wide and panic stricken, and then one of the gunmen slammed his rifle butt into the man's face, thrusting his lolling head back as he was carried forward in the line. Jack grabbed Costas, ducked down and pushed through the cordon. 'Come on. Our cover's been blown. We've got to run.'

They rushed forward past the clusters of people heading towards the square and then ducked down an alley to the left. Jack had no idea where they were going; this was pure survival. Seconds later he heard booted feet pounding down the alley behind him, and a crack of rifle fire. Two men holding Kalashnikovs appeared out of nowhere in front and he and Costas barrelled through them, sending both men sprawling. Jack stumbled, snatching up one of the rifles as he did so, and pushed Costas ahead. 'Run,' he yelled. '*Run*.' He turned, firing a burst into the air above their pursuers, his hands jarring with the clacking of the bolt. Chunks of brick and masonry fell from the upper storey where the bullets had hit the wall, but still the men kept coming. One of them fired back, the bullets striking the walls of the alleyway ahead and filling the air with dust. Jack lowered the rifle, holding the wooden barrel guard to stop it from jumping, and fired a long burst into his attackers, seeing several of them jerking and falling. Another man lunged towards him, only yards away. He pulled the trigger again, but the bolt was open; the magazine was empty. He threw it down, pulled out his Beretta and turned to run, seeing Costas in the dust ahead. A rifle cracked deafeningly behind him, and the air was filled with shrieking and yelling. Suddenly he was knocked sideways and sent sprawling in the dust, and then he was raised on to his knees and pushed against the alley wall, his arms pulled savagely behind his back and his wrists tied. Someone pulled him up by his hair and dragged him along, slamming him against the wall. The pain from his hair was eye watering, but he was too dazed to care. He saw Costas alongside him, spitting blood from his mouth, and was conscious of a circle of gunmen forming around them, Kalashnikovs raised.

Somebody, a leader in the group, was talking, too fast for Jack to understand, but he guessed that their lives were in the balance. He stared at the intricate pattern in the granite of the wall in front of him, trying to focus on that, and breathed in deeply through his nose, smelling the dust and stone. He caught Costas' eye, but they both knew better than to talk. Each knew what the other was thinking: after more than their share of near-misses underwater, of danger they accepted as part of their calling, it seemed a perversity of fate that they should die like this, in a squalid execution in a back alley of Cairo. Jack felt numb; all emotion seemed to have drained from him in the square. The argument behind them stopped, and there was a silence. Suddenly there was a deafening rip of gunfire, and chips flew off the rock above his head. Jack was thrown forward against the wall, and felt a hammer-blow of pain in his right arm. His knees give way, and he fell, seeming to fall a long way as if he were going far beneath the ground, back to that place from which he and Costas had just emerged, into a well of blackness. Then nothing.

25

Jack recovered consciousness moments later as he was being hauled to his feet; he was aware of Costas alongside him as the two of them were shoved ahead by the gunmen down the alley. Costas already had his hands zip-tied behind his back, and Jack felt his own arms being pulled roughly together, causing a jolt of pain to course through him from the bullet wound in his right shoulder. His arm was dripping with blood, and out of instinct he played it up, bending over and yelling with pain each time they tried to pull it back. Someone shouted in Arabic and they relented, tying his wrists in front of him instead. At the end of the alley they were hustled into the back of a pickup, made to lie face down and had hoods pulled over their heads. Jack braced himself as the truck revved up and screeched down the road, trying to keep his head from banging where it had been bruised when he had hit the wall in the alley, knocking him out momentarily.

He forced himself to assess the situation. His right arm was still functional, but he could feel the stickiness of the blood on his hand and the numbness where shock was still overriding the pain of the wound. He knew that they had been reprieved, that someone had stayed their execution; there was some small hope in that. It was not the way of the extremists to carry out mock executions, so someone among the gunmen must have seen something, perhaps their CNN press cards, and ordered his men to fire high. Where they were going now was anyone's guess, back to the killing ground of the square, perhaps, to face the judgment of someone higher up the chain of command, or to some hidden place to await an ignominious end, to join the many like the girl Sahirah who had already been arrested by extremist sympathisers before the coup, and would provide another wave of victims as the extremists finished their first round of executions and swept through the city looking for more. Jack was thankful that Aysha and Lanowski had not been with them in the alley; he desperately hoped that they had not tried to follow but had made their own way to the felucca to make good their own escape.

The truck screeched to a halt and they were bundled out of the back, up a shallow flight of steps into a large space that echoed with shouts and commands in Arabic, and then up a flight of stairs, along a corridor, through some doors and into a smaller space, where they were roughly forced to a halt. Jack's hood was pulled off and he blinked hard, looking around. He was standing beside Costas and they were in an office, that of a minor government functionary by the look of it, with a desk and filing cabinets and a glass screen to the corridor outside. Two gunmen with wispy beards and black headbands loitered outside the door, and another two were inside the room facing them. One of them let his rifle hang on its sling, pulled some leaves from a bag and began chewing on them, and the other asked for some, in English with a broad Yorkshire accent. Jack stared at the man with contempt. He knew that the gunmen included radicalised Western sympathisers, just like the extremist groups elsewhere. Jack glanced at the gunmen in the corridor, and then back at the two who were chewing khat; they would be the easiest to deal with if the opportunity arose.

Another man walked into the room; he was short and dapper with a thick beard and wore a white robe beneath his ammunition vest. He was carrying Jack's Beretta with the spare magazines and Costas' Glock, and placed them on the desk. He clicked his fingers at the two men, who slung their weapons on their backs and came up behind and frisked them. Jack could smell the khat on their breath, and stale sweat. They found nothing, and Jack saw that the zip pocket where Costas had put the camera microchips was open and empty. He must have destroyed and ditched them back in the alley as the gunmen were closing in. Jack could barely think about that now; his arm was beginning to throb and he felt faint. The small man perched on the edge of the desk, picked up the Beretta, turned it over, put it down again and then gestured at the press card still hanging around Jack's neck.

'We have been coming across quite a few of these.' His English was accented, but educated. 'If they are being carried by Egyptians, we shoot them on the spot. You are the first Western imposters.'

'We're not imposters,' Costas protested. 'We're journalists.'

'If you carry these false cards, you must have something to hide. You are spies.'

'We're journalists. Read the accreditation.'

'You are spies.' The man was becoming heated. 'Zionist spies.'

Jack thought quickly. The truth might be the best option. 'Okay. A friend arranged the cards for us. We're archaeologists, making our way back to Alexandria.'

'You are lying. You are Zionist pigs.'

'I'm Jack Howard, and this is Costas Kazantzakis. The Antiquities Director shouted my name in the square. We're from the International Maritime University. Look us up online.'

'We have no use for the Internet.'

'Except to show videos of executions,' Costas muttered. 'And burning pyramids.'

The man stared venomously at Costas, and then turned to Jack. 'I will tell you why our forces are in Cairo.' He pointed to a poster on the glass partition, one that Jack had seen gunmen plaster on walls as they had come through the city. It showed an old black-and-white photo of a whitewashed tomb-like structure, the Islamic crescent above it, with words in Arabic lettering below. 'A hundred and twenty years ago General Kitchener swore that he would avenge the death of General Gordon in Khartoum by killing an Arab for every hair on Gordon's head. He had his vengeance at the Battle of Omdurman, but then he went too far. He desecrated the Mahdi's tomb, tossing out the Sufi's relics and parading his head in front of his men. When that happened we swore our own vengeance, and now we are having it. History has come back to haunt you, to haunt all who stand in our way.' He picked up the Glock, and waved it at Costas. 'Kneel, infidel.'

Costas remained impassive, and the man gestured again. One of the gunmen chewing khat came behind Costas and kicked him below the knees and he fell heavily, pushing himself back up off the floor and kneeling.

Jack felt paralysed. 'He's Greek,' he said. 'He couldn't possibly be an Israeli spy.'

'Show me his papers then. No passport? Then he is a spy. You will watch him die, and then it will be your turn.'

He raised the Glock to Costas' forehead and pulled the trigger. In that split-second Jack remembered that the Glock was security-imprinted, that it only recognised Costas' fingerprints. It was a manufacturer feature that Costas had wanted removed, but had not got around to doing. The man tried again, and again nothing. He threw it down in disgust.

There was a sudden screaming in the corridor and a burst of gunfire, and the two gunmen who had been outside the door disappeared. Jack lunged forward, grabbed the Beretta off the desk and fell backwards, emptying all fifteen rounds into the three men in the room. The man on the desk crashed back against the glass partition with blood pumping from a hole in his throat, and the other two dropped instantly with multiple wounds to the chest and head. Jack scrambled up, ejected the magazine and loaded another from the two on the table, chambered a round and shot the small man in the head. He put down the Beretta, picked up a knife from the slew of blood on the floor and quickly cut the tie between Costas' wrists, holding out his arms while Costas did the same for him. They both grabbed their pistols and spare magazines and dropped down together beside the doorway, huddling out of view. The two gunmen who had been outside were sprawled motionless in the corridor in a pool of blood, and a ferocious gun battle was raging in the direction of their entrance from the lower floor.

'I know where we are,' Jack said, shouting above the noise. 'It's the Ministry of Culture. You can read it on the label on the desk. This is where they're holding the girl Sahirah, and where Aysha's cousin Ahmed was going to try to break her out. Chances are that's what all this gunfire is about. He's ex-Egyptian special forces, trained with the SAS, and knows what he's doing. Now's the time I would have chosen for an assault if I were in his shoes, while most of the focus among the jihadis is on the executions in that square.'

There was a sudden clatter of boots down the corridor and the sound of doors being kicked open, followed by bursts of gunfire. Seconds later two men in civilian clothes with Egyptian paratrooper M4 carbines rushed in, weapons levelled, taking in the scene, seeing that they were still alive and aiming at them. Neither of the men was wearing the black headband of the gunmen, and both looked Egyptian. Jack dropped the Beretta and waved the press card at them. 'CNN,' he shouted. 'Journalists.'

Another man came in, glanced at them and gestured to the others to lower their weapons. 'Dr Howard,' he said, crouching down. 'Remember me? Aysha's cousin Ahmed. We're in here to find Sahirah.'

Jack raised himself, picking up the Beretta. 'Where's Aysha?'

'I sent her on to the felucca. She's gone with your friend the Sufi.'

Jack closed his eyes. *Thank God for that.* He helped Costas up, and then turned to Ahmed. 'I can help you. I've been in here before, when I came with Aysha's husband to see the Antiquities Director. He made us wait for hours, and I went down to the archaeological conservation labs. Aysha told me that's where they're holding prisoners. The previous regime turned the labs into interrogation chambers. I can lead you there.'

'Okay,' Ahmed said. 'We've cleared this corridor and the ground floor. There are probably still gunmen in the basement. But we don't have much time. Someone will have reported back to the commanders in the square, and they'll probably send a couple of truckloads of gunmen here. I only came in with five guys, and one's already down.'

'What if there are other prisoners still alive?' Costas asked. 'Sahirah was probably one of many.'

Ahmed shook his head. 'We get her out first. Anyone else waits inside until we're sure we've cleared the building. If there are many of them and we try to get them out together, it will be chaos and a massacre.'

Jack heaved Costas to his feet, grimacing from his wound, and then approached the door with the Beretta held ready. He glanced back at Ahmed. 'You good to go?'

'On your six.'

Jack nodded, turned and stepped cautiously into the corridor, peering to left and right and then making his way quickly to the stairway and down to the entrance foyer. Bodies were strewn everywhere, and Jack saw Ahmed's other two men guarding the street entrance. He could orientate himself now and turned along a ground-floor corridor through a swinging door and down a flight of stairs to the basement level. The labs lay through two more doors ahead, visible through the glass partition. He turned to the others, putting a finger up for quiet, and slowly opened each door in turn, leading them forward until they all stood silently in the corridor outside the labs. The walls were still covered with archaeological posters, one showing artefacts from the travelling Tutankhamun exhibition, the same one that Hiebermeyer had in the institute in Alexandria, and another advertising a forthcoming conference on the Cairo Geniza, a section of medieval manuscript text in Arabic prominently displayed beneath it.

Jack turned to the first of the labs, slowly raising himself until he could see through the glass partition that divided it from the corridor. The scene inside was like something from a horror film. The lights were off, but he could see a body strapped to a chair with electrical wires attached to its hands. Another body was suspended from a hook that had once been used to raise heavy artefacts on to the lab bench. Neither of the bodies had been a woman, and he turned back to Ahmed, who was crouched behind him, and shook his head. He moved forward to the next lab, crawled along to the door and slowly raised himself up, holding out his hand for the others to wait. He was expecting the worst, but this one was different. The lights were on, bright fluorescent bulbs used for archaeological work, and he could see that the lab was filled with crouching people, perhaps twenty-five or thirty of them, their hands behind their heads and their faces down. Against the back wall were two gunmen with black headbands, chewing khat and fingering their Kalashnikovs, evidently left to guard these people while a decision was made about what to do with them.

Jack slowly dropped down and turned his back to the door. It was impossible to make out any faces, but if Sahirah were alive and in the labs this was the only place where she could be; there were no other rooms. He looked at his Beretta, his hand stuck with his own congealing blood to the grip, and opened the slide to check that a round was chambered, letting it back silently against the spring. He ejected the magazine, checked it and slid it back in again until it clicked in place. He looked back at Ahmed and Costas and the other two, putting his fingers to his eyes and pointing towards the door, holding up two fingers, and then raising his hand for them to stay where they were. If one of them tried to come up to him and dropped his weapon or made any other noise it might provoke the gunmen to open up inside, causing carnage. Jack slowly turned towards the door and shuffled back a metre or so, keeping low so that he was invisible from inside, holding the Beretta out in front of him with both hands. He would have to ignore the pain in his shoulder when he struck the door. He closed his eyes, and counted down. *Three. Two. One.*

He leapt up and crashed into the door, pushing it hard against the people squatting inside, turned to the left and fired twice in quick succession, hitting both gunmen in the head, the blood and grey matter splattering against the wall behind as they crumpled to the floor. The crack of the Beretta had deafened him, and for a moment he sensed only the smell of the smoke curling up from the muzzle. The people began to look up at him, their faces contorted with fear, the men with days of stubble and the men and women alike streaked with dirt and dried blood. A figure stood up and detached herself from the rest, a young woman, and lurched towards him, falling into his arms. He realised that he was shaking her by the shoulders, the pistol still in his left hand, trying to snap her out of her shock, shouting at her to pull herself together. He had never spoken to her before, had never even seen her except in Rebecca's photograph, but in that split second she was all that mattered to him. His hearing came back, a hiss and then a roar that became yells and screams and gunshots, and he heard himself shouting at her. 'We've come to get you out of here. Stay close behind me. Everyone else has to remain here until the building is clear. You tell them.'

Sahirah turned and spoke quickly in Arabic, her voice shaky and hoarse, repeating herself more loudly as several men got up and tried to push themselves towards the door until others pulled them down. Jack turned back, holding her wrist with his right hand and the Beretta with his left. Two gunmen rushing down the corridor were cut down in a hail of fire from Ahmed and his men, the bullets smashing through the glass screens and pinging off the pipes overhead. He crouched down, the girl behind him, and poked his Beretta into the corridor. A voice yelled her name, and Ahmed showed himself at the end of the corridor, his M4 aimed. Jack pushed her ahead and turned back, emptying his Beretta down the other end of the corridor where more gunmen had been shooting at them. He dropped the magazine, inserting the last one and releasing the slide, and then followed Sahirah and Ahmed. He was conscious of Costas ahead of him, and Ahmed's men firing bursts behind them as they ran. Seconds later they were outside, running down an alley towards a street. As they turned the corner a pair of trucks hurtled by, the gunmen aboard oblivious to them, heading in the direction of the execution ground in Fustat.

Ahmed pulled Sahirah under an archway and the rest came after him, Jack following. One of the men spoke rapidly in Arabic to Ahmed, who bowed his head briefly and put a hand on the man's shoulder before turning to Jack. 'We're down to three men. We lost another in the foyer. But there are others like us around the city, pockets of fighters. Every able-bodied Egyptian man has done military service and knows how to use a rifle, and they'll start coming to us now. That bloodbath in Fustat is going to work against the extremists, a sign of weakness, not strength. While they're focused on executions we're going back into the ministry to kill any others in there and collect their weapons and ammunition, and get those other people out. Now is the time to rally resistance, not later when the gunmen have come down off their high and begun to establish order.'

'I take it you're not coming with us.'

Ahmed gave him a bleak look. 'What would you do in my position? Even if there is Western intervention it will be too late to save most of my family and friends. This is my country, and I haven't seen an Egyptian face among the gunmen. I will stay and fight.'

Ahmed turned to Sahirah, embracing her. He released her and peered out into the street. 'It's about three hundred metres to the river. I'll hold this position until we see you safely on the felucca. Then I'm back inside to help my men get those people out. Walk quickly, but don't run.'

Costas turned to Ahmed, and clasped his hand. 'God be with you.'

He nodded, squeezed Costas' hand and released it, and glanced again at Jack. 'And with you too, my friends. Now go.'

Dawn was just breaking as the felucca finally motored clear of the last dilapidated dwellings of northern Cairo, the way ahead of them now clear through the delta towards the sea. It had been a tense hour since they had scrambled on board, with gunmen in trucks careering along the banks and firing bursts into the air, but Ahmed had been right; all attention appeared to be focused on the feeding frenzy in the centre of the city. Lanowski had been in satellite contact with *Sea Venture* and the IMU security team, who had modified the extraction plan in the light of the events of the past twenty-four hours. With the Egyptian air force dysfunctional and the extremists having no air capability, the Israelis had total air superiority over northern Egypt and the Sinai. Ben had liaised with their contacts in the Israeli Defence Force and arranged for air cover for a revised helicopter extraction deep within Egypt, only a few kilometres ahead of them now on the east bank of the Nile. Not for the first time Jack was grateful to David Ben-Gurion, whose reserve rank in the IDF had allowed him to pull off something which would never have been officially sanctioned. Israel would undoubtedly maintain her presence in the air over Egypt to secure a buffer zone, but her ground forces were needed to the north and east where the threat of invasion was greatest, by organised, well-equipped forces rather than ragtag gunmen in pickup trucks;

any hint of intervention by Israel in Egypt would only provoke the crisis further, leading to all-out war and extreme acts of terrorism not only against Israel but also against the Western powers which were perceived to be her allies.

Mohammed slowed the engine and veered closer to shore, his son making ready the boarding plank. Jack shifted from where he had been lying and looked at his upper right arm. The bullet had glanced off the bone, leaving a gaping exit wound but no apparent damage to major blood vessels. Aysha had done her best to patch it up, cleaning it and applying a shell dressing, but there were no painkillers in the first-aid kit strong enough to have much effect and there was nothing more to be done until they reached *Sea Venture* and her bolstered medical team, already on standby to receive Sahirah and any others escaping Egypt who might need assistance.

Aysha clambered over the thwarts to him now, leaving Sahirah with a water bottle looking out over the Nile. 'How is she?' Jack said quietly.

'Physically, it's nothing more than bruises, dehydration and exhaustion. Mentally she's obviously traumatised, and desperately worried about Ahmed. She knows his chances are slim.'

'She doesn't have to worry about her own future. We'll see to that.'

'How's Costas?'

Jack jerked his head towards the space under the bows where they had hidden away on the voyage towards Cairo the day before. 'The first thing he did was to burrow in his kitbag for some sandwiches he left there. A reserve supply, apparently. Ever since then he and Lanowski have been in there hunched over something technical on the computer. Costas is a rock. Guys like him don't get traumatised.'

'That's why you love him, isn't it?'

Jack paused, the pent-up emotions of the last twenty-four hours suddenly welling up. He swallowed hard, looking away. 'Not the word I'd use.'

'No, of course not. Men like you don't. But you know what I mean.'

Jack took a deep breath. 'We just look after each other, that's all.'

She held his arm. 'And you, Jack? You've seen some terrible things. You've killed people. Don't tell me that will all wash over you.'

'It won't. But I've been here before. I'll be fine.'

The felucca came alongside the riverbank, and the plank was laid ashore and tied to the gunwales. Jack gestured at Mohammed. 'What will your uncle do?'

'He'll go back to Alexandria. He's not like Sahirah, not like me, people who can carve out lives for themselves anywhere in the world. Mohammed is a Nile fisherman and a felucca captain, and his whole life is here. If people like Mohammed were to leave Egypt then it truly would cease to exist. They are her past, and her future.'

'If there is one.'

'There will be. Inshallah.'

'And you, Aysha?'

Her face hardened. 'If it hadn't been for my son and Maurice, I'd have been with Ahmed right now killing extremists. But I'll never turn my back. One day the flag will fly again over our institute in Alexandria. You'll see.'

The boy jumped ashore, laying the plank and holding the bow by the painter. Aysha got up and led Sahirah across to the plank, and Jack followed, pausing to shake hands with Mohammed and his son. He was followed by Costas and Lanowski, who brought the two empty kitbags, Lanowski's laptop and any other evidence of their presence with them. Jack crouched down on the riverbank, picked up a handful of dust from the ground and let it fall through his fingers. 'So near, and yet so far.'

'What do you mean?' Costas said.

Jack peered up at him. 'You and I know what we saw, but the rest of the world will only be able to take it on our word. It could be a lifetime before anyone gets the chance to explore where we went again.'

Costas went rigid, and put up a finger. 'Ah. I nearly forgot.'

'What is it?'

He dug in his pocket and pulled out a small package wrapped in tissue. 'Two microchips, from your camera and mine. All the video we took.'

Jack stared, stunned. 'Where did you hide that?'

'You don't want to know. It was in the alley just before we were captured. I don't know how I did it, but I did. Must have looked pretty odd to anyone watching. But there was no way I was going to ditch those chips after all we went through. No way.'

Jack stood up, feeling suddenly more elated than he could remember. 'Costas, you know sometimes I really do . . . *appreciate* you. Yes, that's the word. *Appreciate*. Brilliant. You just tied a big red bow around this whole project.'

Costas pushed the package back into his pocket and zipped

it up. 'Glad to be of service.' He pointed into the air. 'Looks like we've got company.'

Two Israeli Air Force F16s streaked far overhead, and in the distance Jack could see the Lynx swooping in low from the north, the sound of its rotor reverberating off the waters of the Nile. He shook the rest of the dust from his hand and stood up. 'That was quite a night,' he said.

'And now a new day dawns.'

'Yes, it does.' Jack turned and watched Aysha and Sahirah slowly make their way from the felucca to the landing site, followed by Lanowski. 'You know that feeling when you've been weighed down by a big project, a really important one, and it's gone on and on because you've wanted to get it right, and then finally you've nailed it and it feels as if the whole world has lifted off your shoulders?'

'It makes everything ahead seem that bit more exciting. The little things. A holiday on the beach. Gin and tonics. Sandwiches.'

'The big things. That Phoenician shipwreck off Cornwall. Who really were the first Europeans to reach America. Whatever *did* happen to Akhenaten.'

'Some down time with Maria? A little holiday with your daughter?'

'That too.'

Lanowski came over to them, his robe and artificial beard removed but his face still darkened with polish. 'Well, boys,' he said, holding up one palm of his hand. 'Did we do it, or what?'

Costas high-fived him, and Jack put a hand on his shoulder. 'You made the team, Jacob. Good work.'

'I've been meaning to ask.' Lanowski squinted into the dust, watching the helicopter begin its descent. 'Is it always like that? I mean, the bad stuff? The present day?'

'Not always,' Jack said, following his gaze. 'Sometimes the adventure's all in the past.'

'I think,' Lanowski said, putting a finger to his lips and furrowing his brow, peering at Jack, 'don't get me wrong, I'm not complaining, but I *think* I'd prefer that.'

Jack suddenly felt dead tired; he was feeling the pain in his arm continuously now. He nodded slowly. 'Wouldn't we all.'

They crouched against the downdraught of the rotor, waiting until the Lynx had landed and powered down. Lanowski hurried off to help Sahirah and Aysha on board, and Costas got up, holding the rim of his hat against the dust. 'I had a brainstorm just now in the boat about Little Joey,' he said, his voice raised against the noise. 'Well, it was Lanowski, actually. It was about the microprocessor for the robotics, and also a small problem with how he swims. If you want a state-of-the-art robot to explore that Phoenician wreck, look no further than our new creation, Little Joey Four.'

Jack cracked a smile. 'The big things.'

'You got it. Come on, Jack. Time to let Egypt go.'

Epilogue

Five days later Jack sat under an awning on the aft deck of *Seaquest*, gently easing his arm out of its sling and attempting to raise a water bottle to his lips. It was still too painful, and he let it down, gasping as he slid the arm back into the sling and sat back again. With his other hand he picked up his phone and looked at the picture Rebecca had just sent him from Greece, showing Maria far above climbing a rope ladder to one of the monasteries on Mount Athos. Jack suddenly remembered a promise he had made to himself. *Maria*. He made a mental note to contact her when he was back in action again. He put on his sunglasses, pulled down the peak of his cap and looked disconsolately at the Mediterranean, wishing above all things that he could be diving into those crystal-clear waters right now. The hatch clanged behind him and Costas came sauntering out, wearing a spectacular Hawaiian shirt and knee-length shorts, his feet bare. He sat down heavily on the deckchair beside Jack, cracked open a can of drink from the selection on the table and put on his sunglasses, pushing aside a map of the world that Jack had been perusing. 'How's the world's worst patient?' he said.

'Don't ask,' Jack grumbled. 'The doctors say three weeks until I can dive. *Three weeks*. I can make it one week, no more. It wasn't even a compound fracture.'

'The small matter of a bullet hole.'

Jack looked scornfully at the dressing on his arm. 'That's nothing. Hardly even hurts.'

'Right.'

'Has Macalister said when we're leaving?'

'He's finishing the formalities with the Spanish authorities now. We should be underway within half an hour, course set for home. He wants to do a complete shakedown on the derrick and winch apparatus before she goes to sea again. He never wants to see an escapade like ours again. ' Costas leaned over and slapped the base of the derrick, the arm now secured to the deck in preparation for the voyage into the Atlantic. 'It's hard to believe our dive in the submersible was only ten days ago, isn't it? I meant to say, Jack, I'm not sure if I said it properly, but . . .'

'Don't mention it,' Jack replied, wincing as he shifted. 'Don't mention anything about diving at all. Now that really is painful.'

'Well, some other friends of yours have arrived to cheer you up.'

The hatch had opened again and Hiebermeyer, Aysha and Lanowski came out, Hiebermeyer looking decidedly uncomfortable in a shirt and tie and Lanowski affecting an attempt at formality that looked like an ill-conceived safari suit. They all sat down around the table and Aysha opened her laptop, showing Jack a photo.

'That's Maurice cutting the ribbon, with the Mayor of Valencia and the Spanish Minister of Culture officiating,' she said. 'There were about a hundred TV cameras behind me when I took this.'

Hiebermeyer loosened his tie, the sweat beading on his face. 'Not my favourite way of spending an afternoon, but it was a good outcome.'

'Are they still planning to keep the sarcophagus on the waterfront?'

'They're building a museum around it, with UNESCO and IMU providing the funding. They've taken up your idea of showing the sarcophagus within a virtual representation of the pyramid chamber as well as on the wreck, so the viewer can alternate from one to the other. The multibeam sonar data will allow a half-size model of the wreck, and there are plans for a permanent camera on the wreck site for live-stream imagery. That was an inspirational idea, Jack. To cap it all, *Seaquest* is due back next season to raise two of the bronze guns for the museum, one of them the cannon you spotted with the East India company markings.'

'I still hope that one day the sarcophagus can go back to Egypt,' Jack said.

'We all do,' Aysha said. 'But it's a pretty remote prospect now. Have you seen the news?'

'I've just been watching Al Jazeera. It looks like the apocalypse.'

'Our only hope now is for military intervention. It can't destabilise the region any more than it is already. Israel has just carried out a massive pre-emptive airstrike against extremist positions in Syria. The US Sixth Fleet is now within easy bombing and cruise-missile range of Cairo, and the president is due to make an emergency address at the White House within the hour. We all just hope that if there is an intervention it's on a big enough scale to destroy the extremists as a fighting force, and not result in a long-term insurgency war.'

'Have you managed to make contact with Sahirah's parents?'

'They know she's safe in England.'

'I just wish we could have got them out too.'

'I wish we could have got *everyone* out. But you have to draw the line somewhere. They're hugely grateful to you and Costas and Jacob.'

Jack had a flashback to the final desperate minutes of their escape from Cairo. His ears were still ringing from the gunfire, but he felt nothing about those he had killed, men whose humanity was already long extinguished, only a surge of satisfaction that they had managed to get the girl out and had escaped themselves without fatality. He gave Aysha a penetrating look. 'We arranged for her to go straight to Oxford, where she's got an open-ended position at the institute funded by IMU to work on our Geniza finds. Jeremy thinks that she stands a very good chance of getting a place as a graduate student and that there could be a doctorate in it for her.'

'Ah. Speaking of Jeremy.' Aysha tapped the laptop. 'While we were at the ceremony he sent me an enhanced image from your film of the papyrus Costas found on the dead caliph's skeleton. He and Sahirah have been working on it day and night since they got to Oxford. Maurice and I brainstormed the translation in the Zodiac on the way back here from Valencia this afternoon, and we think we've nailed it. We have no doubt from the appearance of the hieroglyphs that it dates from the New Kingdom period, to the time of Akhenaten.'

Jack had forgotten his arm, and stared at her. 'I can't wait.'

She opened a text file and began to read:

All wisdom comes from the Aten and is with him forever.
Who can count the grains of sand in the sea, and the drops of rain, and the days of existence?
Who can discover the dimensions of heaven, and the width of the earth, and the depths of the sea, and the entirety of wisdom?
I come to you like a stream into a river, like a water-channel into a field.
I said, I will water my orchard and drench my garden;
And lo, my stream became a river, and my river became a sea.
I will make wisdom shine like the dawn,
And leave it for future generations.

They were silent for a moment. 'It's Akhenaten's manifesto, his creed for the City of Light,' Jack said. 'He's telling us that his library comes through the Aten, and that he bequeaths it to us. Those words could be inscribed above the entrance to any great library or university today, only here it was one built over three thousand years ago beneath the desert sands of the Giza plateau.'

'It's even more incredible than that.' Lanowski's voice was hoarse with emotion. 'I've heard those words before, many times in my yeshiva as a boy, growing up studying the Talmud and the holy scriptures. Substitute Lord for Aten and those words are almost exactly the words of the Ben Sira, the Book of Wisdom.'

'Hang on,' Costas said. 'You're telling me that a Jewish sacred book was originally an Egyptian text, written in hieroglyphs?'

Aysha stared at him. 'Some of the oldest fragments of the Ben Sira come from the Cairo Geniza, and it's thought to have been first set down in Hebrew in Egypt, in Cairo or Alexandria during the Hellenistic period. But this shows that its composition dates almost a thousand years earlier than that. They were one and the same. The revelation of the one god came at the same time to Akhenaten and to Moses, and their sacred texts spring from the same wellhead.'

'We've got another Geniza on our hands here,' Jack said quietly, shaking his head. 'Thousands of papyrus scrolls. It's going to take an army of scholars a lifetime even to begin to tackle it.'

'We're ready, Jack,' Hiebermeyer said, eyeing him determinedly. 'Aysha and her team are the best hieroglyphics people anywhere, and they'll be training up more translators in preparation. The day that Egypt opens up again is the day that we'll be down there.'

'And remember, there's a guardian,' Costas said, his voice thick with emotion. 'Little Joey's in sleep mode, but he's triggered by motion sensors and I've programmed him to put the fear of God into anyone who tries to get in there. He'll make the curse of King Tut's tomb seem lame.'

'And meanwhile, mum's the word,' Aysha said. 'Nobody outside our group knows anything about it.'

Hiebermeyer nodded, looking serious. 'One slip of the tongue, one inadvertent lapse online, and word of a discovery like this will spread across the Internet like wildfire, and before we know it the extremists will find it and torch the entire place.'

'One question,' Costas said. 'Caliph Al-Hakim wouldn't have been able to read hieroglyphs, right? Of all the thousands of papyrus documents lying around in that chamber, how come he chooses the one that's so significant?'

'Ah.' Aysha nodded to Hiebermeyer, who scrolled through a series of photos on the screen. 'The answer lies in the memory chip that you so carefully,' she coughed, 'concealed on your person.'

'Excellent. My treasure trove. I knew it would come in useful.'

'These pictures are the most incredible I've ever seen, outstripping even those famous first images Howard Carter took of Tutankhamun's tomb,' Hiebermeyer said. 'Without these pictures and that scrap of papyrus, we'd have nothing tangible to go on. I for one owe you a very large gin and tonic.'

'There it is,' Aysha said, pointing at the screen. The photo showed the huge golden sarcophagus, the lid slightly ajar where Jack had tried so hard to push it. Hiebermeyer zoomed into the central part below the crossed arms holding the sceptre and the Ankh symbol. A curious blackwood embellishment like a picture frame lay on the lid below, its interior edges jagged like the broken remains of a window-pane.

'I get it,' Costas exclaimed. 'Al-Hakim found that papyrus inside that frame.'

Aysha nodded. 'You can see where he tore it out. He couldn't read it, but he guessed that it must be some kind of holy text. He held it close to him as he died.'

'There's something else we want to show you, Jack,' Hiebermeyer said. 'Something else to close the story.'

'Go on.'

Hiebermeyer tapped the laptop and an image of a stone slab covered with hieroglyphs came into view. 'This is the so-called Israel Stele, set up in Thebes in the late thirteenth century BC to commemorate the conquests of the Pharaoh Meremptah. It's famous as the only known reference to Israel in an ancient Egyptian inscription. But it now takes second place to Rebecca's find of the Israel cartouche under Temple Mount in Jerusalem, dating at least a century earlier to the time of Akhenaten or shortly after. Here you can see the two cartouches side by side, showing how they contain identical hieroglyphs.'

'Tell them Rebecca's theory,' Aysha said.

Hiebermeyer sat back in his chair, looking pensively at the image. 'When Rebecca emailed me her photo of the Jerusalem find she outlined a startling idea. The other conquered enemies listed in the Stele – Canaan, Ashkelon, Gezer, Yenoam and Syria – were all city-states or confederations, whereas the determinative hieroglyph written in front of the word for Israel shows that Israel was regarded as a people, not a city. And yet at this date it seems hardly plausible that a nomadic people or a marauding band of warriors would have the strength to oppose an Egyptian army, to be considered opponents worthy enough to list in this fashion. Rebecca then pointed out one city that was missing from the list.'

'*Mât Urusalim*,' Jack said. 'Jerusalem.'

'Exactly,' Hiebermeyer continued. 'Jerusalem was a significant citadel, on a par with the coastal cities and a gateway for any Egyptian army intent on conquering further north. Either the alliance revealed in the Amarna letters with Akhenaten still remained in force, or, more likely, *Mât Urusalim* actually is there in the list, only under a different name.'

'Israel,' Jack murmured.

Hiebermeyer nodded enthusiastically. 'Here's a scenario. In the century or so between their arrival as refugees from Egypt and the campaigns of Merenptah, the Israelites had taken over and transformed Jerusalem, strengthening it with their knowledge of Egyptian engineering and winning over the people to their new religion. Rebecca thinks the origins of the Jewish state lie then, not several centuries later with the arrival of King David as the Old Testament would seem to suggest.'

'So who exactly were the Israelites?' Costas asked.

'I think they may originally have been a tough hill people of Canaan, a large enough component of the prisoners captured by the Egyptians in earlier wars of conquest for the name to have stuck. But the migration from Egypt recounted in *Exodus* probably included peoples of diverse origins. Imagine the composition of a Roman slave revolt, for comparison. At certain periods it would be dominated by prisoners from the current wars, Gaulish, Spanish, or Macedonian, for example, but there would always be others from different parts of the ancient world, some very exotic. In the same way you can imagine the followers of Moses predominantly claiming Canaanite origins but including a diversity of others who the Egyptians had enslaved, from captured sailors of the Red Sea and Indian Ocean to Nubians and Saharan nomads. This ethnic diversity may well have been one of the strengths of the early Jewish state and religion.'

Lanowski pointed at the first hieroglyphs in the cartouche, the determinative of a throw stick, a sitting man and a woman. 'That's what does it for me. Israel was a people, not a land. A people is always restless, always wanting to be on the move, seeking a promised land that lies just out of reach. The refugees from Egypt may have settled in Jerusalem, but that yearning was always in their blood. You can see it in the history of the diaspora, in that tension between the lure of the Holy Land and the spiritual and creative strength that came from not quite getting there. You can see it in the life of a man like Joshua Halevi. Would he have been such a great poet if he had reached the Holy Land as a younger man?' He turned to Jack. 'Would you be such a great archaeologist, such a good storyteller, if your Holy Grail didn't lie most of the time just over the horizon, just beyond your reach?'

'Speaking of horizons, I wonder what really did happen to Akhenaten,' Aysha said.

'The sun rises in the east, and sets in the west,' Costas murmured.

'What did you say?' Jack said.

'Well, if you're going to worship the sun, you look east or you look west. It's too bright in the middle.'

'Moses and the Israelites went east,' Lanowski said.

'So which way did Akhenaten go?' Jack tapped his pencil, staring at the image of the empty coffin, and then swivelled the map on the table so that his line of sight took him from Egypt across North Africa and beyond, due west.

'Uh-oh,' Costas said, peering at him. 'It's that look again.'

'You know all those theories about the origins of the pyramids in MesoAmerica?' Jack said. 'We need to look at every scrap of evidence, and I mean *every* scrap, for Egyptian exploration to the west. If Akhenaten set off in the search for his own promised land, it could be anywhere west of Libya.'

'I'm on to it,' Lanowski said, sliding the laptop in front of him, brushing his fringe aside and pushing up his little round glasses. 'I'll start with the fringe stuff first. I'm pretty good at working out which of those theories are crackpot, and which have a modicum of sanity behind them. Some of those guys are alarmingly like me.'

'Maurice?' Jack said.

Hiebermeyer stared at the map, and slowly nodded. 'After finishing at the mummy necropolis, my new project was going to be an excavation near Mersa Matruh, a trading site on the Mediterranean coast of Egypt close to the Libyan border. Aysha and her team had already begun to evaluate all of the known evidence for Egyptian trade further west. One of the most intriguing reports comes from the early Phoenician outpost at Mogador, on the Atlantic coast of Mauretania, where surface finds have apparently included fragments of New Kingdom pottery.'

'Fourteenth century BC?' Jack said.

'It's possible.'

'We have a standing invitation to excavate there,' Aysha said.

Costas slapped Hiebermeyer on the back. 'There you go. Just say yes. Egyptology lives on.'

Jack turned to Costas, cracking a smile. 'And you, my friend, have free rein to go and tinker with submersibles. There's a possible Egyptian wreck off Sicily I've always been meaning to visit that might just need your expertise. It might just provide the stepping stone we need to take this theory forward.'

Costas' eyes lit up. 'That's even better than a beach holiday, Jack. *Way* better. With Maurice's gin and tonic, of course. And you'll be amazed at what my guys have come up with while we've been crawling down slimy tunnels under the desert. I can't wait to show you.'

They began to disperse, and Jack sat back, exhausted but elated. The horizon had suddenly opened up for him again, and the possibilities seemed endless. He stared at the map, his eyes narrowing. He had that feeling again, the overwhelming instinct that he was on to something big, as big as any quest he had pursued before. He felt the ship's engines begin to throb, and he looked out to sea, already planning the next few days, his mind racing.

Game on.

Author's Note

Hidden wisdom and concealed treasure: what is the use of either?

From *Ben Sira* (*Ecclesiasticus*, the Book of Wisdom),
c 3rd – 2nd century BC, in the Cairo Geniza

The idea that the Giza plateau in Egypt might contain underground passageways and chambers has long fascinated archaeologists, particularly following the discovery in the 1950s of two pits beside the Pyramid of Khufu containing the pharaoh's funerary boats. The existence of mortuary temples, man-made harbours and canals leading from the Nile has long been known, and was given further credence when digging for a new sewage system under the adjacent suburb of Cairo in the 1980s revealed tantalising evidence for further structures – one of them a huge mud-brick wall interpreted by some as part of a 'palace' or priestly complex. The engineering feat in cutting these waterways is in many ways as extraordinary as the construction of the pyramids themselves. Despite being one of the most intensively studied sites in the world, there is much about the Giza plateau that remains open to speculation, including the possibility of subterranean complexes that have been inaccessible to exploration and lie beneath the range of ground-penetrating radar.

A further possibility, that such a complex might contain an extraordinary revelation, a secret hidden away by a heretical pharaoh, is the basis for this novel. By the time of the New Kingdom, more than a thousand years after the pyramids had been completed, it seems likely that the cults of the three individual pharaohs of the Giza pyramids had coalesced into one, and that this unified cult had become associated with the worship of the sun-god Ra. When Amenhotep IV – the future Akhenaten – discarded the old religion in favour of his new sun-god, the Aten, and changed his name accordingly, he may have sought a new cult centre away from the traditional focus of priestly power in Thebes, and chosen instead a place that remained the oldest and most powerful expression of kingly power in Egypt and already had a strong association with the worship of the sun. Akhenaten was one of the greatest builders of all the pharaohs, with new temples at Heliopolis, not far from Giza, and at Luxor, not to speak of his magnificent new capital at Amarna, and the idea that he might have directed that energy to a new complex at Giza – drawing on all the experience in rock cutting, canal building and large-scale schemes evident in the Old Kingdom structures – is a compelling one, and plausible in terms of the engineering and architectural ambitions that his builders were capable of realising.

Some of the inspiration for this idea of a later pharaoh 'reinventing' the Giza site comes from the Pyramid of Menkaure itself, where the archaeological evidence suggests a complex picture of restoration and reuse and even the reburial of the pharaoh some two thousand years later in the 26th dynasty, in a wooden coffin that you can see today in the British Museum – the only artefact collected by the British Colonel Richard Vyse from the pyramid in the 1830s not to have disappeared with the sarcophagus in the wreck of the *Beatrice*, the coffin fragments having been despatched in a separate shipment that made it safely to London.

As well as being a builder, Akhenaten was a thinker; for most of the other pharaohs we can say little about the life of the mind, constricted as they were by the kind of priestly ritual and control that the young Amenhotep IV clearly despised, but the fact of his conversion makes him intellectually the most interesting of all the pharaohs. I have speculated that instead of mysticism his revelation may have stimulated a clarity of thought that led him to gather together all of the ancient knowledge and wisdom as an expression of his cult, and that the same kind of incentive that we might identify in the foundation of the Great Library of Alexandria almost a thousand years later was rooted in a memory of this centre of learning lost in the desert of the Giza Plateau after Akhenaten's death. Its very secrecy, buried out of sight and known only to a select priesthood, would have reflected Akhenaten's certainty that his new cult would not long outlast his death, ensuring that knowledge of the place was quickly lost and showing how such a complex might have survived intact without being looted through the ages to the present day.

The possible association of Akhenaten with the Old Testament prophet Moses has been another constant source of fascination. In his book *Moses and Monotheism*, Sigmund Freud speculated that Moses was in fact an Egyptian of royal birth, and came close to conflating the two. It is certainly striking that the monotheism of Aten-worship and the revelations said to have been experienced by Moses could have been contemporaneous, and that Moses and Pharaoh are presented in the biblical narrative in such close connection with each other. If there was indeed a revelation in the desert, shared perhaps by an Egyptian prince and an Israelite slave, then it was to be in the Judaeo-Christian tradition and later in Islam that the monotheism arising from that revelation survived, with Egyptian religion reverting back to its traditional polytheism after Akhenaten's death.

I have imagined Akhenaten foreseeing this outcome, and engineering the escape of the Israelites to a place where their religion might flourish – doing so by finding a haven for them in the city of Jerusalem, a place whose allegiance to Akhenaten is revealed in the clay tablet archive from Amarna – as well as bringing about the destruction of his own chariot army in the pursuit of the Israelites, the basis for the famous accounts in Exodus and the Qur'an quoted at the beginning of this novel as well as for the fictional Red Sea discovery made by Jack and Costas in the Prologue.

★ ★ ★

In Fustat, the Old City of Cairo, blocks of masonry thought to have come from Akhenaten's temple at nearby Heliopolis have been found reused in the medieval walls, the basis for the fictional discovery in this novel of a block beside the Ben Ezra Synagogue containing a hieroglyphic cartouche of the pharaoh. If you visit the synagogue today you may be told that the infant Moses was found in the reeds of a tributary of the Nile that ran up behind the precinct, a fascinating foundation myth by a people who had been forced out of Jerusalem by the Babylonians and the Romans and had returned to Egypt with their religion now strong enough to survive persecution and the vicissitudes of history.

For me one of the most powerful images of the demands of scholarship is a famous photo taken in 1912 of the Cambridge academic Solomon Schechter surrounded by boxes and table-loads of fragments from the Cairo Geniza, shortly after the collection had been removed from the Ben Ezra Synagogue to Cambridge University Library. The image of a man bowed down before a project which he knew would occupy far more than his lifetime has added poignancy because the dust he inhaled when he first sorted through the scraps in the synagogue severely damaged his health and probably short-ened his life. The story of the recovery and study of the Geniza documents is one of the greatest in the history of scholarship, and its discovery should rank alongside that of Tutankhamun's Tomb in the annals of Egyptian research.

In a fictional addition to the hundreds of thousands of fragments recovered when the Geniza was cleared out in the late 19th century, I have imagined a new exploration of the empty chamber revealing a hole in the wall with a few additional fragments overlooked in the clearance and restorations of the synagogue. The scrap with superimposed texts found by Jack and Maria closely mirrors actual palimpsests from the collection in which an earlier text on vellum has been scraped away to allow the sheet to be reused, but where the original text is still visible beneath; some of the oldest of these texts have been fragments of *Ben Sira* (*Ecclesiaticus*), the Book of Wisdom thought to have been first written down by Ben Sira in the third century BC. The overlying text, a fictional letter from the prolific Spanish poet Joshua Halevi, draws inspiration from other texts in the archive related to Halevi, one of the most appealing of the individuals of the early medieval period who come alive again through the archive. The letter contains phrases from a number of actual letters and poems by him, examples of which can be seen on the Cambridge University Schuchter-Taylor Project website and the many other websites from researchers around the world who continue to work on the Cairo Geniza.

In 1196, Malek Abd al-Aziz Othman ben Yusuf, son of the caliph Saladin, spent eight months removing stones from the north face of the Pyramid of Menkaure, causing a degree of damage not to be visited on the pyramid again until Colonel Vyse used explosives to blast his way into the burial chamber in the 1830s. For Malek the pyramid would have been a quarry for building stone, the cause of damage to many of the pyramids at this period, though some extremists in recent years have imagined a religious motivation and have threatened to complete what they regard as unfinished business, on much the same grounds that led to the destruction of the Bamiyan Buddhas in Afghanistan in 2001.

Another caliph who figures in this novel is the erratic Al-Hakim bi-Amr Allah (996–1021), founder of a public library in Cairo and patron of the sciences but also a persecutor of Jews and Christians – he ordered the destruction of the Holy Sepulchre in Jerusalem as well as the Ben Ezra Synagogue – and whose strange nocturnal behaviour and disappearance in the desert added further to his mystique. Whether or not he was seeking some kind of spiritual redemption or simply relished the solitude is unclear; all that is known with reasonable certainty is that he took to wandering alone in the desert south of Cairo at night, and after his disappearance all that was found was his hobbled donkey and blood-stained clothes.

I have imagined that the place he discovered was the same one entered from the Nile by my fictional Corporal Jones, who also appears in my novels *Pharaoh* and *The Tiger Warrior*. Of the two men I have imagined accompanying Jones on that night in 1892, the French diver is fictional, though his gear is based closely on the compressed-air cylinder and reduction valve that had been developed recently by the Frenchmen Rouquayrol and Denayrouze; it is fascinating to think of the military and civil impact had a fully functional demand valve indeed been developed in secret by this date, as in my story, and not lost beneath the Nile. The second character, Charles Chaillé-Long, is historical, and one of the more colourful of the adventurers to make their way to Egypt at this period. An American of Huguenot French ancestry – hence his surname – he had fought in the US Civil War, served under Gordon in Sudan, explored Lake Victoria, and worked as an international lawyer based in Alexandria, and later made a name for himself in America with his sometimes embellished tales of his adventures in deepest Africa. Chaillé-Long was one of some sixty veterans of the US Civil War from both sides to accept commissions in the Khedive's army in Egypt, a little-known but fascinating episode which – though unofficial – marks the first major involvement of Americans in the affairs of the Middle East, in the employ of an Islamic regime but one that was ultimately to be reined up against the growing movement of the Mahdi in Sudan.

Fustat and the Ben Ezra Synagogue would have been intimately familiar to another historical character of this period, Howard Carter, the future excavator of Tutankhamun's tomb, when he first arrived in Egypt as an impressionable teenager in 1891. Before being whisked off to work as a draughtsman on the excavation of Akhenaten's capital at Amarna he would have learned much about the characters and byways of Old Cairo, knowledge that would have stood him in good stead after he resigned from the Antiquities Service in 1905 and became an antiquities dealer. The diary entry from him in this novel is fictional, though it reflects a constant curiosity and quest for new finds that ultimately were to lead him back to the Valley of the Kings and fame. During his years in Cairo after his resignation he would undoubtedly have come across men like the fictional Corporal Jones, former British soldiers who had stayed to try their hand in Egypt but had fallen on hard times, some of them Sudan war veterans disturbed by their experiences and with tall stories to tell of tombs and mummies that might nevertheless just contain a kernel of truth.

* * *

The tomb of the chariot general in the mummy necropolis in the Faiyum is fictional, though the necropolis itself is based on reality and the region has produced tombs of officials of New Kingdom date; it features as well in my novel *Atlantis* where a crucial papyrus is discovered as a mummy wrapping. Despite many claims and several hoaxes, archaeological evidence for the destruction of the chariot army described in the Book of Exodus and the Qur'an has never conclusively been identified. What is well substantiated, though, is the evidence for Minoan influence on New Kingdom Egypt, in particular Queen Ahhotep's epithet 'Mistress of the Shores of Hau-nebut' found on a stele set up by her husband Ahmose at Ipetsut in the temple of Amun, and evidence for Minoan connections in her grave goods. If 'Hau-nebut' does indeed refer to Crete, and if she was therefore Minoan, it is fascinating to imagine her bloodline influencing the character of the pharaohs in subsequent dynasties; whether this lay behind Akhenaten's tastes or it was simply his receptivity to external ideas, the wall paintings from his palace at Amarna are strikingly similar in naturalism and colour to those seen in Minoan Crete.

The oldest known reference to Israel, and only known reference to Israel in a second millennium BC Egyptian inscription, is on the so-called 'Israel Stele' from Thebes; the two other occurrences of the hieroglyphic word in this novel are both fictional. The stele, in the Cairo Museum (JE31408), is a slab of grey granite over three metres high erected by the 19th Dynasty pharaoh, Merenptah, in his funerary temple in

Thebes, and commemorates his conquests in the lands of Syria-Palestine towards the end of the 13th century BC: 'Their chiefs prostrate themselves and beg for peace: Canaan is devastated, Ashkelon is vanquished, Gezer is taken, Yenoam annihilated, Israel is laid waste, its seed exists no more, Syria is made a widow for Egypt, and all lands have been pacified.' In the hieroglyphic word for Israel, the 'determinative' – the first hieroglyph in the group – signifies a people rather than a place, a fascinating indication that the sense of identity as a people that was to become so much a part of Jewish history may have been evident well before the diaspora.

The development of Jerusalem in the second millennium BC remains scantily known, with many modern accounts using the Old Testament as a framework and little being certain in the written evidence before the foundation of the 'City of David' about the beginning of the first millennium BC. It seems clear, though, that Jerusalem was a substantial settlement by the time of the Egyptian New Kingdom in the late Bronze Age. Among the most fascinating of the 'Amarna letters' from Akhenaten's capital in Egypt are several from the ruler of Jerusalem confirming the loyalty of *mât urusalim* – the Land of Jerusalem – to the pharaoh, presumably Akhenaten himself, and from the same period comes the oldest writing from Jerusalem itself in the form of a fragmentary cuneiform tablet.

Whether or not any part of the Israelite Exodus from Egypt reached Jerusalem is a matter for speculation, but is the type of question that taxed the many foreign archaeologists who descended on Ottoman Palestine in the 19th century, Bibles in hand. These included a remarkable group of British officers of the Royal Engineers who carried out the first detailed mapping of the city and its environs, working officially as well as on their own initiative – among them several officers who were to achieve fame in the war against the Mahdi in Sudan and feature extensively in my previous novel *Pharaoh*, including Charles Wilson, intelligence chief in the 1884 Gordon Relief Expedition, Charles Gordon himself, doomed defender of Khartoum, and Horatio Herbert Kitchener, whose desecration of the Mahdi's tomb at Omdurman in 1898 satisfied his promise to avenge Gordon but set the stage for the resurgent extremist movement generations later that forms a fictional backdrop to this novel.

Two of the books by these men, Gordon's *Reflections in Palestine, 1883* (1884), and Charles Warren's *Underground Jerusalem: an account of some of the principal difficulties encountered in its exploration and the results obtained* (1876), provide accounts of exploration beneath Jerusalem, the latter detailing extensive investigations that resulted in the discovery of a vertical hole still known as 'Warren's Shaft'. Much of the prehistoric rock-cutting beneath Jerusalem is likely to have been associated with securing the water supply – opening up vertical shafts to reach the level of springs and horizontal tunnels to channel the water to convenient points beneath the city. One of the most remarkable finds detailing this type of work, now in the Istanbul archaeological museum – a legacy of Ottoman rule in Jerusalem – is a stone block from the 'Siloam tunnel' with an inscription in Palaeo-Hebrew of the early first millennium BC, the inspiration for the fictional inscription that Rebecca discovers in Chapter 17 of this novel.

Whether or not undiscovered man-made spaces exist

beneath Temple Mount, perhaps including tombs and storage chambers, may only become apparent when the authorities allow further exploration, though one underground passage is known to exist to the east of 'Wilson's Arch' beside the Western Wall leading towards the temple site. Meanwhile, in the area surrounding the temple precinct several recent excavations have been carried out which closely parallel those presented fictionally in this novel, and suggest the revelations that may await those who one day may be able to resume the explorations of Warren and his colleagues and penetrate even further into the spaces beneath Temple Mount where access is currently forbidden.

You can read about Jack and Costas' exciting discovery of the wreck of the *Beatrice* in my previous novel *Pharaoh*. The actual wreck site from 1837 remains undiscovered, though south-east Spain and the scenario for her wrecking presented in this novel fits the available evidence, including the likely wind patterns at that time of year for her voyage from Alexandria via Malta and probably Livorno. Since carrying out my initial research I have unearthed more details from *Lloyd's Register* and other sources about her structural changes after a refit, including the addition of iron knees, and about her armaments. The idea that these might have included guns made initially for the East India Company was inspired by the discovery in 2014 of EIC guns on a merchantman wreck in the English Channel, and by the idea that EIC weapons requisitioned by the Crown during the Napoleonic Wars before being shipped to India may have included naval ordnance that was sold off afterwards when neither the Crown nor the EIC had any use for it.

★ ★ ★

The hieroglyphs that appear as a heading through this novel are taken from the Israel Stele in the Cairo Museum, mentioned above, and show the ancient Egyptian word for Israel. Of the quoted material in this novel not already attributed, the wording of the fictional inscription found under Jerusalem in Chapter 17 is based closely on the Siloam Tunnel inscription, in the Archaeological Museum, Istanbul, and the Amarna Letter quoted by Rebecca in the same chapter is no. 287: 60–64. The text of the fictional papyrus document shown by Aysha in the Epilogue is inspired by a translation of passages of the *Ben Sira* (*Ecclesiasticus*, the Book of Wisdom) by Adina Hoffman and Peter Cole in *Sacred Trash: the Lost and Found World of the Cairo Geniza* (2011, pp 53–4), also the source of the pithy quote at the beginning of this note.

Since completing *Pharaoh* I have discovered a fine contemporary watercolour depicting the *Beatrice* a few years before her loss, and you can see that, a drawing by Colonel Vyse's draughtsman Edward Andrews of the sarcophagus of Menkaure in the pyramid before he removed it, the photo of Solomon Schechter with the Geniza archive, Corporal Jones' medals and many other images related to the novel and the facts behind the fiction at www.davidgibbins.com and www.facebook.com/DavidGibbinsAuthor.